Michael W. Sherer

MISTAKEN

IDENTITY

MICHAEL W. SHERER

Mistaken Identity

"Sherer keeps the live wires of his complex plot sparking and distinct. Jenny is a ticked-off but highly capable heroine, whose family of cops adds depth and texture so that motivation and revelation keep coming to the very end. This is a sharp and satisfying thriller." —*Publishers Weekly*

"*Mistaken Identity* revs up as characters are introduced and then goes all out in a high stakes Indy race of a novel. You come to know the characters. You know who you're rooting for, but the plot turns fast. It's fingers crossed until the last turn and the redemptive end."
—Kirk Russell, author of *No Hesitation* and *Gone Dark*

"Sherer is a master at creating unforgettable characters. Take Jenny Roberts. She's smart, complex, a little bit broken and totally kick-ass. *Mistaken Identity* starts your adrenaline flowing and ramps to a frenzy. A thriller that's impossible to put down." —Chris Goff, author of *Red Sky*

Stolen Identity

"...high-octane, compulsively readable thriller from Thriller Award finalist Sherer...is a first-rate hijacking of any thriller reader's attention." – *Publisher's Weekly*

"This book is terrific. Well plotted, all the elements of a classic thriller with a fresh take on the characters, especially the hero. It paid off every promise and more." —S.G. Redling, bestselling author of *Flowertown* and *Trigger*

"Love it!" —Timothy Hallinan, author of *Street Music*

Night Drop

"Looking for an adrenaline rush? You'll find that and more in *Night Drop*. Blake Sanders is back, and that means the action is nonstop!" —Alan Russell, author of *Multiple Wounds* and *Burning Man*

"I LOVED this story. *Night Drop* is a fast-paced, tension-filled thriller that will grab you by the throat until the very last page.

Blake Sanders is one of the most intriguing characters I've read in years. This is definitely Sherer at his best."
—KT Bryan, author of *Team EDGE*

Night Tide
"A great, great read! Even better than *Night Blind*, and that's not easy." —Timothy Hallinan, author of *The Fame Thief*

"A cracking good story and a first-rate thriller."
—J. Carson Black, *New York Times* and *USA Today* bestselling author of *The Survivors Club*

"A tight, well-constructed story and characters that leap from the page. I'll definitely be back for more."
—Robert Gregory Browne, author of *Trial Junkies 2: Negligence*

Night Blind
"An appealing, empathetic lead."
—*Publisher's Weekly*

"This is an exciting, well-crafted thriller and most certainly a satisfying one."
—*Mysterious Reviews*

"Thriller writer Sherer renders a sympathetic lead character and an engaging . . . story line in his latest."
—Allison Block, *Booklist*

"Loved every page of it."
—Brett Battles

"A tightly paced page-turner that's impossible to put down. Terrific!"
—Allison Brennan

"Pay attention. You won't want to miss a word."
—J.T. Ellison

"Rich, complex, and deeply satisfying."
—Bill Cameron

Also by Michael W. Sherer

Stolen Identity

Blake Sanders Series

Night Strike
Night Drop
Night Tide
Night Blind

Tess Barrett Thrillers

Blind Rage
Blind instinct

Emerson Ward Mysteries

Death on a Budget
Death Is No Bargain
A Forever Death
Death Came Dressed in White
Little Use for Death
An Option on Death

Suspense

Island Life

MISTAKEN IDENTITY

by

Michael W. Sherer

Cover Design: Anne Kaye-Jewett

Girls rule.

MICHAEL W. SHERER

14

MISTAKEN

IDENTITY

JENNY

1

Teeming hordes of morning commuters stream through Union Station in every direction. Metro and regional rail and bus lines service more than 90,000 passengers daily, and additional pedestrian traffic through the station's 135 retails shops and restaurants bring the total number of visitors each day to nearly 100,000. To my eye the swirl of motion resembles nothing so much as an anthill on steroids. The flow of people heading one way stops when it encounters a stationary cluster or torrent flowing the other way until those in the lead find their way through or around the impediment, and those behind sweep into the hole, a river jumping its banks and undulating through the landscape.

The sheer scale of the station, the kaleidoscopic swirl of color and motion, and the constant din strike first-time visitors dumb in their tracks, gawking at the spectacle. Besides the worker bees, intent and focused on getting from point A to B in as short a time as possible, and the open-mouthed tourists, at least two other generic "types" move through the wide corridors and cavernous halls. One prowls, stalking prey, eyes constantly shifting to find a victim to cull from the herd. The other includes Amtrak officers and local D.C. cops patrolling the space to discourage most pickpockets, perverts and panhandlers, but a few occasionally get through their defenses.

If I allow myself, I can be as awestruck and mesmerized by the spectacle as any greenhorn. But I'm here to catch a train, and my training automatically kicks in. I mentally remove myself from the sensory dump and take in the whole scene, looking, smelling, sensing the things that are out of place, that don't fit the milieu. I stop and lean against a balustrade to make a phone call I should have made days, maybe years ago. That's how I spot the team of pickpockets working the crowd in the main hall.

From an upper level of the main concourse, under the barrel-vaulted, coffered ceiling, I watch a couple, a boy and girl barely in their teens, separate, hurriedly walk in opposite directions, then turn and approach each other. They pass each other without acknowledgement. When they're thirty yards apart, they both turn and advance toward each other again.

This time, however, the boy raises his hand as if to wave to someone far down the concourse and bumps into a businessman in a suit. The boy half-turns and says something, maybe a mumbled apology, and keeps going. Twenty feet behind the commuter, the girl draws closer carrying a large shopping bag. The teens pass each other again without acknowledgement, so close they nearly brush. I almost miss the handoff except for the ripple in the shopping bag, as what I assume is the businessman's wallet falls inside.

Nettled by their audacity, I check my watch. I don't have much time, but I pocket my phone and head for the stairs, keeping the girl in sight. I stay well back, but she's not hard to keep in sight despite being nondescript enough to blend in. The bag is the giveaway. It's from a high end department store, which doesn't fit with the girl's ratty jeans, baggy T-shirt and dirty brown hair hanging in rasta ropes down her back.

When I see her heading for a bank of lockers, I close the gap. I'm hoping the boy is scouting potential victims. Then maybe I can circle back and reel him in later. Right now, my focus is on the girl as she heads straight to a specific spot and digs a key out of her pocket. As soon as she has the locker open, before she stuffs the bag or its contents inside I swoop in, grab her wrist and twist her arm up behind her back. She yelps.

"What'cha got there, princess?" I say. "A little contraband?"

She struggles against my grip. I push her up against the lockers and pin her with my weight, and now I get a whiff of her that confirms my suspicions. She hasn't showered in a while.

"What are you doing?" she squeals. "Let go of me!"

Leaning over, I rustle through the bag with my free hand, pull out the wallet and hold it up next to her face. "I don't think this is yours, is it, sweetheart?"

"Hey!" a voice yells. "Leave her alone!"

My head swivels to see her partner running a zig-zag pattern through the crowd toward us.

"Stop her," the kid shouts. "She's trying to rip off my girlfriend!"

The girl struggles harder, and I drop the wallet to control her with both hands. Heads turn, and some people stop to look.

"Keep still," I tell the girl. "Don't make me hurt you."

She tenses, her head craning to see past me. I twist to follow her gaze and see not only the kid still barreling straight at us, but a uniformed Amtrak officer hot on his heels.

"Here comes a cop," I say. "It's all over."

"I don't think so," she says through gritted teeth.

She raises her free hand, slams the locker shut and twists the key out of the lock just as the kid slams into me, knocking me away from her. I lose my grip and go down hard onto the marble floor, arms twisted up in my backpack straps. The kid scrambles to his feet and takes off after the girl just as the Amtrak cop runs up.

"Don't move!" he says.

"I'm a cop!" I say.

Still on my side on the floor, I stretch my arms over my head, twist up to a sitting position, and slowly reach for my ID.

But the shield I always wear on my belt isn't there.

2

I feel as if I've been hosed down with lemon juice, and my mood puckers. A whole day wasted. It took a good twenty minutes to convince the Amtrak cop that I was legit, at which point another officer arrived on scene. I spent another twenty minutes explaining what happened. They finally let me go, but the train I hoped to be on was long gone. I hitched the backpack into a more comfortable position on my shoulders and hips and walked home.

No more butting into other people's business. I have to remember, for the time being at least, that I'm not a cop anymore. But the encounter still sticks in my craw hours and hours later like bad sushi.

The sound drowning out the noise from the street outside reminds me of the hiss of steam from a brake valve on an old locomotive. It comes from me. The pile of clothes on my bed mocks me. I eye it warily. I know how to pack. I've done it countless times, traveling to all sorts of places around the world. So why is it so freaking hard to figure out what to bring on this trip? I've unpacked and repacked the backpack three times now since I got home.

When it comes right down to it, all I need is clean underwear, running shoes, workout clothes, a couple of pairs of jeans, low-top boots. A few assorted tops that go with the jeans, some conservative, demure, some sexy—for me, not some imagined notion that I'll encounter another need for them—and toiletries. I've never been one to wear much makeup, nor did I need to, due to my job, genetics and a general aversion to wasting time better spent elsewhere. Other than a brief bout of acne during my early teens, I've been blessed with clear skin, naturally dark eyebrows, long lashes, and what I'm told is a perfect mouth, with lips a natural shade of pink that will never go out of style. Not that I put much stock in flattery.

With a determined sigh, I systematically select and pack the items I've listed in my head once more, ticking off each one as it goes in the suitcase. When the checklist is complete, I reach for the Glock 23 semi-automatic I normally wear in a holster on my hip, intending to unload it and lock it in a gun case before packing it. I sigh again when my hand swings at empty air. Like my shield, my service weapon isn't there, either. I never really liked the Glock anyway.

Lately, I've spent what little range time I have with a backup gun, a Sig P320 Compact. I thought the 9mm Sig was a lock to replace the .40-caliber Glock anyway as the agency's "official" weapon. Then again, what do I know? I'm presently persona non grata. Besides, the bureau always knows better. It chose the new Gen 5 Glock 19M. I still like the Sig.

I move to the living area of my small apartment, which takes only a few steps even with my relatively short gait, and retrieve my backup piece. As I thumb the magazine release, and check to make sure no round is chambered, I reconsider. My weapon's been an essential part of my wardrobe since I graduated from high school. Like panties. On the basis of parental advice, and personal protection, I never leave the house without clean versions of either.

I have a concealed-carry permit. No way am I tucking my now-only weapon into a gun case inside a bag where it would be nearly inaccessible. The gun is small, yet too bulky for an ankle holster. But I have some slacks that might work. Then again, the weather is crappy enough to warrant wearing my black leather jacket, and that has a roomy enough cut that I can wear the weapon on my hip, like I'm used to, and choose comfortable jeans instead of slacks.

Nodding, I set the gun aside for a moment and sit at the "dining" table, a round, two-top that barely fits in the floor space supposedly set aside for eating. I know why packing and organizing for this trip is so difficult. The longer I procrastinate and do mental gymnastics about which service pistol is better, the longer I can put off the most unpleasant task of all. The one I avoided in the train station. But I can't avoid it forever.

I perch on the edge of the couch and pick up my cell phone from the coffee table, staring at it for a good half-minute, working up the courage to dial, then shake my head. I've drawn down on murderous al Qaeda members and lived. I've thwarted ISIS plans to bomb a market in Lyon, France. A simple phone call shouldn't scare me. I look at my watch. Close to midnight, but the time is an hour earlier there. A shiver runs down my spine as I dial a number I know by heart, though I haven't used it in years.

"Yeah? Roberts." His voice sounds exactly the way I remember it.

So many emotions rush through me so fast that for a moment I freeze, speechless. "It's Jenny," I choke out.

"Been a long time," he says softly.

I toy with a strand of hair. "How are you?"

"I'm fine. You?" He sounds cautious.

"I'm okay. Been better, but I'm okay, actually." I pause. "I'm coming home."

He remains silent.

"Just to visit," I rush on. "I'm not coming to stay."

He sighs as if the weight of the world sits on his chest, forcing the air from his lungs. "What happened?"

I flush, heat rising into my face. "Don't you pay attention to the news? Or do they still not cover anything outside the state up there?"

"If you're talking about that terrorist attack there in Washington, I heard. And don't take that tone with me, girl. Your brother was caught up in that whole thing, too."

My anger immediately turns to worry. "Billy?"

Roberts snorts. "God, no. What the hell would Billy have to do with it? Bruce. We got called in to back up the feds at FCI Oxford. I had a situation here, so I sent Bruce and Don Tinsley. So don't go all high-and-mighty on me just 'cause you're a fed."

"Was," I say softly.

Roberts doesn't reply right away. "That's why you're coming. They fired your ass."

I feel my face twist into a grimace as the words find their mark. "Not quite, but close. Administrative leave until they can figure out where to put me. Alaska, maybe."

"What'd you do? Sounded like a righteous shoot from here."

"Well, I didn't kill anyone."

"Then what...? No, don't tell me. We'll talk when you're here. If you want, that is. When are you getting here?"

"Day after tomorrow."

"You coming by horse and buggy?"

"I'm taking tomorrow's train." I don't tell him that I missed today's. "Figured it would give me time to sort some things out."

"Well, can't argue that, I guess." He pauses, and sighs again. "You getting a car, or do you want me to have someone pick you up?"

"I'll get a car. No need to put anyone out."

"I suppose you expect to stay here?"

I squirm on the edge of the couch cushion. "If it's not too much trouble."

"You know where the spare key is. Guess I'll see you when I see you."

"Thanks, Dad."

Before the words leave my mouth, the connection goes dead.

3

After tossing restlessly, I finally fall into a troubled sleep and dream…

*****

The scent of browned lamb, rosemary, celery and carrots fills the air, which means dinner is almost ready. It won't be long before Mom calls us to the kitchen to help set the table, carry bread, butter and condiments into the dining room. In the meantime, Robbie has shut himself in his room, which means he's shut Bruce and Doug out. They're roughhousing and playing tag, chasing each other through the old four-square-style farmhouse we live in. Billy, who's only two, sits on the kitchen floor surrounded by pots, pans and plastic blocks that picture animals on their many sides. He seems content to put them into the pots and pans and then fish them out again, his hands barely big enough to grab them.

I'm curled up on a chair in the living room with one of my favorite picture books that I've learned how to read, the letters spelling out words on the page having magically revealed their code. My best friend Liza, a stuffed bear, sits next to me, quietly taking in the story as I read it softly to myself.

The boys run past, whooping and hollering, Bruce in the lead. Doug darts to the side on the way past and snatches Liza from the chair. I know that Mom won't intercede if I complain, so I scramble out of the chair and give chase. After one circuit of the first floor, we end up in the living room again, and the boys decide to play "Monkey in the Middle," tossing Liza back and forth as I wave my arms wildly and jump for her every time one of them tosses her over my head.

Tears sting my eyes and blur my vision, but I choke back the sobs that try to escape from my chest. I won't give them the satisfaction, or the ammunition to tease me even more. But the longer I participate in the game, the angrier I get, until I change tactics and let the anger take over. I charge Doug fast and hard. He's strong and wiry, but at nine he's still small enough that I knock him over. I scrabble my way onto his stomach and pound on his chest with my small fists. He still holds Liza with outstretched arms over his head, but now he's laughing.

"Bruce, come get the bear," he gets out between peals of laughter.

When Bruce comes closer, Doug tosses Liza up over my head. I keep pummeling Doug, my anger like a white-hot sun inside me burning its way

27

out. Now that his arms are free, Doug catches my wrists in his hands and holds me tight. Then he bucks his hips and rolls me off onto my back and straddles me. I wriggle and struggle to get free, but he's too strong. His grinning face looms over mine. Now I want to cry from humiliation, but fury keeps my tears at bay. The rage consumes me to the point that I can barely see his face as he lowers it next to my ear.

"You need to toughen up, little girl," he whispers.

*****

I rise just after dawn. With time to kill, I don a spandex sports bra top and capris, ankle socks and running shoes, and go for a run. From my apartment in the Fort Dupont neighborhood, I jog over to Minnesota Avenue and down to Randle Circle, where I turn left to go around the large Fort Circle Park. Normally, I'd take a route through the park itself, but at this time of day that could be asking for trouble, so I stick to city streets. My feet and knees take more of a pounding on the pavement, but my sense of security improves, allowing me to relax somewhat. A mile into the run, I find my rhythm, my steady breathing and heart rate emptying my head of the aimless and fragmented thoughts that spoiled my sleep.

I cover the three-mile circumference in less than twenty minutes, far from my personal best but fast enough to get my heart rate up. As soon as I slow to a walk to cool down, the thoughts that haunted me during the night intrude once more. I want to tip my head back and scream, rail at the gods of misfortune that have turned my life upside down. But I can't. I played a part in it, so in a sense have no one to blame but myself.

I am—or was—a member of an elite "fly" team, a multi-skilled group of counterterrorism agents tasked to enter a foreign theater, identify hostiles, infiltrate their networks, and ultimately target and destroy their leaders. Three days ago, everything I worked for, everything I accomplished, vanished, pulled out from under me, leaving me standing on unfamiliar ground. And I can't help replaying the incident over and over in my mind, recalling every word of the conversation, as one-sided as it was.

Roger Beamis, my team leader's supervisor, called me into his office, not unusual in the aftermath of a major incident and agent-involved shooting. I'd already been relieved of both service weapon and field duties for the duration of the investigation but was happy to ride a desk because it meant I still had a job, a career that meant something to me. I sensed bad news immediately at the sight of Beamis's tight-lipped grimace. The second clue was my team leader Terry Hunt's presence. The fact that he sat in a corner of Beamis's office and refused to meet my gaze put a hot bowling ball in the pit of my stomach. The first words out of Roger's mouth confirmed my

28

worst fears.

"I've read your report," Beamis said. "Can you explain the discrepancies between yours and Special Agent Hunt's?"

My face burned and my mind reeled. Sandbagged. I refused to look at Terry. "No, sir, I can't. Not without knowing what they are."

Beamis tried to smooth it over. "No one disputes that your actions—along with those of Special Agent Hunt—prevented a national tragedy and saved untold lives. But I've got LEOs in at least three states, not to mention a couple dozen field office SACs, breathing down my neck demanding answers—and howling for retribution, I might add—because of the way you handled your team's investigation."

The heat in my faces rose to my hairline, and I'm sure my complexion was bright scarlet by then. Hunt was the team leader. It was *his* investigation, I wanted to scream. It was Hunt who'd gone off the rails, grown myopic in his quest for personal vengeance on the man he held responsible for his parents' death. It was Hunt who'd refused to see the bigger picture, the greater dangers posed by one of the boldest and most heinous terrorist plots ever conceived. And it was Hunt who'd taken a bullet dead-center mass in his Kevlar vest, causing him to spend two days in the hospital with a bruised sternum, coughing up blood while I was thrust into the media's glare to answer questions about what the hell had happened. I'd tried to avoid the cameras, the microphones, the reporters' shouted questions as much as possible, deferring to higher-ups, but I'd been caught unprepared in the immediate aftermath, becoming the focal point for the media's insatiable appetite, my face plastered on television screens for two days until the agency regained control.

It was Hunt's investigation, but I'd been the one to nudge him back on track, move him in the right direction. So, instead, I force myself to breathe.

"I believe my record speaks for itself, sir," I said calmly. "I've performed as well or better than every agent out there, and take pride in the results this team has produced. More than a dozen infiltrations in the four years I've been on the team, with scores of bad guys, from Taliban to ISIS, either captured or killed."

I worked toward the job for most of my career without knowing it. My stint in the military taught me to fight and to stay tough no matter how difficult the path ahead. I joined the agency without a clear sense of what I wanted other than fieldwork. But when I learned about the FBICTG's counterterrorism teams, I immediately applied. The job description instantly pressed all my hot buttons. I finally earned a spot on a team headed by Terry Hunt, a long-time agent who scouted me after losing a team member in Libya. I heard about him almost as soon as I discovered the existence of the fly teams. Hunt brought me in under his wing, taught me the ropes, and I soaked up the knowledge that slowly poured from him like syrup from a stack of pancakes. I love the work.

"Are you suggesting your record is better than SA Hunt's?" Beamis snapped. "Youngest fly team leader ever appointed in the bureau's history, an unparalleled record of tracking and neutralizing targets for the past decade?"

I shake my head. "No, sir. Simply that—"

"Then are you suggesting he's lying?"

The hot dread in the pit of my gut turned to anger. "My report states facts, sir. I take full responsibility for my actions."

"This isn't Afghanistan, Roberts," Beamis said through clenched teeth. "And it isn't Yemen or some other third-world country. We have protocols—laws, even—that you follow, no matter what. We do things by the book here. Since your role in all this indicates you don't agree, I'm relieving you of duty until the investigation is finished and I decide what to do with you."

"But, sir—"

"But nothing, Agent Roberts. You're on administrative leave until you hear otherwise. Understood?"

"Yes, sir," I mumbled. On my way out the door, I turned and glared at my team leader and former partner, who still refused to look at me.

I'm damned good at what I do. Or I was. Now I wish I'd never heard of Terry Hunt.

I shake my head to brush away the memories like cobwebs. One thing I know is that if I don't let go of the anger, it will eat me up, burn until my insides are hollow and empty. I sigh and let my shoulders relax as I walk, let tension flow down my limbs and out the tips of my fingers and toes.

Look at it like a vacation. You haven't taken time off in a couple of years.

The trouble with this "time off" is, I don't know if I'll be coming back.

4

I love trains. Ever since I was little I've been fascinated by their power and diversity. The tracks near the town where I grew up carried huge orange locomotives pulling mile-long strings of box cars and flatbeds with stacked containers aboard that held, in my imagination, treasures of all sorts—bejeweled silk dresses, high-heeled shoes, fur coats—bound for cities with department stores big enough to cover an entire block. Or large black locomotives pulling a funereal procession of black tank cars filled with inky oil bound for a refinery to turn it into gasoline to run their automobiles.

The best days were those when we were caught at a crossing on our way somewhere and I watched the shiny cars of a passenger train streak past in a blur of silver, a river of mercury glinting in the sun. If I focused on a single car and turned my head to follow it, sometimes I could see people on the other side of the smoked-glass windows, reading a newspaper or gazing out at the countryside. Every so often, one of those passengers saw me hanging out the car window and waved to me. I made up stories about the passengers on those trains, the places they traveled to.

When my brother Bruce got a train set for Christmas one year, I was the one who helped populate it with life-like scenery—trees and shrubs and grass painstakingly created by hand from whatever materials I could find. I also talked my father into driving me and my brothers the three hours down to the railway museum in Union, Illinois, on one of his rare days off.

Taking a train back to Wisconsin feels natural, but the closer I come to Union Station's Amtrak counter to pick up my ticket, the slower I move. It feels the same as getting my feet mired in mud as an army grunt at Ft. Leonard Wood. When I get in line, uncertainty rises inside me faster than a fire hose filling a bathtub, making my stomach queasy. I turn to leave, but two people are already queued up behind me, so I grit my teeth and face the counter. First the cop, now this. I don't know what's wrong with me.

"Where to, miss?"

I look up startled to see that I stand at the head of the line. A fifty-ish black woman almost as broad as I am tall sits on stool behind the counter. Red-framed reading glasses hanging on a colorful beaded

31

chain stand in stark relief against the woman's voluminous white uniform blouse.

"Huh? Oh, home."

The ticket agent dons her glasses and peers at me over the top of the frame.

Feeling heat rising into my cheeks, I fumble for words. "Sorry. I... I meant... Wisconsin. I'm going to Wisconsin."

In a soft voice the agent says, "Where in Wisconsin, hon'?"

I unsling the backpack and paw through a side pocket. "I'm sorry. I don't know what's gotten into me." Going home... I haven't called it home for ten years. What am I...? I pull a sheet of paper from the pack and hold it up. "I have reservations. I just need to pick up a ticket."

The agent extends a hand. I step forward and give her the reservation.

The agent gazes through the lenses perched on her nose and taps the keyboard in front of her. "ID, please."

I hand her my driver's license.

"Thank you..." She inspects the license and hands it back. "...Miz Roberts. Going to see your folks?"

"No. Yes." I pause. "My dad. It's complicated."

"Families are like that," the woman says gently. "Haven't seen my sister in ages."

"What happened?" The words are out of my mouth before I realize I shouldn't ask.

The woman looks up and shrugs. "She lives in St. Louis. Never had time to make the trip. Her kids are almost grown now." She hands me a ticket.

I can't think of what to say. And I don't need to hear the woman's problems; I have enough of my own. I start to turn away.

"My point," the agent says, surprising me, "is that any time you have a chance to visit family, you ought to take it. You just never know."

I consider her words as they sink in. "Thanks."

5

I haven't shied away from a challenge in twenty years, not since I was a kid, really. Growing up with only boys for siblings can do that to a girl. And I've run away from only two things in my life. One's an ill-fated marriage that I knew I shouldn't have entered into in the first place. As far as the other thing goes, I like to think I hadn't run away so much as I'd run to something else. I think about that as I walk through the train car looking for my seat.

I grew up in a family of cops, and it's all I ever wanted to be. My father is a county sheriff, a job he took over from my grandfather. My four brothers unknowingly instilled in me the drive to succeed, to learn to use the assets I have since I'm not as big, strong or fast as many men. They taught me how to fight fair when the playing field was reasonably level, and how to fight dirty when the odds were stacked against me. Competing with all that testosterone at home, though, was a lost cause. If I wanted to become a cop, I had to do it on my own terms, somewhere else.

Nate Tattersall was my ticket out of town. Nate was pretty nerdy in high school, but nice, not a spazzed-out dweeb like most of the geeky kids, or a brain-dead jock like some of the farm boys. I found it possible to have an intelligent conversation with Nate, and discovered I liked him. He was socially inept in a way that really intelligent people often are, a brainiac who found it easier to talk to computers than people. We had enough in common to find each other approachable, and enough differences that we had our own interests and didn't have to be attached at the hip like kids who went steady. We didn't even think of each other that way. At least I didn't. I considered us more than casual acquaintances and less than best friends. But Nate had a car—a beat-up old Gremlin— and big dreams.

My prospects if I stayed were limited and about as inviting as a case of crabs. I couldn't afford college, even with grades good enough to get a scholarship at UW–Madison. That left waitressing at a Ground Round to pay for a long commute to a community college somewhere—maybe LaCrosse or Baraboo—in order to qualify for a better job like clerking for some county department. After that, marriage and kids. It wasn't a matter of expectations; it's just what people where I lived did. I wanted more. Some people are suited to small town life. I wanted to see other places, do different things. If I stayed, I'd always be so-and-so's sister or the sheriff's daughter.

Nate told me that after graduation he planned to leave town. Said he wasn't interested in college, but couldn't settle for the kinds of jobs on offer in rural Wisconsin, so he was headed out. Jokingly, I said I'd marry him if he took me with him. After the initial shock wore off, his expression grew thoughtful and he said we had a deal. A day or two later he produced a certificate of marriage he got online and said he'd take it in to the county clerk's office so he could get a marriage license to make it all legal. After my shock wore off I decided that getting out of town was worth the sacrifice. I was seventeen and—I won't say stupid—naïve.

We left three days after graduation. I didn't know where we were going and didn't care as long as it was at least a day's drive away. Turned out Nate had a plan. A family friend who knew about Nate's mastery of computers had tipped him to a job possibility in Kansas City. So, that's where we went. Nate had a large enough stake from repairing computers in his spare time during high school to cover a security deposit, first and last month's rent on a small apartment. The little start-up company he heard about told him to come in for an interview when he called. Once he showed the principals what he could do, they hired him on the spot at a starting salary about three times what I might have made after thirty years at the county clerk's office back home.

With our financial situation in pretty good shape, Nate said that I didn't have to work if I didn't want to, that he'd be happy if I cooked a meal here and there and kept the place clean. I'd brought along my life's savings from summer jobs and didn't feel right mooching off Nate, even though we were officially married and living together. I found a waitress job pretty easily and started out working lunch shifts that no one else wanted. That left me time to keep the apartment straightened up and make dinner for Nate if we didn't feel like going out or ordering something for delivery.

The problem at my workplace was the manager, a self-styled Lothario twice my age with a receding hairline and grabby hands. He realized how good I was at my job and added dinner shifts to my schedule, too. Women who'd been there longer resented me. And the more hours I worked, the less I was home and the less Nate and I saw of each other. I could tell it bugged him, and he reminded me grumpily one night after I came home tired and more than a little tetchy that I didn't have to work. I tried to explain to him that, yes, I did, if only for my own self-esteem. We went a few weeks like that, with our relationship steadily deteriorating until we barely grunted at each other if we happened to cross paths in the apartment.

On my eighteenth birthday, I found the nearest army recruiting office and signed up before my shift. When I got home after work that night, Nate had already fallen asleep. I sat on the edge of the bed next to him and listened to his even breathing and gazed at his tousled hair on the pillow. After what seemed like hours, I mustered the courage to wake him gently. Bleary-eyed, he listened to me explain that I was leaving in the morning because I, too, had plans. Big plans. And if I didn't see if I could live up to them, I'd forever regret not taking the chance. The words—mostly the wrong ones—came in a torrent, all the thoughts and feelings I'd bottled up over the months. Years, even, counting my time in the frustrating and stifling patriarchy in which I'd grown up.

When I finally finished, to my surprise, Nate put a hand on my shoulder, leaned in and bussed me on the cheek.

"I get it, Jenny," he said gently.

"Really? Are you sure? I mean after all you've done, I—"

He shushed me with a finger on my lips. "I understand. I do. I wondered how long it would take you to outgrow this." His head swiveled as he gazed around the dark, shadowy room. "This is only temporary, for both of us. It just took you longer than I thought it would to figure out what you want to do with your life, where you want to go. It's okay. I'm happy for you."

"Thanks, Nate."

In typical guy fashion, he rolled over and pulled the covers up around his ears. Unsure of what to do, I hesitated a moment then rose to leave.

He craned his neck. "Oh, Jenny. Happy birthday." With that, he fell back asleep.

I wanted to be a cop. I come from a family of cops and couldn't remember ever wanting to do anything else. I just hadn't seen a way to do it back home. And it didn't seem a realistic option in Kansas City. So, the day after I told Nate, I boarded a bus bound for Fort Leonard Wood, Missouri, to start basic training. After the ten-week program, I put in for the military police school, was accepted and went through the twenty-week course to become an MP. I was a week away from completing training for 31D—criminal investigations special agent—when the Twin Towers came down in New York, and my career plans took a different tack.

Language courses and certification in close-protection and intelligence-planning along with officer-training courses put me on track for promotions up the ranks and, finally, a deployment to Iraq. I served there for two tours, talking to local women through interpreters to get intelligence on al Qaeda movements until I was comfortable enough with the language to speak for myself.

I took online courses at night, so when I got reassigned stateside to Fort McNair in D.C., I finished my degree requirements in only two years. With a college diploma in hand, I applied to the Bureau. Sounds like a cakewalk, but when I look back on what I accomplished, and the hell I went through to do it, I realize that some people probably thought of me as an overachiever. Any woman who's taken on a job in a traditionally male world knows what I mean.

All that reminiscing brings me back to the other challenge I ran from. In all those years, I've never been back home. Now that I'm headed that way, memories seem to be unlocking a Pandora's box of insecurities. I find my seat as the train gently lurches away from the platform, then stow my backpack on the shelf above, thinking that twenty-eight hours on a train might give me a little too much time to ruminate on subjects I'd rather forget.

MICK

6

"I hate this fucking job."

Mick stared through the smeary windshield at the rain slanting down into the cones of light ahead of the car. An unsettled feeling gnawed at his intestines. He clenched his ass cheeks in reflex, not only to prevent an accident, but to ward off the sense that the car was going somewhere from where it couldn't return.

George's big head swiveled. "Why do you have to be like that, huh, Mick?"

Mick gestured at the darkness beyond the windshield.

"Well, look at it. Why do we gotta brace this guy out here, in this pissing rain?"

George stared at him even longer this time, so long that apparently he didn't see the critter on the road up ahead.

"George! Look out!"

The big man jerked his head forward and swerved left and right.

"Stop the car!" Mick said.

"What?"

"Stop the fucking car."

George jammed on the brakes, and the heavy vehicle yawed to a stop on the wet pavement.

Mick threw open the door and ran back, straining to see in the rain and the dark. The cold, blue light from his phone did little to cut through the murk. There, still thirty feet away, a dark shape grew out of the black asphalt. Mick approached it slowly, unable to determine if it was dead or alive.

"Aww, jeez, George," he muttered to himself. "Couldn't you have watched where you were going?"

He rushed up to it and bent down to peer more closely at the ball of wet fur. He didn't see any blood, but the critter didn't move. Mick hated seeing roadkill, innocent victims of bad timing just left on the road to rot like no one cared. The least he could do was move this one off the road. He pocketed his phone and scooped his hands under it. As he lifted it, it uncurled and jumped out of his grasp, startling him, chittering indignantly as it scurried across the lane to the safety of the grassy shoulder.

Mick laughed with relief, and watched it scuttle into the trees. He jogged back to the car, shaking the rain off his hair and climbed in.

"It's okay," he said. "You missed it."

"Missed what?" George said.

"Possum."

George shook his head and put the car in gear.

Minutes later, George slowed as they approached a curve, and the headlights glinted off a car parked well off the road.

"Okay, this is it," George said, pulling ono the shoulder. "You set to go?"

"Yeah, I got it."

The dread Mick used to feel before a firefight in Afghanistan was back again. He pressed the earbuds more tightly into his ear canals, got out of the car, and walked past the parked car.

Cold drops of water sloughed off Mick's hair, down his neck and under the collar of his already damp shirt. Drizzle slanted in white streaks through the bright headlights that penetrated the gloom for only a few yards beyond him. It shifted and billowed, a gray curtain against the blackness of the woods outside the direct light of the twin beams. Hunching his shoulders did little to keep the dampness from spreading across his back, and icy droplets kept finding their way down warm, dry patches of skin under his clothing in thin rivulets. It pasted his hair to his forehead and hung on his eyelashes, blurring his vision. He blinked and swiped a sleeve across his face. His suit was probably ruined.

The suit worn by the man facing him, shielding his eyes from the headlights, however, was dry and impeccable. Doubtless he'd paid far more for it, but karma had a way of evening the score. Kevin Cummings, a junior congressman from Illinois, owed Mick's boss money, a lot of it. Mick was supposed to remind Cummings of that.

Cummings eyed him from under his umbrella as he approached. Rain beaded on the tops of his black Italian loafers, the drops glittering in the light. The shoes probably cost more than Mick's entire wardrobe.

"What the hell is that for?" Cummings said, pointing.

The metal felt cold in Mick's hand. He hefted the wet aluminum bat and waggled it to give Cummings a better view. He liked the feel of it. Not too heavy. Good swing weight. Fairly balanced but slightly end-loaded.

"You missed your payment," Mick said.

"You think I don't know that?" Cummings said. "I'm a congressman. Tell your boss I'm not stupid. He's got pictures, for God's sake. You don't need to use that."

Mick sighed and stopped a yard away. He knew he wasn't the

brightest bulb in the box, otherwise his employment opportunities might be better than what he'd more or less been forced to accept. But this arrogant, naïve prick standing in front of him had driven out here to Rock Creek Park in the middle of the night by himself as if he didn't have a care in the world.

He didn't give a shit about the asshole in front of him; whatever the man got was well-deserved. Still, foreboding filled him with doubt, the feeling that this task was a fork in the road, but it didn't matter which direction he chose. There was no way back.

"I hate this fucking job," Mick muttered again.

With a flick of his wrist, he twirled the bat to build up a little head speed, stepped in and smacked it one-handed against the side of Cummings's left knee. Cummings howled in pain and dropped to the muddy ground on his other knee, the umbrella slipping from his grasp and skittering sideways in the wind. Now Cummings's suit was wet, too, and dirty.

Mick stepped back and swiped the rain off his face. Only the misery on the face of the man cowering a few feet away made his own discomfort more bearable.

"A couple of days," Cummings pleaded. "C'mon. That's not too much to ask."

Mick shook his head, and more water ran down his face. "You know I can't do that."

"Why not? Who's to know?" Cummings clenched his jaw, his face white with pain. "Jesus fucking Christ, you just ruined my knee. Isn't that enough? I'll get the money."

"Yeah, you keep saying."

"Just tell your boss to give me a few days."

"Can't do it." Mick jerked a thumb over his shoulder at the limo parked behind him. "George is in the car. Besides, I'd know. Do a job right or don't do it."

Cummings's eyes widened, bugging out of his head. "What are you going to do?"

Mick shrugged. "I don't know. The other knee, maybe?"

"Change of plans, Mick."

Mick stiffened at the sound of George's voice in his ear. George had been watching, listening on the open cell line the whole time, but Mick had tried not to think about it.

"Boss called on the other line," George said. "Says the congressman's healthcare plan will buy him a new knee. Figures Cummings is a lost cause. He wants to make an example of him."

Mick's stomach roiled, and for a moment he felt like he might puke. He choked back bile. No way he'd get sick in front of

Cummings. Or George.

"Just do it and get out of the rain," George said.

Mick sighed, and his shoulders drooped. This was what he had dreaded. He saw no way out. For the briefest moment, the expression on Cummings's face lightened, as if he still held out hope. Mick twirled the bat in a circle, light reflecting off it in arrows that shot into the trees and were swallowed in the darkness. He watched Cummings's eyes follow the movement. Before the frightened man could react, Mick swung the bat up in an arc and brought it down with two hands on the top of Cummings's skull, summoning all the anger and frustration he felt for getting himself in this position in the first place, the blow crushing bone and brain matter. Cummings collapsed in a heap as if a puppeteer had cut his strings.

Mick stared at the body for a moment, then took two steps and heaved the bat as far as he could. It spun end-over-end, disappearing into the black, rain-filled sky. A second or two later, over the constant drumming of raindrops he heard a clank as the bat landed on the rocky creek embankment.

He turned and walked back to the body. Squinching his face in distaste, he rifled through Cummings's pockets and found the key fob to his car. Mick wrestled the tail of Cummings's suit jacket up and over the man's crushed skull and grasped the body under the armpits.

"Come on, George," he said as he dragged Cummings's body towards his car. "Give me some help here.

While Mick grunted and strained to pull Cummings's weight, George slowly levered his bulk out of the limo and lumbered across the wet ground, meeting Mick behind the trunk of Cummings's car.

"About fucking time," Mick mumbled. He thumbed the key fob, popping the trunk lid. "Grab his legs."

George wrapped meaty hands around the congressman's ankles as Mick regained his hold on the corpse's torso.

"On three," Mick said, lifting his end of the body. The two of them got the body swinging nicely as Mick counted down, "Three, two, one…"

They heaved him into the trunk. Mick wiped the key fob thoroughly with his own wet coattail and threw it in on top of the body, and then slammed the trunk lid.

He took a deep breath, let it out, and followed George back to the limo.

9

Mick stared into the darkness as the limo wended its way back to the heart of D.C., a finger idly tracing abstract patterns on the cold glass. He felt the car's slight rocking motion as George shifted and resettled his bulk in the driver's seat. The big man would have squeezed all the air out of a smaller car. As it was, Mick had to lean toward his door to avoid the massive elbow that jutted over the center console.

"Why you being a mope?" George said.

Mick didn't answer.

"It had to be done, Mick," George said gently. "You know that. Guy wasn't taking his responsibilities seriously. Mr. S. figured he'd just cut his losses. Besides, a statement like this makes everyone else behave."

Mick let out a breath. "Yeah, I know."

"Okay, so why the long face?"

Mick turned his head and saw George glancing at him with a worried expression.

"You knew about this, didn't you?"

George's eyebrows shot up. "No, honest, I didn't." He glanced at Mick then turned his eyes back to the road. "I didn't, really. But I had a feeling. I've been down this road before with Mr. S. Well, not this road, exactly, but...well, you know what I mean."

"I guess I do."

George snuck another sideways glance. "So, what's bugging you?"

"That was a really nice bat, George. It had a good feel to it. Now I gotta buy another one. You know Mr. S. ain't gonna pay for it."

George roared with laughter, raised a big paw, and clapped Mick on the shoulder. "Oh, that's rich. You're sitting there looking like you lost your best friend, and all because you had to toss the bat." He chuckled. "Good one, Mick."

Mick forced a smile and willed himself not to rub the spot where George had smacked him. Yeah, all one big joke to these *goombahs*, but what really worried him was the video he knew George had taken of him bashing in the congressman's head. With George's attention back on the road and a smile on his face, Mick faced the window again and looked for answers to how the hell he'd come to this.

It wasn't like he'd been born to a life of crime. Fact was, Mick Costanza had done everything he was supposed to. Stayed in school long enough to get a high school diploma and recognize that he'd never make the grade in college. So he'd joined the Army. He had the physical presence and the athletic ability to do well as a grunt, and he respected authority enough to follow orders. The pay wasn't great, but with three squares a day and a place to bunk, it wasn't as bad as flipping burgers.

He'd done two tours in Iraq then two more in Afghanistan. Most guys he knew had either gotten out after a couple of tours, decided to make the military a career and advanced through the ranks, or had done those two hot spots in reverse. He knew he'd probably never make sergeant, but he was good at training soldiers how to dress, maintain their equipment, and fight. He'd spent his second pair of tours "consulting" with the Afghan security force along with a team of officers and specialists. The work not only had included training wet-behind-the-ears grunts how to stand, sit, fight and shit, but leading sorties against the Taliban when they got too close.

Back stateside, he'd tried going into law enforcement, but hadn't been able to pass the tests anywhere he'd applied. Not even State Patrol in his home state of Wisconsin, which was part of the state's department of transportation, for God's sake, and did little except set and enforce speed traps around the state. None of the agencies he'd applied to had ever told him whether he'd failed the knowledge tests or the psychological ones. Physically, he knew he could compete with any cop out there. He could run ten miles with a forty-pound pack in under an hour and twenty minutes. He could score ninety-five percent or better on the army rifle qualification test every time, and was even better with a handgun. He'd picked up enough street-fighting techniques over the years that he could hold his own against mixed martial arts fighters.

None of it mattered, apparently.

But no way was he heading home to pump gas or work a c-store counter. Still, he knew that the only things he was good at were doing what he was told, and killing people. He called around, networking with the guys he'd met in the service. A lot of them had the same problems—trouble adjusting to civilian life, training that did little good in landing them jobs in the real world. He ran into a lot of discontentment among those who'd taken the jobs available to them. Who really wants to stock inventory at Walmart for ten or twelve bucks an hour? Most of them struggled to make ends meet, and their relationships with girlfriends, wives and children suffered under the strain.

He'd even tried his hand at being a rent-a-cop, but the few security jobs he'd actually worked had bored him to tears. He'd nearly been fired from an office-building gig for falling asleep on the job because he couldn't find enough to do in the middle of the night in the quiet lobby to keep him alert. And the mall cop thing.... Definitely not his cup of tea. At nine bucks and change per hour, it was about the most humiliating work he'd ever done. The hot housewives shopping with their husbands' money had looked down on him with scarcely concealed distaste, and the teenagers had all snickered behind his back. None of them, of course, knew what he'd seen and done in the military to ensure their right to act like the assholes they were.

He shook his head, and felt George's eyes on him again.

"What's the matter?"

Mick pressed his lips together; George wouldn't let it go.

"This wasn't what I had in mind when I took the job, George."

George reared his head. "Whoa. You called me, remember? Pretty desperate at the time, as I recall."

"Security, you said. At a club. I figured that meant bouncer. Bust a few heads occasionally when the patrons get rowdy."

"This is a hell of a lot better than some sleazy strip joint, don't you think? I never lied to you, Mick. I told you straight up that Mr. S. runs a high-class place. I said you'd be asked to provide security for the club and Mr. S. personally sometimes. Whatever it took."

Mick sighed. "Yeah, you never lied."

George snuck another silent glance at Mick. "You did your job. Cummings was a security risk, to the club and to Mr. S."

"I got it." Mick gritted his teeth, the retort sharper than he'd intended.

The silence in the car grew thick and heavy, weighing on Mick's chest, making it hard to breathe. George wheeled the limo through the gentle curves of some city boulevards not far from the Naval Observatory. Mick idly wondered if the vice president was in residence, and how he had spent his evening. Probably not the way Mick had.

The view outside Mick's window suddenly filled with five feet of brick topped with spiked wrought iron, signaling they had arrived. The fence walled off a large mansion from the street, its roof barely visible over the top. It made a tasteful but firm statement to those on the outside that those inside its perimeter valued privacy. As large as many of the foreign embassies in the area, the house and grounds stretched the full length of the block.

George turned at the next corner and followed the wall to a narrow gated entrance. He thumbed a small remote, barely visible in his big hand, and the gates slowly opened as the limo approached. A lane barely wider than the car led to the rear of the house. George steered the limo in and stopped short of an open garage door.

"I gotta wipe the car down." George sounded almost apologetic.

Mick climbed out and watched George swing the car in a tight semi-circle, and back it into the slim stall. His head drooped in the light drizzle. He shook it once and headed for a rear door that accessed the mansion's kitchen. Inside, his stomach growled at the smells being produced by the pair of cooks still on hand, even at this hour, preparing some dish for a hungry guest, or maybe Mr. S. himself.

One of the cooks noticed him by the back door and raised the pair of tongs in his hand in greeting. "Yo, Mick. Want me to fix you a plate?"

Mick jerked his chin up. "Maybe later, Sergio. Gotta see the boss."

Sergio smiled and waved as he turned back to the sauté pan he had working on the big eight- burner range.

Mick grabbed a kitchen towel out of a laundry basket nearby and wiped the rain and mud off his shoes. He tossed the dirty towel back in the hamper and got a clean towel from a shelf to dry his suit coat and trousers as well as he could. He passed through a side door in the kitchen that led to a plushly carpeted hallway dimly lit with glass and brass wall sconces. Solid, carved oak doors on either side of the hall hid business offices from view, those of the chef and food and beverage manager located closest to the kitchen. Mick knocked softly on a door at the end of the hall and waited.

In a moment, he heard a baritone voice say, "Come."

Mick pushed open the heavy door and stepped into a large, formal office. Carpet here gave way to a black walnut hardwood parquet floor adorned with a rich blue and red Persian carpet in the center. Bookcases lined opposite walls with a table and chairs on one side and a comfortable seating area on the other. Straight ahead sat an enormous, ornate walnut desk. A few bare necessities covered a portion of the lustrous surface—green-shaded brass banker's lamp, a sleek computer monitor, and a leather desk pad.

The man in the executive chair behind the desk appeared unassuming. Handsome in a general way, but indistinguishable from hundreds if not thousands of men his age, he had gray hair slicked back and neatly trimmed on the sides. Of average height and weight, Mick guessed him at about five-feet-ten and a hundred seventy pounds, "trim" and "athletic" the words likely to describe him. Immaculately dressed in an unwrinkled, bespoke navy wool and mohair suit, custom-tailored Albini cotton shirt, and an Hermés tie.

Benton Sykes ran the most exclusive gentlemen's club in D.C. Before George had talked Mick into making the trip east and interviewing for the job, Mick's idea of a gentlemen's club was a titty bar in a cinderblock building set back from a busy strip of highway, where night always reigned inside, old '80s rock played over the sound system, bartenders watered down the drinks and charged triple their cost anywhere else, and bare breasts hung on the chests of some of the most plain-faced women in the Midwest. This club was anything but.

It had no name. The mansion offered men of distinction a chance to unwind and relax from the stress and cares of a day running political interference, drafting new trade legislation, doing some backroom bargaining on an energy bill, or entertaining some low-level schmuck from the agricultural department of a backwater Pacific island nation no one ever heard of in order to make POTUS happy. None of that mattered in this place. Inside the fence that walled the mansion off from the rest of the world, members could be as anonymous as they pleased, no matter how recognizable their faces. No deals were done except those conducted privately and with the consent of the members involved. Here, members could simply be, and indulge, themselves.

In addition to lounges decorated in rich, dark woods, leather wingback chairs, heavy velvet drapes and thick oriental rugs, the mansion housed a complete fitness area with workout room, lap pool, squash and racquetball courts, a golf course simulator, steam rooms, sauna, and massage rooms; entertainment including a small movie theater; a live stage, a two-lane bowling alley, a piano bar, and the dining room, of course; and private rooms—meeting and conference rooms on the first and lower levels, and private bedrooms upstairs.

Mick stood silently while Sykes pored over a ledger on the desk, making entries and jotting note on a scratch pad with a limited edition fountain pen that cost more than Mick had earned in his entire life. Sykes worked without looking up until he finally set the pen on the desk pad, closed the ledger and slid it into a drawer. As he closed the drawer, he beckoned Mick by crooking his fingers, palm up.

Taking half a dozen more steps until he stood a few feet from the desk, Mick gestured toward the dark computer monitor. "Why don't you use a software spreadsheet?"

Sykes considered him for a moment. He picked up the pen and rolled it between his thumb and two fingers.

"I enjoy the mental exercise. Anyone can type numbers into a spreadsheet." He paused and glanced at the pen. "Do you know what a gift this is? We're the only animal on the planet—maybe in the universe—that can form and use symbols to communicate. Such a shame to waste it."

Mick shrugged and tipped his head.

Sykes laid the pen down gently. "George said you handled the change of plan readily. Any problems?"

Mick shifted his weight from one foot to the other, squirming inside under Sykes's intent gaze. "Was it really necessary?" he finally blurted.

"Isn't that beside the point? You did your job."

Mick dropped his gaze and stared at a mandala woven into the carpet, trying to pull himself together. He couldn't figure out what it was about Sykes that made him lose his composure, but if he didn't get his shit together he'd be out of a job altogether. Then again, maybe that's what this was all about. Maybe he wasn't cut out for this kind of work. Killing your country's enemies was one thing, but whacking a guy because he was behind on the vig....

"Would I have asked you to do it if it hadn't been necessary?" Sykes spoke softly, as if patiently explaining something to a child.

Mick raised his eyes, steeled his spine and shook his head. "No, sir. But he was a congressman."

"Mick, Mick, Mick." Sykes shook his head. "Time to grow up. Men like Cummings? They're the worst. Politicians, captains of industry, kings...they think they can do whatever they want. I wouldn't be in business if it weren't for them. Cummings was scum, not some American hero you put on a pedestal. He couldn't keep his dick in his pants; he came to the club so he could get his rocks off with pretty girls in private. He owed me money; he couldn't pay. Don't you think he deserved to be punished? Wouldn't a bank punish you if you couldn't repay a loan?"

Mick nodded, feeling miserable.

"Of course it would. Cummings was dirt. Do you know why he owed me money? Because he gambles. And gamblers always lose. But what's worse, he stole from his campaign funds to cover his gambling debts. He begged me to help him, begged me for money to pay back his campaign before it was discovered. And how did he repay me? By gambling the money away. Foolish man. The world is better off without him."

Mick bobbed his head in agreement. But he couldn't get rid of the vision of George sitting in the limo, holding up a smart phone and recording the rainy scene that played out in the headlights, then sending it to Sykes as confirmation. Cummings may have been a bad man, but was what he'd done any better? Mick knew, deep in his heart, his soul, that despite the path his life had taken he really wasn't a bad person. Was he? And suddenly, the resolution to his dilemma took on the crystal clear dimensions of the only other object sitting on the polished surface of the desk—a gold-trimmed smart phone. It appeared in his peripheral vision as he matched Sykes's gaze, and he forced himself to maintain eye contact so he wouldn't look at it. If only there was some way he could get his hands on it.

A soft knock on the door behind him diverted Sykes's attention, and Mick heard the door opened before Sykes issued an invitation to enter. He glanced over his shoulder as Phillip Stevens, the club's second-in-command, stepped inside, hand still on the door.

"Sorry to interrupt," Stevens said, "but an issue requires your immediate attention."

A flash of annoyance bordering on anger crossed Sykes's face, replaced in an instant by cognition.

"The Sheik?" Sykes said. Stevens nodded, and Sykes swung his gaze back to Mick. "You did a good job tonight. Go home. Get some sleep. I have to attend to this."

Mick nodded as Sykes rounded the desk and hurried toward the door, Stevens already launching into an explanation of whatever "issue' demanded their response at that time of night. His pulse pounding, Mick faced the door as their heads leaned in to talk quietly. He took a step backward, then another. His heart hammered his ribs so loudly he was sure they must be able to hear it across the room. He backed up another step and extended a hand behind his back.

Sykes and Stevens moved out of sight now, their footfalls silenced by the thick carpeting in the hallway. Quickly, Mick closed his hand on the phone and slid it silently over the surface of the desk and into his pocket in a single smooth motion. He was a yard or two from the doorway when Sykes poked his head around the doorframe. Without stopping, Mick feigned a yawn and raised an arm to his mouth.

"Yeah, coming," he said. "Sorry."

Sykes took a step back to avoid a collision as Mick walked through the opening and pulled the door shut. He brushed past Sykes, the phone in his pocket burning against his thigh.

Michael W. Sherer

10

All Mick's instincts had screamed at him to run like hell. He'd exercised every scintilla of restraint in his command, casually walking out of the neighborhood as if he belonged there, and he'd kept on walking, meandering for hours on a circuitous route through the capital. The rain had stopped, but the air felt heavy and laden with moisture. His damp clothes hung on him limply as if they couldn't muster the effort not to curl up with the same exhaustion he felt. His sodden shoes weighed him down, gluing him to the pavement with each step. He trudged on, thoughts as murky as the clouded night sky.

He wondered when his life had gone to shit. In the military, maybe, when Uncle Sam had taught him how to kill. No, earlier than that, he decided. He'd spent most of his high school years barely a step ahead of the local cops, staying under their radar by being just a little faster than anyone he knew—except for one kid. One kid back in grade school had been just as fast, and almost as drawn to trouble as he. Ironic, since the kid's dad had been a cop. They'd had a grudging respect for each other and ended up on the same relay team in high school track. Yeah, the truth was, Mick had been skirting the edges of disaster most of his life.

He couldn't blame it on abusive parents or a deprived childhood. As far he could tell, his upbringing had been about as normal as that of most kids he'd known, and pretty typical for a small town in the part of the world where he grew up. His family struggled, like a lot of families—though he had no proof, he was pretty sure his father had cut a few corners here and there, done a few jobs that weren't exactly legal to make ends meet. But they had enough food to eat, and enough money each month to keep the lights lit and the heat on. So where had he gone wrong? When had he turned a blind eye to what was right instead of simply doing what was asked of him, no matter how questionable?

Now, as the sky lightened to gray, he found himself sitting on some steps in the Lower Senate Park, staring at the damn phone he'd taken from Sykes's office. Without a password it was useless. He cursed his impulsivity. Half-heartedly, he tried a couple of number

51

combinations, but the phone stubbornly resisted his attempts to unlock it. It rang suddenly, startling him so badly that he fumbled it and nearly dropped it. He knew he should let the call go to voicemail, but his arm raised the phone to his ear as if it had a mind of its own, thumb swiping the screen. He held it without speaking.

"Mick." A soft statement, not a question. "I'm disappointed."

Mick's stomach roiled. If Sykes had figured it out that fast, what hope did he have? Too late for regrets. Mick thought furiously to come up with a way to salvage something from his bonehead play. Don't get greedy. That was the key.

"Look, Mr. S., you can have the phone back. It's no use to me. I just want out. That's all."

A sigh came through the speaker. "That's not how it works. You know that."

"The stuff you got on me, what am I gonna say? Who am I gonna tell? Come on, Mr. S. Give me a break. I just want to walk away. Maybe find a job washing dishes somewhere. No harm, no foul. What do you say?"

"You stole my phone. How can I put any faith in what you say after such a breach of trust?"

"I've done a lot worse for you, sir. Never complained. Never asked questions. Did what you said, and kept my mouth shut."

"Until tonight."

"I've been a good employee. I promise I won't say a word about you or the club, or anything. I just...I need to start over. Get my life back."

"You had a pretty good life here, Mick." Sykes paused, and Mick held his breath. "So, what? I give you your freedom, and you return the phone?"

"Sure, after I delete the video. Why not? Honor among thieves and all that."

The chuckle he heard was as cold as a graveyard in February. "Fine. Where are you, Mick?"

"Uh-uh. I disappear, and when I feel safe, I'll get a message to you and let you know where to pick up the phone."

Sykes's voice took on a hard edge. "You're playing a dangerous game. I think you—"

"Gotta go, Mr. S. I'll be in touch." Mick ended the call and jumped to his feet, heat rising to his face and pulse rising.

Sykes didn't have to ask where Mick was; he could track him. Mick couldn't believe he'd let Sykes keep him talking that long. He powered off Sykes's phone and moved away from the spot. Pulling up a location-services app on his own phone, he searched for pack-

and-ship stores and found one a few blocks away. Breaking into a trot, he hustled away from the park, looking like any other schlub hurrying to work.

A hotel stood at the address Mick's phone had given him. He shook off the momentary confusion and pushed the turnstile door, realizing it must be inside. He glimpsed his bedraggled reflection in the glass as he stepped into the lobby. Fortunately, guests checking out kept the front desk staff busy, and the lobby traffic was heavy enough that no one took any notice. He found the storefront tucked in a corner of the lobby next to the gift shop, but the interior was dark. He peered at the sign indicating the store's hours and checked his watch. Another twenty minutes until it opened.

Turning a slow circle, he scanned the lobby, nervous now. Sykes would send someone. Already had, more than likely. If Sykes sent George, Mick might be able to talk his way clear. But he knew that Sykes had more on his phone than the video George had sent earlier. He had no idea what, but he'd banked on whatever it might be as leverage he could use. Now, too late, he realized his mistake. Sykes would be more concerned about the other stuff on the phone than he would about a video that incriminated Mick Costanza. He would surely send others besides George to find him. But who?

The club hired an outside security firm to provide uniformed guards to patrol the perimeter and man the entrances. Sykes wouldn't send any of them. But at least a dozen men like Mick provided security inside the club. Mick knew most of them, but only one or two others, if any, handled the unpleasant chores often assigned to Mick. If Sykes sent them out to look for him, Mick wondered if they'd question why. Sykes himself handled security and could tell them any story he wanted to. Hell, Sykes could even call the police. Mick didn't think it likely, but then what did he really know about Sykes? The man had never directly asked him to do any of the things Mick had done. The orders—or "requests"—always came from George.

He didn't have much time. Bright light spilled into the lobby from the gift shop next door. Racks of souvenir shirts stood on either side of the wide entrance. The bright colors pulled Mick inside the store. He fanned through a rack and pulled out a lightweight, gray hooded sweatshirt emblazoned with "WASHINGTON, DC" across the front. Further in, he found another rack with ball caps, some generic to the city, others in the colors of the city's pro sports teams. He picked one at random, and took the items to the register. Adding a newspaper to the pile, he pulled cash from his pocket and paid.

Leaving the store, Mick spotted signs for the restrooms down a hallway. He scanned the lobby for any signs of interest in his movements but saw none. He went into the men's room and, finding it empty, quickly stripped off his suit coat and put on the sweatshirt. After transferring the coat's contents to his pants pockets, he stuffed the coat into the bottom of the trash bin, pulling the soiled paper towels on top of it. He rinsed his hands in the sink, dried them off, and pulled the cap down low over his eyes. He checked his image in the mirror. Not perfect, but it might buy him some time. He wandered casually back out to the lobby and sank himself deep into an easy chair away from the action in the lobby's center.

When the pack-and-ship store opened not long after, he picked out a padded envelope, then glanced around before slipping the cell phone inside.

The young black woman behind the counter raised a meaty hand to her mouth to cover a yawn.

"Too early for you?" he said.

"More like up too late wit' my kids last night," she said with a rueful smile. "One of 'em's got the flu, or something. Would you like to send a package, sir?"

"Yeah, that'd be great," he said. He didn't pursue her tale of woe, whatever it was.

She handed him a form and a pen. "If you'll just fill this out we can get started."

Mick looked at the form and realized he had no idea where to send the phone. His plan hadn't gotten that far. He stared at the paper, dumbstruck that he couldn't come up with one name, not one person he'd trust to sit on the package until Mick decided what to do. He couldn't think of anyone he could send it to, trustworthy or not. Pretty damn sad state of affairs when he couldn't even rattle off the name of a single friend.

He straightened and tapped the end of the pen against his chin. The memories from earlier came back to him The kid, the cop's son.... Not a friend, exactly, but he'd never gone out of his way to give Mick a hard time, either. Quiet. A loner, like Mick. Mick felt pretty sure the guy would accept the package, no questions asked, and hold it without poking his nose where it didn't belong.

He felt the clerk's gaze, and looked up to see her peering at him. "Are you okay?"

He nodded. "Yeah, just thinking is all. I know who I want to send it to, but I forgot the address." She perked right up. "Oh, I can help you with that. If you give me the name and city, I should be able to find an address for you."

"Really? Okay, name's Roberts." He gave her the name of the town, a Podunk place he thought he'd never see again. Now it seemed like the safest, most faraway place in the world. Her fingernails clacked on the keyboard as she typed, drawing Mick's notice. Black and bejeweled, the two-inch talons reminded him of a Disney wicked witch, maybe the one in Snow White. He wondered how she managed to hit the right keys.

"Lot of folks with that name there. Got a first name?"

Mick gave it to her. She typed, then swiveled the monitor so he could see it. "How 'bout this, then?"

He focused on the spot where one of her fingernails pressed into the screen and nodded. "That'll do."

As the clerk typed in the information and printed a label, Mick shifted his weight from one foot to the other and glanced over his shoulder. When he turned back, she quickly dropped her gaze. Mick sensed her sudden nervousness and cursed inwardly.

"I'm almost done," she said.

He gave her a tight-lipped smile, tried to ease the tension in his shoulders. "That's okay."

She finished the paperwork, and Mick quickly paid. As he left the store and headed for the hotel entrance, he saw two men cross the lobby toward the registration desk. Something about them caught his attention. Maybe the suits, though they blended in with all the others dressed for what amounted to battle in this town—politics, not business. Maybe it was the way the men's heads turned from side to side, as though more attentive to their surroundings than each other. As though looking for someone. Both were heavyset, and Mick's eyes were drawn back to the suits, cut full for broad shoulders and too much gut. And generous enough to conceal most, but not all, of the bulge of a holstered weapon that poked out on one side as they walked. The man on the right was left-handed, judging from the bulge.

As Mick moved for the front door, he realized he'd seen these two before. At the club. *Goombahs* of the worst sort. They worked for a man named Volya Nastase, an oily character who showed up at the club occasionally. More often, Nastase sent "guests" who were comp'd for anything they wanted and whom the staff treated deferentially. Mick had no proof but he felt certain Nastase was a Russian mob boss. These two had always accompanied Nastase, and sometimes escorted Nastase's guests. Sykes didn't like Nastase, Mick knew, always seemed tense when Nastase was in the club. Mick figured they had some sort of quid pro quo arrangement, but he'd known better than to ask.

The names came to him suddenly—Dobrev and Orlov. He shivered, pulled the cap brim down and kept walking. How had they known where to look so fast?

Mick almost smacked himself across the face. They'd tracked his phone. Mick dug it out of his pocket, shut it off, and popped the cover off the back as he walked. He pulled the SIM card and battery out, and dropped the battery in a trash receptacle next to the entrance. He pushed through the revolving door and stepped away from the front windows. As soon as he moved out of view of those inside, he tossed the SIM card a step ahead and smashed it under his heel. He quickly bent and scooped up the mangled chip and dropped it in the nearest trashcan. A block away, he threw away the rest of the phone.

All the while, his thoughts raced furiously. If those two had been set on his scent, either Nastase owed Sykes a big favor, or the phone was more valuable to Sykes than Mick had thought. Either way, Mick was in over his head. He needed to get the hell out of town.

11

Mick put some distance between himself and the hotel as fast as he dared without attracting attention, then stopped when he realized he didn't know where he was going. He hadn't planned for this eventuality, hadn't planned much of anything in life. And now it was going to bite him in the ass. He couldn't go back to his crib. That was the first place they'd look. He had nothing in that rat hole worth going back for anyway. A few changes of clothes. No weapons, no cash. It had been a place to crash. Even meals he'd eaten out, though he'd occasionally fried an egg and some bacon for breakfast on the weekends if he wasn't at the club. Christ, he'd had more to his name when he'd been in the military.

The rain had returned, soaking his shoulders and head through the new sweatshirt and hat. Rivulets of water ran from his hair down the back of his neck. He couldn't remember when his clammy skin had last been dry.

Ducking under an awning over the sidewalk, he turned out his pockets and quickly riffled through a wad of bills, counting out a little less than $500.00. Credit cards were out. He knew Sykes would trace them. That meant that airplanes and rental cars were out, too. He didn't have a lot in the bank, but if he cashed out what he could now from ATMs, he might have enough to get out of town. But how? Bus? Sykes would have people watching the bus station. Get on the subway going anywhere, and find a bus in Maryland or Virginia? The thought made him feel exposed.

He hurried down the sidewalk, wracking his brain, now oblivious to the rain pelting his clothes, and the answer hit him in the face. Across the street on the far side of Columbus Circle stood the arched, white granite façade of Union Station. He could melt into the crowd, pick practically any destination in the country, and get out of town on a train. Darting across the busy intersection against the light, he narrowly missed being hit by a panel truck, the angry blare of its horn following him to the other side. Sweat broke out on his forehead and under his arms. He chastised himself for his carelessness. He didn't need the attention.

Keeping his head down, he cut across the plaza to the station's front entrance. Inside, the din of hundreds of travelers moving through assaulted Mick's ears. Despite the rush of morning commuters, though, the cavernous main hall seemed so sparsely populated that Mick felt conspicuous, vulnerable. He hurried across the marble floor to the concourse, wet clothes clinging to his skin, and ducked into a men's room. The sudden quiet slowed him up, and he scanned the facilities quickly, taking stock as he stepped up to the sinks. He spooled paper towels from the dispenser and mopped some of the dampness from his face and neck.

An older businessman in a suit, a trench coat thrown over one arm, emerged from a stall, propelled by the whoosh of the toilet flushing behind him. He stopped two sinks away, gaze bouncing off Mick's in the mirror before briefly running his fingertips under the faucet, shaking them once and reaching for a towel. A teenager with a backpack zipped up his jeans in front of a urinal and turned to face the sinks as the older man strode out. Mick caught him glancing at him in the mirror. The kid quickly broke eye contact and stepped up to the sink.

Mick gave him another glance as the kid bent toward the faucet and splashed water on his face. Acne marred what would otherwise have been a handsome, square-jawed face. Stubble grew on his face in sparse patches, and Mick couldn't tell if it was deliberate or neglectful. The clothes—torn jeans, dirty Korn T-shirt, stained windbreaker— suggested the latter. Probably a runaway, and homeless to boot.

As Mick did the best he could to blot the excess moisture from his clothes and tried to come up with a plan, he caught the kid surreptitiously glancing at him from under a sheaf of black hair a couple more times. The kid shook the water off his hands in the sink and ran his wet fingers through his hair.

"Traveling?" the kid said.

Startled, Mick faced him. "Yeah, guess I am."

"Where you headed?"

"Don't know." Mick wadded up the soggy paper towels and threw them at the wastebasket.

"That's cool." The kid nodded as if he knew what was running through Mick's mind, then shifted his weight and swallowed hard, eyes darting to Mick's face and down to his feet.

"You need any help, man?"

Mick's eyes narrowed. "What do you mean?"

Thin shoulders bobbed up and down. "I don't know. Like anything. Like train fare."

Mick hesitated, looking him over again. "Why? You got tickets you don't need? Change your mind?"

"No, not like that," he said, hands wiping an imaginary table in front of him. He craned his neck, looking around the restroom to see if they were alone. "I just took a wallet off a guy. Not more'n ten minutes ago. Older. Fancy suit. A congressman, maybe. Guy doesn't even know it's missing yet. You want one of his credit cards?"

Mick considered it. He didn't think the kid was scamming him, not after admitting he'd just stolen a man's wallet. In an odd way it made a kind of moral sense. Sort of like why Mick had taken Sykes's phone after Sykes had made him kill Cummings. Mick thought it through. If he used a stolen card to buy a ticket, the bank would send cops to look for the person who used it when the theft was reported. That wouldn't be too smart.

He waved a hand. "Nah, that's okay, kid. I'm good. You use it. Buy yourself some clean clothes and a hot meal."

The kid's face fell, and his face tipped down as he shuffled past Mick toward the door.

"Yeah, sure," he grumbled. "Well, fuck you, too."

Mick watched the door swing shut. Cash was the way to go. He had a little money in savings that should get him far enough away. After checking his image in the mirror one more time, he straightened his shoulders and turned for the door. He peered down the concourse in both directions before opening the door all the way and stepping out. A businessman approaching the restroom stopped and frowned in annoyance, then sidestepped to let Mick by.

Mick pulled the damp cap down low, put his head down and headed for the nearest ATM, scanning the approaching faces for any that might be familiar. As soon as the machine dispensed a few hundred in cash, Mick made his way to the ticket counter and nervously stood in line, his gaze constantly in motion, watching out for Nastase's men or anyone he knew from the club.

The family ahead of him moved away from the counter. As Mick stepped up to the window he still had no idea where he was going. All he'd thought about was getting as far from this life as he possibly could, using Sykes's phone as leverage to keep him safe. The phone was safe for the time being. But it would be even more valuable if he knew why Sykes wanted it back so badly. If he could get away undetected and find out what was on that phone, he might be able to bargain for more than his freedom.

Follow the phone.

"Where to, sir?" Mick rested his gaze on a balding Amtrak agent on the other side of the counter. "When's your next train to Chicago?" The agent typed something on his keyboard. "Got one leaving in about a half-hour."

"How much?" Mick said, digging in his pocket.

"Coach or business, sir?" Mick hesitated. "How long's it take?"

"The train is scheduled to arrive in Chicago tomorrow at ten-thirty local time. We have one leaving this afternoon that arrives two hours earlier if you need to get there faster."

Mick waved the idea away. "No, the sooner I leave the better. They must have a sleeper car, right?"

"Yes, sir. You can get a roomette on either train. Would you like me to book one for you?"

"How much did you say?"

The agent typed some more and then looked up. "I have one for six hundred four dollars."

Mick grimaced. He hated to part with everything he had, but he still had a little cash he could access the next day, and it would be easier to hide out in a private cabin than in a coach seat. Reluctantly, he handed over most of the roll of bills in his pocket.

The agent counted it out and completed the booking, handing Mick a ticket when he finished. "Track Ten."

"Thanks."

Mick turned away from the counter and headed for the concourse. He hadn't gone more than fifty feet when an earlier thought triggered another one—he needed a new phone. An electronics kiosk stood in the middle of the wide concourse about thirty yards down. As Mick drew closer he could make out signs advertising phones on different networks. He quickened his pace. In moments, he slowly circled the booth looking over the selection of phones. Without bothering to read the plans, let alone the fine print, he picked out two and took them to the register.

A pimply kid with an overbite stood behind the register looking bored. "You know how this works?" he said as he rang up Mick's purchase.

"Yeah, I think I can figure it out. Doesn't take a genius."

The kid shrugged and handed Mick his change.

"Thanks."

Mick turned away from the counter and ripped open both phones, dropping the packaging into a nearby trash receptacle. He stuffed one phone into his back pocket, and thumbed on the power to the other to activate it. He'd have to charge it as soon as he could, but it would be good for a call or two. Once the phone was activated, he called directory assistance and asked them to look up a number. When the operator found it, the call automatically went through. Mick nervously scanned the concourse as the phone on the other end rang three times.

Mid-ring on the fourth, a voice answered, "It's your dime."

"Billy, it's Mick. Hey, man, I know it's—"

A beep cut him off, and it took him a moment to realize that voicemail had answered, not a real person.

"Billy, it's Mick Costanza. I know, been a long time. Look, I sent you a package. Can't talk now. Just hold it. I'll explain in a few days. Gotta go. And thanks."

He disconnected and put the phone in a front pocket, and headed for the platforms. As he passed another kiosk, he saw an Amtrak cop on the other side of the wide concourse bracing the kid from the restroom. Mick averted his gaze, hoping the kid wouldn't see him, but he heard a shout, and a sideways glance revealed the kid pointing at him across the hall and the cop craning his neck to see who the kid meant to single out. Every instinct Mick had told him to run like hell, and his heart felt like it was being ripped out of his chest as he fought to stay calm. The cop already had a perp in hand; Mick was certain he wouldn't let go of one to chase another. But the cop might call for back-up.

Mick glanced at his watch and picked up his pace as if he realized he was late. The archway to one set of train platforms was just ahead. If he could slip through it before the cop sicced anyone else on his tail, he'd be out of sight and might be able to lose himself in the crowd. Another few yards. Arriving passengers streamed toward him. He pushed through the arch against the current, and once past the sightline of the cop behind him, he quickly stripped off the sweatshirt and cap and stuffed them in a trashcan as he hurried past, eyes searching for Track 10.

There.

He broke into a fast jog as he rounded the front of the locomotive on Track 9, ticket in hand, looking like any other harried passenger running late. A conductor and an attendant, several cars apart, helped passengers board the train on Track 10. Mick dodged luggage carts and passengers as he hustled down the platform. Breathing hard, he pulled up in front of the attendant at the farther door and flashed him his ticket.

"Slow down, my man," the attendant said in an easy drawl. "You in an all-fire hurry to get someplace, but this train ain't movin' for another fifteen minutes."

"Thought I was late," Mick gasped.

"Relax. Take your time." The attendant glanced at the ticket again. "Up the steps to the left. You be the second roomette on the left. Welcome aboard."

"Thanks." Heart still racing, Mick quickly glanced over his shoulder, then bounded up the stairs into the car.

12

The train compartment was comfortable enough but confining, and Mick had nowhere to pace or work off his nervous energy. As soon as he'd boarded and found the right cabin, he'd locked himself in and pulled all the curtains. Like a kid on his first trip away from home, he figured out how everything worked, flipping switches, lowering the top bed, folding the table away and opening the bottom bed, checking the tiny closet, flushing the toilet. That took all of three or four minutes.

He washed his face in the sink, then sat down and read all the instruction signs in the compartment. Spotting a slim brochure, he reached for it. It gave a description of the train, hours of the dining car, a map of the route and highlights of some of the sights. He checked his watch for the sixth time since he'd boarded and had to look at it twice before the time registered—one minute closer to departure. He leaned forward slightly, lifted the curtain away from the window with one hand, peered out and instantly regretted it. Jerking his head back, he let the curtain fall back into place, hoping he wasn't too late.

"Fuck!"

One of the *goombahs*—Dobrev, maybe—was standing on the platform next to the train less than ten yards away. Mick didn't think Dobrev had seen him, but he could have kicked himself for making such a bonehead mistake. He stood and smashed the heel of his hand against the now-stowed top bunk.

"Fuck!"

He sighed. At least Dobrev couldn't board without a ticket. As if reading Mick's mind, the floor under his feet gave a little hitch, and the train slowly pulled out. Mick spun into the backward-facing seat and carefully lifted the shade again to peek out. Dobrev had his back turned. Mick couldn't tell what he was doing. Maybe checking out the train on the other side of the platform. The thug quickly disappeared from sight as the train gained speed. Mick's pulse raced as a thrill ran through him.

He just might have pulled it off.

He settled into his seat, emotions bouncing between elation and fear. But as the adrenaline dump wore off and the train fell into a rhythmic rocking motion, the wheels clack-clacking monotonously, his body relaxed and he started feeling drowsy. His eyelids drooped and closed. He shook himself awake. He needed coffee, but he didn't dare leave the compartment yet. He wanted to get away from D.C. first. Wait and see if anyone came for him, give it an hour or so.

The hypnotic motion and noise of the train on the track lulled him deeper into the seat, and his eyes closed again. He jerked awake and slapped his cheek. The all-nighter had taken its toll, and exhaustion rolled over him in waves. He stood up, flipped the sink down and splashed water on his face. He sat down again and tried to concentrate on the view outside, count cars, anything to keep his mind alert and working. But the third time his eyes closed, they stayed closed.

DANA

6

Four stories of unassuming, light gray limestone dotted with rows of equidistant glass rectangles reflected the buildings on the opposite side of K Street. Among other firms, they housed the charitable foundation where Dana Carlisle worked. She'd never really consider the building's architectural aesthetics before, since it seemed to blend in seamlessly with most of the bland mid-rise structures in D.C. The only buildings that stood out were those that the power brokers wanted to stand out, the ones with historical or political significance. Her office building had never expressed any personality before; now it glared at her under the overcast sky, intimidating her with its bulk.

Dana had never been inclined to go to work early. She believed in being punctual, but at $17.00 per hour, her pay didn't warrant more loyalty than that. When she was younger, she thought putting in longer hours, even without pay, would signal to her supervisors that she was willing and able to handle more work, more responsibility. She'd learned that in this town, especially, sheepskin mattered. She was an administrative assistant—a secretary, face it—not a degreed professional, and no matter how hard she worked she couldn't change that. Unfortunately, the lesson had come after a succession of jobs, too late for her to go back to school and get some piece of paper that said she was worth more than what she'd been paid so far. So, now she gave only what the job description called for, no more, no less.

Except she liked this job—loved it, actually—and she liked the organization she worked for. Like Heifer International or World Vision, it fostered a bootstrap approach to poverty and feeding the world's hungry. Instead of asking people to donate food or clothing, it asked people to give money to buy relatively inexpensive tools that people around the world could use to provide for themselves—hand-cranked water pumps for wells so villagers could irrigate crops; flywheel generators that operated like a stationary bike. An hour of pedaling could produce 24 hours of electricity for a single dwelling. She liked it enough that she'd put up with the crappy pay and an overbearing boss for years, hoping that eventually he and the organization would recognize her value and move her up.

She'd kept her head down and done her job for so long that she knew more than almost everybody there except Toby Granger, the executive director. She knew the heavy hitters in town, the whales who would give huge gifts each year if courted properly. She knew which foundations to hit up for donations. She knew the right pitch to each target demographic, the appeal that would strike the right balance between people's sense of guilt and altruism. She knew which direct mail houses delivered the highest response rates, and she could run down the organization's administrative expenses, fundraising expenses and overall program efficiency to within a few hundred dollars.

Still, as her value to the organization grew, the pay and her failure to advance rankled even more. Maybe it was her own fault for not "self-advocating," as they liked to say in management seminars. Then again, maybe Toby was a prick who liked her work well enough to keep her on but didn't want her to get ahead. He'd made a clumsy and crude pass at her during the employee holiday party her first year on the job. She'd been so shocked at being groped that she'd frozen in fear. He'd quickly realized his mistake, acting as if it had been an accident. At work the following Monday he'd pretended it had never happened. She'd steered clear of him since whenever possible, not easy in an office as small as theirs.

About a year after that first incident, Toby had intimated that she could go places, that she had a bright future and had suggested they discuss it sometime. She'd given him a noncommittal shrug but not another thought. Weeks later, he'd asked her to lunch. She'd hesitated and made an excuse about being too busy. He'd persisted, and she'd finally relented, thinking that perhaps he really did value her work.

At the dim, white tablecloth restaurant where he'd made reservations, they hadn't even gotten their drinks—he'd insisted she have wine—when she felt his knee brush against hers. An accident, she'd decided, but when he put his hand on her thigh after the waiter had served their appetizers, she'd politely excused herself to "powder her nose." Instead of going to the restroom, however, she'd simply walked out and gone back to work. And when Toby had returned an hour later, he'd never mentioned it.

But she'd never advanced in the organization after that. She'd watched fresh-faced event coordinators who didn't know a dahlia from a dandelion or crudités from canapés leapfrog over her at annual review time, even though she taught them everything they knew. She'd seen three office managers come and go because they couldn't handle special requisitions or the details necessary to keep the organization working smoothly. One had even managed to kill all the rented office plants, convinced that if she told the service not to come they wouldn't charge the foundation.

Through it all, Dana had kept her head down and done the work because she enjoyed it, and she believed in the cause. Every time she was tempted to quit and look for something better, she thought of all the lives she'd saved, all the money that had been raised because of her efforts, not those of Toby or anyone else in the organization. But seeing others get the promotions she deserved was hard.

Skimming the money had been so easy. Send the organization an invoice from a direct mail firm no one had ever heard of, one that sent e-mails not physical material. Approve a bill from a florist for centerpieces for one of the organization's fund-raising events that totaled many times what they usually cost. Hit up a sponsor of a gala fundraising fête with a fifty thousand-dollar invoice for "live entertainment" even though the headliner cancelled at the last minute and was replaced by a wedding singer with a deejay as his backup band. Or charge another event sponsor a six-digit special consultation and site-selection fee when the site owner had already offered the venue *pro bono*.

The organization had grown large enough to add a number of satellite offices around the country to augment the efforts of headquarters, so unfamiliar vendors providing services some couldn't recall had become commonplace. Only a few people—Toby, one or two directors on the board, and the foundation's accountant—were authorized to sign checks. But several people had authority to approve invoices, Dana chief among them. Since she handled most of the event planning along with managing the office, she had the most familiarity with the organization's vendors and their invoices. All the fake suppliers used box numbers not street addresses, making them difficult to track to a single individual.

The embezzlement had gone on for years. All told, she figured, more than three million dollars had been siphoned off, but it was hard to tell an exact number. The total could be twice that, but it didn't matter at this point.

Someone knew.

She crossed the lobby, getting the barest glance from Ant'wan at the reception desk before his gaze dropped back to his smart phone or whatever was hidden under the lip of the countertop. She'd heard stories from people who'd been around the capital a long time that in the old days staffers, even visitors, could wander around the Harry S. Truman Building in Foggy Bottom and run into foreign dignitaries. That all changed after 9/11. Now, the entire city was on lockdown, not just government buildings.

Dana knew that someone in a back room somewhere watched on a closed circuit monitor as she approached the bank of elevators. The doors remained stubbornly closed until she unclipped her ID badge from her waistband and held it up next to the panel where call buttons normally would be found. The RFID chip in her badge unlocked the security code, and doors on one of the cars slid open with a whisper.

She stepped on nervously, though she'd done this thousands of times before. The doors shut with a soft sigh, cocooning her in silence. Only the lurch in her stomach indicated that the car started its smooth ascent. The fourth floor was deserted, and the carpeted elevator foyer swallowed the sound of her footsteps. She turned to see if she'd left a trail, some physical manifestation of her passing, and saw her ghostly reflection in the glass doors of the law firm that occupied half the floor on the other side of the foyer. Shivering, she faced forward and marched around the corner toward the suite of offices that housed the foundation.

Her ID card opened the outer door. Once inside, she moved with more purpose. She didn't know how much time she had, but figured the hour or so before staff started arriving would be enough. The pirr of air conditioning created white noise that masked street sounds and chilled the office suite to the point that she was glad she'd worn black jeans and boots instead of her usual dress or skirt and blouse. The A/C must have been on to remove some of the mugginess from the air, she decided, because it wasn't all that warm outside.

She dropped her purse on her desk and headed straight for the files. Other companies where she'd worked before coming to the foundation had used purchase orders to control and track what they'd asked for and what vendors had delivered. The foundation was run more loosely, POs viewed as a time-consuming and unnecessary layer of bureaucracy. Instead, the foundation required at least one person to sign off on invoices before they could be paid. And the person paying the invoice had to be someone other than the person who initialed it.

The system had been easy to get around. Dana knew she couldn't take all the bogus invoices out of the files even if she could find them all. They'd surely be missed. But as she methodically worked her way through the drawers pulling the suspect bills, she knew she had to make a record. She wasn't sure why—the mere fact that she'd done it would implicate her, and if someone found evidence of the invoices in her possession, it would be as damning as holding a smoking gun. Nonetheless, a voice deep in her head convinced her to take all the fake invoices she could find and scan them onto a thumb drive.

The monotonous task of riffling through file folders, pulling suspect invoices, putting them on the copier and scanning them, then returning them to the drawers absorbed her. When the muffled sounds of voices and a high-pitched laugh finally registered on her consciousness, she jerked her head up in surprise. An indifferent clock on the wall of the copy room told her it was nearly 9:00, and a tidal bore of panic rose inside her. She snatched the stack of invoices out of the copy machine and yanked the thumb drive loose. Her stomach clenched, and she thought she might throw up as she fumbled the invoices awkwardly into the right file drawers. She nearly ran into a co-worker on her way out the door. Her heart leapt into her throat and her hand flew to her chest.

He quickly sidestepped to avoid her. "Whoa!"

"Jeez, Greg. You scared me half to death."

"Where's the fire?"

Too worried to think straight, she pushed past him and threw an apology over her shoulder.

"Sorry, gotta go."

She heard muttering, then, "Sorry enough to buy me lunch?"

She kept going and didn't look back.

When Toby leaned against the doorjamb and stuck his head in ten minutes later, she was buried in correspondence, the old-fashioned, snail-mail kind. She'd already uploaded the thumb drive contents to a cloud account she'd opened under a fake name, and the correspondence had given her pulse a chance to slow down. Dana felt Toby's presence but kept her head down until he rapped lightly on the doorframe.

"Got a minute?" he said.

The seriousness of his tone set off warning bells in her head. She peered at him from under her bangs, heart again beating faster when she saw the muscles at the corners of his jaw tightening, the pinched nose and lips set tightly in a thin line. It could be nothing. Everyone knew Toby was a drama queen. Still, her stomach turned somersaults.

"Can't it wait?" She lifted her chin and stared at him. "I have a lot of correspondence to get through, and I still have to go over the final menu for the philanthropy awards dinner with the caterer."

His eyes narrowed. "Is that why you were in so early this morning?"

She stared at him indignantly to hide her surprise. "Are you checking up on me?"

"I keep tabs on everyone who works here. You know that."

As she stared, she noticed that he seemed more jowly, and his pasty complexion had flushes high on his cheeks. Taking him in from head to toe, she realized he'd put on weight. The fullness in his face pushed his eyes together, making them look porcine. He didn't look healthy. She clamped her jaw. She refused to feel sorry for him.

"Well, you know that I do my job," she said, "along with a lot of other people's."

"What's that supposed to mean?"

"Exactly what it sounds like. I really don't have time for this, Toby. Unless you're deliberately trying to prevent me from working."

His mouth set in a grim line and his brows dived toward the bridge of his nose. "What were you doing in the copy room?"

The menace in his expression and tone billowed across the room, an invisible cloud of noxious gas enveloping her with fear and doubt. She knew his moods, knew that he could be petty and mean. But she sensed something deeper now, desperation exposing rot at his core. She swiveled her chair, trying to hide the involuntary shiver that ran through her. Her pulse raced, but she pushed the fear back down into her gut.

"I was checking invoices to see what we paid for centerpieces at our last event," she said calmly. "The bid we got seemed high, and I was thinking about getting one from another florist."

He grunted. "I think someone's ripping us off."

Her eyes widened, and her breath grew shallow. She thought furiously. "The florist?"

"For chrissakes no, not the florist, you idiot," he hissed. "Someone inside."

She blinked. "Here? In the office?" She felt a trickle of perspiration run down her side. He stared at her.

"I can't believe it," she lied. "I wouldn't know anything about that."

His eyebrows rose. "No? You've been acting very strangely the past few weeks."

"I don't know what you're talking about," she protested. "You can't possibly think I'd do something like that."

Before he could answer, Dana heard someone in the hall call Toby's name, and he turned his head.

Dana heard murmuring, then Toby said, "All right, I'll be right there."

He faced her again. "We're not done. We need to talk about this."

"Sure. Fine. Whatever you say." She thought she'd be sick. As soon as he disappeared from view she leaned over with her head between her knees and breathed heavily until the feeling passed. As her pulse slowly calmed, a feeling of resolve overtook her. If anything, her fears had intensified, but now that circumstances had forced her hand she saw her course of action more clearly. She was finished here. She knew that now. It was time to leave.

Almost by rote, she glanced around the small office to see that everything had been put away neatly. She checked her purse to make sure she had her keys, phone and wallet. Finally, she stood and lifted the leather jacket from the back of her chair where she'd draped it earlier. She shrugged her arms into it, and pulled it snugly down onto her shoulders. After double-checking her purse for the thumb drive, she slung her purse over her shoulder and calmly walked out.

Her nerves didn't get the best of her until she reached the elevators, and then her knees wobbled and her mind screamed silently for an elevator car to arrive. The silence was broken by the sounds of a door opening down the corridor behind her and heated voices. She didn't dare turn around and peek around the corner.

"Dana!" Toby's voice called. "I know you're out here. Don't you try to walk away from this." She heard the soft tread of footsteps and the next time he spoke his voice was closer. "We need to talk, Dana."

A bell chimed, signaling the arrival of a car, and Dana willed the doors to open with all her might. Toby's footsteps pounded down the corridor now as the doors slid open. She stepped in quickly and jabbed at the "close door" button repeatedly.

"Dana! Come back here."

The air shimmered with the anger and frustration in Toby's voice. Dana pressed herself against the rear wall of the car, trying to disappear into the paneling. The doors slid closed, inching toward each other with agonizing slowness. Just before they shut, Dana caught a glimpse of a suited leg and arm as Toby lunged toward the narrowing opening to stop the doors from shutting. Dana moaned as the doors softly thudded shut against each other and the car descended.

7

She stood in a daze on the corner, barely aware of the traffic rushing by, tires whipping up a fine mist from the wet streets, drenching her. The light rain had plastered her hair to her skull, excess moisture rolling down her face. She would have cried if it hadn't meant even more water washing her make-up down her cheeks, painting them like one of those scary clown faces. A drowned rat would have been wetter, but she stood rooted, not knowing which way to turn. She couldn't go home. That would be the first place they would look for her.

The thought of all that money and no way to get her hands on it nearly caused her to burst into tears. Instead, over the rain's steady patter, the whoosh of traffic on the slick pavement, and the rude belching of car-horns eructed with an angry slap of the wheel by aggressive drivers, she dimly heard someone shouting her name. In a panic, she whirled around, searching for the source. Toby stood on the corner at the end of the block glaring at her through the rain pelting his face. He crooked his arm and jerked it violently in a command for her to return.

She couldn't believe he'd followed her out of the building. Toby standing in the rain in a $10,000 Brooks Brothers suit without a coat or umbrella was as incongruous as Dana would be at a Scottish caber-toss event. Fear welled up inside her as she stood rooted watching Toby swivel his head left to look for a break in traffic. When he stepped off the curb to jog across the busy intersection, she turned and ran, ignoring the stares of startled passersby from under dripping umbrellas. Her boots slipped on the slick sidewalk and she nearly fell. Arms flailing, she found her footing and kept running. Chancing a look over her shoulder she nearly lost her balance again.

Toby kept coming, steadily gaining on her.

Terrified, she stepped off the curb into the path of an oncoming taxi. Horns blared, and the driver jammed on his brakes, car slewing sideways on the wet pavement, tires protesting as they tried to gain purchase. Dana threw her arms up in front of her face, squeezed her eyes shut and held her breath as the taxi slid toward her. When the impact didn't come, Dana opened her eyes and saw that the cab had stopped within inches of her. With her heart threatening to leap from her throat, she bolted around the side of the car, yanked open the door and fell inside.

"Go!" she yelled.

"What the fuck, lady? Are you out of your freaking mind?"

"Just drive! Please." She rummaged in her purse for her wallet, snatched some bills from it and leaned forward to stuff them through the cash slot in the Plexiglas divider.

Toby suddenly appeared on the other side of the car and grabbed the door handle. Dana cried out and pressed herself back into the corner. Before Toby could yank the door open she heard the *thunk* of the locks as the driver muttered, "Who the hell is that?"

"Dana!" Toby shouted. "Out of that cab. Now."

Car horns blared behind them, and Toby pounded on the glass. Rain streamed down his florid face, and his features twisted into a snarl of rage. Dana had never seen him so angry. She cowered, trying to make herself as small as possible.

"Hey!" the cabbie yelled. "Hands off the car, asshole."

Toby pounded the window again. "Get out of the cab, Dana!"

"I'll show him," the driver said. He threw the taxi into gear and hit the gas. The cab's tires spun on the wet pavement for a moment. With a squeal they gripped pavement, and the car leaped forward. Dana craned her neck to look out the rear window. Toby stood in the middle of the street, cars flowing around him, drivers honking angrily.

"Sorry about that," the driver said after they'd left Toby behind. He glanced at her in the rearview mirror. "I thought you were crazy running out into traffic like that, but that guy is a real nut job. Old boyfriend?"

Dana shook her head, unable to speak she was shaking so hard.

"Whatever. He's a jerk. Where to?"

Where to? Good question. Dana looked at the buildings sliding by. "Anywhere that isn't here," she murmured.

The cabbie looked up sharply at her reflection in mirror "What? I missed that."

For a moment, she didn't reply. Where could she go that they wouldn't find her? She needed time. Time to figure all of this out, how someone might trace all the money that had been stolen, and cover her tracks. So someplace Toby wouldn't think of. Somewhere she could lie low, untraceable.

She had no family. Her father had run out on them when she was still in middle school, and by the time she graduated from high school, her mother had drunk herself to death. She shivered at the memory of the funeral—a dozen mourners at most in the cemetery on a steely cold day in spring under a sky so bright it had made her eyes water.

Those in attendance had murmured in sympathy, thinking that she was crying with grief when in fact she hadn't been able to shed a tear for her mother.

Her mother had talked about a best friend, though, a woman she'd known growing up, and Dana wracked her brain to come up with the name. Her mother's friend had even visited once just after Dana's father had left, to help them pick up the pieces of their lives. Dana remembered trying to understand the snippets of late-night kitchen conversations she'd eavesdropped on, the plaintive wailings of her mother's voice, and the calm, collected responses of her mother's friend. The friend had stayed less than a week, leaving with a sad shake of her head, recognition of a lost cause written plainly on her face. But she'd told Dana to visit whenever she wanted.

Aunt Becca. That was it. Not Dana's real aunt, of course. With the name, the rest of it came flooding back—the slip of paper with Becca's name and address written in faint, flowery cursive; the sad smile as she cupped Dana's cheek with a hand, her warm fingers long and slender, her touch as gentle as a soft breeze. Dana had tucked the paper in a favorite book, but after years of no contact, she'd forgotten about her mother's friend. It had been hard enough getting through high school and first making excuses for her mother and eventually becoming her caretaker. The challenges of making a living after the funeral had consumed her.

Dana still had the book. And no doubt the note with Becca's address was still pressed between the pages like a dried flower. But Dana couldn't go back to her apartment to retrieve it. She squeezed her eyes shut and willed her mind to go back in time, to see that paper in her hand, picture the blue ink. And suddenly she had it. Not all of it, but enough. A last name—Thompson— and the name of the small town in eastern Minnesota where Becca had lived.

"Union Station," she told the cabbie, making her decision.

"That's only a block away."

"It's raining," she said. "And I've been through a lot. Please?" She dug in her purse, pulled out twenty-dollar bill, and held it up. "For your trouble."

The driver shot her a last glance then turned his eyes to the street ahead as the wipers slapped away fat raindrops.

8

The train rocked gently as each car's wheels rolled over the switch. It moved slowly, picking through a gritty urban landscape as it made its way out of the city. The rhythmic sway and clackety-clack of the wheels were hypnotic. Halfway down the coach car, a boy and girl, maybe eight and ten, talked excitedly and took turns pointing out the window while an elderly couple seated across from them nodded, smiled and feigned undivided attention.

A young couple in scruffy clothes sat across the aisle from the kids and their grandparents. Both of them wore their hair in matted dreadlocks the color of mud, so she had a hard time telling them apart from behind. They'd wedged two large backpacks, made taller with bedrolls and sleeping bags strapped on, into the row of seats with them, squeezing them so close the girl was practically in the boy's lap. Rather than seeming inconvenienced, they appeared to prefer the closeness to the point of embarrassment.

Two businessmen sat a few rows up, distinguished by neatly trimmed hair framed by starched shirt collars peeking out above dark wool suit jackets. In front of both men, open newspapers rose over the seat backs, rustling loudly as a page turned occasionally. The large sheets of paper hid the passing scenery from view, both men oblivious to all but the day's news.

On the other side of the aisle, a man in rough clothes swayed with the movement of the train, hands resting in his lap, chiseled face turned in profile as he gazed out the window. A flannel shirt buttoned up to his chin was visible under a brown canvas field coat. His hands were large, the knuckles bony. A workman's hands, maybe a farmer's. As if he sensed something, he slowly turned his head until his eyes met Dana's. They contained no emotion, no glimmer of humanity. She shivered and averted her gaze. His stare made her nervous. She clutched her purse more tightly on her lap and focused on the sights outside the window, ignoring him. When she no longer felt his stare, she relaxed somewhat, and let the car's rocking motion settle her further into her seat. Her eyelids drooped, then closed.

As she fell into a dream state, her father's face appeared in front of her, the mottled skin and broken capillaries running like rivers on a map imprinted across his nose and cheeks. Despite the visible signs of the affliction that had rotted him from the inside out and laid waste to their small family, he'd been a good-looking man once. A dash of gray salted his hair at the temples. A craggy brow cantilevered above piercing blue eyes. A hooked nose pointed to a wide mouth that could charm when it smiled. But up close, the cragginess turned coarse, the eyes hooded and calculating. The hooked nose had been broken in a fight, maybe more than once. And the thin-lipped mouth, more often formed into a cruel sneer, didn't smile enough.

In the vision, he barged through the front door of their small bungalow, face reddened by more than the cold outside, features contorted by perpetual anger into a scowl. He removed his coat and carefully hung it on a hook on the wall by the door. Then he unbuttoned the cuffs of his shirt and rolled up the sleeves, revealing thin, veined arms roped with muscle. He disappeared from her view through the crack between her barely open bedroom door and the jamb, but she heard his raised voice from the kitchen quickly turn to shouts and curses. At the first sickening sound of flesh smacking flesh, she quietly shut the door and wedged her desk chair under the knob. With all her strength, she put her shoulder to her dresser and shoved it in front of the small straight-backed chair.

Breathing heavily, she collapsed on her bed. For a few moments, she listened to the muffled shouts and cries. Then she picked up a book from her nightstand and shut the sounds out of her mind, praying that the chair would hold. Or, as happened most nights, he ran out of strength after taking out his rage on her mother and gave up beating on her door in only a few minutes.

A buzzing sound and vibration in her lap startled Dana fully awake, and her eyes snapped open. Disoriented, she needed a moment to figure out what was demanding her attention. Her phone. She dug in her purse and found it. As she pulled it out she checked the screen—an incoming call from Toby.

She shivered again and threw the unanswered phone back into her purse.

SYKES

13

Sykes swiped his keycard on the unobtrusive pad mounted next to the doorframe and opened his office door. He strode silently across the carpet to his desk and slid into the leather chair behind it. Weariness pressed on him like a chorus girl sitting in his lap. He pushed it away, anger clearing his mind. Stevens had followed him inside and now stood quietly in the center of the room, hands clasped, awaiting instructions or dismissal. His second-in-command's calm demeanor settled him, once again affirming Sykes's decision to hire him.

"You debited the sheik's account?"

Stevens allowed a barely perceptible nod. "The girl has been recompensed accordingly, as have the doctor and nurse who attended to her. We remunerated her service for her time off to recover and gave all the other girls a bonus to keep them quiet. And we docked his account another two hundred thousand."

Sykes considered the steps taken, wondering if it would be enough to prevent the night's events from ever happening again. Were it not for the sheik's net worth, not to mention his diplomatic immunity, Sykes would have beaten the man to a pulp himself. As it was, it had taken three of them—Sykes, Stevens and George—to drag the obese, naked, drunk and cocaine-fueled sheik off the battered "escort" in his bed, while another five girls in various states of undress cowered in a corner in horror.

Though the girl looked all of twelve—by special request—thank god she wasn't underage. Sykes was inured to most of the vices of the club's members, but he drew the line when it came to pedophiles. The mere idea disgusted him, and the risks to the club were too great to indulge any member's interest in that particular perversion. He'd been tempted to throw the sheik's naked ass out on the street but knew exposure would be bad for business.

"I apologize again, sir," Stevens said quietly. "If we'd monitored the feed in his suite more closely, it never would have gone that far."

Sykes tapped a finger against his chin, then waved his hand. "No one blames you Phillip."

"I've already alerted kitchen and bar staff still on duty that he's not to be served alcohol," Stevens went on. "I left voicemail for all the day managers to that effect as well."

Sykes nodded. "Good. I'll have a sit-down with the sheik when he sobers up and let him know what we've done. The room feed was recording?"

Stevens nodded. "Of course."

"Then I'll explain that the $200,000 is intended to cover our inconvenience. I also plan to fine him two million, and let him know that if he ever so much as sneezes in the wrong direction anywhere on the grounds, the fine will go up by two decimal points."

Stevens arched an eyebrow.

"Please, Phillip. Two million is pocket change. Two hundred million, though, might sting a bit. It will make him think twice about misbehaving. If he balks, we can show him the video footage."

"Of course," Stevens murmured. "Anything else?"

"The clean-up...?"

"We're using a discreet service that normally handles crime scenes instead of our normal housekeeping staff."

Sykes loosed a small sigh. "Thank you, Phillip. I appreciate your attention to detail, as usual. You can expect a bonus in your account tomorrow."

"It's not necessary, but thank you, sir. If there's nothing else, I'd like to review tomorrow's scheduling." He glanced at his watch. "Or, rather, today's."

Sykes waved him toward the door. "By all means. Thank you again."

As Stevens turned, Sykes reached toward the spot on the desk where he usually left his phone to call the sheik's embassy and let them know he would not be back until later in the day. He frowned when his fingers brushed the polished wood surface. He patted down the pockets in his suit, but felt nothing.

"Phillip?" he called before his assistant was out the door. "Did you see me with my phone earlier?"

Stevens turned with a quizzical expression. "No, sir. Have you misplaced it?"

Sykes let his gaze pan across the desk's nearly bare surface. "It seems I have."

"I'll keep an eye out for it," Stevens said. He pulled the door shut behind him.

Little ruffled Sykes. He dealt with the demands of impatient, powerful men every day, men who expected impeccable service at lightning speed. Some of the club's members were arrogant pricks; others were unassuming and kind. Sykes handled them all with aplomb, never kowtowing or fawning. Obsequiousness was for those with no self-assurance, no chutzpah. But his phone's disappearance rattled him, sending his heart into his throat.

He took a deep breath. The night had been long and tiresome. Cigar smoke from the lounge permeated the fibers of his suit, and he couldn't get the stink of bodily fluids from the sheik's suite out of his nostrils. He wanted nothing more than a hot shower, a few hours of sleep and fresh clothes. They lay beyond his reach until he found his phone. He must have forgotten where he put it due to overwork. Methodically, he opened drawers and searched his desk. When his hunt turned up nothing, he sat back and approached the problem from a different angle, thinking back to the last time he'd seen it.

Right before Phillip had come in to ask for his help with the sheik.

It had sat on the desk in its usual spot. But Phillip's request had been so urgent that Sykes had forgotten to take the phone with him as he normally did when he left his office. And there had been only one other person in the office at the time.

Mick Costanza.

14

Sykes drummed the desk with his fingers, willing the phone on his desk to ring. He'd put every available man on the hunt for Mick, and he knew it wasn't enough. He'd even called in a favor from Volya, as much as the effort had made him cringe. Asking Nastase for anything simply lengthened the time he'd owe the crass banker a favor. Banker. Sykes snorted at the thought. Nastase liked to think of himself as a sophisticate, a man of the world, a businessman on par with, say, the CEO of a Fortune 500 company.

As Sykes had expected, Nastase had loaned him Mikhail Orlov and Alexei Dobrev, a couple of goons with a lot of bulk, most of it muscle gone to fat, and half a brain between them. He swore under his breath. His own staff wasn't much better. Beyond George, who wasn't the sharpest tool in the box, either, Sykes trusted only a few members of his security team to handle a situation like this with discretion. He had no concerns about the security they provided for the club, but he had to manage Mick's sudden defection delicately.

He swore again, audibly this time. Mick's initiative surprised him, and he wondered if he hadn't pushed the kid too far, too fast. George had vouched for him, and Sykes had seen enough gumption and native intelligence in Mick to believe he could be a valuable asset. Until the situation with the congressman, Mick had fit right in and proved himself both loyal and adept at everything they'd asked of him. He'd kept a low profile, exercised diplomacy and good manners with members and guests, gotten physical when needed, and hadn't shied away from the more unsavory aspects of the job. Unless Mick was a lot smarter than Sykes had estimated, though, he'd gotten lucky. Sykes didn't think Mick realized what he'd done when he'd taken the phone, nor what he really had in his hands. And Sykes wanted to keep it that way. He wanted that phone back before Mick could cause some real damage.

And, of course, Mick had to be taught a lesson.

Sykes felt ready to explode, and a headache throbbed around his eyes. He winced and pressed the pad of a thumb hard against his left temple and rubbed in a circular motion. His foot had started tapping in time to the rhythm of his drumming fingers, and he willed it to stop. This nervousness wasn't like him. He drew in a slow, deep breath, picked up the handset of the phone on his desk and dialed an extension.

After one ring, his general manager answered, "Stevens."

"Any word?"

"No, sir. George just checked in. I'm waiting to hear from Joe and Rick. Should be any moment."

Sykes grunted. "Keep me posted."

"Yes, sir."

Almost as soon as Sykes hung up, the phone rang. He snatched it up. "Speak," he growled.

"It's Alexei. The kid isn't here. I mean, he is, but he isn't." Sykes banged the receiver against the edge of the desk then brought it back to his ear. "What the fuck are you talking about?"

"I mean we can't find him in the hotel, but the GPS stopped working, so we don't know where to look."

Sykes wanted to crawl through the phone and strangle the bastard. He absently ran a finger over the dent he'd put in the edge of the walnut desk. Maybe now it qualified as antique.

"He figured out we're tracking his phone, you moron," Sykes said. "He can't have gotten far. The two of you should split up and start working out and back, around the block."

"Out and back where?"

"Get moving!" Sykes shouted. "Now! Find him!"

He slammed the receiver down, hoping the noise busted Dobrev's eardrum. Swiveling his chair, he faced the sleek high-definition monitor on the desk and pulled up a map of downtown D.C. He tried to imagine where Mick would go next, and as he zoomed in on the last location of Mick's phone, a busy hotel, he jabbed the monitor with a finger hard enough to leave a smudge.

"That's where he'll go," he said, and reached for the phone again.

15

Dobrev and Orlov reminded Sykes of a couple of Irish thugs from his Hell's Kitchen neighborhood growing up—Seamus Flynn and Pádraig Boyle, a couple of Cro-Magnon lowlifes if ever there were. Boyle's kid Eoin, no surprise, had been the school bully, at whose hand Sykes had suffered many indignities and bruises. Until the day Sykes had had the foresight to bring a penknife to school and had left Eoin bleeding on a bathroom floor.

Sykes had earned respect that day, and he'd vowed there and then that he would never again be bullied. He'd been two weeks shy of his twelfth birthday.

Now, he called Dobrev's number and drummed his fingers on the desk until Alexei picked up. "Take everyone you've got out there and go to Union Station. He's there. Find him. Now."

Less than twenty minutes later, Sykes looked up at the sound of a soft knock on his office door. Before he could speak, the door opened. Stevens entered, and without appearing rushed, glided across the Persian carpet in an instant.

"They found him?"

Stevens nodded. "Spotted him on a westbound train as it pulled out."

"I need George," Sykes said.

"Already on his way back," Stevens said, his voice as calm as his placid expression. "He should be outside the rear entrance, ready to go in a few minutes."

Sykes grunted, already focused on what he would need. Not much. He unlocked a desk drawer and took out a Taurus PT 709 9mm semi-automatic. The little gun was virtually undetectable when holstered under his suit jacket. He'd had it modified, though, adding a threaded barrel so he could easily screw a sound suppressor onto the gun.

"You're not expecting trouble, are you, sir?" Stevens said.

"No. But it's better to be prepared."

"Of course, sir."

"He needs to be taught a lesson. I'm very disappointed in him."

"Mick did hold a lot of promise." Stevens let out a small sigh. "Are you sure he doesn't have some sort of explanation?"

Sykes glanced at him sharply. "He's running, Phillip."

"He doesn't strike me as the sort to divulge information."

"I can't take the chance." He saw the consternation on Stevens's face. "Fine, I'll give him a chance to explain himself. Perhaps you're right. Maybe it's all a misunderstanding. But he stole from me. I can't just turn a blind eye. He has to learn there are consequences in life for the choices he makes."

"A lesson we've all learned at one time or another," Stevens murmured. He stepped closer to the desk and held out his hand. "As soon as you informed me of Alexei's call, I got the itinerary for that train."

Sykes glanced at the papers in Stevens's hand and reached for them. "Thank you, Phillip."

"There's a train ticket for you in there. Without knowing your plans, I thought it best to err on the side of caution and give you some time to find him, so I booked you through to Cincinnati."

"That's fine. As always, you've done well." Sykes came around the desk and opened the door to a small closet, retrieving an overcoat and deerskin gloves. He lifted a briefcase from the desk, and faced Stevens once more. "I don't expect to be on the train for long, but I'll keep you informed. You know what to do here."

"Of course." Stevens inclined his head. "Everything will run smoothly, as usual."

Sykes nodded and walked out, heading for an exit that would take him out to the rear driveway. George was already there in the car, engine running. Sykes slipped into the back of the town car, and George pulled away without waiting for instructions. Sykes consulted the itinerary Stevens had given him and glanced at his watch. He didn't think they had time to reach either of the train's first two stops ahead of schedule. But knowing George's driving prowess, he felt confident they'd arrive at the third stop minutes before the train.

"Culpeper, George. We have a little more than an hour."

George glanced at him in the rear view mirror. Without a word, he pulled out of the drive and tapped their destination into the car's navigation system.

Sykes lowered the seatback tray table and retrieved a notebook computer from his briefcase, glad for George's silence. Despite this interruption in his day he still had work to do. As indispensable as Stevens was in running day-to-day operations, the club belonged to Sykes, and not even a sightseeing trip by train would force him to abrogate his responsibilities. And, if only for a little while, he wanted to put aside his anger. He would have time to indulge it later, but letting it consume him now was counterproductive. He barely noticed the trees whipping past the windows, nearly stripped now of their fiery autumn foliage, or the loud hiss of tires whisking water on rain-soaked pavement.

He glanced at his watch in surprise when George announced they were five minutes outside of Culpeper. He made some notes to himself, powered off his computer and put his work away just as they pulled up to the quaint, century-old brick train station.

"Thank you, George," he said as he gathered his things and opened the door. "Nice bit of driving."

George glanced furtively in the mirror, but said nothing. Sykes shrugged and swung a leg out of the car. He was straightening when George blurted, "I'm sorry, Mr. Sykes."

Sykes bent down to peer at him over the back of the seat. "About what? You have nothing to be sorry for."

George glanced down before answering. "I brought him in."

"You recommended him," Sykes corrected. "I'm the one who hired him. He's my responsibility, not yours." The assertion didn't dissuade George from looking miserable. "I appreciate the sentiment, and your loyalty. You did nothing wrong."

George nodded and swallowed.

"I'll call you with instructions when I'm ready," Sykes said, and turned away.

Checking his watch again, Sykes hurried through the station out onto the platform. He felt the reverberation of the train under his feet before he heard the blast of the horn as it neared a crossing, then the rumble and clack of steel wheels on the rails. Before long, the locomotive hove into view around a curve. Sykes willed himself to remain calm.

This was a long shot at best. Dobrev had only caught a fleeting glimpse of what he thought was Mick's face through a window on this train. Sykes had called him and insisted that Alexei tell him exactly where he'd seen Mick. Alexei had said Mick was in the second-to-last car, left hand side, second window from the rear.

As the train rolled slowly into the station, Sykes noted the last two cars were sleeping cars. Mick had gotten himself a berth, it seemed. Which meant he intended to run far. If Dobrev was right, Mick's assigned berth was on the other side of the train. A conductor with a step stool in hand hopped onto the platform from a car closer to the engine. He took a couple of running steps as the train came to a stop with a hiss of air brakes.

"'The Cardinal,'" the conductor called, setting the stool in front of an open door. "Service to Charlottesville, Staunton, Cincinnati, Indianapolis and Chicago. All aboard!"

Sykes strolled up the platform toward the open door, letting other passengers board first.

"Morning," the conductor said, touching the brim of his cap as Sykes hopped up.

Sykes waited in the vestibule while the conductor looked up and down the platform, and waved as he spoke into a walkie-talkie to the engine crew. The conductor grabbed the stool with one hand, a bar next to the door with the other and swung himself up as the train started to move. Sykes showed him his ticket.

"Business class is that way, sir." The conductor opened his hand toward the rear. "Just past the dining car."

Sykes nodded and oriented himself as he entered the dining car, quickly forming a mental picture of the train's layout—engine, two coach class cars, lounge car with cafe, business class and two sleepers in the rear. The dining car was nearly full. He scanned the faces as he walked through, not expecting to see anyone familiar, but taking stock. Putting himself in Mick's shoes, he figured the traitor would lie low and let some time pass before feeling confident enough to venture out.

He steadied himself in the vestibule between cars as the train picked up speed and swayed on the tracks. Through the door inside the business-class car, he went on a higher level of alert, taking note of everything, judging each passenger on their expression, attire, mannerisms. A businessman here in shirtsleeves, focused on a laptop in front of him, likely on board only to Charlottesville or maybe White Sulphur Springs for a conference at the Greenbrier. Someplace too far to drive but too close or inconvenient to fly. Older couples dotted the car in a checkerboard pattern, some with books, others gazing out the windows, retirees traveling the country. An attractive woman he guessed to be in her early thirties sat alone, preoccupied by something troubling, a corner of her lower lip caught delicately between white teeth, stare fixed on the passing scenery.

Sykes noted the location of his own seat, but continued walking through the car, his gaze returning to the single woman. Something contradictory about her had snagged on a corner of his consciousness. Stylish clothes—leather jacket, silk blouse—but a backpack, albeit leather, not a purse or bag. Traveling light? Or pragmatically? Features that bordered on beautiful, but chestnut hair pulled into a utilitarian ponytail that downplayed her looks. A woman who wanted to be taken seriously. He stared a moment too long. Feeling his gaze, she turned, her eyes meeting his briefly before he looked away, feigning disinterest. He had a task to accomplish, and limited time.

At the end of the car, he opened the door to the vestibule and stepped through. The clacking of wheels on the rail joints, squeal of steel on steel and wind rush more than doubled in volume here. He stepped up to the door of the first sleeper car and looked through the window before opening it. No one on the other side. As he stepped through, he turned to look back through the glass into the business coach. No one followed. A little hallway led to the right and along the side of the car to skirt the large family suites. He stopped and quickly knelt, putting his briefcase on the floor and popping the latches. From a pocket in the lid he removed a stun gun and slipped it in his coat.

The narrow corridor jogged left then right, now taking him down the middle of the car, with roomettes on either side. The door curtains in one or two had been pulled back, giving him a glimpse of their occupants as he passed, but most passengers had opted for privacy. The empty corridor suggested that the attendant had made his rounds and retreated to his own room, the last one on the right, across from the communal shower, and one behind Mick's. If Mick is on board. Feeling his adrenaline spike, he quickened his pace. The timing was good, since many people had gone to the café for lunch.

Now he could see the attendant's door standing open. Curtains hung over the door of the roomette in front of the attendant's. Sykes stopped just shy of the attendant's door, eased the briefcase to the floor, and stuck his head around the door jamb with a smile on his face. The attendant looked up from some paperwork on the small table between the seats under the window.

"Can I help you?"

Sykes nodded as he stepped into the small space. The attendant started to rise out of his seat, curiosity on his face starting to turn to alarm when Sykes continued to close the gap between them. Sykes quickly jammed the stun gun against the attendant's chest and thumbed the discharge trigger. The man jerked in pain and surprise, and his body shook violently as fifty-three million volts coursed through him, disrupting his nervous system. He collapsed in the seat, flopping a few times like a fish on a dock before lying still. Sykes quickly grabbed the key ring on the man's belt, ripped it off and stepped back into the corridor.

THE CARDINAL

17

"Tickets! Tickets, please."

Mick lurched out of sleep, sweaty and disoriented, heart pounding at the sudden knocking sound. For a moment he thought he was still in George's limo, but as the conductor's request for tickets rang in his ears, he remembered. He couldn't believe he'd fallen asleep. He swiped the back of his hand across his mouth and checked his watch. He'd been asleep nearly an hour. *Smart, Mick, falling asleep on the job.*

Now, he frowned, blinking away the sleepiness that still fogged his brain. The attendant had checked his ticket when he'd boarded.

"What do you mean?" he said loudly. "I showed my ticket when I boarded."

"That was the attendant," said the voice on the other side of the door. "I'm the conductor. Sorry for the inconvenience, but I need to see everyone's ticket."

Confused, Mick rummaged through his pockets and pulled out the wrinkled ticket. He stood and reached for the door. As he put his hand on the lock, he had second thoughts and stretched out his other hand to move the curtain aside. A sudden jolt of pain ripped up his arm like lightning into his chest and through the rest of his body, jangling his nerves and ringing his head like a bell. He twitched spastically and fell back, bouncing off the table onto the floor, paralyzed.

While part of his brain tried to figure out what had just happened, dawn broke over the rest of his consciousness, and with a brilliance that outshone the sun the realization hit him that he was well and truly fucked.

18

Pangs of hunger roiled Dana's stomach, and she involuntarily bent at the waist and groaned. As the pain passed and she was able to straighten, she flushed and glanced at nearby passengers to see if they had noticed. She glanced at her phone to see the time and realized that she hadn't eaten since dinner the night before. No wonder she was hungry. She dug her wallet out of the purse on her lap, and looked through it, ruefully counting the few bills that remained.

The enormity of what she'd done loomed above her, a rogue wave that curled, frothing and seething over her head. She had no job to go back to, no place to live, and barely enough money to eat for the duration of her trip. She had no idea where she was going or who might be there at trip's end to help her, give her shelter and comfort. She could definitely use some of those millions now, but where the hell had they gone? Where was the money? Her chest constricted, and her breath grew shallow as panic welled up inside her, threatening to choke off her air supply. A small sob escaped her lips, and this time she felt someone's gaze boring into her.

Get a grip.

She sucked a deep breath in between clenched teeth and looked around casually. The creepy guy a few rows down across the aisle was staring at her again. Screw him. She'd gotten away from Toby, and with enough insurance that she'd figure out a way to come out of all of this ahead. She'd find the damn money, figure out where it had gone. And she definitely wouldn't let some halfwit get inside her head.

Lunch sounded like an excellent idea. She knew how expensive the food was aboard a train, but until they reached a large enough city with a long enough layover for her to run to a nearby grocery or deli and buy some food, she was stuck. Maybe she'd just get something to tide her over—a piece of fruit, or a muffin—and then explore the rest of the train. Warming to the idea, she put her wallet back in her purse, checked her reflection in her compact mirror, and gathered herself. Standing, she smoothed her jeans down over her thighs, pulled the hem of her leather jacket down, clutched her purse under her arm and turned into the aisle to walk to the café car.

19

Before he even heard the thud of the body on the other side of the door falling to the floor, Sykes had worked the attendant's master key—more like a hex wrench—into the lock and rolled the door aside. He nearly grinned with satisfaction at the sight of Mick on the floor twitching, drool running down his chin. He reached down with both hands, grasped the front of Mick's shirt, and dragged him up into a seat. Mick feebly tried to swat his hands away but his motor skills remained scrambled. Grabbing his briefcase from the corridor, Sykes slid the door shut and quickly went to work. In less than a minute he'd bound Mick's wrists, ankles and knees, stuffed his mouth with one of his own socks and taped it shut.

Mick's eyes grew bright with fury as the effects of the shock wore off and Sykes further immobilized him with each new strip of tape. Sykes had no doubt that Mick's bravado would soon vanish like a wisp of smoke in a stiff breeze. The sooner he could make that happen the better. Time was his enemy now. He risked discovery with every passing moment. He ripped off two more lengths of tape, used one across Mick's forehead to snug his head to the back of the seat. He looped the other length under Mick's chin, pulled it tight against his throat and stuck the ends against the wall above the headrest.

Satisfied Mick wasn't going anywhere, Sykes quickly let himself out into the corridor, shutting the door behind him and stepping back into the attendant's room. The attendant was still in his seat, but was stretching his arm out and down. Sweat covered his face, showing Sykes the amount of effort the man had expended in trying to shake off the paralysis and pain caused by the electric shock. Sykes directed his gaze at the floor where the attendant's trembling fingers stretched. His estimation of the man's determination went up a notch at the sight of the two-way radio on the floor. Too bad the attendant had dropped it.

Sykes poked his head back into the corridor and looked both ways. With no one in sight, he rolled the door closed, then confidently and methodically unholstered his pistol, took a suppressor out of his coat pocket and threaded it into the barrel. The attendant watched him with widening eyes, mouth working as if to say something, emitting only soft grunts in his effort to yell for help. Sykes twisted the silencer one last time to tighten it, leaned back against the door to prevent blowback from soiling his clothes and shot the attendant in the head. He carefully tucked the now- elongated gun into the holster under his suit coat, let himself back out into the corridor and locked the attendant's door.

Mick watched him warily as Sykes entered Mick's roomette again and lifted his briefcase onto the covered sink and opened it.

"I'm disappointed in you, Mick." Sykes rested his palms on the edge of the countertop, fingers curled over the edge of the open case. "You stole from me. Why would you do that? I took you in on George's word, no questions asked. I paid you generously, treated you well. And this is the thanks I get?"

Mick shook his head, wide-eyed. "No? No, what? No, you didn't steal my phone? No, I didn't treat you like one of my own?" Sykes back-handed Mick across the face, the pain across his knuckles enough to take the edge off his rage, keep him calm enough to do what had to be done.

In a calmer voice, Sykes said, "Okay, here's what we're going to do. I'm going to ask you a simple question. You have once chance to answer it. If you don't, or if I'm not satisfied with your answer, then this will go very hard for you. Do you understand?"

Mick hesitated, then gave a single nod.

Sykes reached down and ripped half the strip of tape away from Mick's face, eliciting a wince, and took the sock out. "Where is my phone?"

Words tumbled out of Mick's mouth in a rush. "Look, I don't want any trouble. I just want to disappear somewhere, go back to living a normal life—"

Sykes slapped him hard. "Last chance. Where's my phone?"

"I don't have it. It's not here."

Savagely, Sykes jammed the sock between Mick's teeth and pulled the tape tight over his lips. From the briefcase, he removed a pair of pliers and an antique brass and ivory handle *balisong* he'd taken from a very drunk and irate Japanese businessman at the club one night. CEO of a major international conglomerate, the man had been experimenting with a tincture of sativa, the psychoactive effect of which had been nearly a hundred times stronger than that of a Brainstorm Haze joint, and started hallucinating. Running naked and screaming through the upstairs halls, he'd threatened some of the staff with the butterfly knife. Security had disarmed him, and Sykes had kept the knife.

He unfolded it and used the point to rip a gash in Mick's shirt. He tore it open further with both hands until he bared Mick's torso. Then he brought the razor-sharp blade of the knife to a spot just above

Mick's beltline, midway between his navel and hip. He pressed the point into Mick's flesh and flicked it up toward his chest, slicing a two-inch cut that oozed then dripped blood. Mick sucked in a breath through his nostrils. Sykes moved the point of the blade half an inch to the left of the first cut and sliced a second one parallel to the first. Mick started to buck, and Sykes had to lean his weight on Mick's chest to hold him still enough to make a third cut joining the other two at the bottom, forming a U in blood.

Mick grunted now, eyes wildly flicking back and forth in their sockets. The knife was sharp enough that Mick wouldn't have felt pain at first, but three cuts probably stung a bit. Soon he'd feel real pain. Sykes found a towel, opened it and laid it across the open briefcase. He placed the *balisong* on the towel and slowly picked up the pliers, giving Mick plenty of time to think, to anticipate where the pain would hit him next.

There's no time. Get on with it.

Sykes opened the jaws of the pliers, jammed them into the cut at the bottom of the U on Mick's stomach, squeezed and ripped the half-inch strip of skin up and off the underlying layer of fat. A scream gurgled from Mick's throat as his chest heaved and his hips bucked like a bee-stung horse.

20

The terrain flashing past the window is both foreign and familiar. The last time I traveled this deeply into the Commonwealth of Virginia was a few weeks back, when I talked my partner into chasing down a lead on a fugitive who managed to rabbit after we raided his house in Ypsilanti, outside Detroit. I thought we were chasing the wrong man, a case of stolen identity. My partner—ex-partner now—didn't see it that way. Hunt had such a hard-on for this guy that I figured the only way to catch the bastard we were really after was finding the fugitive and clearing up the confusion.

That bullshit about stuff that doesn't kill you making you stronger is just that, cow manure through and through. At least that's what it feels like. I worked my ass off to land a spot as an FBI field agent, and even harder to attract Hunt's attention. After all, he led of one of the bureau's most elite counterterrorism fly teams.

Once I became part of Hunt's team, the real work began—convincing an egocentric, old-school, no-nonsense, long-time agent known for playing by the book that I had valuable skills and experience to share. Five years as a field agent, then three more as Hunt's partner before he started listening to me and taking my advice. All that went down the tubes in the space of forty-eight hours.

Technically, my leave should last only as long as it takes to investigate an agent-involved shooting. But after the dressing down from Beamis, scuttlebutt around the office is that I screwed the pooch and will likely be reassigned to some burg in the hinterlands where the only activity more exciting than naval-gazing is mole-hunting, an equally futile and meaningless pursuit. Of course, that's if the bureau doesn't quietly let me go.

The shooting was righteous. A known terrorist wounded my partner, threatened a young boy and his grandfather, and planned to bomb the Rotunda in the National Archives, destroying the Charters of Freedom, the three most important documents in our country's history. Not to mention the fact that he was taking potshots at me, which made self-defense well within my purview and more than justified.

I don't think the bureau even had a problem with me shooting the guy. It wasn't like I killed him. Not that I missed, either. I've always been a crack shot, even as a kid plinking at cans with BB guns with my brothers, and my skills haven't waned. I hit that bastard center mass with five slugs before the grandfather got up behind him and blasted a load of tungsten buckshot into the base of his skull with a replica of an antique gun from Vietnam War days. Turns out, the s.o.b. was wearing a Kevlar vest, so my slugs didn't kill him, only cracked a few ribs, according to the M.E.'s report.

The problem, at least from my perspective, is that Hunt had a personal grudge against this particular terrorist and a blind spot so big that half the time he couldn't see past his zeal to get the man. As his partner, rather than cause discord by objecting, I gently steered him in what I considered better directions. The upshot is that we found and stopped the right guy.

At issue with Beamis and his boss Havlicek, the counterterrorism division director, however, is the fact that I didn't follow protocol to get Hunt to track the real terrorist. And there isn't anything the bureau hates more than rule-breakers who don't respect authority. As if that fits me to a T. I couldn't have gotten as far as I did in the army, let alone the FBI, without following orders.

What I still can't understand is Hunt's willingness to hang me out to dry. Everything I did not only benefitted him, but actually saved him from a fate far worse than what I'm about to suffer. Well, that might not be totally true since I don't know yet what the bureau plans for me. And instead of facing it—fighting it, even—I turned tail. I'm running away again, and what faces me at the destination I chose could turn out worse than staying in D.C.

I shake my head like a chaperone at a middle school dance, put away my whiny violin, and take in my fellow passengers. As I do, I recall seeing a man walk through the car. I'm not sure the image would have stuck in my head except that I don't see him anywhere now. As I form a mental picture—elegantly dressed, gray hair, youthful face— I feel I should know him.

As hard as I try, I can't place him. Since I didn't see him come back through, I assume he has a seat or a berth in a car behind me.

I wonder where he's gone.

21

No stranger to pain from his stint in the military, Mick couldn't comprehend the agony he experienced now. The white-hot, searing pain consumed him, filled his brain to the point of bursting. He'd tried not to cry out at first, not give Sykes the satisfaction of seeing how weak and pathetic he was. But he'd screamed anyway, the muffled, strangled sounds lost under the steady staccato castanets of the train on the rails. No one would hear him, and now even he was no longer sure that the mewling whimpers sounding in his head came from him.

As soon as he'd seen Sykes's face, not Dobrev's or George's, he'd known it that it was all over. Anyone else's face coming through that pocket door and he might have had a chance. But Sykes himself...? Mick was a dead man. Taking Sykes's phone had been the dumbest fucking thing he'd ever done, an impulse that would now cost him his life. Killing that congressman hadn't been so smart, either. Had it only been hours earlier? Now, he could see that working for Sykes meant he'd had no choice from the beginning. Maybe that had been his dumbest mistake, accepting the job offer.

Even from Sykes, Mick hadn't expected this level of pain. Pain so excruciating that he would have done anything, promised anything, to make it stop. Maybe he deserved this agony for what he'd done. Maybe it was karma for pissing away his life. Mick knew he wasn't a good person, but he had a conscience, and in the end he'd tried to get out. Too late....

Incapable of rational thought now, he held onto one prayer, one hope. He would not fuck up anyone else's life just because he'd made a mess of his own. He wouldn't give Sykes shit. He had no idea why Sykes wanted that phone back so badly, but the one good thing Mick could do with his remaining minutes on earth was keep his mouth shut. And despite all the agony, he thought he might just make it. Sykes had screwed up. Mick could feel it, sense it. Even through the white haze, he'd felt Sykes's rage at his refusal to give up any worthwhile information, to offer anything except his smothered shrieks of pain. Sykes had pressed too hard—literally.

Mick felt something give way inside, felt his senses receding and his strength ebbing away. Through the blur of tears and sweat in his eyes, Mick saw Sykes's face come close, faintly heard him growl in his ear.

"Where is it, Mick? Just tell me, and I'll end your pain."

As his vision turned black, Mick managed a wan smile.

Too late, motherfucker. See you in hell.

22

After standing in line for nearly twenty minutes for a crappy Danish and overripe banana that cost more than a decent glass of pinot grigio at the bar in the Hay-Adams Hotel, Dana ended up taking the food back to her seat because the café was full. She chewed slowly, taking a bite of each every time so the mushy banana made the sawdust Danish less dry and tasteless. She ate self-consciously, aware that the odd man continued his staring with the intensity of a stalker.

She didn't want to be here. She didn't want to be on this train to who the hell knew where. She hadn't done anything to deserve a life on the run. All her life she'd kept her head down, her nose clean. She'd worked hard, gotten ahead, had a nice life. Well, an okay life. Better than many. She'd earned enough to pay her bills, live in a decent studio apartment, feed and clothe herself, take a one-week vacation every year as long as she budgeted frugally. And now this. It felt so unfair. Running away. No job, no place to live. Always looking over her shoulder for Toby or whoever he sent after her.

She bit her lip and blinked back tears. She had all the insurance she needed in her bag. Surely Toby would figure that out and realize that she'd managed to stalemate him. She didn't think he'd risk it once he thought it through. Then again, he'd already come after her, had followed her onto the street and tried to pull her out of a taxi. He could be angry and crazy enough to keep coming. Unless she figured out how to use the leverage she had in a more offensive manner. Follow the money. She had to find out where the money had gone. She needed to work this through.

She folded the banana peel and soiled napkins into the bag that had held the Danish, and brushed the crumbs from her lap. As she had thirty minutes earlier, she gathered herself together, slung her bag over her shoulder and stepped into the aisle with the intent of heading to the lounge car to think. From the corner of her eye she saw the stalker get up. Her pulse took a syncopated triple jump to nearly twice its normal rate. She quickly turned away. Walking with hands out, ready to grab something to steady herself against the rocking of the train, she headed for the end of the car and glanced over her shoulder.

He's following me. Oh, God, he's following me.

She couldn't imagine that Toby had sent him. He didn't know

where she was going, and he wouldn't have had time.

He's coming.

She tried to calm herself. As weird and perverted as the man appeared, he wouldn't dare try anything with all these people around. Even so, she hurried. When she reached the vestibule, she wrinkled her nose. Only an hour or so out of D.C., and already the restrooms emitted an unpleasant odor. She wondered how bad it would be after another twelve hours. She quickly pushed through the door and crossed to the next car. Pausing a moment as the door closed behind her, she chanced a quick glance through the pane of glass set in the door, and saw the stalker enter one of the restrooms in the other car. Her shoulders sagged with relief.

Boisterous laughter and a hum of conversation greeted her inside the lounge, and she was dismayed to find that what seemed like half the train's passengers had shared her idea. Discouraged, she lowered her head and trudged through the lounge, past the snack bar and down the center aisle between the dining tables in the other half of the car. She still couldn't believe this was happening. But she couldn't assume the insurance policy she'd taken out that morning in the copy room would keep her out of jail, or worse. She had to do something, take some kind of action to protect herself.

She wracked her brain as she crossed over to the next car, struck by the comparative silence as she moved through the car. The train's motion threw her off balance, and her rolling gait made her feel like a duck waddling down the aisle. The car wasn't full, but the hush seemed to come more from the fact that those in the car all sat quietly, preoccupied with reading or work. The plush leather seats seemed to demand respect and quiet. The passengers here were better dressed, more genteel than the folks in coach, a better class of people.

No, she chided herself. Just because her father had been a wife-battering alcoholic and her mother a weak-willed, co-dependent domestic abuse victim didn't mean that Dana was less-than. Just because she'd grown up poor and couldn't afford the right schools, or fashionable clothes or any other trappings of the "upper" class did not mean that these people were any better than she. Toby, especially, wasn't her superior in any sense of the word. Not anymore. She pressed her lips into a grim line and marched through the car with her head held high.

An even bigger hush blanketed the next car. As she sidled down a narrow hallway first to her right, then left a few steps, then a quick jog left and right again, her momentary resolve left her, and her anxiousness returned. She pushed it aside, forcing her mind to work on the problem at hand. By the time she reached the end of the last car she had a glimmer of an idea. As she worked her way back through the narrow hallway of the last sleeper car, she thought it through. Toby may not have had time to block her access to the foundation's bank accounts even if he was smart enough to think of it. She could pull up photo images of cancelled checks, try to match those to suspicious invoices and see who had endorsed them and where they'd been deposited. She might find a pattern.

Deep in thought, she'd just reached the second sleeper car on the way back when the train braked suddenly. As she lurched forward to get her footing, the curtains inside the roomette on her left swung open, a hand grasping one edge as if to keep from falling. Trying to maintain her balance, she caught only a momentary glance inside from the corner of her eye, and then she was past it. The enormity of what she'd seen suddenly registered. Her knees went weak and she thought she might vomit.

Oh my God.

Putting a hand to her mouth, she lowered her head and stepped up her pace. Two men. One standing, holding the curtain, then quickly swinging it back across the glassed door. One half-lying on a seat in shadow, face turned toward her with empty eyes and a mouth forming an O, as if in surprise or pain, she couldn't tell which. But was the image of his bare torso that stuck with her, roiling her stomach and filling her with fear. A mass of blood and muscles bared under strips of skin that hung from his ribcage like fat noodles.

Oh God, oh God, oh God.

She waited for the sound of a door sliding open behind her as she rounded the little jog in the hallway, but it didn't come. She broke into a run, a sob escaping her lips.

111

23

Sykes pounded the mirror above the fold-down sink in the small roomette with the heel of his fist, sending a spider web of cracks expanding out to the edges. He contemplated the body slumped in the seat. Devoid of life, it bore almost no resemblance to Mick. If only the prick had done his job and kept his mouth shut. Sykes grunted, giving Mick some grudging respect for holding out as long as he had.

That stoked his fury even more, but now he aimed the anger at himself. He'd been too impatient, too intent on getting the information he wanted out of Mick. And he hadn't been careful enough. The smallest jostle at the wrong moment as the train travelled over an uneven section of track had caused his hand to jerk, embedding the knife too deeply in Mick's abdomen. He must have nicked an artery. He hadn't seen much bleeding beyond what he'd caused by flaying Mick bit by bit, and he'd stanched that with towels. But the veteran must have been bleeding out internally for some time.

Sykes confronted the mess. The physical scene was easy enough to leave behind, but the problem Mick had created remained. Sykes needed that phone. And, after searching the roomette thoroughly, he had no clearer idea now what Mick had done with it than he'd had when Mick stolen it earlier that morning.

Methodically, he lowered the fold-up sink, rinsed the knife under a thin stream of water and wiped it clean. He closed the sink, placed the knife and stun gun in his briefcase and snapped it shut. He wouldn't strip off the latex gloves until he was clear of the sleeper car. He leaned forward to inspect his reflection in a small portion of the mirror that wasn't crazed to see if he'd gotten any blood on his face or clothes.

As he reached for the briefcase to leave, the train braked suddenly and he lost his balance. He fell backward and grabbed the curtain with one hand to keep from cracking his head on the wall behind him. He instantly realized his mistake as he caught the barest glimpse of someone passing by in the hallway outside the roomette. Leather jacket, dark jeans—maybe black—longish dark hair. The image was gone in a flash, and Sykes could only hope that whoever it was hadn't noticed the horror inside the small cabin.

He sighed. Another loose end. He would have to deal with it. He checked the holstered pistol under his coat. It was unwieldy with the suppressor attached, but the breakaway holster was designed to accommodate it, and the length didn't hamper his movements too much when he stood. Sitting was another matter.

Picking up the briefcase, he checked the roomette once more for anything he might have forgotten, then drew the curtain open a few inches to check the corridor. Seeing no sign of life, he quickly slid the door open, slipped out, and turned to close and lock the door.

As he took a step up the hallway toward the first-class coach he had his most pleasant surprise of the day so far.

24

It's my nature to be nosy, a good trait for a cop. Cops question everything.

Curious now, I decide to stretch my legs and see the rest of the train while I look for him. I stand and turn to step into the aisle, almost getting knocked on my keister as a woman about my age rushes past. She's wide-eyed, as if a ghost is on her tail. No one is behind her, but if she was confronted by some phantom I probably couldn't see it anyway. I shrug. Something on her mind, maybe.

But given the direction she's just come from, I'm even more curious. I start over, glancing over my shoulder to make sure my backpack is padlocked and stowed in the overhead rack. Then I step out into the aisle and head toward the rear of the train.

The train slows, the steady *clickety-clack* of the wheels gradually reduced to a lethargic *clack-clack*. Outside the windows, rolling meadows and copses of trees give way to signs of civilization, the industrial businesses that rely on rail for transport of supplies and finished goods and that often mark the outskirts of a town. I slide the vestibule door open, cross over to the next car, and muscle that door open, too. From the vestibule, the difference between the two cars is immediately apparent. A narrow corridor along one side of the car skirts two large bedroom suites, making the car's purpose clear. The corridor wraps around the end of the second suite, then jogs right in the center of the car.

As I round the corner I see the man who piqued my curiosity earlier. He smiles pleasantly from the other end of the car when he sees me, and raises his hand as if in greeting. But my eyes lock on what he holds in his hand, my brain trying to comprehend it. I recognize it instantly as a small sound-suppressed semi-automatic. What my mind seems to have trouble with is placing it in context with the well-dressed man with the friendly smile.

My body, thank God, reacts instinctively, adrenal glands dumping epinephrine, cortisol and a cascade of other hormones into my system, triggering my flight response. In other words, I'm already backpedaling before he has the gun raised to shoot me, and just as he pulls the trigger, the slowing train brakes. Not hard, but enough to throw off his aim.

By the time the *thwok* of a bullet hitting a bulkhead registers, I'm around the corner out of sight, and I run for the vestibule as fast as my legs can carry me. My own pistol rubs against my hip as I run, but engaging a strange man in a gunfight in close quarters on a train invites collateral damage. A decision I hope I'll live not to regret.

I don't have much time. I feel a dragon's breath at my back, the same one I felt in Baghdad every time I ran for cover. But there, we always ran toward enemy fire, blazing guns of our teammates laying down covering fire. Here, I have no choice.

In the vestibule, instead of opening the door to cross over to the next car, I cut right, down the few steps to the exit door. I yank the emergency handle, shove the door open with my shoulder and jump as the train comes to a stop. The rocky shoulder of the track bed is rough and uneven, and I nearly go down when my ankle turns. I stumble downslope a few feet to more level ground. Thankful I'm wearing low-heeled boots with nonskid soles, I manage to keep my balance and run alongside the train on hard-packed gravel. The ankle feels okay, but might be sore later. A hundred yards ahead, the train straddles a crossing, cars stopped at a lowered guard-arm and the steady ding-ding and flashing red lights of the signal. I sprint for it, intending to flag someone down, or at least ask where to find a local cop.

About halfway there I risk a glance over my shoulder. The shooter has gotten off the train, too, and follows, albeit more slowly, weighed down by the briefcase he carries and the long coat he wears. Still, the center of my back develops a sudden itch, and I cut at an angle to my right, changing plans. If my pursuer is crazy enough to take shots at me on the train, he'll likely try again out in the open. I figure I'm far away enough to make a shot difficult, but if I can find some cover, I might be able to return fire, and or at least put more distance between us. The prickle between my shoulder blades spurs my legs to churn faster.

Only roofs and trees are visible on the far side of the road, suggesting the ground slopes away. Darting between two cars, I take one stride over a curb onto a sidewalk and another before vaulting a steel railing to a grassy slope on the other side. Still concerned about confronting the shooter with so many civilians in the way, I decide to keep going. Risking another quick glance behind me, I see no one following.

The grassy patch quickly gives way to paved parking lots of commercial businesses that front the street. I pass a dry cleaner, pizza restaurant, and a fast food restaurant before facing an intersection and another decision. The cross street looks like a main drag through town, and surrounding myself with more obstacles feels right. Turning left toward town, I fall into an easy rhythm, the way I do on my morning runs, ignoring the weight of the gun on my hip and the warmth of my leather jacket as the sun breaks through the morning's rain clouds.

My mind races. The conductor didn't announce a stop aboard the train, and it's too early for the train to have arrived in Charlottesville, so this is a town along the way, and the train has stopped for a track signal. As if confirming my hunch, a train horn blows from the tracks a block or so away. Through an empty parking lot, I see a freight train travelling parallel to the street I'm on, heading back toward D.C. at a good clip. One question resolved. The bigger ones are why a man with a silenced weapon shot at me on board and why he seems familiar in some way.

An answer to the first part comes to me in a flash—he wasn't shooting at me at all. The woman on the train who seemed so frightened is dressed similarly to me—black jeans and white top of some kind covered up by a leather jacket. She's his target. But why? Why risk shooting someone in such a public place? And how did he mistake me for her? We resemble each other in only a general sense— clothing, dark hair, about the same height though she seems heavier than me. Suggesting he doesn't know her. Or what she looks like. A case of mistaken identity?

Behind me, the shooter's nowhere in sight. I don't believe for a moment he's given up, but maybe he's changing strategy. I slow to a brisk walk so I won't attract as much attention, mind still working furiously. If the other woman is a contract hit, he would have confirmed her ID.

She saw something she wasn't supposed to.

My first instinct is to find her and warn her. But I realize that as long as the shooter is chasing me the woman is safe. And if she saw something, she might tell someone, like the conductor. Another reason the shooter may have followed me off the train. He risked a lot taking a shot at me. If he already killed someone on board, his hasty exit makes even more sense.

As I reach an intersection—one with a traffic light this time—I change plans again. My purse is in my backpack on the train, but I have my phone, a gun, and my FBI badge holder minus badge, in which I always carry my FBI ID, driver's license, a little spare cash, and an unused, black American Express Centurion card. I get the phone out of a jacket pocket, and pull up a GPS map to find out where I am. The cross street on my right leads to Charlottesville. I turn the corner, step off the curb and stick out my thumb.

117

25

Dana choked back the bile in her throat, sure she would vomit in the aisle at any second. She hurried back to her seat, trying to push the image of what had been done to that poor man in the tiny cabin in the sleeper car, the strips of fatty skin writhing on his skin like bloody snakes, his lifeless face turned toward her, sightless eyes boring through her as if blaming her for his horrific death.

The train slowed beneath her feet, gentle braking at one point causing her to stumble into the back of a seat. She hurried on with a mumbled apology to its occupant, and the train's jerk to a final stop nearly threw her into her own seat. A sheen of sweat coated her face and dampened the hair at the back of her neck. Her breathing grew fast and shallow, and her heart thumped so hard against her ribs that she feared she was on the verge of a heart attack. She leaned back trying to relax, force her thoughts into a rational internal monologue. But her muscles twitched involuntarily, and tremors in her hands made her suddenly crave a cigarette, a glass of wine—no, a very, very strong vodka and tonic—anything to calm her down. Tears lurked in the corners of her eyes, begging for release, and she bit her lower lip to keep from making a scene.

One moment she wanted to bolt out of her seat and run to the nearest exit, the next she felt paralyzed, convinced she would die. She rummaged through her purse and found tissues to mop the sweat off her forehead and neck. The train car seemed to spin in a slow circle, frightening her even more, filling her ears with the racing *ka-thump* of her heartbeat. She wondered when she'd outgrown her bra size, the intimate apparel suddenly feeling like a whalebone corset squeezing her chest and constricting her breathing. She grimaced and caught the creep across the aisle looking at her again.

"What?" she screamed. "Stop staring at me! Leave me alone."

Heads throughout the train car bobbed up and turned in her direction with startled expressions. The strange man quickly turned his head away, toward the window, his face turning scarlet. She hadn't wanted to cause a scene, yet she'd done just that. With good reason. Serves him right. Behind him, the windows darkened suddenly as a freight train rumbled past.

119

Her moment of moral certitude and gratification lasted an instant before panic overtook her again, this time prompted by a new fear. What if the killer saw me? She leaned into the aisle and craned her neck to look back the way she'd come. She saw no one, but the fear only swelled inside her. She half-stood, then melted back into her seat. Straightening, she perched on the edge, hands unconsciously rubbing her thighs so hard that her palms grew hot. She didn't know what to do.

I'm going to die.

Her head swung wildly. Like a cornered animal, she saw danger in every movement, smelled it in the myriad scents wafting under her nose—the sour, slightly soiled fabric seats, diesel exhaust, fried food, her own fear. She felt nauseous again, and turned her face toward the thin stream of air coming from the vent. Motion outside the window caught her attention, but her mind couldn't quite comprehend what she saw—a mirror image of herself running away from the train toward a line of cars stopped at the crossing. An out-of-body experience? She lifted her hands from her lap and turned them inward to inspect her palms.

More movement pulled her gaze back to the window. Almost directly below her, a man ran with a wobbly gait, arms spread to maintain his balance on the uneven gravel shoulder alongside the tracks. The same man she'd caught the barest glimpse of in that sleeper car cabin. The sophisticated clothes, long overcoat flapping at his legs as he ran, the immaculately groomed salt- and-pepper hair. She still only saw a portion of his face in profile as he passed.

She slumped in her seat, trying desperately to manifest the image of Alice after she downed the "Drink Me" potion. Her thoughts churned, irrational ones slowly spinning off into oblivion until clarity, and her sanity, began to return. Slowly, she raised her head and peeked out the window. The woman was gone. The man still followed, now well past her window.

She stood, pointing, and announced to no one in particular, "That man killed someone."

Looking around the car, she saw only quizzical looks on the faces turned toward her, and most were busy looking in any direction but hers.

"Can't you see he's getting away?" She heard the shrillness in her voice.

No one answered. The train lurched gently forward, and she almost pitched into the seat in front of her. She grabbed the seat back and swayed in time with the train as it slowly gathered speed.

"I have to find the conductor," she said, bustling into the aisle. "The killer's getting away!"

26

Sykes watched the woman ahead of him gracefully vault an iron railing on the far side of the road and disappear. Proud of his physical condition despite his age and the demands of the club— handball twice a week, weights and cardio in the gym most other days, helped—his breathing felt labored. Running on rough terrain in full business attire while carrying a heavy briefcase and an awkward weapon taxed him more than he thought it would. And he recognized a runner when he saw one. He had no chance of catching her.

For the first time in as long as he could remember, uncertainty crept into his consciousness. The day had gone badly as few did for him, thanks to his meticulous planning and foresight. People said, "hope for the best; plan for the worst." Sykes *expected* the best because he planned for the worst. He'd been behind the curve, however, since the day started. And all because of Mick making a move Sykes had never seen coming. He didn't believe Mick even knew what he had, only that it was valuable.

So, he'd dealt with Mick, but without getting the information he needed. He shouldered the blame for that. He'd been too impatient, too concerned that someone would go looking for the sleeping car attendant and find him dead. Too worried, in fact, that he himself would be discovered before the train arrived in Charlottesville. And his fears had come true. That had been sheer bad luck. Worse, now, his one, easy shot at the witness had gone astray, another bit of bad luck. If bad luck came in threes, he'd hit the trifecta.

Time to start planning.

He slowed to a brisk walk and weighed his options. Unless the woman was a complete idiot, she'd be looking for someone to report him to by now. He needed to get out of the open first, and then get out of town as quickly as possible. With the train straddling the crossing, he had no choice but to follow in the direction the woman had taken. When he reached the spot where she'd disappeared, however, he saw that the street approaching the crossing curved left and down the slope in the other direction. He stayed on the sidewalk as it curved alongside the street, conscious now of blending in.

His free hand found his phone, took it out and speed-dialed

George's cell. George answered on the first ring.

"Yes, sir?"

"Come get me."

"Where are you?"

"Hang on." Sykes pulled the phone away from his ear, pulled up a GPS app, and noted his location. He looked up and scanned his surroundings slowly as he walked. Spotting a red-roofed fast food restaurant a little more than a block away, he got back on the line.

"A town called Orange."

"I know it. I'm fifteen, twenty minutes out."

"Good. Meet me at the Hardee's on Route 15. Madison Street."

"Got it."

"George," Sykes said quickly before George could disconnect. "As fast as you can get here."

"Right. On it."

Sykes crossed the street and cut through a strip mall parking lot, feeling more out of place each passing moment. He passed a hardware store, tax preparer's office, souvenir store, its window full of kitsch and Halloween décor, a barbershop, coin laundry, gift shop and lawn equipment store. A sparse collection of pickup trucks, SUVs and older sedans dotted the big lot, and the few people strolling to or from their vehicles wore clothing in colors and patterns that hurt Sykes's eyes in fabrics he considered an affront to human skin.

In the restaurant, Sykes went to the restroom to wash his hands and check his clothes in case he'd missed spots of blood while cleaning up on the train. On the way out, he looked for a door to the kitchen and an exit out the back. At the counter, he bought a cup of coffee and took it to a table as far from the entrance as possible. He sat in a chair that faced the door, set his briefcase on the floor at his feet and took a sip. He grimaced involuntarily. The best thing he could say about it was that it was hot, but the only other way in which it resembled coffee was its color. He leaned back in an effort to appear relaxed, but his gaze never stopped moving, assessing.

Five minutes into his wait, Sykes spotted a town police cruiser slow as it drove past on the street outside. He tensed, sitting up a little straighter, waiting to see what it would do. At the corner, it turned left out of sight. Sykes's shoulders started to ease, when a second cruiser came into view and turned directly into the lot. As it turned into a parking slot, the first cruiser reappeared, driving around the corner of the building. It pulled into the empty slot alongside the second cruiser, and an officer got out of each.

Too soon. They're only coming in for coffee, maybe lunch.

Sykes slipped his hand inside his suit coat and grasped the semi-automatic snugly, covering his arm with the flap of his coat. Sliding forward to the edge of his chair, he picked up the briefcase and set it on the table in front of him. He couldn't believe they were onto him already, but he was ready to bolt out the back or engage if necessary.

One officer approached the door and pulled it open, holding it for the second cop. As the second officer entered, he automatically scanned the restaurant. Sykes had seen it many times before. It was what cops did; they assessed every situation they came across, looking for suspicious behavior, possible dangers. When the cop's gaze met Sykes's, Sykes gave him a small nod, and tipped his head toward his coffee cup, taking another sip of the vile brew. Sykes felt the cop's eyes linger on him for a moment, then saw him move toward the counter from the corner of his eye. Keeping his eyes averted, Sykes watched them in his peripheral vision confer at the counter, one of them nodding his head in Sykes's direction causing the other's head to swivel toward him. They turned.

Sykes's grip tightened on the pistol. Bolting now would only convince them he was guilty of something. The cop's every step closer bumped Sykes's pulse up another ten beats per minute. His hand tightened on the gun to the point that the knurled grip dug into his palm. A gunfight would be suicide, but Sykes feared he had no option. He slowly drew the gun out of the holster as the cop approached, and suddenly realized the cop's gaze wasn't directed at him, but past him. He unclenched his fingers and withdrew his hand, sat back in an open, relaxed manner, and put a smile on his face as the cop walked past to an empty table beside him.

The other officer turned away from the counter carrying two cups of coffee. Halfway to the table, both cops' radios crackled to life, a garbled voice emanating from the speakers of their two- way radios. One of them unclipped the unit from the epaulet on his uniform, thumbed the mic and gave a short response. The dispatcher's distorted instructions put grave expressions on the cops' faces. Immediately losing interest in Sykes, they hustled out the door and roared out of the lot on squealing tires, sirens blaring.

Sykes pulled his phone out and dialed George. "Where are you?"

"Two minutes away."

27

Like a dry fly on a trout pond, my extended thumb hooks a passing pickup truck in seconds, and I reel it in to the curb. I look it over as I hustle down the street toward the passenger door. It's a pewter Ford F150 Supercab with a matching Leer cap over the bed, maybe nine or ten years old, dirty but no dings. I note the license plate and commit the number to memory. The window is down, and the weathered face of a sixty-something man with shaggy gray hair sprouting from under a worn and faded red Massey Ferguson cap leans across the seat.

"Where you headed?" he says.

I step onto the running board, rest my forearms on the sill and take a quick gander at the interior before meeting his gaze. Open carry without a permit is legal in Virginia, but I don't see a weapon or a bulge anywhere he might carry concealed if he does have a permit. His manner is friendly, and though I don't doubt my gender has as much to do with him stopping as my charmed thumb, he's a small man and I'm confident he'll be no trouble.

"Wherever you're going."

A smile spreads across his face, revealing a gap where a lower incisor used to be. "Footloose and fancy-free, eh? Hop in."

I check the street behind me as I climb in, but see no sign of my pursuer. The driver looks at his side mirror and waits for traffic as I buckle the seatbelt, then pulls away from the curb. He drives with his right wrist draped over the top of the wheel and his left forearm on the armrest in the door.

"Name's Chet," he says.

"Jenny," I reply. It's as much as he's going to get from me.

I consider calling the locals to report a shooting, but the details of what I can tell them are so vague that I wouldn't believe me if I got a call like what I have in mind. The FBI resident agency office in Charlottesville will have what I need. So I settle in for the ride instead.

"You ain't from around here, are you?" Chet says, shooting a quick glance my way before putting his eyes back on the road.

I shake my head. "Just passing through. Much obliged for the ride."

"Happy to have the company." He chances another glance at me as we hit the outskirts of town and gain speed. "So, what do you do, anyway?"

"If I told you, I'd have to kill you." I watch him to see how he takes it. After a moment's surprise, he offers that gap-tooth grin again. "Seriously," I say.

His grin vanishes, and he goes silent. Blue and red flashers ahead speed toward us. A county sheriff's patrol car zooms by at a good clip, running without siren. I wonder if it's responding to whatever happened aboard the train.

The countryside slides past the windows, rolling hills of pastures turned brown by the late summer sun and copses of trees holding onto their fall colors. The first ridge of Appalachian foothills miles to the west are ablaze, lit by shafts of sunlight beaming through the pewter clouds. The pavement under the truck's wheels is still damp, but there's been no rain since I ran earlier in the morning.

"Not sure I can figure you out," Chet says after a mile or two. "You're dressed nice, so I expect you got a job, maybe some money put away. But you ain't got no car, or it's maybe in the shop, and 'stead of taking a bus or the train, you hitched a ride. You're goin' somewheres, but you ain't got no bag, not even no purse. So, what's your deal?"

I take a breath and huff it out my nose. I don't want to be impolite, but I need some think time.

"Chet, like I said, I appreciate the ride. If you want to talk UVA basketball or whether Massey Ferguson or John Deere tractors are better, fine. You want to tell me all about what you do, or complain about how the missus mistreats you, I'll listen. And I'll pay you for gas if you take me as far as I'm going. But just so it's clear, any discussion about my personal or professional life is off limits. I don't mean to offend you. My parents raised me not to talk to strangers is all. Okay?"

"Heck, a real challenge. Yeah, okay, I can live with that, on one condition. We each get one question."

"Fine. One."

"Where you going?"

"Charlottesville."

He looks startled, cheated. "That's it? That's as far as you're goin'?"

I nod. "Right now, yes. My turn. Assuming you'll take me all the way, how long's the drive?"

"She-it, hon', it ain't more'n forty, forty-five minutes."

"Make it thirty-five minutes and I'll throw in a twenty on top of gas."

He doesn't stomp on the pedal, but I feel the truck accelerate. The two-lane road meanders, but we don't sit behind traffic long before a straightaway gives him a chance to pass. The big truck engine powers us past three cars with barely any strain before Chet glides back into the right lane and lets up on the accelerator.

"You a basketball fan?" He glances in the rearview mirror.

"I enjoy watching a game now and then."

"I'm more into football."

"Redskins? They've gotten some nice draft picks recently. Some terrific receivers."

"Yeah, but they still got no decent running backs."

"Give Perine a chance. He'll grow into the job."

"Could be. Got us a good high school team there in Orange. Maybe you'd like to see a game."

Not wanting to encourage him, I don't reply. For the time being he seems fresh out of things to say. Grateful for the silence, I search my mental file drawers for an image matching the face of the shooter on the train. I get so lost in thought I don't notice the truck slowing until Chet has already turned onto a side road.

"What are you doing?" I ask quietly, breaking into a sweat.

He turns and grins at me. "I thought you 'n' me could have a little fun."

For a moment, fear tries to commandeer my sense of reason and whisk me in a time machine to a juncture in my life I'd rather forget. Based upon many discussions with a therapist who took only cash to ensure our sessions were private, I recognize the sweating, elevated pulse, rapid breathing and aborted flashback as PTSD symptoms. With the help of some emotional security guards—years of grueling self-defense training, anger, and the gun under my jacket—I hip-check the fear out of my way.

I slow my breathing and wait to see where Chet's taking us. The road curves, putting us out of sight of the highway. He drives the truck onto a grassy shoulder and stops. My cantering heartbeat belies the calm exterior I present him.

Throwing the gearshift into park, he leans over and boldly places his right hand on the leather covering my left breast. I sigh but there's no pleasure in it. Why are men so damn predictable? I place my right hand on his with the barest hint of a smile. His face lights up with a smug grin that I quickly wipe away with a wristlock that twists his arm and forces him to turn away so no bones will break. I use the surprise and all my strength to keep rotating the wristlock until it's up between his shoulder blades and his face is mashed against the

127

steering wheel. I'm on my knees on the seat now. He struggles, tries to swing his other arm back far enough to hit me. I twist his arm harder and higher, eliciting a howl of pain.

Leaning forward to put my weight on his arm, I take one hand away to pull my gun from its holster. Blood sings in my ears, and I barely hear his grunts and cries of pain as I press the barrel of the Sig against his cheekbone. The cold metal gets his attention, and he immediately stops struggling and complaining.

"That's better," I tell him. "You obviously know what this is."

His eye—the one I can see—rolls back toward me like that of a spooked horse, trying to get a look at the thing tormenting him.

"You really should learn some manners," I say. "Ladies don't like it when men try to cop a feel on the first date. They *really* hate it when they're not even on a date. It's demeaning, Chet."

"How the fuck was I supposed to know? I thought you liked me."

"When did I ever give you that indication?"

"When you got in my truck?"

"I needed a ride, asshole."

"What are you gonna do?" His voice has a tremor in it now.

"I want you to use your other hand and slowly open the door. I'm very good with this gun, Chet, and I will use it if you try anything."

"Okay, okay. Then what?" He pulls the door handle and shoves the door open.

"Then you get out—slowly—and assume the position by the back wheel. I'll be right behind you. Don't fuck up if you want to live through this. I am one sincerely pissed-off lady right now. Got it?"

"Yeah, I got it."

I can taste the bitterness in his voice, but he does what I ask. I let go of the arm behind his back, but stay close as he gets out so he doesn't have a chance to do something stupid like slam the door on me. He shuffles toward the back of the truck, makes an exaggerated quarter-turn when he reaches the back wheel, and slaps his hands on top of his cap dramatically. His stands with his feet close together, facing away. I tap the inside of his thighs with the gun, and he replants his feet a yard apart. Pressing the gun against the back of his head, I kick him in the groin from behind.

He screams, grabs his crotch with both hands and falls to the ground. While he writhes in pain, I fish in an inside jacket pocket for some of the plastic zip ties I always carry on the job instead of handcuffs. I toss two at him and they land on his face. He stops moaning and looks around to see what hit him.

"What the fuck, bitch?" He moans. "I think you busted one of my balls. I oughta call the cops."

"And tell them what? You tried to feel the 'bitch' up, and she kicked you in the nuts?"

He grits his teeth from the pain. "What do you want from me?"

"I want you to put those zip ties on your wrists. And I don't want to see any slack."

I waggle the gun to remind him who's in charge. He sits up, picks the zip ties up out of the dirt and fastens them around his wrists.

"Stand up," I tell him. "Face the truck and put your hands behind your back."

He does what I tell him, and with my gun to his head, I string another zip tie through the loops on each wrist, and with some difficulty manage to find the dexterity to thread the end of the tie into the lock, and yank it tight. As distasteful as I find the task, I pat him down to look for any weapons and to get his keys. Thankfully, no gun. I pat the rectangular bulge in the seat of his pants.

He glances at me over his shoulder. "What, are you gonna rob me now?"

"Shut up." The wallet in his hip pocket has a Virginia driver's license and credit cards issued to Chester Haynes along with close to sixty bucks in cash. I stuff it back in his pocket. "Happy?"

"Suppose you want me to thank you for not ripping me off."

I'm momentarily thrown by the lack of keys, then realize they're still in the ignition. I sidestep away, keeping the gun aimed at his head. "Don't move, Chet."

The driver's door is still open, and I reach in and feel around the steering column for the keys, never taking my eyes off him. I have to stretch to get my arm in far enough without leaning into the truck, but my fingers find the keys and wiggle them loose.

I approach him again and motion with the gun barrel. "Around the back."

He hangs his head and shuffles around the back of the truck. I motion him aside, unlock the camper shell and tailgate and open them. Inside, the truck bed is a jumble of tools, mechanical parts and junk that smells of grease, dirt, sweat and stale sex. A filthy sleeping bag and old pillow are wadded in a corner, suggesting that he sleeps off a good drunk in h is truck or I'm not the first woman he's hit on while driving around. My stomach churns in disgust.

"Hop in," I tell him.

He looks at me wide-eyed. "You're kidding."

I raise the pistol level with his heart. "Do I look like I'm kidding?"

He walks up to the tailgate, turns around and jumps. His ass bounces on the metal gate and he nearly falls off. His bound arms are of little use, so he throws his weight backward in a panic and rolls into the bed. When he sits up and blinks at me from the dim interior, he's covered in dirt. I slam the tailgate shut.

"Hey!" His shout is muted. "Hey, you can't leave me back here."

I holster my gun, get in the driver's seat, fire up the engine and make a U-turn back to the main road.

28

The big sedan glided almost silently through town, buffered from the outside world by tons of insulation and acoustic-laminate glass, big twenty-inch wheels, and a computer-controlled suspension system that continuously dampened the effects of bumps in the road. It offered an oasis of calm in a chaotic world. With the doors locked, it even felt like an impregnable fortress on wheels. Sykes knew better, but was glad he—or, rather, the club—had made the investment. He also knew that George loved the combination of power and cushiness the car provided in exchange for the cushiest job George had ever held.

George glanced at the rearview mirror and met Sykes's gaze. "Where to, Mr. Sykes?"

"Charlottesville. Let me know when we're close and I'll tell you where to go."

"Yes, sir."

Sykes leaned back in the plush leather seat and closed his eyes for a moment, letting the remaining tension in his body drain away. He'd acted too hastily, too impulsively. Killing Mick had given him no satisfaction, though it had ultimately been necessary. Instead, Sykes was more frustrated than he'd been before deciding on this course of action. He should never have boarded the train. He should have sent someone to intercept it at some point along the route and bring Mick back. He could have held Mick indefinitely in the confines of the club and dealt with the situation at his leisure in a controlled environment.

He was furious with himself for making the amateurish mistake of letting his emotions rule his actions. He could think of only two prior incidences where he'd allowed his feelings free rein, but in both cases he'd calculated the risk first. He never did anything without a plan...until today.

Now he had to evade the potential consequences of his rashness while still finding a way to rectify the situation. He tried to put himself in the girl's shoes. She had to believe he wouldn't get back on board the train. But she was going somewhere. So, she might figure that the train was the safest place and either try to backtrack quickly and reboard while the train was still stopped at the crossing or head for the train's next stop. Sykes thought that's what he would do in her place. Charlottesville was the first place he'd look for her.

In the meantime, he needed to figure out what Mick had done with the phone. Sykes had found only a couple of cheap burner phones in Mick's compartment on the train. Which meant that Mick had left Sykes's phone back in D.C. A locker in Union Station? No, or else he would have found a key among Mick's things. Sykes mentally retraced his steps that morning. Not many minutes had passed between the time Mick had answered Sykes's call to his own phone and the moment Dobrev and Orlov called from the hotel where the GPS signal from Mick's phone last transmitted. He left it at the hotel. With the concierge, maybe. Or he had the front desk put it in the hotel safe. Too easy, but he'd have Dobrev check anyway.

His mind churned, then settled on a more likely answer: He mailed it, sent it somewhere. Leaning forward, he said, "What can you tell me about Mick?"

George's head jerked up. "Like what?"

"You two were pretty close in the service, right?"

George looked uneasy when his gaze met Sykes's in the rearview mirror. "Well, yeah, I guess."

"So what do you know about him?"

George shrugged. "I don't know what I can tell you that you don't already know. Back then, he was a stand-up guy. When you're out on patrol or an offensive mission, you want to know that the guys on your team have your back. Mick was one of those guys."

"Where'd he grow up?"

"Midwest someplace. He didn't talk about himself a lot. I got the feeling it wasn't a happy place. Like that's why he joined the military."

"Thank you, George."

Sykes sat back, raised the glass partition, and dialed a direct line at the club.

"Stevens," a voice answered.

"Phillip, I need you to do something."

"Things didn't go as planned?"

"Not quite. Do some research for me. I need more background on Mick than we have in his personnel file. Find out where he grew up, went to school, any friends he might have had."

"Certainly, sir. Anything else?"

"Yes. A young woman may have seen more than she should have. She's in the wind, but I have an idea where she might be headed. However, it's a big world out here, and I may need some back-up. Find out if our friends Alexei and Mikhail are still available and on loan to us."

"And if they are?"

132

"First, have them check with the hotel concierge and front desk to see if my phone was left with them for safekeeping. Then send them to Charlottesville, and tell them I'll be in touch when I need them."

"Very good, sir. I'll get back to you with information as soon as I have it."

"Good."

Sykes ended the call and relaxed into the comfortable leather. His problem was a long way from being fixed, but he felt better than he had fifteen minutes earlier.

29

The conductor quickly slid the compartment door shut and faced Dana, his blanched face twisted in shock.

"You saw this?"

Dana nodded and swallowed hard. "I caught just a glimpse."

"And you say you saw who did this?"

Fear and uncertainty squeezed the air from her lungs. "I don't know," she managed. She tried to moisten the desert inside her mouth with her tongue and forced herself to take a breath. "It all happened so fast. I saw someone else in there, a hand grabbing the curtain for balance when the trained slowed down. I'm sure it was a man, standing over the body. He wore a topcoat. Black, I think. A suit under it. Older, but not old. You know?"

"But he's gone?"

"I went back to my seat as fast as I could. I didn't know what to do." Dana felt panic rising up from the pit of her stomach. She took another breath. "Something outside caught my eye, and when I looked out I saw him running alongside the tracks, following a woman."

"What woman?"

"I don't know. Another passenger. She was sitting in the first class car earlier. And she was dressed like me." The words came out in a rush.

The door of a compartment up the corridor slid open, turning both their heads. A short, bald man in shirtsleeves stepped out into the corridor and looked both directions. When he spotted Dana and the conductor, his brow furrowed and he headed toward them.

"What's going on?" he said. Dana felt the anger and annoyance in his voice before she heard the words. "Where's the attendant? I've been waiting nearly an hour for extra towels."

"We have an incident," the conductor said, his voice calm.

"What sort of incident?" The man's eyes narrowed.

"Nothing to concern you," the conductor went on smoothly. "It appears a passenger has fallen ill. I'm sure the attendant will accommodate you as soon as he's able."

"He better," the man said.

"I'll see to it, sir. Can I get you anything besides towels?"

The man stood with hands on hips for a moment, staring. Then he shook his head and disappeared inside his compartment.

"Where is Dennis?" the conductor muttered to himself. He turned around and stepped in front of the next compartment. He knocked lightly and tried to slide the door open but it didn't budge. Pulling a key ring from his belt, he inserted a master key and unlocked the compartment door. Dana quietly crowded him from behind and stood up on tiptoes to look past him into the compartment. She quickly clamped a hand over her mouth to keep from retching at the sight. The uniformed attendant sprawled in a seat, part of the headrest and window behind him splattered with blood and brain matter.

"Jesus!" The conductor whirled on Dana. "Did you know about this?"

She clutched at her chest, wide-eyed with terror. "No," she whispered. "I swear."

"I can't believe this," he said. "Who would have done this?"

The conductor took another long look at the man in the compartment, then closed and locked the door. He pulled a two-way radio from his pocket, thumbed the mic and spoke into it rapidly. Almost immediately the train began to slow. When he finished, he turned to Dana.

"Come with me, please," he said. "I have to call the authorities, and they'll want to question you about what you saw."

"I didn't see anything," she protested, "except a glimpse of that poor man in there." Another shiver ran through her.

The conductor shook his head. "Doesn't matter. They'll want to speak with you. Let's go."

Dana followed him back through the first class car to the dining/lounge car, heart pounding faster with each step. She hadn't thought it through. Reporting what she'd seen had been her only option as far as she was concerned, but she'd figured that her responsibility would end there. The cops would take over. But of course they would want to talk to her. And cops were not high on the list of people she wanted to confide in. Not now.

Passengers filled half the lounge, and some looked at them with curious expressions as they passed. The conductor ignored them and had her take a seat at one of the empty tables. He dialed 911 on a cell phone and walked to the vestibule at the end of the car to speak with a dispatcher. Dana turned her gaze out the windows and saw that the train had stopped, the town's houses and streets replaced by trees and meadows again. She wondered how long they'd be stuck there.

A moment later, the conductor's voice came over the loudspeaker. She turned and saw him speak into a microphone at the end of the car.

"Ladies and gentlemen, I apologize for the delay, but we have a medical emergency on board, and we've stopped here for assistance. In a few minutes, you're likely to hear sirens and see flashing lights of emergency vehicles. There's no cause for alarm. Bear with us, and we'll get back underway as soon as we can. Thanks for your patience."

Dana heard murmurs of, "What's going on?" and "I wonder what happened?" around her, and two passengers rose from their seats to intercept the conductor as he walked back to Dana's table.

He held them off with a raised hand and a low comment that Dana couldn't hear. He slid into a seat across from Dana and extended his hand.

"Julien," he said. His wan face still reflected her own shock, and beads of perspiration dotted his forehead.

She hesitantly gave his hand a quick squeeze, and pulled hers back into her lap. "Dana."

"The police should be here any minute."

She squirmed. "I really didn't see anything. Can't you tell them everything they need to know?"

He leaned toward her and in a low voice said, "I don't know what's going on here, but it looks to me like someone killed Dennis to get a key to the compartment next door. Dennis is—was the attendant. I've known him for nearly twenty years. His daughter's graduating from high school next spring. Now he won't be there to see it. He deserved better. What you saw might help the cops catch the monster who did this. I don't know about you, but it's important to me."

The distant wail of a siren penetrated the thick glass windows. Dana's stomach knotted, and gray blotches appeared in her vision. Her chest hurt, and her limbs tingled as if she'd downed a pot of coffee, making her want to crawl out of her own skin. Fear built up inside her. She didn't know which she feared most, Toby's wrath, an unknown killer covering his tracks, or the cops.

She was about to find out.

30

Twenty minutes after getting back on the highway, I turn the truck into the lot of a car rental agency in Charlottesville, park and go inside. The adrenaline dump has left me feeling tired and cranky, and a headache is forming at my temples. I put on a smile for the agent behind the counter, though, and walk out ten minutes later with the keys to a small, nondescript SUV. Muted banging and shouting drifts across the lot from Chet's truck as I find my rental. The truck gently rocks on its suspension. Despite what he had in mind not long ago, the image of him rolling around in his truck bed amuses me. Small consolation. With all the ruckus he's making, he won't have to wait long before someone discovers him. He's not likely to confess what happened, but I left the keys in the truck, and I don't want to be around when he's let loose.

I drive off the lot with an app on my phone already giving me directions to the resident agency office in Charlottesville a little more than a mile away. The modern four-story brick and glass building sits in an office park where the nearest neighboring office buildings are a couple of football fields away, separated by an undulating landscape of green grass dotted with copses of trees that reminds me of a golf course.

There's no indication the bureau resides in the building until I read the tenant list in the lobby. I take the elevator up to the requisite floor and find the office without any trouble. There's no receptionist at the front desk, but in a resident agency office like this, I don't expect one. I barely have enough time to look around the small reception area before a young man in slacks, dress shirt and tie appears from a hallway and greets me as he crosses the floor to stand next to the front desk.

"Can I help you, ma'am?" he says. His tone and smile are polite, but his demeanor is all business.

I pull out my badge holder which still contains my bureau photo ID and flash it at the agent. "Jenny Roberts, D.C. headquarters. Is your SAC in?"

He turns evasive. "I'm not sure. Maybe I can help you."

I consider him, trying to figure out what my play is. I'm in so much trouble with my own office, I decide straight up is best.

"Not quite an hour ago, a man aboard the Amtrak 'Cardinal' headed from D.C. to Chicago took a shot at me. I want to report it, and I'd like a look at the mug shot files to see if I can ID him."

"Took a shot," he says with raised eyebrows, "as in tried to hit you? Tried to hit on you?" With that, his eyes leave footprints from my head to my toes.

"No, Special Agent...?"

"Mulcahy. Tom."

I nod once. "Took a shot as in fired at me with a suppressed semi-automatic pistol. A compact model. I couldn't tell the make."

His eyebrows rise a notch higher, but his expression remains unchanged—friendly, polite.

"Why would someone fire a weapon at you on board a train?"

"That's what I'd like to find out."

"What did you do after this man shot at you?"

"Got the hell out of there. Are you going to help me or not?"

"You didn't return fire?"

I shake my head. "I didn't think it prudent. Too much chance of collateral damage."

"So, you ran?" The corners of his mouth twitch enough to suggest amusement.

"Laugh all you want, Mulcahy. When you find yourself in the same position, come find me and tell me what you do. I made a strategic retreat, which is why I'm here asking for the damned mug shot files."

He holds out his hand. "May I see your ID again, please?"

Reluctantly, I give it to him. He compares my photo to the real deal, and looks at the holder again. His eyebrows return to their normal position. He doesn't ask me about the missing badge.

"I'll see if the SAC is around and let him know you're here, then set you up in the conference room with a laptop so you can look at mug shots."

I let some of my anger drain away, and the tension in my shoulders dissipates. "Thank you."

Mulcahy deposits me in a small conference room dominated by an oval table with blond wood veneer surrounded by eight wheeled office chairs upholstered in gray cloth. I sit and look out the window at a retention pond set in a hollow of the manicured grounds. A fountain in the middle of the pond shoots spray skyward in a *fleur de lis* pattern. When I sense too much time has passed, I check my phone, then lay it gently on the table with a sigh.

They keep me waiting another fifteen minutes before Mulcahy

opens the door. A small man with skin as smooth and dark as a latte under a head of close-cropped curly, gray hair precedes Mulcahy through the door and sits at one end of the table. He's impeccably dressed in a well- tailored light blue suit, regimental tie, and silk dress shirt. He leans forward, clasps his hands and rests his forearms on the table. French cuffs fastened with gold links peek out from the sleeves of his suit coat. He contemplates me for a moment while Mulcahy takes a seat to my left and sets a micro recorder on the table.

The older man doesn't take his eyes off me as he tilts his head toward the recorder and says, "Any problems with that, Roberts?"

I shrug. "Not exactly what I asked for."

Mulcahy turns the recorder on.

"I'm Special Agent in Charge Dan Corbett, Charlottesville," the suited man says. He rattles off the date and time, and names those present. "The thing is, Special Agent Roberts, you don't seem to be in much of a position to ask for anything. You're on administrative leave, according to your superiors, and no wonder. Your name sounded familiar. Guess you're the one who brought a fly team leader into my territory and took over a crime scene without so much as a howdy-do. Didn't even give the Richmond field office the courtesy of a phone call, let alone us. We don't mind entertaining visitors from time to time, but we like to have a little advance notice."

It's obvious he knows who I am and what I did to help Terry Hunt and the rest of my former team track down and stop one of the world's most notorious terrorists. I don't see any point in confirming it.

He stares me down, but I used to play that game with older brothers. He blinks first. "Want to tell me what you were doing on that Amtrak train?" he says.

"Going home, sir." I say softly. "Since I'm on leave."

"And where's that, Agent Roberts?"

"Wisconsin, sir."

He taps the tips of his forefingers together for a moment. "A man fired a weapon at you aboard the train, is that right?"

"Yes, sir."

"But instead of reporting it, calling it in, you waltz in here asking to see mug shots."

I nod. "And to report it now, sir, in person."

"You're suspended." His voice is more forceful now. "You're not on active status. Do you understand that you can't investigate diddly right now?"

"Sir, I'm simply trying to report a felony—assault and attempted murder of a federal officer—with the most accurate information I can. I thought identifying my assailant might help."

"You waited an hour to report it. Why?"

"The assailant pursued me off the train on foot. My first priority was to remove myself from danger. I came straight here. Well, with a few short detours."

His head bobs at my phone on the table. "You couldn't call in?"

"I believed I recognized the shooter but wasn't sure. This is how I intend to identify him." I pause. "Excuse me, but what the hell is going on, sir? Why the third degree?"

He leans back in the chair and rests his chin on his hand as he watches me, deciding what he wants to tell me.

"The scene you left is a clusterfuck, Agent. It was barely on our radar when you walked in. We hadn't even gotten a call from the sheriff's department or state patrol. We only knew that they responded to a 9-1-1 call from the conductor. Yet you may be the only person able to ID a man who shot and killed an Amtrak employee, and tortured and killed another man on board that train."

My eyes widen in surprise, but the shooter's behavior makes sense if what Corbett says is true. "I knew none of this, sir. Who was the victim?"

"You don't get it, Roberts! Along with whatever else you've done to sabotage your career, you have really screwed the pooch here. We can't share anything about the investigation even if we wanted to. You have no official standing with the bureau."

A waterfall of sound fills my ears with a dull roar, and his voice starts to fade. I want to defend myself, tell him I've had a shitty day so far, scream at him that already today one man tried to kill me and another tried to rape me. I want to tell him to fucking walk in my shoes for a day and see how he likes it.

I do neither.

Though the waves crashing in my head nearly drown out his words, he goes on. "Worse, by taking your own sweet time coming in, you prevented any possibility of setting up a perimeter and tracking down this asshole. If you were still an active agent, I'd arrest you for obstruction."

Black Rorschach inkblots obscure my vision. I rest my head on my arms on the table as the dragon I managed to hold at bay earlier rears up and spreads its wings, cloaking me in darkness.

31

Twenty yards from the tracks, vehicles started lining up nose to tail on what appeared to be a seldom-used frontage road alongside a highway. To Dana, it looked for all the world like the staging area for a Memorial Day parade in the town where she grew up. Local police arrived first in two cars. The two officers who approached the train seemed surprisingly young, too young to be cops.

Julien stood and leaned toward her. "Stay put," he said, so quietly Dana strained to hear him. "And if anyone asks what's going on, tell them you don't know."

The conductor strode to the end of the car and disappeared. A few moments later Dana saw him reappear outside and meet the two officers. The three of them stood in a small knot, and while Julien talked and gesticulated, one of the cops asked an occasional question and took notes on a little pad while the other observed. After a minute or two, the conductor led them back toward the sleeper cars instead of into the lounge. Dana breathed a sigh of momentary relief. She knew her turn would come soon enough, and she dreaded it.

A county sheriff's car pulled up next. A deputy got out, stood next to his open door for a moment while his hands patted pockets, holstered gun, and utility belt before he shut the door and slowly walked toward the train, his gaze taking in the length of it, stopping every so often as if checking gauging a passenger's expression on the other side of the glass or taking in some minor detail. A moment or two after he stepped out of her view, she heard muted conversation from the café. Shortly after that, the deputy strode into the lounge and looked around.

"Y'all know where the conductor is?" the deputy said.

Passengers looked at the deputy blankly, then at each other.

Dana raised her arm and pointed behind him. "Sleeper car, two cars back."

The deputy nodded and turned his shoulders, then looked at Dana again and approached. He was an older man with gray hair and a weathered face, but trim. The Kevlar vest under his uniform jacket and shirt, along with all the gear around his waist made him look top-heavy on top of wiry legs. His tan, lined face seemed world-weary and suggested that he'd seen just about everything during his years of duty. But the gentle smile that broke on it went all the way to his eyes, making Dana feel a little less queasy.

"I'm Frank," he said, sticking his hand out.

"Dana," she said, giving him her fingers to squeeze briefly. She saw the name badge on the breast of his jacket: Frank Landon.

"Mind if I sit?" he said, gesturing at the empty seats on the other side of the table. She shook her head. "I see a couple of officers from town got here ahead of me," he said, "so I'll wait until they suss out the situation. I take it you have some idea of what's going on."

She hesitated, nerves starting to make her itch. Julien had told her not to answer questions, and the last thing she wanted to do was talk to a cop. But he was a cop, which didn't give her much choice. She nodded tentatively.

"Did you witness what happened?"

Dana quickly glanced around her to see if anyone had heard his question. A few people watched them but were too far away to hear. Most of the others in the lounge had tried to find other things to do—read, chat in low tones, gaze out the window—but their worried expressions said they wondered, too. She turned and saw Frank following her gaze around the car.

"I'll take that as a yes," he said in low tones. "Care to tell me what happened?"

Again, Dana hesitated, this time due to the fear that rushed back through her, paralyzing her.

"Take your time," the deputy said. "I know this is hard. I heard a man was killed."

A tremor went though her. "Two men."

The deputy raised an eyebrow but said nothing.

She leaned forward, and in a voice barely above a whisper said, "Look, I really didn't see anything. I only caught a glimpse of something, something horrible, and I told the conductor. He found the dead men."

"Because of what you saw, though, right? Sometimes a glimpse is enough. Why don't you start at the beginning and tell me what happened."

Dana glanced behind her once more to make sure they weren't overheard, walked him through her movements and told him what she'd seen. When she finished, he nodded.

"That was good. You remember a lot of details. What's your last name, anyway?"

She froze. For a moment she couldn't quite catch her breath and through the panicky pain gripping her ribs she wondered if she might just pass out. "Carlisle," she finally choked out.

"Carlisle," he repeated. "Spelled like Kitty Carlisle?"

Dana looked at him blankly, the oddness of his question making her forget her panic.

He waved a hand. "Sorry. Before your time. A singer. I used to watch her on 'To Tell The Truth' when I was a kid."

"Oh." Dana didn't know what else to say, and the momentary silence felt awkward.

"Where did you board the train?" The deputy's voice sounded casual, but Dana saw his eyes search her face.

"Washington. I live there."

"And where are you headed?"

"Minnesota. I'm taking some time off work and going to see an old friend of my mom's."

"Sounds nice."

The deputy opened his mouth to say something else, then looked up at something behind her. She craned her neck to look over her shoulder. Julien and one of the officers from town approached them.

The deputy slid out of his seat and stood in the aisle. "Hey, Bill, good to see you. You check out the scene?"

"Yeah," the officer sighed. "It's bad. Gonna need your help on this one."

Frank nodded. "Who's with you?"

"Russ Jones. He was looking a little green around the gills, so I told him to tape off the scene and stand guard until I come get him."

"Good. I'll call and see who's free to take over the investigation. It'll probably be Liz." He turned to Julien. "You're the conductor? You called it in?"

"Yes, sir." Julien nodded. "But as for your people taking over, I'm afraid that our Special Operations will want to head up the investigation. I've already called them."

"They have someone coming from D.C.? That's fine, but it'll take two-plus hours to get here, and I'm sure you and all your passengers would like to get back underway as soon as possible. Why don't I have our investigator start collecting evidence and interviewing passengers, and we'll update your people when they get here."

The conductor hesitated. "I guess so."

"Good. Have you said anything to the passengers yet?"

"I announced that we stopped for medical attention for a passenger."

"Sounds like we're way past that," the deputy said wryly, "but that was probably smart not to panic the passengers. Stick with that if anyone asks. Would you please stay here with Ms. Carlisle? Bill, you can show me the scene, then start a canvass of the passengers in the car where it happened. We'll set up interviews here, and take over the dining area if we need more space."

The town cop headed toward the rear with the deputy in his wake calling in on his two-way radio. Dana's shoulders slumped as some of her tension receded along with the deputy, but the worry churning the acid in her stomach didn't lessen. The conductor slid into the seat the deputy had vacated, but he remained silent.

Dana watched outside the window as more official vehicles pulled up—a fire truck and two EMS medic vans, one from the Orange County Rescue Squad and the other from Lake of the Woods Fire & Rescue, according to the lettering on the door, another county sheriff's patrol car, a state police cruiser, a county sheriff's van, and an unmarked car at the back of the line. Many still had their flashers or the light bars on their roofs turned on. None of the men or women those vehicles disgorged had come into the lounge car yet. Dana assumed they'd all gone to gawk at the gory scene in the compartment two cars behind her. She didn't know how long they'd been sitting there, but it couldn't have been much more than twenty minutes since Julien had called 911.

The conductor fidgeted in his seat. "I have a train to run."

He stood and headed toward the front of the train.

"Where are you going?" Dana asked. She didn't like feeling as if he was babysitting her, but the thought of being confronted by more cops without his presence worried her more.

He stopped and turned. "To speak with the crew and then tend to my passengers. Stay put."

As soon as he was gone, Dana felt the eyes of a half-dozen or so passengers in the lounge on her back, their accusatory stares blaming her for preventing them from getting to destinations where loved ones, new jobs, business deals or vacations awaited. She refused to turn around and look. Though the waiting seemed interminable, only a few minutes passed before she heard voices approaching. She swiveled in her seat. Frank was back with a frumpy, strawberry blond not much older than Dana in tow, along with a tall man in his forties wearing a state trooper's uniform with brush-cut brown hair and a military bearing. They stopped short of the table where Dana sat and finished their conversation.

"We can't hold them off forever," the woman said. "Seems like that'd give them something picturesque to focus on instead of this damn train. I don't want anyone nosing around the scene until the evidence techs have combed every inch. Gerard's just about done with his prelim, and as soon as we finish getting pictures, they can get those bodies out of there."

"Sounds fine, ma'am," the trooper said. "I'll get over there and set it up. And I'll get someone else on patrol to come in and help me with traffic control."

The trooper turned smartly on his heel and marched out as the woman sat across from Dana.

The woman flashed her a quick smile and held her hand out. "Sorry. I'm Elizabeth Stinson. Liz. I'm an investigator for the county sheriff's office. Nice to meet you, Dana. Wish it wasn't under these circumstances. I know you spoke with Deputy Landon, but I have just a few more questions for you."

Dana grasped the woman's warm, dry fingers, and her estimation went up several notches. She looked more like a harried young mother than a cop, curly tendrils of reddish-blond hair framing a plump but attractive face set with piercing blue eyes. But now that she was sitting across the table, she looked older than Dana originally thought. Wiser, too.

"Can't hold who off?" Dana said.

"The media." Stinson waved at the window.

Dana's gaze followed the woman's hand. For the first time she noticed that the line of emergency vehicles formed a barricade against a phalanx of television and radio news vans parked on the other side of the highway.

"Oh, God," Dana groaned, unable to stop the tears springing to her eyes. "You can't tell them who I am. Please, oh, God, please don't give them my name. He's still out there."

As she spoke the words aloud, the terrifying mental images of two faces, not one, now loomed in Dana's mind.

CHARLOTTESVILLE

32

"Charlottesville, Mr. Sykes."

Sykes glanced up from his work and saw George watching him in the rearview mirror. He looked away. Stately homes on rolling pastures behind white rail fences—horse farms, some of them, others made to look that way—gave way to corners with traffic lights and gas stations.

"Where to? UVA?"

Sykes frowned. "No, George. I'm not interested in going back to school."

The big driver went silent, but Sykes saw him glance in the mirror.

Sykes sighed. "Use your head. Why Charlottesville? Why not turn around and go home?"

George's features contorted, as if thinking was physical torture, but they eventually smoothed into an expression of understanding.

"This is where the train stops next."

"Good, George."

Now it was George's turn to frown. "Why would you want to get back on the train? You just got off."

"That IED in Iraq really scrambled your brains, didn't it?"

George's head jerked up, and his nostrils flared.

Shaking his head, one corner of his lip curling involuntarily, Sykes waved him off. "I'm not getting back on the train. We're going to try to keep someone from boarding, but if that fails, you're getting on the train, not me."

George's brows shot up. "Me?"

"We need to find someone. A woman. You're going to help. Young brunette. Long hair, black jeans, white blouse, black leather jacket. Got that? Now, let's get to the station."

"Yes, sir."

Sykes wondered why he hadn't gotten rid of George a long time ago, but knew the answer before the question fully formed. Loyalty. The only reason he sat in the car far from the office where he belonged,

151

or better yet the soft bed that waited for him at home, was that Mick lacked what his compatriot, his fellow-in-arms had given Sykes in spades. Unquestioned loyalty. To Sykes, it was a rare and valuable commodity.

George threaded the big car through downtown traffic and pulled into a large parking lot. Sykes admired the two red-brick Neocolonial buildings in the far corner as George slowly circled the lot. They represented the kind of classical architectural style he appreciated, one of the reasons he loved D.C. so much. Formerly Charlottesville's original train station, the larger two-story building now housed a restaurant. The squat building next door had been added on in the early 1900s as a baggage handling facility, and Amtrak had put its ticket office and waiting area there when it took over the station in the 1970s.

George angled the car into a shady spot with a good view of the station's two platforms and left the engine running.

"Very good, George," Sykes said. "If we spot the woman, you can simply walk up to her and convince her to come back to the car with you."

"How am I gonna do that?"

"I think holding her at gunpoint ought to do the trick."

George's head jerked as if he'd been punched.

"Discreetly, of course," Sykes said. "And if we don't see her on the platform, then you'll look for her on the train."

George met his gaze in the mirror. "But I—"

Sykes cut him. "It shouldn't take long to search the train—as far as the next stop, maybe."

"Guess I'll go buy a ticket," George said to the windshield.

Sykes nodded, already engrossed in the work in front of him again. He heard the door open, and the car shifted as George eased his bulk out of the car.

George leaned over and stuck his head into the car. "Can I get you anything?"

Glancing up with a sigh, Sykes said, "I'm fine, George. Just go get the woman."

33

A drop of water formed along the seam of the suit jacket hanging on the coat tree in the corner, and finally grew large enough to fall and land silently on the plush carpet. Toby Granger's nose wrinkled in disgust. He didn't know if the suit could be salvaged after being out in that downpour. Thankfully, he made a point of keeping a clean set of clothes at the office, and had changed as soon as he'd returned to the office. But it pissed him off that chasing after that bitch, Dana, might have cost him two weeks' salary.

It wasn't the money so much as the principle. He didn't deserve that sort of treatment— running out into the street in the rain, for fuck's sake. She was an employee, a peon. She should have obeyed his commands in the first place. He choked off a harsh laugh. His therapist was going to have fun with this one. Executive director of a multi-million-dollar foundation and he couldn't get a subordinate with a high school education to do what he asked. He wanted to kick something, but the thought of ruining two pairs of Bruno Magli shoes in one day squelched the impulse.

He could blame it all on dear old dad, of course. The legendary Jedediah Granger had cashed out of the family tobacco business at an opportune time and gone into politics at a young age. Putting a tiny percentage of the family fortune into his first campaign, Jed was voted to the U.S. Senate from the Bluegrass State, the Commonwealth of Kentucky. He'd thrown over Toby's mother for a Senate intern during his second term, when Toby was eleven. Naturally, at that age, Toby had chosen to live with his mother, and Jed, the bastard, had never spoken to his son again.

Toby remembered the years of struggle with bitterness, his mother's shouting matches with Jedediah every month over child care and alimony, her attempts to hold a job to bring in extra cash, the taunts at school because of the second-hand clothes he'd had to wear. His fists clenched at the thought of the few times he'd gone to his father's office during his teens to confront him about his lack of support, and how he'd been turned away by the staff each time with the excuse that the great Jedediah Granger was too busy—too important—to see him. How impotent Toby had felt that he couldn't get an appointment to see his own father.

That had all come to an unresolved end with the elder Granger's death. Celebrating after his reelection to a sixth term with yet another intern who he intended to make his third wife, Jed had dropped dead of a massive myocardial infarction on top of his desk in the Senate Office Building. Jed hadn't left a dime of his still-considerable estate to Toby or Toby's mother. Never inclined to forgive the son of a bitch for what he'd done, Toby's biggest regret was that he hadn't been there to watch his father die. And he'd promised himself that he would never be poor again.

Beads of sweat broke out on his upper lip. He took a handkerchief from his pocket. As he lifted it to his mouth, his hand shook. The whole incident earlier had set him on edge. Why would Dana have taken off like that unless she knew something? He didn't for a moment believe that she'd ripped off the foundation. She wasn't the type. When he thought back to the times she'd turned down his subtle hints that he might be interested in helping further her career for a little quid pro quo, she'd been such a goodie-two-shoes that it seemed impossible.

She didn't seem smart enough, either. Smart or not, there was no way in hell she was fucking up his career. He'd worked too hard to become someone in this town besides the forgotten progeny of a six-term senator. He was a mover and shaker in D.C. now. His fundraisers were A-list events, the foundation's cause both righteous and trendy. No way was he going to let that bitch get away with whatever she had planned.

"Greg!" he yelled. "Get your ass in here!" He fumed, wondering what was taking so long.

The office door burst open. Greg rushed in, gesticulating wildly.

Before Toby could open his mouth, Greg said, "You need to see this. Hurry."

Toby frowned, irritated at being cut off. Was there no such thing as respect anymore?

"What are you talking about?"

"I'm not kidding, Toby. You've gotta come quick." Greg turned and rushed out without waiting. Curious now as well as pissed, Toby followed his assistant out to the reception area where a small knot of staff members stood staring open-mouthed at the large-screen television that usually was tuned to C-SPAN or CNN. Toby's head swiveled to see what had captured their attention on the screen.

At first all he could discern was an unmoving Amtrak train in a background shot behind an on-camera reporter. Then the camera zoomed in on the train over the reporter's shoulder and slowly panned back and forth. He thought his staff had gone mad until he

154

suddenly spotted a familiar face behind a window on the train. *Dana*.

"Turn it up," he barked.

The startled receptionist grabbed a remote and pointed it at the screen, and the reporter's voice gained volume.

"...two men have died aboard that train. Authorities have not yet indicated how the men died, or released their names. For now, the investigation continues. We're live outside Orange, Virginia."

"Isn't that...?" Greg said.

"The woman on that train looks like Dana," someone piped up.

Toby nodded grimly.

"I thought she was acting strangely this morning," Greg said. "I nearly ran into her outside the copy room."

Toby felt a chill run through him.

"Wasn't that Dana you tried to stop at the elevator earlier?" Greg said. "Why would she be on that train? She didn't have a trip scheduled, did she?"

"I'll take care of this," Toby said. "Okay, back to work, people. We have a world to save, remember?"

As the group disbanded, Toby motioned Greg aside. "I'm going to handle this personally. Route all my calls to my cell phone."

"What's going on? Why's she on that train?"

"I don't know, but I'm going to find out. Watch things while I'm gone. I'm not sure when I'll be back."

"What should I tell people?" Greg said as Toby turned away.

"Just say I had to take care of an emergency," Toby called over his shoulder. He was already thinking about what he was going to do to Dana when he caught her.

34

I'm connected to my brother Doug in the unspoken way that my friends Lanie and Jeanette are. They're twins in my third-grade class with blond braids and perky noses who say that I can't possibly be linked to my brother in the same way because he's nearly three years older than me. But I am. I've felt it since I was old enough to walk. Doug tells me I'm full of crap, and it mystifies him how I know what he's thinking. But I know there are times he feels it, too, when he knows what I'm thinking. Now is one of those times.

Four of his besties—Sweets, Toad, Jim and Ralph—swivel their heads, alternating their gaze from Doug to me, their expressions cycling from expectancy and impatience to disdain and back. Doug's eyes never leave my face. He knows I have him over a barrel, and he's calculating the risks of doing what he wants versus what he should. The five of them are going to play ball at the middle school. I want to go and play, too. Since I'm a girl, they don't want me tagging along, but Doug's supposed to watch me while Mom's out running errands. If he wants to hang out with his friends, he has to take me, and he's not happy about it.

"Fine," he says. A chorus of groans erupts, and he raises his voice to talk over them. "But you have to do what I tell you."

The groans subside somewhat, but Ralph and Sweets grumble under their breath. I nod at Doug. There's always a price. I want to stick out my tongue at the others, but I know to quit while I'm ahead.

"Well, no sense standing around," Doug says. "Let's go."

The others scramble onto their bikes and stand on the pedals to see who can peel out fastest. Doug hangs back to make sure I'm okay on mine, but once he sees that my bike is steady and I'm just fine, he stands up and pedals furiously to catch up with his friends. They part to make way for him. He's obviously the leader of this group. I'm not as fast, but I know my way, so I don't care.

The wind whips my hair around my face, and the weight of the summer sun presses down on my bare shoulders and arms. The blue sky is so bright it hurts my eyes. I squint, but the wind drags tears out of the corners anyway and across my temples where they vanish in the hair over my ears. I smell summer in the air as I pedal—food seared over charcoal fires, fresh-cut alfalfa, and since we live miles out of town, what Wisconsinites call "our dairy air." Even third-graders know that's a play on the French "derrière," which is universally understood. And anyone who's been near a dairy farm knows that cows produce about as much methane as milk.

I'm just happy I get to go with Doug and his friends. It's not that I like playing baseball so much. But I don't like being treated like a baby. Billy's the baby in the family now. And I know that the guys will do something even more fun afterward, like ride into town for ice cream or go swimming.

Ahead of me, the boys drop their bikes in the grass at the edge of the diamond and run into the outfield with their gloves, laughing. By the time I run out to join them, they're in a circle warming up their arms, tossing the ball to each other. I squeeze in between Doug and Sweets, shoving my fingers as far as I can into an old mitt I got from Robbie, and they reluctantly shift and make room for me. The mitt's still too big for me, but since it was Robbie's first baseball glove, it was too small for Doug, so it was handed down to me.

The others pointedly avoid throwing the ball to me. I know it's because I'm a girl. I almost don't mind because I'm still a little fearful of catching the ball. It hurts if I don't do it right. But Doug taught me how to throw, how to turn my body, reach back and extend my arm in the follow-through instead of pushing the ball from the shoulder the way most girls throw. So when he softly tosses it to me underhanded, I catch it easily and drill it across the circle to Ralph, surprising him. I see Doug hide a grin even though I know he's still mad at me.

Four more boys show up a few minutes later. They're a year or two older, but Doug and his friends know them, and he immediately asks if they want to play.

The tallest of the four shrugs and glances at his buddies before he says, "Sure, us against you guys."

Doug says, "Six against four wouldn't be fair. We should pick teams."

"Six?" Jeff looks around, a confused look on his face before his eyes light on me. He laughs. "You mean pipsqueak, here? Okay, sure. Let's pick teams."

The two groups of boys line up facing each other, and the picks begin. To no one's surprise, Jeff picks his friends, Doug picks his, and I'm the last player standing, which means I'm on Jeff's team. A coin toss says we take the field first.

Jeff looks at me and points to right field. "Stand out there and don't get in anybody's way."

I do as I'm told. It's an easy job since no hits or players come anywhere near me. I'm okay with that. The sun is warm on my face, and I watch bees lazily hop from clover to purple clover in the grass. At least I'm on a team. When it's my turn at bat in the bottom of the inning, though, a monkey-faced kid with big ears shoulders me aside on the way to the plate.

"Hey!"

"What's the deal?" Sweets calls from first base.

"Designated hitter," Jeff answers loudly.

"Come on," Doug says, scuffing a toe in the dirt on the mound. "You

158

can't do that. Let her hit."

There's a chorus of "Let her hit" from Doug's teammates. Jeff lifts a shoulder, lets it drop. Looking at me, he nods his head toward the plate. Monkey-Face scowls at me as he stomps back to the bench. I step up to the plate and go down swinging at the third pitch.

Two innings later, Slim Jim pops a fly to right field. I hear loud groans and someone shouting at me to get out of the way. But I'm transfixed by the black dot arcing in the blue sky and growing larger as it descends toward me until it seems as big as the moon. I stick out my glove and cup it with the other hand the way I watched my brothers do it. My heart thumps so loudly in my chest that I'm barely aware of the shouting and don't even hear the pounding footsteps coming toward me. The ball rushes at me until fear overtakes me and I squeeze my eyes shut at the last second. When the ball smacks the leather where the palm meets the webbing, I automatically close both the glove and my other hand around the ball, trapping it.

And then someone barrels into me like a freight train, knocking me over and tumbling me in the grass. My breath leaves me with a whoosh, and when I open my eyes I'm on my back, arms clutched to my chest, gasping for air. The bright sun stabs at my sight, nearly blinding me. I close them to slits and lie there, chest heaving until I can suck in a huge breath. I hear shouting again.

"Why'd you go and do that, you turkey?"

"She had it, man. You blew it."

"What were you thinking, idiot?"

"Where's the ball, anyway? Anybody see where the ball went?"

The weight of my hands presses into my chest, and I feel the roundness of the glove. I can't help smiling as I raise my glove hand and hold the ball aloft. As we change sides, my teammates look at me with something close to respect. But the looks from Doug's friends are different, as if they are both fearful and envious. They fuel my determination to get a hit, or at least make contact with the ball, even if I don't get on base.

When it's my turn at bat again, I try to remember everything my brothers told me about hitting. Choke up. Step into the pitch. Swing early. Keep the bat level. Follow through. The advice is my mantra on my way to the plate. I repeat it over and over as I dig my sneakers into the dirt and focus on the ball in Doug's hand. He starts his motion and everything around me disappears except the ball. I start my swing almost as soon as the ball leaves his hand, and I'm as surprised as everyone else when my bat connects with a satisfying thwok and drives the ball between first and second.

Voices scream, "Run!"

I drop the bat and run as fast as my legs will go, and watch the ball bounce and roll into the outfield.

"Keep going!" someone yells as I reach first.

Sweets chases the ball into the outfield as I round the corner and head for second, where Ralph faces me with a foot on the bag. But he's looking into the outfield, and suddenly I see the ball wing through the air toward him. He stretches, but the throw is way off, and the ball flies past. Toad scrambles after it while Doug runs from the mound toward third.

My teammates are yelling from the bench, "Go! Go! Go!"

The ball is still bouncing and rolling past the foul line, so I put my head down and run faster. But when I step on the bag at second, Ralph sticks his foot out and trips me, launching me head over heels into the dirt. I land hard and slide, the rough, dry earth sanding skin off my forearm and knee. I choke on the dust swirling around me, and blink as it gets in my eyes. Then the pain kicks in, and my watery eyes tear in earnest now. My arm and knee are on fire, and I can feel trickles of blood from both wounds running down my skin. My tailbone is sore from landing so hard.

I bite my lip to keep from wailing, but as I struggle to my feet, Ralph says, "Oh, don't be such a crybaby."

Anger fills me, white hot. I forget about running to third or going back to second and standing on the bag. Ralph's smug face fills my vision, and though I can't stop the tears from streaking down my dusty cheeks in muddy tracks, I can wipe the look off Ralph's mug. I march up to him.

"Whatcha gonna do, crybaby?"

Without saying a word, I kick him in the nuts. He howls and folds in half before falling over and writhing in the dirt. His teammates come running, which prompts my teammates to clear the bench. Within seconds it feels like the whole world is descending on me.

*****

The anger pushes the darkness away. I listen to the purr of air from the overhead vent and the faint ticking of someone's watch. My cheek is warm where it rests on my forearm, but the table feels cool under my arms. I compose myself, relaxing the muscles in my face so my features will reveal nothing of what I feel, and slowly raise my head.

Corbett looks at me quizzically, as if I'm an animal he's never encountered before. Reassured when I don't say or do anything, he's back on familiar footing.

"You're done here, Agent," he says quietly. "Give Mulcahy a description, and leave a contact number in case we have more questions. Then keep going. Go home if that's where you were headed, and forget you were ever here."

"And the investigation?"

"We'll handle it," he says sharply.

I nod. He stands and looks down at me for a moment, then turns and leaves. When the door shuts behind him, Mulcahy looks at me with what seems like genuine concern.

"Are you okay?"

"Yeah, fine." Weariness settled over my shoulders like a shawl.

"You sure? You didn't look too good there for a moment."

"I'm fine, Agent." It comes out sharper than I intended. "Sorry. It's been a rough morning."

He regards me for an unnecessarily long moment before speaking. "We'll pass on your description of the perp, don't worry."

I nod, and while he lifts his pen and holds it poised over the legal pad on the table, I start telling him what happened aboard the train.

35

Dana abruptly slid out of her seat, dragging her purse behind her, and wildly looked around the car for another seat as far away from the media cameras peering through the windows as possible. The other passengers in the car stared at her. She saw the fear in their expressions. They knew she was connected to the events on the train, maybe even thought she had caused them, but they had no idea what she'd been through, what she was still going through. They didn't know the fear she experienced, the fear she still felt. She wondered how they could possibly be afraid of her.

Spotting an empty table in the front corner of the car, she hurried over and squeezed in as far as she could, shrinking against the bulkhead out of sight of anyone outside. Liz Stinson got up and slowly followed, a frown on her face. She eased into a seat across from Dana and rested her forearms on the table, interweaving her fingers.

"Want to tell me what that was all about?" she said in a quiet voice.

Dana shook her head. "I just don't want my face all over the evening news. That terrible man is out there somewhere. I don't think he got a good look at me, but he will if the media knows who I am." She leaned across the table and gripped Stinson's forearm. "You have to protect me. Please. Don't let them know who I am. You can do that, can't you?"

Stinson looked down at her arm. Dana followed her gaze and realized with horror that her nails were digging into the deputy's arm hard enough to draw blood if not for the sleeve of her blouse. Dana yanked her hand back.

"What aren't you telling me?" Stinson said in the same quiet voice, as if she hadn't even felt Dana's grip.

Dana sat back quickly and blinked, composing herself. "Nothing."

Stinson peered at her. "Look, I can keep your name out of the press, and do my best to keep the cameras away, but you need to help us help you. If there's something else going on...."

"Nothing. Really." She paused, but Stinson didn't look convinced. "You saw what he did, right? My God, what kind of a monster can do that to another human being?"

Dana tried to keep the desperation out of her voice, but every time the vision of what she'd seen in that roomette flashed through her mind, her stomach roiled and she wanted to puke.

Stinson tipped her head slightly and glanced at her hands. When she raised her eyes to look at Dana, her mouth was drawn thin with determination.

"Yes, I saw what he did. You have a right to be scared, Dana, but you have my word that we'll do everything we can to keep you safe. We already put out an APB based on your description. I'd like to have you talk to a sketch artist, though. It would help to—"

"No! I told you, I didn't get a good look at his face."

Stinson, studied her for a moment before relenting. She pushed herself upright with her forearms and stood. "We'll get this guy. I promise. I have to interview some other people and see how things are going. I'll be back to check on you in a bit."

She turned, but Dana stopped her. "Do you have any idea how much longer this will take?"

Stinson paused. "I don't know. Our crime-scene techs are just about finished with the scene, but we're still waiting for Amtrak investigators to get here, and we don't know if they want to bring anyone else on scene."

"Who else is there?" Dana's tone drew the hint of a smile from Stinson.

"FBI, maybe."

"I can't stand being on this train. I can't help thinking about what that man did. It gives me the creeps." She shuddered. "You don't think they'll hold us here, do you?"

Stinson's brow furrowed. "You mean after we get Amtrak investigators caught up? I don't see why they would, as long as they believe we've processed the scene properly. If they hold the train, I'm sure they'll provide buses to take you at least as far as Charlottesville."

"Can't happen soon enough," Dana muttered. "I have to get off this train."

36

Sykes wasn't used to having idle time on his hands, and the waiting made him nervous, something he hadn't experienced for years. Normally, he would be starting his day at the club after five or six hours' sleep, sipping a Turkish coffee and going over the previous night's receipts while he waited for his breakfast of fresh berries or melon in season, half a cup of Greek yogurt topped with granola, a single soft-boiled egg and croissant or brioche to go with it. Instead, through sheer dint of bad luck, he sat in a stuffy car in the middle of Virginia chasing after some forgettable young woman who may or may not have seen squat but would surely remember the man who'd taken a shot at her.

No, he decided, it wasn't the disruption in his routine, or the lack of sleep, or even the waiting that had set him on edge. It was the fact that he'd fucked up. He'd made a mistake. Not just one but many. And that made him doubt himself, made him wonder if there was something physically wrong with him. A brain tumor, perhaps. Or early onset Alzheimer's. He snorted. *Preposterous.* Sykes knew that if he didn't rein in these emotions—the anger fueled by this odd feeling of inadequacy—he might continue to make mistakes.

He couldn't afford more mistakes. And now time had become a factor, adding to the pressure to clean up the mistakes as quickly as possible and get back to what was important. If the woman had gone to the cops, they'd circulate his description around town. Someone from the restaurant would probably remember him, maybe even have seen him get into the town car when George picked him up. He shuddered to think that someone may have jotted down the license plate number. No, they couldn't have known at that point.

He was taking a huge risk that the woman would somehow make her way to Charlottesville and re-board the train. The more he thought about it, the more he realized the enormity of his mistake. He'd made an assumption based on what he would have done, trusting that his was the most logical course of action. She had any number of choices. If she went to the police, she might ask for their protection and stay in town until she could board the next train headed wherever she was going. If she were on the run, she could rent a car or fly out of Charlottesville. He couldn't believe he hadn't killed her when he had the chance. How could he have missed?

Just solve the problem.

He took out his phone and dialed.

Philip's trusted voice answered, "Stevens."

"It's me. Anything?"

"Not yet, sir, but I am working on it. I'll ring you as soon as I have something."

"And our two friends? Are they on the road?"

"I believe so."

"Good. Thank you, Philip."

"Of course, sir."

Sykes disconnected and punched in another number.

"*Da*," Dobrev answered.

Sykes figured the white noise he heard in the background was wind rush and highway noise from a moving car. "It's Sykes," he said. "Where are you?"

"Don't know. Wait, please."

Sykes heard crackling on the phone, then a muffled, "Mikhail, where in fuck are we?"

"Never mind," Sykes said loudly. "It doesn't matter. Alexei!"

"*Da*, I'm here."

"Good. Change of plans. I want you to go to Orange."

"Orange? What is this?"

Sykes heard roaring in his ears. "Use your GPS, you dumb fuck!"

"This Mick you want us to find, he is in town of Orange?"

"Mick is dead! I'm looking for a woman, probably late twenties, brunette, hair down to her shoulders. She's wearing black jeans, nice ones, a white blouse and a black leather jacket. She was on the same train as Mick, but she got off in Orange. She might still be there."

"Where should we look?"

"Go to the police station first."

"Are you *psikh*? Is not such a good idea."

"No, I'm not crazy. She saw Mick, and she saw who killed him. She might have gone to the cops to report it."

"What's woman's name?"

"I don't know what her fucking name is. Just go there and ask if a woman of that description showed up, and if so, where is she now?"

"*Dumaeš', ja durak*? You think I'm stupid? What you want me to say to cops?"

"Tell them...tell them you're her brother or cousin or something. Tell them you know she was on the train, but you haven't heard from her, and you're worried."

166

"And if they don't know anything about a woman?"

"Christ, Alexei, do I have to spell it out for you? Ask around town. See if the train is still there."

"And if we find her?"

"Kill her! I don't care how. Just get rid of her. Got it?"

"*Da*," Dobrev grumbled. "Got it. Going to cost you."

"I'll take that up with Nastase. Just get the job done. And let me know what you find out from the police. If they don't know what you're talking about, that will change things, and I'll have new instructions for you two."

"Okay, okay."

Sykes disconnected and had to restrain himself from throwing the phone at the windshield as hard as he could. As if admonishing him, the phone buzzed in his hand. Startled, he looked at the screen, and read a text from George.

Train is all over the news.

He sighed and texted back.

Do they know who they're looking for?

He waited a long couple of minutes before George replied.

Two bodies. (WTF?) No names. No leads.

Sykes leaned back in the seat, some of the tension in his body easing away. The media, of course, might have no clue about what was really going on. It depended on how much information law enforcement wanted to give them. The phone in his hand buzzed again as another text from George came in.

Train's still sitting on the tracks somewhere.

Good. Hurry, Alexei.

37

Toby kept the radio in the BMW tuned to an all-news station and listened with half an ear as the countryside sped past the windows in a blur. No way was he letting Dana slip away this time. She knew something about the missing money—either who'd taken it or how—and he was going to find out what.

Greg had rolled a seven for him when he'd spotted her on television. Toby would have to find a way to thank him that wouldn't entail nearly as much as the cost of the raise Greg had been whining for the past six months or more. Now, though, his thoughts were consumed with Dana and what the hell she'd done on that train. Two men dead? Murdered? What the fuck was she into?

Of course her presence on the train could be totally coincidental to those men getting killed, but after the strange way she'd acted earlier in the morning, Toby had to wonder.

He smacked the steering wheel with the heel of his hand. Why couldn't women be more like cars? Perform on demand, and when they wore out or their looks faded, just trade them in for a new model. No, he definitely wasn't going to let her get away with whatever she planned to do with what she'd learned.

He reached over, opened the glove compartment and curled his fingers around the knurled butt of the baby Glock 9mm pistol he kept there.

38

I've never thought of Kathryn Jennings Roberts as pretty. With so many boys in the family, there's little in the house that's frilly or feminine, and she's so down-to-earth and practical that I've never seen her in any other role but mother. As she daubs away the blood on my skinned knee with a cold, damp washcloth in one hand and tweezers in the other, her scent reassures me. She smells like oranges and vanilla, a combination that has always signified security—safety from night terrors, fairness in sibling squabbles, comfort in times of trauma—and given me what will probably be a lifetime love of Creamsicle bars.

The sides of her wavy, shoulder-length, chestnut hair are swept up into a ponytail high on the back of her head, but an errant strand is curled damply against her cheek as a bead of perspiration slides down from her temple past a delicate earlobe. The pink tip of her tongue pokes out of the corner of her mouth as she focuses intently on a tiny pebble lodged under my abraded skin. I am holding my breath, lower lip quivering, and wincing in anticipation.

To keep from crying, especially in front of Doug and Robbie, I concentrate on this sense of seeing the person ministering to me in a new light. Some feeling compels me to catalog everything about her, to capture this moment on mental VHS tape.

Her flawless complexion is devoid of make-up, yet it has a healthy glow from time spent outside under the summer sun in the garden, running errands, taking us swimming. Wearing her typical summer uniform of sleeveless cotton blouse—yellow today—and beige Bermuda shorts. Her exposed skin—shoulders, arms, legs—has a lovely matte, tan finish. I have her nose—straight, pert, with a small bump on the bridge—and strong chin, but not her eyes, which are wide-set and the color of a hazy summer sky, not the intense cornflower blue of today's.

I suddenly see her as more than a mom; I realize she's a beautiful woman, and my entire perspective shifts. Moments, gestures, glances and conversations both spoken and wordless take on new meaning. Like most children, I've always seen my parents as protectors, instructors and occasional disciplinarians, but this new and sudden view—no longer childlike but not quite adult— reveals them as so much more. I see how individual they are, how different in personality, almost mirror images of each other—one serious and sober about life's realities, the tragedies that could *befall any family, any person, in an instant of bad luck, yet possessing a silly, fun-loving side; the other a joyful, playful soul who faces each day and its challenges with a smile and a kind word, yet someone thoughtful, deliberate and deeply spiritual. I see how they make a perfect team, each bringing strengths to their roles as parents and providers.*

A flood of memories rushes through my head. My father, still in his county sheriff's uniform, one of his big, calloused hands gently resting in the small of my mother's back as he leans over her shoulder to smell what's cooking on the stove. Her slender fingers touching his cheek before he walks out the door on his way to work, the expression on her face conveying more information, more emotion, than any words could ever impart—pride, joy, contentment, concern, longing, love. His goofy grin and goggle-eyed look of what I now know is adoration at the dinner table as he watches her act out a scene at the grocery store involving local crazy lady. The murmured conversations salted with stifled laughter I hear coming from their bedroom sometimes when I wake up to get a drink of water. The chaste kiss in the kitchen when any of us kids are there that lingers too long to be just a show of affection between two adults.

They love each other. I already knew that, but to my surprise I now have an idea of what that means. As parents, they are a team, but as husband and wife they are an inextricably linked couple, heart, body and soul. They have a life outside of us, one that "family" and we kids give them little time for, but if they're lucky, one that will grow and enrich them when we get older and leave the nest. I see signs of it already. Robbie has a job and a driver's license. Bruce puts almost all his spare time into learning how to be a cop alongside Dad even though he's still in high school.

"There," Mom says, standing back to admire her nursing skills.

I look down to see what seems like an awfully small bandage on my knee to match the one on my elbow. I didn't feel her put it on, and with the scrape cleaned up I see that it's all I need.

Robbie steps forward and chucks me under the chin with a knuckle. "Pretty brave, kid. Did you really kick Ralph in the nuts?"

I giggle and see a smile flash across my mother's face before she quickly wipes it away with the back of her hand and replaces it with an all-business expression.

"Okay, Douglas," she says. "No more taking off with your friends without checking in first, especially when I ask you to watch your sister."

"I don't need him to watch me."

"Aw, Mom," Doug groans. "We were just fine. Heck, if you and Robbie hadn't stopped the fight I think Jenny would have beaten the crap outta all of them."

"Watch your mouth, young man." *She uses her schoolteacher's voice. But her eyes crinkle with amusement.*

*****

I joined the army, then the FBI, to save people, to save lives. I wasn't able to save anyone back then. As it turns out I wasn't even able to save myself, but I'm determined to do what I can to save the woman on the train, or at least warn her. From what I learned in the field office, the man who took a shot at me killed two others aboard the train. He didn't strike me as the type to leave loose ends. He will find a way to hunt her. Or me. Or both if he figures out what I already suspect.

I drive like an old lady. My anger has left me shaking and primed with adrenaline, and only sheer force of will prevents me from driving like a reckless teen. My right foot itches to punch the accelerator pedal through the floor. I don't want to attract attention, and can't afford another run-in with law enforcement today. After the racial unrest and the death of one young woman when a punk kid with neo-Nazi leanings drove his car into a crowd a few years back, Charlottesville cops are on high alert. And my experiences today have soured me on my own kind, disillusioning me with how many, in a profession that vows to serve and protect, view the world monochromatically when they pin on the badge, to the point that some think they're a law unto themselves.

The five-minute drive takes me ten, but I arrive safely without a black-and-white on my tail. My route takes me down West Main Street, and when I spot the train station off to the right below me, I realize I'm crossing over the tracks. From here, the parking lot looks too exposed, and I find myself suddenly pulling over and parking at the curb in response to commands from a cautionary voice in my head. I shut off the engine and take stock.

It's a decent vantage point, with a view of most of the parking lot next to the station. I sit tight, maintaining a constant vigil to see if anyone seems interested in me. I don't know why they would be. Who could possibly know I'm here? Unless Corbett had me followed, and I've seen no evidence of that.

When my pulse slows and my paranoia is properly stowed deep in my prefrontal cortex and firmly tamped down, I get my phone out. Despite my disenchantment, I know I need help from someone with access to resources I don't have. I swallow my pride, pull up a number from my contacts list and dial.

A gruff voice answers, "Machowski."

"Chris, it's Jenny... Roberts," I add lamely, as if he'd forget me in a day.

"Why are you calling me?" His voice is now soft, like he's trying hard not to be overheard.

I feel the anger still on simmer in my belly. Machowski is a misogynistic throwback, but a damn good agent. I was sure he'd been sympathetic during the aftermath of our most recent case, but now my confidence is shaken.

"I'm selling raffle tickets for the Juvenile Diabetes fundraiser. Jesus, Chris, why do you think I'm calling? I need help."

"I'm not supposed to talk to you. You know, until your, uh, thing is resolved."

"Maybe not, but you're still on the phone. A tiny favor. That's all." He doesn't say yes, but doesn't say no. I plunge ahead. "What have you heard about the Amtrak shooting?"

"Bare bones is all. Why?" He's curious now.

"I saw the shooter, Chris. I was on the train. Heading home to Wisconsin."

"As in witnessed?"

"Not the shooting, but the guy, yeah."

"You can ID him?"

"That's my problem. Yes, I could pick him out of a lineup. But I need to know who he is."

"What? I'm supposed to know?"

I sigh. Sarcasm has always been one of his strong suits. "You have access to wanted lists, mug shot files, people who've worked cases. I don't."

"Got a photo, a sketch, anything?"

"No. Just a description."

The line is silent long enough that my lungs let me know I'm holding my breath. I suck in more air as he answers.

"It's a long shot."

"This guy tried to kill me, Chris. He's in the wind. I need to know who I'm dealing with."

It's his turn to sigh. "I'll see what I can do."

I give him a description in as much detail as I can remember and manage a quick "thanks" before he hangs up. I put the phone away and survey my surroundings once more.

Slipping out of the car, I check traffic and dart across the road. A set of stairs on the other side leads down to the street level below, another parking lot, and the train platform that stretches nearly a block. It's empty, so no one is waiting for the delayed westbound train. With UVA classes in session, I think most passengers would be heading east anyway, to D.C., or up to New York.

I look back in the direction I came from; I'm hidden from view of the main parking lot. I cross the street again to my car. This is as good a spot as I'm going to find. I climb in the driver's seat to wait, and instantly wish I'd stopped somewhere to pee.

39

The maelstrom in Dana's mind raged, wind-torn thoughts tossed on heaving emotional seas. She wanted to scream, to wake herself from this nightmare that wouldn't end. Or at least run from the train and go as far and as fast as she could until no one could find her. That was it. She could bolt from the train like that other woman...and run right into the waiting cameras and microphones of the media horde. She frowned and sat up a little straighter.

How had that woman gotten off the train? Jumped?

With the killer behind her, Dana probably would've done the same thing, but whoever her lookalike was, the woman was fast on her feet, in more ways than one. And she had moxie. Dana wished she had that kind of courage and quick-wittedness. As she thought about the woman, Dana's heartbeat and breathing slowed, and some of the tension in her body eased.

I'm smart, too, damn it, even if I don't have a degree.

So smart she nearly forgot why she was on the damn train in the first place. Instinctively, her hand dived into her purse and fumbled around, fingers digging, digging, until they touched.... She grasped the object and pulled it from her bag triumphantly. The thumb drive. More precious than gold. Suddenly, she dropped it back into her purse as if it had burned her fingers, and glanced around the lounge car, stomach churning. She had to guard it with her life, but it did her no good unless she figured out a pattern in what she'd found.

Think!

She closed her eyes and rewound her day until she could see herself in the copy room that morning, mindlessly scanning. She forced herself to focus, to zoom in on the invoices she thought were out of place, from companies as fictitious as city government workers in Chicago. Names floated off the sheets of paper and danced in front of her eyes. She mentally snatched them out of the air and filed them alphabetically in a specially marked drawer. When she had a half-dozen, she snapped her lids open and dug in her purse for her phone, hoping she wasn't too late. Toby might have already called to take her name off the accounts.

Quickly, she thumbed through her contacts list and found the name of the person she thought would be most sympathetic and helpful. She dialed and waited, knee bouncing under the table, as the phone on the other end rang and rang before it was finally answered.

"Hey, Dana."

Relief flooded her system, and she wanted to shout out her gratitude that he'd picked up. Caution warned her to play it cool, sound normal. "Hey, Jared. How are you?"

"I'm okay, but you are in trouble, girl."

Her relief vanished, and she barely squeaked out, "Why? What happened?"

"It's been far too long since we had lunch. I'm beginning to think you don't love me anymore."

Dana wanted to laugh but knew if she started, she might go into hysterics. "Of course I do. But I don't see any invitations in my inbox."

Jared chuckled. "Touché. So, if you didn't call to ask me to lunch, what can I do for you?"

Dana thought quickly. "Toby's all over me about some possible discrepancies."

"In your account?"

"No, no," she assured him. "Differences in what we think we've paid some vendors and what they claim we owe them."

"Oh, got it. How can I help?"

"Rather than try to back through our statements online, Toby wants me to get copies of the cancelled checks. Can you do that?"

"Uh, sure. Might take me a little while, depending on how many you want."

"I have about six names for you. Ready?" She rattled off the names she recalled.

"How far back do you want me to go?"

"Let's say three years. Five would be better, but I know that's asking a lot."

"Honey, that's what computers are for. They do the work while I sit and sip my Starbucks. I suppose you want this yesterday?"

"You know Toby."

"Yeah." Even the one-word response conveyed his distaste, for which Dana was glad.

"You're a lifesaver. I need images of front and back. Text whatever you find to my phone. I'm out of the office today. And I promise I'll call you about lunch."

"When?"

"Soon. I mean it. How's Anthony?"

"He's good. About ready for another show. We'll let you know."

Jared's partner was an artist who'd begun to establish a significant following; a number of companies had commissioned pieces for their offices.

"I look forward to it," she said. She wanted to get him off the phone, but didn't want him to regret the favor he was doing for her.

"I'll text those copies as soon as I can," he said. "Call me about lunch."

"I will. Promise."

The line disconnected. Dana put her phone away and thought about the woman again. She vaguely remembered seeing her in one of the cars... Business class. Looking around the lounge car, Dana realized that the more she focused on problem-solving, the calmer she became. She could do this if she approached it methodically, logically, the way she did her job. Jared was going to help her follow the money. Now it was time for her to find out more about the woman who'd been mistaken for her. Maybe she could switch places with her on a more permanent basis. At least until she found a way out of this mess.

All the investigators had gone elsewhere on the train. Dana felt pretty sure that they weren't planning on talking with her again anytime soon. Julien had left, too, maybe to go wait for the Amtrak cops. Dana stood, hooked her arm through her purse straps, steeled her resolve and made her way toward the rear of the car. She drew only a few curious glances. The other passengers in the lounge looked subdued, resigned to a fate of waiting until someone with authority told them what they could or couldn't do. Dana was done waiting. No one stopped her or challenged her, and she straightened as she walked, putting more purpose into her stride.

She crossed over to the business class car, and slowed her pace, casually taking in the entire car, looking both left and right as she went. Five steps inside the car, she spied the backpack on the luggage rack above a row of empty seats about two-thirds of the way down. Bingo! She held her excitement in check, maintaining her pace. When she reached the row, she casually swung in and plopped into the window seat where she remembered the woman sitting. None of the business class passengers paid her any attention. She sat there a while, looking out the window, checking out the other passengers she could see in the car, trying to relax and look as if she belonged. But her heart thumped loudly in her chest.

When she thought enough time had passed, she stood and reached up for the backpack on the shelf above her. She pulled it down and set it on the seat next to her, casually examining it. A small padlock held the zipper pulls together on a front pocket, but the knapsack's largest compartment was unlocked. Dana unzipped the main compartment, bent over and pawed through the contents. Neatly folded articles of clothing were stacked carefully inside, larger, bulkier items on the bottom and filmier, lighter items—a couple of nice silk tops along with pretty, lacy lingerie that while not Frederick's of Hollywood was racier than anything Dana owned—on top. Digging her fingers all the way down, Dana found two pairs of shoes, what felt like the fabric and rubber of athletic shoes and leather flats.

Pulling some of the top items up far enough, she checked the tags in a T-shirt and a zip-up nylon windbreaker. Her size. She breathed a sigh of relief. This could be a huge help. The locked compartment no doubt contained the woman's valuables—maybe jewelry.... She could find out later when she had some privacy. The lock looked as if she might be able to pick it with a hairpin or a nail file. If not, a good whack with a hammer would open it. She straightened up the contents, zipped up the compartment and sat back to think. If she was lucky, the locked pocket might have some cash, or a credit card. The way things had been going, she couldn't count on it, and since her resources were limited, she needed to find out if her ticket would still be good if she got off the train at the next stop. She had to find Julien.

When she looked up, she caught the elderly man across the aisle staring at her, a scowl on his face. When her eyes met his, he turned away. A woman who appeared to be his wife sat next to the window, an open book in her lap. The man swung his head back toward Dana, and again frowned at her. Nervous now, she gave him her best smile. Instead of returning it, the man averted his gaze and leaned toward his wife and muttered something. She didn't even look up, just waved a hand and shushed him with a murmur.

Dana swallowed hard and tamped down her rising panic, calmly gathering up her purse. She threaded an arm through one of the backpack straps and shouldered it as she stood. Stepping into the aisle, she smiled down at the man as sweetly as she could before striding up the aisle. His stare bored a hole in her back all the way to the end of the car. Biting her lip, she fought the urge to run.

No shouts or footsteps followed her out to the vestibule between the cars, and she breathed easier as she continued on through the lounge car again. She didn't stop this time, continuing on until she reached her seat in coach. Legs weak and wobbly, she sat heavily and slid the backpack on the floor to the bulkhead under her feet. No one had taken note of her return despite how long she'd been gone. Most of the other passengers busied themselves with reading or quiet conversation to pass the time. Some remained glued to the windows to watch the law enforcement and media activity outside.

The only person who acknowledged her presence was the same

nitwit across the aisle. He turned his baleful stare toward her as she shifted in her seat. A shudder ran through her, but she met his gaze, refusing to be intimidated. His flat affect and blank eyes reminded Dana of the bottomless black holes of a shark's eyes. She'd known only one other person with eyes like that.

For a brief moment, Dana had a vision of her father as he'd been when she was little, shirtless, hitting her mother, blow after blow, with no expression on his face, no anger, no regret, no pleasure, either. Only sweat from the effort and concentration on the task at hand, his eyes as empty as Dana's tummy the day before he got paid at work.

Wrenching the memory aside, Dana forced herself back to the present. Bile rose in her throat as the face of the man across the aisle swam back into focus. She didn't know this man, didn't know if he was capable of the things her father had done. He probably went to church, had never gotten so much as a parking ticket, and was an upstanding member of his community. But she wouldn't trust him to hold her place in line at the store.

She thought of the dead man in the compartment a few cars behind her and the well-dressed man standing over him, and she would have bet everything she owned that his eyes looked the same. And she vowed that she would never let someone with eyes as soulless as theirs get within ten feet of her.

The stalker looked away then, as if reading her thoughts, and she nodded to herself in triumph. With a sudden jolt, the train moved forward slowly, making her decision for her. Grabbing the backpack, she stepped into the aisle and headed for the restroom.

Time to become someone else.

40

Sykes had always been a patient man, willing to bide his time until he felt the moment was right. After all, timing was everything. He'd learned that quickly in his chosen trade, and not without some hard lessons.

By the time he'd reached high school, Sykes was getting jobs from the Westies, and then from others. Hits on small-timers, fuck-ups and losers, people no one would miss and whose deaths would garner little time and attention from the cops.

He was careful, cautious, meticulous even, both in his planning and execution of each job. He took care to keep as much distance as possible between himself and those who hired him. He embraced the Internet as it grew because it made remaining anonymous easier. He made clients deliver burner phones to his dead drops pre-programmed with a single number.

To avoid leaving trace evidence at a job site, he wore generic clothing that covered most of his body—long-sleeve shirts and trousers, hats—and disposed of it every time. Latex gloves worn inside leather gloves ensured that gunshot residue wouldn't get on his skin and his fingerprints couldn't be lifted from inside the leather gloves, if by some miracle investigators found them in a landfill or charred in a steel drum near a homeless encampment.

Taking jobs by referral only, he reserved the right to refuse any contracts that could put him or his reputation in jeopardy. Client deposits—half the contract fee—were nonrefundable, even if he aborted the job. It had happened only once.

A fence he knew had referred a client, but the job had been a set-up designed to take Sykes off the board. Sykes had managed to kill the assassin, and had barely escaped. He'd found the fence later that night in his pawn shop a few blocks from the river off West 34th. After nearly an hour in the back room the fence had given up name of the client. Sykes had let him live, but the client who'd set Sykes up was dead before dawn.

Sykes derived no particular enjoyment from killing people, but he'd gotten tremendous satisfaction and had taken great pride in a job well done. The thrill had lain in evading detection and avoiding getting caught. He'd been good at it, and had made a lot of money, enough that he'd been able to put a substantial down payment on the D.C. mansion that became the exclusive club he now ran. Patience had served him well, but his fingers drummed softly on the soft leather armrest. He had too much on the line now.

When the phone on the seat next to him rang, he snatched it up fiercely and answered before the second ring.

"It's Dobrev. Cops don't know what in fuck I'm talking about. Never heard of your *moorzilka*. They're all at train looking for their dicks. We drive around, don't see nothing."

"Fine. Don't waste your time. Get to Charlottesville as fast as you can. Amtrak station."

"Whole day is waste of time. *Der'mo burya*—a shit storm—if you ask me."

"No one's asking. Get here now."

Sykes savagely stabbed the disconnect button.

41

The springs on the big sedan groaned as Alexei settled his bulk into the driver's seat. Mikhail turned his head at the sound and the car's motion, and stared.

"What?" Alexei waited, but the slightly smaller man simply shook his head and turned his gaze forward.

Alexei started the car and pulled onto the street with a spurt of gravel. He'd purposely parked half a block away from the police station. At the corner, he glanced at the navigation screen to get his bearings then turned onto the highway, west back through town.

"Now where?" Mikhail said after a moment.

Alexei grunted. "Charlottesville."

"I don't understand. Why do we chase our tails out here in the country? This Sykes makes you look like *durak*—a fool. Both of us."

"We don't do this for him. We do this for Volya. You know this."

"But why? This is stupid."

"Because it is one more favor that Sykes will owe."

"*Polnyi pizdets*," Mikhail muttered. "Sykes is going too far. What did this Mick do that would make Sykes risk it?"

Alexei didn't answer. He'd wondered the same thing. They knew who Mick was, of course, from their visits to the club with Nastase or on his behalf. Quiet kid. Nothing but respectful. Capable of handling an altercation. And now dead, apparently. And Sykes's voice on the phone....

Sykes was one cool customer, even around Nastase, but Alexei had heard a note of desperation that had never been there before.

"I don't think you'll have to worry for long," he said finally. "I think he's going to fuck up big time. And soon."

"As long as he doesn't drag us down with him," Mikhail said. "I got wife and kids. Who takes care of them if something happens to me?"

Alexei fell silent again. He'd driven a couple of miles out of town before a sight by the side of the road ahead broke him out of his contemplation. Flashing lights. Lots of them.

"The train," Mikhail said.

"Yes," Alexei replied softly. The scene of everything that had caused their present concerns. He braked softly as they approached a line of vehicles stopped on the highway.

"You think the woman got back on?"

"If she did, Sykes is lucky son of bitch."

"Da."

The big sedan came to a gentle stop, and they waited patiently, inching forward as the line moved. The battalion of emergency vehicles made Alexei nervous. He didn't know why. He and Mikhail had done nothing wrong, not today. He had a permit for the gun he carried concealed. Sure, the armaments in the trunk were illegal, but without probable cause, cops had no reason to search the trunk. Alexei wasn't about to give them one, either.

Cops had always given him the willies. His distrust stemmed from the fact that Soviet military police under the direction of a GRU colonel had smashed down the front door of his family's house in Luhansk, Ukraine, before dawn one morning and arrested his father. Alexei had been a kid at the time, but he could still hear the screams of his mother and younger sisters as uniformed men smashed furniture and pointed guns at them all while others beat his father with rifle butts and heavy boots as they dragged him through the house and down the front steps.

He'd sworn then that he would never kowtow to a cop, and he'd made it his life's work to thumb his nose at the law. Funny thing: along the way he'd discovered that one side wasn't all that different from the other. Most cops had their price. He tapped his finger against the top of the steering wheel, and suddenly had the feeling they were moving even though his foot firmly pressed the brake pedal.

"Train is moving," Mikhail said.

Alexei glanced to his left. Sure enough, the train was pulling forward, slowly gathering speed. He chafed, sitting straighter, looking around for a way to get through the traffic.

"It's okay, Alexei," Mikhail said. "We're almost there."

Soon, they had a clearer view of the cop directing traffic at an intersection ahead. A few minutes later they pulled up to the crossroad, and the cop waved them through. As Alexei smoothly accelerated away from the intersection, weight lifted from his shoulders. They would help Sykes handle the situation in Charlottesville, and then they could go home.

A drop of rain splatted on the windshield, followed by another, then more in close succession. Alexei leaned forward to peer up at the darkening sky, and turned the wipers on. The gleam of headlights in the mirror caught his attention. A vehicle was coming up fast behind them. He checked the speedometer and his surroundings before looking in the mirror again. The lights had closed in on them quickly and now rode their bumper. Oncoming traffic made it impossible for the car behind to pass.

The tailgating irritated Alexei, but he wouldn't have minded so much if the driver dimmed his headlights. Moments later, a gap opened in the oncoming traffic, and the large, white BMW behind them pulled out and started to pass. Alexei thought the driver was cutting it close. A pickup truck in the oncoming lane didn't appear to be slowing at all. With a rumble of its engine, the BMW pulled abreast and accelerated past them. Alexei gave the driver the finger as it swerved into the lane in front of them.

"*Zasranec!*" Mikhail muttered.

Alexei laughed. "World is full of assholes, Mikhail. Including us."

Mikhail peered at him from under a bushy shelf of brow, a scowl on his face. Slowly, the corners of his mouth turned up in a grin.

42

The long procession of cars slowed almost to a standstill. Toby craned his neck, trying to see over the top and around the side of the line to figure out what was holding up traffic. The damn train must be close. He could see the tracks running parallel to the road no more than a hundred feet to his left, and he was already four miles out of Orange. He swore and smacked the steering wheel with the flat of his hand. As the car ahead inched forward, he nosed out to the center stripe. There had to be twenty cars in front of him, and no way to get around them. Looky-loos, no doubt, slowing down to gawk at the train.

Letting the space in front of him grow, he spun the wheel the other way and pulled over to the shoulder. He was about to gun the engine and drive around the entire line, but up ahead the shoulder was still crowded with television vans and cars trying to merge into the line. He swore again. Easing back into line, he heaved a sigh and crawled at a snail's pace along with the rest of the swill.

Another five minutes rolled off the clock before he drew abreast what remained of the phalanx of media vans that had been parked along the side of the road. And there, traffic stopped. A black man neatly dressed in khakis and navy windbreaker stood by the side of an unmarked white van. A younger guy in jeans and sweatshirt, long, dirty blond hair pulled back into a ponytail loaded a video camera and folded tripod in the side door. Behind them, a row of low evergreens screened an old but well maintained house set well back from the road. A neatly lettered sign planted next to the middle of the row designated it the office of a steeplechase foundation. Below it, another sign said, "Races First Saturday in November."

Toby rolled down the passenger window and leaned across the center console. "You know what's going on up there?" he called.

The black man turned at the sound of his voice and took a few steps in Toby's direction. Toby had to stop himself from pulling back reflexively. Put the man in jeans and a hoodie in D.C., and Toby never would have rolled the window down.

"You kidding?" the man said. "Turn on your radio."

"The Amtrak thing? Yeah, I heard. Where's the train?"

"Gone, man."

Toby's stomach dropped. He wanted to scream, but he pasted a smile on his face, trying to be pleasant. "So, what's the hold-up?"

The man gestured to his right. "Everybody's moving across the street to the station building up there. Cops are holding a press conference."

"How come you're still here? Didn't want a front-row seat?"

The man grinned. "Nah, we're freelance. Figured the press conference is just talking heads. We're heading to Charlottesville to see if we can interview some of the passengers when they get off the train."

"Doesn't look like any of us are going anywhere soon."

The man's white teeth shone against his dark skin. "We got this." He turned and hustled back to the passenger side of the van as the young guy climbed behind the wheel and slammed his door. The engine started with a roar, and he threw the van into reverse. The black man waved at Toby through the windshield, his grin widening. Making a two-point turn, the van bumped along the grass shoulder toward another, larger old building with an antique gas station sign hanging out front, the gas pumps long gone. Once the van hit the pavement in front of the former gas station, it veered off at an angle.

Toby started to follow immediately, almost hitting the rear bumper of the car ahead of him, cursing himself for not thinking of the maneuver first. He slammed on his brakes, shoved the gearshift into reverse, spun the wheel the other way and backed up a few feet. The driver in the car behind him honked his horn. Toby jockeyed forward, then accelerated onto the shoulder in quick pursuit of the van, holding his arm out his window in a one-fingered salute.

The van had cut across a hundred feet of grass to a lane that led out to a road perpendicular to the highway. By the time Toby reached the crossroad, the van had reached the corner and was turning back onto the highway. Toby now saw the reason for the jam. A cop stood in the middle of the intersection directing traffic, his police cruiser squatting across the highway behind him with lights flashing. He diverted the media to the quaint, refurbished train station on the other side of the intersection, hanging up the highway traffic. Toby gunned the accelerator up to the corner before the cop started letting highway traffic proceed, and made the turn on squealing tires back onto the highway toward Charlottesville. He caught a glimpse of the cop's disapproval, but he didn't care. He'd broken free of the logjam, and he knew where to find Dana.

He pressed the accelerator harder.

43

The wait seems interminable. I check the train platform every minute or so, watch the few cars coming and going in the parking lot below. The people who emerge from and get into those cars all appear to be patrons of the restaurant in the old station building, not Amtrak passengers. I fidget in the seat, but that reminds me how full my bladder is.

My mind wanders, not a good thing when I'm supposed to be paying attention to my surroundings, but I figure this once I can multitask. I think of my dad, a man I haven't seen since I was in high school—or just out—and I wonder if he's proud of me, of what I've accomplished. We haven't talked, but I suspect my brothers have kept him apprised of my career if not what little of my personal life I've shared in phone calls and e-mails. I know he's been paying attention—he said as much on the phone last night. Was it only last night? It feels like a week ago.

I'd like to think he's proud, but as the only girl in the family I don't think he ever had any expectations. Not like he did with my brothers. He'd never admit it, of course. He'd say he didn't care what any of them did as long as they were happy. I suppose he might have thought that about me, too. But then why did all of them follow in his footsteps in some fashion? Why did I? We'd all become cops of some kind. Even Billy, the youngest. The rebel. Billy has a private investigator's license, but he mostly earns a living from bounty hunting. The only one of us who hadn't gotten into law enforcement was Doug. Because he'd never had a chance.

No sense in chasing phantoms down that road. I shake that thought out of my head and bring my attention back to the here and now of sitting in an uncomfortable rental vehicle with a full bladder, a growling stomach, no job and other worries to occupy my idle time. The sky outside the windshield has darkened, the clouds more threatening now, and a couple of raindrops plop on the glass and sadly trickle toward the bottom edge in rivulets like tears until there's no moisture left in them. I hope it doesn't start coming down any harder. I don't have an umbrella, and I'd rather not get the leather jacket wet if I can help it.

When I catch myself nervously biting a nail—a habit I haven't been able to break for twenty years—I know I need a bigger distraction than reminiscing about a family I haven't been part of for a long time. I call Machowski again.

"Yes, sir," he answers, "let me finish something here and I'll get right back to you."

The line disconnects. I stare at my phone in confusion, and I'm about to dial again and ask him what the hell he did that for when my phone rings.

"Machowski?"

"Are you out of your mind?" His voice is low with a note of anger and a hint of panic in it.

"What's wrong?"

"You're suspended. I can't just drop everything to do you a favor. I have real work, Jenny; we have real cases."

"And what I'm in the middle of isn't?"

"I didn't say that." He's uncomfortable with my indignation.

"So, you don't have a name for me, I take it."

"No, and I'm not going to find one, either. You're radioactive. SAC of the Charlottesville office called and raised hell. Said this is the second time that you've come in and tried to undercut his authority."

"Come on, Chris. You know what happened when Terry and I were chasing down a lead on Keator."

"No, I only know what you told me, and you two had me doing busy work back here."

"We didn't have time for niceties, Chris. We were after a major terrorist, remember? All of us. So, we didn't tell Corbett we were coming. He's a jerk anyway."

"He's SAC. He outranks you."

"Yeah, well, so no surprise that I'm the one who got hung out to dry, not Hunt. What's so damn important that you can't get me one lousy name?"

"You haven't heard?"

"I've been a little busy trying to stay alive."

His voice turns even more serious. "Congressman Cummings was killed this morning. Murdered in Rock Creek Park."

I'm trying to digest this news when he adds a kicker.

"Don't call me anymore, Jenny. I can't help you."

I look at the disconnected phone in disgust. Machowski is actually the one person who can help me, but he's just made it painfully obvious he won't. Thoughts whirl through my head as I consider my options. It's a moment before the sound of a train horn dimly registers. It sounds again from a distance as a train approaches a crossing, but it's closer now.

Game time.

I scan my surroundings, and get out. Hunching my shoulders against the few drops of rain, I dart across the road and down the stairs to the end of the platform farthest from the station. The platform isn't as crowded as it would be in the morning with people headed into D.C., but it's more populous than it was earlier. Westbound passengers may have been warned off by the news the train was delayed and chosen to wait in more comfortable environments than the front seat of a small SUV.

Down the tracks to the right the train's oscillating headlamp signals its approach. I look left and scan all the eager and anxious faces marking the train's progress. I don't have a plan. I'm working without a net. I've followed orders most of my life. As an MP and a field agent I've had to think on my feet—it's expected—but always by a set of rules, and always with someone or some authority at my back. Last time I improvised, things didn't turn out so well. Not for me, anyway. But I don't have much choice. I can't leave this alone. Killers running around loose offend my sensibilities. Creating order out of chaos is why I became a cop.

I search the crowd for familiar faces or for anyone who seems to take an interest in me. At the far end of the platform stands a large man in a black suit. He's not close enough to make out his features; it's his size that sets him apart. But there's something else incongruous about him. It takes a few moments before I realize what bothers me. Like me, he doesn't carry anything. He has no briefcase, no suitcase. He bears watching. In the meantime, I intend to stay as far away as possible. I drift toward a group of what looks like students—friends, apparently—and put them between me and the big man.

The train slows and pulls into the station. The conductor hops off one of the coach cars almost directly in front of the big man while the train is still moving, a step stool in hand. Closer to me, an attendant steps down from the door to the business class car. Like the conductor, he places a step stool on the platform in front of the door. The students head down the platform. I stay with them until I'm at the business class car, and climb up the steps. First thing, I check the rack above my seat. My backpack is gone. I look around frantically. None of the other passengers still on board will meet my gaze.

I force myself to take a deep breath. Losing the pack, as I've already learned, is not the end of the world. It's the thought that someone has stolen my things that rankles, and my mind races in pursuit of a culprit to blame for the theft. No matter, I need to find the woman, so I hustle down the aisle toward the front of the train. Looking out the window to see who's coming and who's going, I spot a woman heading away from the train toward the parking lot. I don't recognize her at first.

Her hair is twisted up into a bun on the back of her head, and she's wearing a quarter-zip sweater over dark jeans, not a leather jacket. But she's brunette, carries a backpack identical to mine, and the pullover is my favorite color—teal.

The kicker, though, is the Green Bay Packers hat pulled down low over her eyes. I don't believe in coincidence. I remember the day I got that hat with crystal clarity. Packers vs. Lions, November 3, 1996. Sunny fall day, temperature hovering in the low- to mid-40s. Dad's always been a fan, ever since his father gave him a football signed by every member of Green Bay's 1963 roster. Practically the only way to get a ticket to a Packers home game is if a season ticket holder offers you one. My dad somehow managed to get six tickets to that game. My mother was happy to see us go. Packers came out on top 28-18, and went on to win the Super Bowl that season. I got the hat as a souvenir, and I've kept it ever since.

Swearing under my breath, I turn and run for the door I entered. Leaping down the steps past a startled attendant, I sprint down the platform toward the station house. The woman has almost reached the lot and a line of waiting taxicabs. I want to scream at her to stop, but I'm already attracting enough attention.

She's at the head of the line now, and shrugs out of the backpack straps while the driver hops out and opens the passenger door, a rare sight in larger cities. I realize I'm not going to catch her, so I change direction and head for another set of stairs up to the street above, where I left the rental. Heart pounding, I keep one eye on the cab as it pulls away from the curb, and take the stairs two at a time.

Reclaiming my backpack from the thieving little witch almost takes precedence over the friendly heads-up I intended to give her. But I'm trying to save her life, and mine. And when I'm determined, there's little that can stand in my way.

I reach the top of the stairs at the same time the cab turns out of the lot. Lungs burning and legs aching, I race for my rental.

44

"Where to?"

Dragging her gaze away from the train platform receding in the rear window, Dana considered what to do next. She had to find somewhere she could lie low for a day or two, let the authorities catch the guy, and plan her next move. She couldn't do much about her situation until she heard back from Jared at the bank. She began to think that running away to Minnesota might not be the best course of action. She could still follow the money. And her Amtrak ticket would remain good if she needed it. She took a breath.

"Can you take me to an inexpensive hotel? Somewhere close?"

The driver glanced at her reflection in the mirror. "Sure. There's a place not far—just off campus—where a lot of university students' parents and families stay when they visit."

Dana nodded and glanced over her shoulder again.

The cabbie turned left out of the parking lot, waited for the light to change at the corner, and turned left again. Dana glanced out the window at the street sign.

W. Main St.

45

A huge fist wrapped itself around his heart and squeezed. Toby could barely take a breath as he turned into the Charlottesville Amtrak station lot. There was no sign of the train, and he was sure he'd missed it. He circled the lot, frantically looking for a space where he could park for a minute, get his panic attack under control and think this through. He drove wildly through the lot before forcing himself to breathe and calm down. Spotting a space near the entrance, he goosed the accelerator and aimed at it before anyone else could claim it.

As he shut off the engine, he heard the long deep blast of a train whistle. Relief flooded through him, and he twisted in his seat to watch the train pull into the station. He thought for a moment, trying to decide how to find Dana. He was too far away to see passengers getting off, so he climbed out of the car, turned up the collar of his overcoat to ward off the chilly mist already dampening his hair, and walked toward the platform. The heavy gun in his coat pocket thumped his hip as he walked, a reminder that he would brook no resistance from Dana. This time she'd do whatever he told her.

Passengers emerged from the two cars with open, attended doors, and descended the steps to the platform, quickly comingling with those waiting on the platform before separating from the throng and heading off in different directions. Toby strained to watch both doors, head swiveling between the two. If she didn't get off, he'd have to board the train, find her, and make her get off. The mist and fading light made it hard to see clearly. He picked up his pace.

Suddenly, there she was, bursting out of the door of the rear car, bounding down the stairs and running down the platform. He turned to intercept her, hand on the gun in his pocket, nearly breaking into a jog now. She crossed fifty feet in front of him, and he frowned. She was Dana, but not Dana. Same coloring, same clothes as those he'd seen Dana wear earlier, but different. More athletic. Prettier.

He looked to see what she was running toward, and his frown deepened. The station? No one waited for her that he could tell. Abruptly, she changed course, heading diagonally across the lot the other way. He stopped and stared as she now ran behind him, away from the station. He whirled back toward the station, eyes searching for what might have changed her mind. No one pursued her. No one paid her more than casual attention. What the hell had she seen?

He stopped in his tracks and stared, all thoughts of the Dana who was not Dana chased away by the sight of a woman lowering herself into the back seat of a taxi. A woman who, despite the change of clothes and baseball cap, definitely *was* Dana. And she was too far away for him to do anything but watch as she shut the door and the taxi rolled forward.

Toby turned and ran for his car, legs and lungs immediately protesting his lack of exercise. He ignored them. He'd gotten this far. No way in hell the bitch was getting away now.

46

Sykes tried working but couldn't concentrate. Even if he could focus on the numbers on the spreadsheets, he knew it didn't matter much anyway. Phillip kept a close eye on all the figures at the club. He knew when food costs were running a percentage point too high, or when a bartender was skimming because liquor costs went up half a point against sales. Phillip ran a tight ship, which is why Sykes had hired him.

The figures in front of him, though, weren't those that truly mattered anyway. The club turned a nice profit, but the real money was off the books. It came from the members who didn't want their peccadilloes known to the outside world, or whose businesses needed a quick infusion of cash that the club would generously lend, with interest, or who wanted services—rather expensive services, since they weren't exactly legal in most cases—that the club could provide.

Those transactions resided on a private server. Only Sykes knew its location, and he had the only means of accessing it. It had its own secure VPN that wouldn't recognize any computer. The server recognized only one device, a device that only Sykes could open, one that required both passwords and biometrics—fingerprint or facial recognition. Since he didn't have the device with him, all Sykes could do was fret. He didn't like it, didn't enjoy this worry creeping into his thoughts, his psyche. He needed to fix this and move on.

He raised his arm and glanced at the watch on his wrist. Only three minutes had passed since the last time he'd checked. He sighed, shut down his laptop and closed it, idly drumming his fingers on the lid as his thoughts roamed. He wondered how long it would take the cops to process the mess he'd made earlier and let the train move on.

No word yet from Phillip, either, which provided yet another irritation. Like mosquito bites, these nagging loose ends itched, and he wanted to scratch them bloody until they stopped. Unconsciously, his arm started to rise again. He willed it to stop, told himself it didn't matter what fucking time it was. He had no timetable now, only goals, objectives he had to meet or he would put everything he'd worked for in jeopardy.

The loud deep blast of a train's air horn corralled his wandering thoughts, and brought his focus back to his surroundings. A light mist had coated the car windows, and the collected moisture beaded and rolled down the glass in rivulets. Sykes wrapped his overcoat tighter around his body. He hadn't realized how chilly the car had become without the heater on.

George stood at the edge of the platform as the train rolled up. Too far away to see his features, Sykes had homed in on his bulk and dark suit. He sat up straighter, peering through the gray dampness, gut tightening involuntarily. He'd reached make-or-break time. If George didn't find the woman here, he had to cut his losses and move on, wait for Phillip to finish researching Mick's background and figure out how to locate his phone.

The train disgorged its Charlottesville passengers. The number of people now on the platform along with the weather and the distance all conspired to make it impossible for Sykes to identify anyone. He didn't dare go look in person and potentially spook the woman he was after. He had to count on George, and he didn't like to rely on anybody.

George climbed the steps into the train car; Sykes had no other choice now. His abdominal muscles tightened further, and acid churned in his stomach. He realized he hadn't eaten since sometime the day before. He pushed the discomfort aside and concentrated on the scene outside the town car's windows.

A running figure caught his eye, coming from the right, a woman, threading her way around the knots of people still on the platform or walking to their cars. She cut across the parking lot toward the station house. Sykes's pulse rose as he took in her dark clothes and leather jacket.

That's her!

But where was George? And why didn't Sykes have a spare key fob for the damned town car? Sykes whipped out his phone and dialed George's cell. It rang and rang.

"Come on," he muttered. "Answer the fucking phone."

He opened the door and started to climb out. He'd chase the woman himself if he had to.

Suddenly, she changed course and ran away from the station. He blinked. He was sure she hadn't seen him, and he hadn't seen anything else that might have startled her. He hurried after her, then saw where she was headed—a set of stairs leading up to the street above that ran over the tracks. He stopped, phone still pressed to his ear. She was too fast.

George finally answered. "Yes, sir?"

"She's here. She's making a break for it. Get back to the car, now."

47

"In one-quarter mile, turn right on 7th Street Southwest."

At the sound of the GPS app's female voice, Alexei glanced at the phone lying on the center console.

"Is like my wife," Mikhail said. "Always telling me what to do."

"Yes, but this one, she has on-off switch. I don't have to listen if I don't want to."

"But you like her voice, *da*?"

Alexei shrugged. "What's not to like?"

"In five hundred feet, turn right on 7th Street Southwest."

Alexei peered through the windshield to look for the upcoming intersection. The traffic signal at the bottom of a long incline, now red, seemed the likely spot. He started to lean back when movement on the sidewalk ahead caught his eye. A woman raced across the walk and burst out into the street between two cars. Alexei swerved over the center line to make sure he avoided her, drawing an irate honk from an oncoming car.

"*Ebanatyi pidaraz!*" Mikhail flung out his arm and braced it against the dashboard as Alexei swung the car back into his lane.

Alexei already had his eyes on the rearview mirror and saw the woman get into a car parked at the curb. His excitement grew as his eyes darted back and forth and his mind rapidly assimilated facts with what had just happened.

"Fucking motherfucker is right," he said. "That's her!"

Mikhail gave him a puzzled look. "You know this how?"

Alexei swung the car to the curb and glued his eyes to the rearview mirror. "The way she is dressed. She is brunette. And she is running. There she goes."

Mikhail craned his neck to see what Alexei already knew—the woman's SUV pulled away from the curb and did a U-turn. Alexei did the same and pulled onto the street a hundred yards behind her.

"We take care of this now," Alexei said.

"What if she's not the one?"

"Don't worry so much, Mikhail. If she isn't who we look for, we go back to train station and tell Sykes we got stuck in traffic."

Alexei snuck a glance at him. Mikhail didn't look convinced.

"I promise, friend. I will have you back to your family tonight."

48

Between the lowering clouds and oncoming dusk, visibility isn't great. Mist coats the windshield as fast as the wipers can push it aside. It's like driving underwater, but the taxi's roof light makes it easy to follow. I swipe a hand across my forehead to push my damp hair aside, and wipe the moisture off on my jeans, wishing I had a bath towel.

Five minutes later, the cab turns into the motor entrance of a motel. It's a five-layer brick sheet cake decorated with wrought iron filigree. I follow but turn into a parking lot across from the entrance. As I hurry to the entrance, I take in the details. The wrought iron forms railings for wrap-around balconies that gird the entire building and provide access to guest rooms. There are stairways at each end. As I enter, I see a sign for elevators and another stairway that lead up from the lobby.

Inside the lobby, the woman stands at the registration desk on the right. I duck into a gift shop and peruse the merchandise while a clerk helps the woman check in. I don't want to spook her or cause a scene in the lobby. I move around a magazine rack so I'm facing the front desk but still half-hidden. The woman is about my age, and from what I can see of her hair under the hat—my hat—it's about the same color as mine. She fills the teal sweater though, and it's a little baggy on me, which is how I like to wear my casual clothes. That makes her both larger in the bust and a good fifteen pounds heavier than I. But she looks enough like me that we could be mistaken for each other at a distance, or if someone got only a glimpse of one of us.

Her head swivels as she looks around nervously. I step back as her gaze travels across the entrance of the gift shop to the corridor leading to the motor entrance. She's afraid she's been followed, not knowing that I'm her tail. I nearly slap myself as I suddenly realize that in my haste, I forgot to check for my own tail. Stupid. And I'm a trained field agent. Was. Maybe I deserve the kick to the curb if I'm dumb enough to forget "Spotting and Losing a Tail: 101."

She picks up a pen from the desk and scribbles on a piece of paper the clerk handed her, and bends to retrieve the backpack from the floor near her feet. As soon as she turns for the elevators, I cross the lobby at a pace that won't attract her attention but that's fast enough to be close if the elevator is waiting. It's not, but when she pushes the call button, the elevator dings immediately, and doors open on one of the cars. She gets on and turns to push the button for her floor. I get on. She glances at me and does a double-take, her eyes widening with fear.

"You're the woman from the train," she says disbelievingly.

Her mouth sets in a grim line. I anticipate her next reaction and block her as she bolts for the doors. They close before she can recover and the elevator rises.

"I'm not here to hurt you," I say. "We need to talk."

She shakes her head vehemently, the fear in her growing toward panic proportions. "How did you find me? Did you follow me? If you found me, then he can find me. You have to leave. You have to get away from me. Now!"

The words tumble out of her so fast that they're barely intelligible. I hold up my hands to calm her. "I'm here to help. Really. I just need to talk to you so we can figure out how to stop this guy."

She shudders. "You don't know what he did."

"You saw it?"

She nods. "Just a glimpse, but it was horrible."

"Well, he tried to kill me, so I figured it must be pretty bad."

She moans. "Oh, God, oh, God. If he finds out it was me, not you, he'll kill us both. Please, just leave me alone."

She squeezes her eyes shut, and a tear leaks from one corner and rolls down her cheek. I'm not unsympathetic.

"Look, I'm an FBI agent. I can help you, but you have to help me figure out who this man is."

She opens her eyes and looks at me, and there's hope there, or desperation. "Really? You're with the FBI?"

I flash my ID at her. The elevator slows and a muffled ding sounds through the door. I stand in front of it and face her.

"Will you help me?"

Her head bobs once. The doors open, and I step out to let her lead the way to her room. At the end of the short corridor leading to the outside balcony, she pushes through the door and turns right. I follow. She passes the first door but stops in front of the second and pulls out her keycard. Hearing footsteps, I turn my head and look over my right shoulder. Two large men in suits walk toward us from the far end of the building. I wait for them to stop at a door, but they don't, and my stomach knots.

I hear the lock on the door release, and the woman turns the knob and opens the door. The bigger of the two men starts as if he's seen a ghost, then smiles at me and stops. But the other one keeps coming and slips a hand inside his suit coat. I want to wet my pants now. It's too late for me to go for the gun on my hip.

"Good evening, ladies," the man says as he approaches. His accent sounds Russian.

The woman is halfway inside, but she stops and turns her head, startled. Her mouth opens to scream, but the man puts a finger to his lips and shakes his head as he pulls out a gun.

"No noise, or I shoot you." He wags the gun. "Inside, please."

"*Yo!*" says a voice from the other end of the balcony. "What the fuck are you doing? Leave the women alone. Dana!"

All four of us turn toward the voice, and now the woman does scream at the sight of another, younger man walking toward us. He, too, is immaculately dressed in a suit, one that looks far more expensive than those the big men are wearing, with a long, cashmere polo coat over it, and his accent is all-American. His hair is slicked back from a receding hairline, and he carries a few too many extra pounds—a different animal altogether from the goon squad. I have no clue what's going on, but I don't have time to think about it.

The Russian next to me raises his gun and points it at the newcomer. "Who in fuck is this? Boyfriend?"

Without hesitation, the younger man raises a semi-automatic he's been holding alongside his thigh hidden by the folds of his overcoat, and shoots the Russian next to me. I hear the slug smack into flesh, as if he was slapped. He grunts, spins back into the wall next me and slides down in a heap. The younger man keeps walking toward us, but aims and shoots at the bigger man who's been guarding against any escape attempts by the woman and me. The big man fumbles to get his own gun out, and as a second shot whizzes past his head, he turns and lumbers down the balcony in a zig-zag pattern, and manages to squeeze off a shot of his own over his shoulder.

In the confusion, I pull out my own gun and fire at the young man. When he ducks and spins in confusion, I grab the woman by the collar and yank her back out onto the balcony and swing her toward the corridor we came out of.

"Go!" I yell at her over her screaming. "Go! Back the way we came. Use the stairs."

The Russian at my feet is reaching for the pistol he dropped, so I stomp on his hand hard enough to drag a scream from his throat. I fire another shot at Mr. Slick—that makes him think twice and sends him running back the way he came. I whirl around to check on the big guy. He's at the end of the building, peering around the corner. I take a shot in his direction to keep him honest, then bend down and grab the pistol away from the Russian.

He moans. "Does everybody in America have fucking gun?"

I don't waste breath on a reply. The woman is in the wind, and both the big guy and Mr. Slick could beat me to her if I don't get a move on. I sprint for the inside stairwell, and when I burst through the door, I hear the clatter of footsteps two floors below me. I race down two steps at a time, getting into a rhythm, and by the time I hear the door on the ground floor bang open, I'm half a flight of stairs behind. When I come through the door, the woman is still in the corridor, wild-eyed, whirling one way then another. I grab her arm and pull her toward the motor entrance.

"Keep up," I growl. "And if you want to live, do exactly what I tell you."

I see a glimmer of resolve on her face, and let go of her arm to fish in my jacket pocket for the key fob to the rental car. I still have my gun in my other hand, and I hold it close to me in hopes that the sight of it doesn't panic anyone in the lobby. Two women sprinting through attracts enough stares as it is. The glass doors to freedom beckon at the end of the corridor ahead and open automatically as we run.

I put my arm out and bark, "Wait!"

She stops, and I quickly move to one side of the doors and look outside the opposite way, gun ready. No one there. I do the same on the other side, then wave at her to follow me out. As she does, I hit the button on the key fob that unlocks the SUV. She sees the lights flash and runs. I follow a little more slowly, looking for hostiles at one end of the building and then the other. A startled bellman bolts for the entrance.

I don't know why, but instinctively I think we have more to fear at this point from Mr. Slick. I think the big guy stayed to help his partner get out before the cops arrive. Sure enough, a moment later the loud report of a handgun echoes off the brick, and I see a flare of orange from the muzzle blast at the corner of the building. Chicken won't show himself.

I stop, assume a Chapman shooter's stance and squeeze off three quick shots toward the spot. My fast response buys me enough time to sprint to the lot and get in the SUV. The woman is already belted in, wearing the expression of the next victim in a slasher film. She cranes her neck for a look out the rear window as I crank the engine.

"Get down, damn it," I say a split second before a bullet blows a hole in the rear window. I throw the gearshift in drive and peel out of the lot on squealing, smoking tires.

49

Dana thought her heart was going to explode. Every time she believed it couldn't beat any faster, some new terror amped her system's supply of adrenaline, throwing it into an even higher gear. Surely, it couldn't take much more before it just blew a gasket and burst inside her chest. She couldn't understand how the woman next to her remained so calm behind the wheel, keeping the SUV's speed only a few miles per hour over the speed limit. She noted, though, how the woman drove evasively, turning corners or changing lanes at the last second without signaling, never drawing the ire of other drivers.

Neither of them spoke. Dana wasn't sure if she'd ever find her voice again, convinced that it had been frightened out of her body permanently at some point during the past ten minutes. She found it nearly impossible that such a short time has passed since she'd collected a room key and headed for a quiet evening of television holed up where no one could find her. Somehow, the whole world seemed to know where she'd gone.

A small moan must have escaped her lips because the woman driving glanced at her sharply. Then, apparently satisfied that Dana wasn't in distress, the driver turned her attention to the navigation screen on the dashboard, fiddling with it until it glowed brightly with a map, lighting her face with a bluish cast.

The sky outside had turned almost completely black now as dusk turned to night. Headlights and streetlights reflected off the wet pavement. As they drove, the arrow on the map indicating their position crept along a colored line representing the two-lane road. It pointed west.

Dana finally screwed up the courage to ask, "Where are we going?"

"Away from here," the woman muttered. She checked the mirrors for the umpteenth time.

Silently, Dana agreed that was probably the best course of action.

"Dana, right?" the woman said.

"Yeah." She didn't offer her last name.

"Nice to meet you. Jenny, in case you didn't catch it on my ID."

Dana didn't reply. Her heart and head seemed to have switched places suddenly, her thoughts racing faster and faster as her pulse returned to normal.

"Why didn't you have backup?" she blurted. "How could you let those people follow you?"

"What makes you think they followed me?" Jenny said quietly. "I never saw those Russians before in my life. And seems to me, you and Mr. Slick are on a first-name basis. Who is he?"

Dana hesitated. "His name is Toby. Toby Granger."

"Who is he?" Jenny repeated.

"My boss," Dana said, her voice so feathery the soft whistling sound from the star-cracked hole in the rear window nearly snatched the words away.

Jenny stared at her long enough to make Dana afraid she might drive off the road. But she eventually turned her gaze forward and drove silently for a few moments.

"Maybe you ought to start at the beginning," she said finally. "What do you do?"

"I work for a non-profit NGO, kind of like Heifer or World Vision, if you're familiar with those." Dana paused. "Or, I did."

"What happened?"

Dana squirmed in her seat. "I can't talk about it."

"Can't? Or won't?"

Dana didn't reply.

Jenny glanced at her. "Look, I can't help you if I don't know what's going on. There are too many players in this now to keep straight, and I have no idea who any of them are. You, at least, know one of the people trying to kill us. Why? Why is he trying to kill you? And what did he mean you're not getting away from him this time?"

The import of her words registered. Suddenly, it was all too much, and Dana sobbed. "I don't know. I don't know why he's trying to kill me. He said he wanted to see me at the office this morning. I just had a feeling it was something bad. So, I left. But he saw me get on the elevator, and he followed me out to the street. He tried to attack me in a taxi. All I could think of was getting out of there, leaving town. I went to the train station. I couldn't think of anywhere else to go."

The words poured out her as fast as the tears streamed down her face. She hiccupped and sniffed.

"There are some tissues in my backpack if you want," Jenny said.

"That's okay," Dana said, calmer now. "I have some in my purse." She pawed through her bag, pulled out a pack of tissues, and blew her nose loudly.

"That still doesn't tell me why your boss was chasing you."

Dana slumped in her seat. "He thinks I did something."

"What kind of something? Must have been pretty bad."

"I can't tell you."

Jenny sighed. "We're back to that?"

Dana bit her lower lip and clammed up. She looked out the window, avoiding the gaze of the woman next to her. She reminded herself that Jenny was with the FBI, a thought that was more cause for concern than comforting. Raising a finger, she absently toyed with a strand of hair, then caught herself and stuck her hand between her knees.

Silence filled the car, expanding faster than the bullet hole could let it leak outside until Dana was sure the windows would blow out. She wondered why she hadn't heard from Jared yet, and the thought gave her something to do, a valve to release some of the awful pressure building up inside her. She found her phone and checked for e-mail, expecting to find her organization account closed. But Toby either hadn't thought of it or hadn't had time. Even so, her inbox was empty.

She checked for messages she might have missed in all the excitement on the train, and found at least half a dozen from Jared, each with attachments. She opened one to find no message, but a bunch of attachments. She clicked on one, and a file opened with a scan of cancelled checks filling the page. She expanded it to try to read the endorsement signatures and depository banks. They all appeared to be the same depositor, but the checks were hard to read on her phone. She'd try later. In the meantime, she downloaded all the files to her phone just in case.

Dana put the phone away, and looked out the windshield. She glanced at the navigation screen on the dashboard to confirm they were still heading west. Another ten minutes passed before she felt the silence about to crush her.

"Where are we going?" she asked again in a small voice.

"I'm going home," Jenny said without looking at her. "Wisconsin. You need protection until we figure this out, so I'm taking you with me. Don't worry, I come from a family of cops. We're up to the job."

Dana groaned. "I can't. Please. Just drop me off somewhere. I'll be fine."

"Why not? What's the matter?"

The FBI agent was bound to find out sooner or later, and Dana had what she needed from Jared. Maybe, just maybe she could stay out in front of this thing. "Someone's been stealing from the foundation I work—worked for. Toby—my boss—thinks I know something about it."

There was no response for a moment, then Jenny said. "He thinks you're the thief. That's why he's so pissed. How much are we talking about?"

"Millions. It's been going on for years." She paused. "It wasn't me. I didn't do it."

When she screwed up the courage to look, Jenny's expression was impassive, eyes flicking back and forth as she concentrated on driving.

Dana wondered if she'd put enough conviction in her voice.

50

The big car glided down the dark, wet streets like a beautiful, mahogany Riva *motoscafo* plying the canals of Venice. From where Sykes sat, their journey so far seemed more nightmare than European dream vacation. George had been driving aimlessly through town for ten minutes or more, and Sykes had seen no sign of the dark gray SUV that had pulled away from the curb on the street above so quickly. By the time George had returned to the car and they'd gotten out of the lot, the SUV was long gone.

"I didn't see her," George muttered. "I swear to Christ I didn't see her."

"You don't hear too well, either," Sykes snapped. "Why didn't you put your fucking phone on vibrate?"

"I did." George Sybiled from indignant to sheepish in a millisecond. "I just don't feel it sometimes when I'm moving around. I'm sorry, Mr. S., but you really don't have to speak to me like that. It hurts my feelings."

Sykes took a breath to modulate the anger seething through him. "If you had any clue what's at stake right now, you'd realize that your feelings are less important than the lint on my coat. We're not playing a game here."

"That's still no reason to swear at me," George pouted.

"How the fuck did you get through army basic training?" Sykes sighed. "If I didn't like you so much, I'd put a bullet in your brain right now just to put you out of my misery. Now, are we square?"

George met Sykes's gaze in the rearview mirror. "Yeah, I guess so. If you're really sorry."

"Good. Now, listen to me carefully. You work for me, George. I'm not some kindly old uncle who's doing you a favor. I'm your employer, and I'll speak to you any fucking way I please. And if you don't like it, you can leave. After which I will follow you out the door and personally shoot your ass, and then shoot you in the head for good measure. Am I making myself clear?"

George's head bobbed. "Yeah," he grumbled. "I got it. So, where do you want to go, sir?"

Sykes turned his head to hide a brief half-smile. He really did like George, but the big oaf had the IQ of a shoe. And Sykes had real problems on his hands. The woman was in the wind, and they had no way of finding her now. Sykes had been trying to raise Dobrev, but he wasn't answering his phone. Sykes wasn't ready to give up just yet.

"Try moving out from the center of town in a widening square," he told George. "If you see a motel, we'll check the lot."

"There've got to be a million gray SUVs in this town."

Sykes's brows dove toward each other. "Maybe we'll get lucky."

George stiffened. "Yes, sir."

They drove for a few more minutes before the wail of sirens disturbed the silence. One of them grew louder as the flashing blue strobes of a patrol car careened toward them. Sykes tensed in his seat, but George merely pulled over to give the cop room as he barreled past, leaving a reminder in his wake: Sykes was running out of time. He needed to catch a fish or cut bait. Trolling was getting him nowhere. And he was out of ideas. He leaned forward to tell George to head for home when his phone rang. He answered.

"Phillip here, sir. I have that information you wanted."

"Talk to me." Sykes grabbed a pen and notepad from the open briefcase on the seat. He scribbled as Stevens spoke for the next minute or two, then put the pen down.

"Thank you, Phillip. You've been most helpful. Everything all right there?"

"Nothing we can't handle, sir."

"Good. Based on what you've told me I may not be back for three or four days."

"We'll manage somehow," Stevens said in a cheery voice.

"You always do. Thank you."

He disconnected the call and leaned forward. "Change of plans, George. We're going to Wisconsin."

51

"*E*banatyi pidaraz!"

Dobrev bent over the figure slumped against the wall. He pulled Mikhail's hand and coat away from his side to see where the bullet had hit. He saw surprisingly little blood and no exit wound. That could be good, but judging from Mikhail's condition it likely was very, very bad.

Mikhail raised his chin off his chest. "Stop crying. I'm the one who takes bullet."

"We have to get out of here. Let me help you up."

Alexei took his friend's wrist and wrapped it around his neck. He put his other arm around Mikhail's waist and strained to lift the smaller man onto his feet.

"Can you walk?"

"I will try." Mikhail took a hesitant step. "I don't want to die here, Alexei. I want to die at home in my bed."

The sorrowful song of sirens wailed in the distance.

"You are not going to die. Come, quickly now."

Alexei bore his friend's weight as they hobbled to the end of the balcony and around the corner of the building. He pushed through the door and helped his friend to the stairs they'd climbed earlier. Mikhail pressed his hand to his side and groaned as they descended. Alexei glanced at him sharply. Mikhail's face was pasty, the color of pie dough dusted with flour.

"How bad?" Alexei said.

Mikhail managed a tepid smile. "Is like case of gas I got after eating your wife's *pirozhki*."

"Ex-wife." Alexei smiled back, but the sound of the sirens outside growing louder wiped it away. He moved faster, almost pulling Mikhail down the stairs, doing his best to ignore the grimace of pain on Mikhail's face.

A door closed with a bang below, and voices floated up the stairwell. Alexei stopped, let go of Mikhail's waist and slipped his hand inside his suit coat. Mikhail silently shook his head. Alexei hesitated, then nodded and continued to help his friend down the stairs. On the way down the last flight, they met an elderly couple coming up who looked at them suspiciously.

"Food poisoning," Alexei said. "I'm taking him to hospital."

"Oh, my," the woman said. "He didn't eat in the hotel, did he?"

Alexei shook his head as they passed on the stairs. "Downtown."

She seemed appeased, but the man still wore a frown. "Y'all didn't hear shots, did you?"

Alexei stopped. "Shooting? Here in hotel? Is not possible. Is no place safe in this country? Come, Mikhail. Maybe hospital is safest place for you."

"Well, you take care, y'all," the man said, turning to watch them go down.

Alexei bore more and more of the wounded man's weight, and as they pushed through the door at the bottom leading outside, Mikhail moaned. Alexei risked a glance over his shoulder to see if the couple on the stairs had noticed, but thankfully they'd turned the corner on the landing above.

Out in the open, the sirens sounded even louder, spurring Alexei to redouble his efforts. He practically carried Mikhail down the sidewalk past the hotel's restaurant entrance. For once, Alexei welcomed the drizzle that plastered his hair to his forehead and trickled down his neck into his collar. The rain and the darkness made them less visible, less noticeable. Just two businessmen walking to their car, shoulders hunched against the damp.

The whoop and wail of first responders sounded only blocks away now, so loud that they almost blotted out Mikhail's sudden cry of pain. Alexei staggered as Mikhail's knees buckled, but the proximity of the cop army about to descend on the scene flooded his system with more adrenaline, amplifying his strength. Gritting his teeth and shutting out Mikhail's cries of pain, he gripped Mikhail's belt and hoisted him up an inch or so onto his hip and increased his pace. Mikhail's shoes dragged on the sidewalk as they reached the end of the block and crossed the narrow alleyway leading to the hotel parking lot and motor entrance.

The black, wet pavement now turned intermittently blue as two cruisers turned onto the street behind them and roared toward them. The wail of their sirens nearly deafened Alexei now, and he risked a glance over his shoulder. A patrol car swung hard nose-in to the curb in front of the restaurant entrance and screeched to a stop. The other roared toward them, and Alexei felt his stomach fall as he started to lose hope. At the last second, the cruiser turned the corner on protesting tires into the alley behind them.

Relieved that he'd had the foresight to park the car down the street, Alexei hurried the final few yards and dragged Mikhail around

212

to the passenger door. Mikhail sagged, nearly folding onto the pavement while Alexei fished for his keys. He popped the locks and wrestled the door open, then tumbled Mikhail into the seat. He swung Mikhail's legs into the car, slammed the door, and hurried to the driver's side. By the time he climbed in and started the engine, Mikhail had passed out. Alexei took a moment to lean over and cinch the seatbelt around him. Slowly and carefully, he pulled out of the lot and turned onto the street away from the madness at the hotel behind them.

He drove in silence like an old *babushka*, obeying every traffic law, every rule of the road, until he got out of town. Then he jammed his foot against the accelerator, hoping he wouldn't be too late. He couldn't take Mikhail to a hospital—too many questions. But he knew a Belarusian guy named Dzmitry living not far from him in Maryland who had studied to be a doctor in Minsk.

Turned out the one thing Bethesda didn't have was a shortage of doctors. Alexei's boss had helped the guy get a union membership, so he'd ended up working as an electrician when he got his green card. Alexei figured he could pressure Dzmitry into helping. Anyway, it was the best shot Mikhail had at staying alive.

Thoughts raced through his head, but as hard as he tried, he couldn't make sense of what had just happened. It was a simple job. Find the woman; take her; kill her. Finding her had been the most difficult part. But suddenly there were two women who looked enough alike they could have been sisters. And the one—the good-looking one—had seemed strangely familiar.

But who the hell was the dressed-up guy with the pistol? He looked like a civilian. They were supposed to play by the rules—no guns. Only cops and bad guys had guns. They couldn't all be bad guys—or gals—could they?

He blamed this on Sykes. If Sykes had kept his people under control, he and Mikhail would not have been chasing across the countryside for Mick, first, and then the woman, second, whichever woman it was.

Not sure of how long he'd been driving, Alexei noticed the darkness first. Trees lined the highway, their overhanging branches in various states of undress, from full fall colors to bare gnarly bones. Dead leaves drifted down, flashes of amber, agate, sunstone and garnet in the beams of the headlights, turning black as they hit the pavement or the wet windshield.

A hitch in Mikhail's breathing snagged his attention. As Alexei glanced over, his friend emitted a gurgling, strangled breath and seemed to shrink in the seat. Alexei reached over and placed two fingers against Mikhail's jowly throat, rasp of the man's stubble like sandpaper to the touch. He felt no pulse. Keeping his eyes on the road, he tried again, fingers walking up and down Mikhail's neck. Nothing. Alexei's shoulders slumped, and he felt something drain out of him that he knew he'd never get back, as if a piece of him died with his friend.

Ahead, a red traffic light signaled that he'd literally come to a crossroad. Straight, and the road led to the entrance to the regional airport. A right turn would put him on the highway heading north and east back toward D.C. But Mikhail had no need of anything now. When the light changed, Alexei drove straight. Instead of entering the airport, however, he took a right and headed back out into the countryside on a county road.

Within a mile or so, pavement had given way to gravel, and the narrow road wound through woods and past open meadows, the breaks discernable primarily by the increase in rainfall on the windshield. The rear end of the big car slewed occasionally where the road had turned to mud.

Alexei slowed down and still nearly missed seeing the low guardrails on either side as the road crossed over a small creek. He stopped and put the car in reverse until the headlights illuminated the end of the bridge and the embankments leading down on either side. He eased the car forward until the nose was even with the near end of the guardrail and put the gearshift in park. Leaving the engine running, he got out, rounded the trunk and opened the passenger door. Rain dripping from the wet trees dampened his hair and rolled under his collar.

He unbuckled Mikhail's body, wrapped his arms under Mikhail's armpits and clasped his fingers over the dead man's chest. With a grunt of effort, he heaved Mikhail's bulk out of the car and dragged it backwards down the slippery embankment, cursing when he lost his footing and went down on his knees in the mud. At the bottom of the slope, he rolled the body under the bridge and stepped back to assess his handiwork. Out here, it might be days before the body was found. Alexei grunted again, this time in satisfaction, and scrabbled up the slope, grasping at the branches of a fallen tree to help pull himself up.

When he reached the top, water was rolling down one cheek, and he swiped at it with the back of a huge hand. Alexei tried to convince himself that it was the pissing rain, but it didn't work. He was crying. He, Alexei Zelenko Dobrev, a six-foot, two-hundred-seventy-eight-pound leg-breaker was crying for his *schlub* of a friend Orlov.

They'd known each other since they were kids, had run in the same wolf packs in Luhansk near the Russian border. They'd gotten out of Ukraine on a merchant marine vessel and never looked back. Now, almost thirty-five years later, Mikhail was dead, a meat carcass in a creek bed under a bridge in Podunk, Virginia. He wondered if the few tears he was shedding were as much for himself as for Orlov. Alexei wasn't a young man anymore. He didn't know where the time had gone, and Mikhail's death was a reminder that he didn't have forever.

Breathing hard, Alexei screwed the heels of his hands into his eye sockets, and rubbed his hands on his thighs. Muddy and drenched, he eased into the front seat and turned up the heater and fan. Who to phone first? His boss, Nastase, or Ellie, Mikhail's wife? He dreaded both. With a sigh, he pulled out his phone and frowned. He had a number of missed calls from Sykes, the prick. As he stared at the screen, the phone rang.

"*Da*," he said softly.

"Where the fuck have you been?" Sykes. "I've been trying to reach you for damn near an hour."

"What do you want?"

"I need you and Orlov to go to Wisconsin. I'm on my way now."

"Fuck you."

"What did you say?" Sykes's voice turned cold, full of menace.

"You heard me. Orlov is dead."

"Dead? How?"

"We found the girl. Both of them. Someone else wants them. Everybody got guns, and someone shoot Mikhail. Gut shot. He bleed out before I could get him to doctor."

"What the hell are you talking about? You're not making any sense. What do you mean, 'both' women? There's only one."

Alexei shook his head as if Sykes could see him in the dark car on the deserted road. "Two. Enough alike, could be sisters. I don't think so, but could be. New one look familiar."

"How familiar? Do you know who she is or not?"

"Don't know. Don't care."

"And this new player? Who is it?"

"You tell me. Easy job, right? Find girl. We find her. Now Mikhail's dead."

"Yeah, I'm fucking crying here. Now get on the road and start driving."

"Go to hell."

Alexei cut off the call.

52

He'd gone too far this time, Wile-E.-Coyote-off-the-cliff too far. His hands trembled and his body vibrated in the plush leather seat of his car, but from excitement, not fear. He'd gone past the point of no return a long time ago, he realized; shooting a man simply confirmed it. But this cliff he'd gone over took him to a whole new level. He could rationalize every action he'd ever taken as acceptable. Shooting a man in cold blood stepped over his moral boundaries. He wondered if the second time would be any easier. It felt natural to assume, at this point, that eventually there would be a second time.

Dana's companion had surprised him. The pair looked enough alike that he wondered if Dana had called a sister for help. But to the best of his recollection she had no siblings. A mystery woman. With a gun. An electric current ran through him. And she'd shot at him. The thrill of that thought and adrenaline converged on his groin, and he felt himself growing hard. That was the kind of woman he wanted.

He'd been less surprised, somehow, by the Russians. He wasn't going to spend a lot of time and energy trying to figure it out. He had to assume that they'd sniffed out the money, or at least gotten a whiff of it. Since Dana had seemed the focus of their interest, it made sense that his suspicions had been correct—she knew something. One thing he knew for sure: the Russians weren't bulletproof. His snort of amusement in the confined cockpit of the BMW brought him back to the scene in front of him for a moment.

Rain percolated through the canopy of trees overhead, and steadily dripped onto his car, bringing dead leaves and conifer needles with it. Each time the tree crowns above him twisted in a gust of breeze like dogs shaking themselves after a swim, showering small twigs, moss and debris on the car, he winced. They beat a tattoo on the roof, one that he was convinced would leave marks. He squelched his irritation, knowing that the mess would leave his white car less visible.

The red taillights of the car ahead shone through the rain, their tiny reflections winking in the drops dotting his windshield. The car sat unmoving, and Toby eyed it warily, unsure whether he'd ducked into this side road four hundred yards behind quickly enough to avoid being seen. He'd followed the car for miles, the last few on this dirt track in the middle of nowhere without headlights, the mud so slick in spots he was sure he'd plow the Beemer into a tree.

After that other bitch—the bitch who was not Dana—took a potshot at him outside the hotel, he'd decided not to press his luck and gotten the hell out of there. Someone would have spotted him sooner or later, and the fewer witnesses, the better. He'd calmly walked back to the small hotel where he'd left his car, fuming over his lost opportunity and wracking his brain to figure out how he would find Dana now.

The answer had come to him at virtually the same instant he'd turned to get in his car and seen the two Russians across the street walking down the sidewalk as cop cars converged on the hotel. Staggering would have been more accurate. The big one had half-carried the man Toby had shot. The Russians had found Dana somehow. Or the bitch who wasn't Dana. No matter; the two women were paired now. All Toby had to do was follow the Russians, and they'd lead him right to them. And then he'd find out what this was all about, what the hell Dana knew.

But so far, the crazy bastards had led him on a wild goose chase through the miserable, wet Virginia countryside. Now their car had sat still on the shoulder for what felt like a long time. He could barely see through the rain-spattered windows, but he didn't dare use the wipers.

He yanked on the door handle, then caught himself before he shouldered it open. He dialed down the rheostat and turned off the dome light first, then shoved the door open, pulled up the collar of his coat, and swung his loafers into the muck that passed for a lane. As quickly as he could move without leaving his shoes behind in the mud, he made his way to the end of the lane and peered through the raindrops.

He saw movement down the road. The door on the driver's side of the car ahead swung open, turning on the dome light and illuminating the interior. The driver got out, his bulk silhouetted as he circled behind the trunk of the car and opened the passenger door. Light spilled onto the ground next to the car. The driver reached in, and a moment later, the passenger tumbled sideways into the pool of light, obviously lifeless. Toby shivered. He'd done that.

The big man dragged the body forward. Toby could make out a guardrail at the edge of the car's headlights. The big man dragged the body to the right of the guardrail and it disappeared from sight as the big man's dark form grew shorter until he, too, vanished. Not too long after, his head and torso rose from the darkness into the shadows cast by the headlights. Toby backpedaled toward the Beemer as the big man reappeared by the car alone.

Toby nodded to himself, understanding now why they'd led him out to this godforsaken place. When the driver turned his back to get behind the wheel Toby slipped the gearshift into reverse and quickly backed up so he'd be less visible from the road. He waited calmly for the Russian to turn his car around and drive back the way he came.

Virginia

53

I hate rain.

As a little girl, I found the sound of rain on the roof comforting. I loved putting on boots and jumping in puddles after a hard rain in the spring or fall, and squishing mud between my bare toes in summer. At night, when big thunderstorms rolled in from the west or northwest, I'd watch the fireworks from my window like my own, private son et lumière. During the day, if a storm front threatened, we'd play outside until the very last minute, until the wind kicked up and the first big drops signaled the imminent arrival of an advancing wall of water. Sometimes we'd wait to see if we could outrun it when it came, tumbling with laughter through the front door whether dry or soaked to the skin.

But the relentless onslaught of water pelting the windshield reminds me of the incidents that changed my feelings about leaden skies weighted with God's tears. I do my best to avoid thinking about the first time I saw rain in a different light. But that makes it impossible not to focus on the event that clinched my aversion.

*****

More rain falls on Dallas in a brief thunderstorm than Baghdad gets during its entire rainy season between November and March. It's so hot here that when the clouds are heavy enough with moisture to form raindrops, the rain evaporates before it hits the ground.

Occasionally, like today, precipitation comes in the form of mist that barely cools the air. It also can't conceal the destruction—twisted metal, broken glass, crumbled masonry, melted plastic, splatters of blood, and bits of flesh and bone—wrought by a suicide bomber. Nor does it do much to tamp down the clouds of dust and smoke raised by the explosion, or dissipate the smells of arid dirt, unwashed animals and people, putrefied garbage, and shit from goats, chickens and feral dogs roaming the city, open sewers, and exploded entrails painting the walls of the buildings lining the street.

The perimeter of Baghdad's Green Zone has experienced a number of these attacks in recent weeks, and my team and I roll up on scene in an M1117 armored security vehicle—ASV—within minutes of the blast, along with others that quickly spread through the neighborhood to search out and destroy any other threats. Too little too damn late, as usual. The damage has been done, the death toll in the dozens, and I'm both discouraged and angry. I'm not used to it yet, but already I'm growing more immune to the emotional effects. What gets to me is that my job is to protect our forces in Baghdad, and these bombers are wreaking havoc on our watch. My mood does not improve when a Humvee pulls onto the block and stops close by. Master Sergeant Carl Woicik, my direct superior, climbs out accompanied by an interpreter and four Iraqi cops who are learning police tactics from us.

Bomb experts will roll in shortly, along with a forensics team to assess the scene. My team and the crew of another ASV are fanning out to help with crowd control and give us a chance to start canvassing witnesses. MSG Woicik watches us—me—deploy the team, explaining through the interpreter what we're doing. I go strictly by the book. Woicik is pushing forty, close-cropped brown hair just starting to gray at the temples. He carries a hundred and eighty pounds on a six-foot frame, with broad shoulders and a craggy, Marlboro Man face.

When I started my tour and came under his command, he seemed tough but fair, the kind of superior officer who's been where his troops are and expects no less of them than was required of him as he made his way up the chain of command. A few weeks in, a different picture began to emerge. There was innuendo in the mess hall when no one else was around. I tried to laugh it off. It got worse. He suggested that my tour could be a lot easier if I did a few favors for him. "Quid pro quo," he said. I finally told him to go fuck himself, and avoided him when I could.

As my company leader, however, he has my life in his hands, and I can feel him staring at me, can practically hear the wheels turning in his head. As I get caught up in the work at hand, I forget about him. The job is what's important, catching the assholes who set off these bombs, getting them to lead us to the bigger assholes who build them. The problem is that half the time, the bombers vaporize in the act.

We've interviewed half a dozen witnesses before I glance in Woicik's direction to see how his team is doing. Woicik is interrogating a young woman dressed in traditional abaya and asha through the interpreter, and a couple of the Iraqi men encircle her. Their voices are loud, her replies murmured with downcast eyes. Suddenly, one of the Iraqi men slaps her across the face. Woicik does nothing to stop it, merely waits for the woman to regain her balance and stand cowed and trembling. He asks another question. She replies and the Iraqi cop raises his hand to hit her again. This time Woicik stays the blow with a raised hand until the interpreter has finished translating the woman's reply. Then Woicik backhands her, knocking her to the ground.

I tell my corporal to take over for me and walk over slowly enough to get my anger in check. I put in for this tour to help these people and bring the rule of law back to a country ruled by a despot for a quarter-century. I know women are second-class citizens in this country, but what I just saw isn't the *way we treat witnesses in the States, and not the example we should set for Iraqi cops.*

I throw Woicik a quick salute as I approach. "Problem here, master sergeant?"

Woicik's eyebrows go up a fraction at the more formal address I used. His stare could freeze water in a more temperate clime. "Nothing we can't handle, Roberts."

I nod. "I couldn't help noticing that the witness seems unresponsive. I thought perhaps she'd be more forthcoming if questioned by someone of her own gender."

I also know that I'm in Iraq because the brass wants to try new ways of gaining the locals' trust. I'm a woman and I speak Arabic.

Woicik's eyes flick toward the Iraqi who'd slapped the woman and back to me. I see him calculating behind his impassive gaze. His head tips almost imperceptibly toward the woman.

"Go ahead."

He wants me to fail. I step toward the woman and give her a reassuring smile. I have to pick my words carefully with the interpreter standing there.

"Where were you going when the bomb went off?" I ask in Arabic.

"On my way to the market to get food for my family." Her eyes are downcast when she speaks, but I detect no sullenness or resentment in her tone.

"How many in your family?"

"Eleven." She lifts her head and looks at me as she lists her relations.

"Are they home?"

She nods. "All except my father, who is working."

"And they had nothing to do with this." I wave a hand at the destruction.

She shakes her head vehemently. I turn, cup my hand to my mouth and yell across the street to my corporal, "Johnson!" When he turns I flag him over. As he trots across the street, I turn back to the girl. "Where do you live?"

She tells me and provides directions. I turn to Corporal Johnson and translate for him.

"Take two men," I tell him. "Go to the house and check out her story. If she's telling the truth, bring back the oldest male in the house to escort her home or wherever she wants to go."

The Iraqi cops all babble at once, voicing their objections, but Woicik holds up a hand and silences them. Johnson is six-feet-five-inches of Godiva-covered muscle who dwarfs my tall-for-a-girl five-seven. He's a good size for a point guard or tight end, but stands frozen, uncertain as a five-year-old with his hand in a cookie jar. I don't blame him, but I'm pissed that he doesn't just follow orders. I'll dress him down later for it, in private.

"What are you waiting for, son?" Woicik asks him. "Sergeant Roberts

gave you an order."

Johnson takes off running.

Woicik addresses the Iraqis. *"It's an acceptable compromise. We'll wait."*

He moves on to the next witness his troops present him, and I cross the street to see how my team, or what's left of it, is doing. Johnson and crew return in less than fifteen minutes with a kid no more than twelve in tow, so I excuse myself for a minute to meet them in front of Woicik and his entourage. Woicik crooks a finger to summon the young woman, and the kid runs to her side. She halts in front of the pack of men, gaze directed at her feet. The boy at her side stares at the men defiantly, cheeks red with anger. He is obviously her brother, and it doesn't take long for him to corroborate her story. Woicik lets her go with an admonishment over some weak protests from two of the Iraqis.

By the end of what turns out to be a long day I've all but forgotten the incident. I nearly run into Woicik, though, on my way out of the mess tent after chow.

"Just the person I was looking for," he says. *"Got a lead on this morning's bomber. Let's go."*

"Me, sergeant?"

"You see me talking to anyone else here, Roberts?"

"No, sergeant." I shake my head, less a response to his question than bewilderment.

He leads the way to a Humvee parked not far from them mess tent, and waves me toward the driver's side. I do as he requests, but as I get in behind the wheel I'm more confused. There's no team inside the vehicle.

I reach for the ignition and hesitate. *"Sergeant?"*

Woicik stares out the windshield. *"We'll get back-up if we need it. Gunnerson and Talbot have squads on patrol tonight, and they're both aware of what we're doing."*

I zip my lip, start the engine and pull out. Once we're off the base, Woicik gives me the general direction he wants us to go. We're in the Red Zone—essentially all of Baghdad except the Green Zone, Camp Victory and the airport—which makes me nervous. It's what I do every day, but with a team that's part of a larger squad I command. Now it's just me and my MSG. Alarms are going off in my head. Everything we're doing is against protocol, but my direct superior is calling the shots.

I know the dangerous sections of Baghdad—Sadr City, al-Shaab, abo-Greeb, al-Khazaliya— but soon we're in a part of the city I don't know, and Woicik isn't talking. His stony expression hasn't changed the few times I've risked glances in his direction. Driving at night in Baghdad is hard enough without the kind of misty fog we've had all day, and I don't even know what we're looking for. The streets are dark, and we meet few vehicles. Figures on the sidewalks scurry, whether furtively or fearfully is impossible to tell from the Humvee.

When the rain finally comes, the dry, hardpan desert is as impervious as concrete, giving the water nowhere to go. The dusty streets turn into rivers of mud. The wipers on the Humvee slap at the moisture, whisking it to the side, but it's replaced just as quickly by more drops falling out of the darkness.

"Slow down," Woicik growls.

Startled, I jerk my foot off the gas and the Humvee coasts to a crawl. I peer out the windshield, wondering what he sees that prompts his command. Fear gnaws a hole in my gut. I wonder if Woicik has gone over the edge. Nightfall has turned the normal palette of beiges, browns and umbers to shades of gray, and the sharp edges of the mostly two- and three-story buildings on either side of the street are distorted by the raindrops.

There are pockets of this neighborhood that bombs have reduced to empty lots of rubble. This is not the sort of place to go sightseeing even during the day. The headlights briefly illuminate a figure walking by the side of the street, shoulders hunched against the rain, face obscured. Dress, in this part of the world, doesn't always distinguish one gender from another, at least not in the dark. But Iraqi women aren't allowed to go out at night, especially not alone. And the figure looks taller than most women.

Woicik suddenly cranes his neck to look behind us. I glance in the mirror and can't see the figure we passed.

"Pull over," Woicik says.

Before I've even stopped, he opens the door and steps out, breaking into a run back the way we came. I try not to panic. He's not supposed to get out of the damn vehicle without me. We travel in nothing less than pairs in Baghdad. Worse, I have no idea where he's going. While half-turned in my seat to watch him through squinting eyes, I grab the comm unit and thumb the mic.

"Charlie Delta Three to base. Do you copy? Over."

"Base to Charlie Delta Three, we copy. Over."

"MSG is pursuing a suspect on foot. I'm going after him. Alert all units in our vicinity. Over."

"Roger, Charlie Delta Three. What's your position? Over."

Woicik has disappeared down the block as I radio our coordinates and sign off. I grab my M16 and run down the block through the rain after him. I can't imagine what he's thinking, running after a suspect without his weapon and without any backup on the way. I can only hope that this is either a wild goose chase or the cavalry will arrive in time if we find ourselves in trouble.

I dart into the side street where I thought I saw Woicik last. There's no sign of him, but a flicker of light up ahead around the corner of a building attracts my attention, and I run toward it. My ACU is nearly soaked through now, the added weight slowing me. I stop at the corner of the building and cautiously poke my head around the edge. Empty lots stretch away from me, what's left of the buildings that stood in them bulldozed into tall mounds.

227

Fifty yards away, the wavering light silhouettes one of them. The pile of rubble is tall enough to obscure whoever is holding the light and whatever is taking place.

I move forward silently, using the debris as cover, and round it slowly. My heart pounds in my chest and I have to force myself to breathe. The guttering glow grows brighter, and in a moment over the shoulder of the mound I can see the person wielding it.

Woicik picks his way through the ruins, swinging a big Maglite back and forth, sweeping its beam over the wreckage—broken furniture, burned out rusted husks of cars, empty steel oil drums—to search for hidey holes. Other than the rain spattering the ground, I hear no sign of anyone else. If the man we saw earlier came this way, he's gone now.

Stepping out from behind the mound, I call out softly, "Sergeant?"

He turns and waits as I approach.

"It's not safe out here," I tell him. "We need to get back to the vehicle."

I can't read his expression. He pivots to aim the flashlight at the rubble a few yards in front of him as I stop by his side.

"You're right," he says, voice barely audible above the patter of the rain in the mud.

The beam of light swings wildly, barely giving me enough warning to jerk my head back, so the Maglite hits my helmet not my face. But it's enough to ring my bell and knock me off balance, and I'm not so lucky with the backhand swing. The heavy flashlight catches me on the chin, clacks my jaw shut and knocks out a tooth. I taste blood. My mind is in shock that I'm being attacked by my superior officer.

Instinctively, I swing my rifle toward him, but he's already inside its arc. He knocks it away and rams the butt end of the Maglite into my solar plexus with two hands. Air leaves my lungs in a whoosh, and my chest heaves trying to replace it.

"You were an embarrassment out there today," he says, contempt dripping from the words like the falling rain. He punches me twice in the face, and blood spurts from my nose. I taste its metallic salinity as it runs down the back of my throat. "A disgrace to the uniform."

What comes next is mostly a blur. He grabs my shoulders and spins me around. A fist thuds into my kidney, and the pain nearly makes me black out. The next thing I know, I'm draped face-first over the top of a barrel, and my uniform trousers are yanked to my knees. Raindrops tap the backs of my thighs and trickle across my bare skin.

I want to scream but I still can't get enough air into my lungs, and fear grips my heart with an ice-cold fist. He rips my Army-issue underwear off like tissue, and presses one hand into my back to pin me to the barrel. I suddenly feel him between my legs. A jolt of electricity goes through me, and I buck involuntarily. He smashes the flashlight into the back of my helmet.

Lightning and thunder crackle in my brain, and my ears ring.

Suddenly, with a stabbing pain unlike anything I've ever known, he's inside me, pushing the hurt so deep I fear it will never leave me. He leans over me, his face so close to mine I can smell his breath, and my stomach roils.

"Don't ever make me look bad again," he snarls. "And don't even think about reporting this because no one will believe you, and it'll just happen again."

Shock has rendered me incapable of movement, of speech, of coherent thought. I try to block out the pain, the humiliation, the violation I feel, compartmentalize it, put it in a place where it's happening to someone else, not me.

"Are you listening to me, soldier?" he screams in my ear. "Did you hear me?"

The metal flashlight whangs off my helmet again. A brocade of sparks explodes in my head.

"Sir, yes, sir!" I blubber through the blood coating a lip that's blown up like a balloon.

Tears roll down my cheeks and drip into the mud alongside the raindrops.

*****

I swipe my coat sleeve across my face. I fucking hate rain.

I glance at Dana. She's lost in her own thoughts and doesn't seem to have noticed my discomfort. I can't let my mind wander like that anymore. I need to focus on possible scenarios.

We're on the run from at least two different factions with divergent objectives but a common desire to kill us both. They don't know where we are at present or where we're going, but they can probably take a guess based on the destinations we had as Amtrak passengers. Of the two forces arrayed against us, I figure the killer from the train is the more dangerous, assuming the Russians belong to him. Dana's boss is an amateur, but a wild card. With a gun.

I no longer have allies in the bureau. I'm not sure if I can count on family since I ran out on mine, but that's where I'm inclined to go. I need more information, need to know what we're up against. I can think of only one person to call, and the last time we spoke was more than a decade ago.

54

For the first time in weeks, Dana had started to feel safe. She'd thought it over and decided that being in the company of an armed FBI agent, even if the agent wasn't officially on duty, in a moving vehicle, the location of which no one knew, was probably a hell of a lot safer than almost anywhere else she'd been in the last day except, perhaps, her own bed. Now they'd finally turned onto an interstate highway, relieving Dana of the fear that she might get dumped on a backcountry road at night. Alive or dead still a harrowing thought.

Suddenly, Dana realized that Jenny was crying. She didn't know why and it made her nervous. She was about to ask—after all, it could have been something else, like seasonal allergies, or an eyelash stuck under her lid—when Jenny wiped her face, sat up and acted like nothing was wrong. Then Jenny initiated the car's hands-free phone and began dialing digits, and Dana realized she didn't feel safe at all.

"What are you doing?"

Jenny threw her a glance that could have withered a cactus.

"No, I mean who are you calling?"

"We need information. Since I'm on leave, the agency won't help, so I'm calling someone I trust."

"Like who?"

"My husband."

Dana blinked. There was no rule that said this woman shouldn't be married. Dana shouldn't have been surprised, but she hadn't seen a ring, and Jenny didn't seem the type.

"What does he do?" Dana said finally, feeling lame.

"Not sure," Jenny murmured. "Last I knew, writing killer apps for smartphones."

"Last you... Wait. When's the last time you saw him?"

Jenny lifted a shoulder and let it fall. "I don't know. Ten years, maybe more."

"Your husband?" Before Jenny could answer, the call went through and a man's voice came over the speakers.

"I wondered when you'd call."

"Hello, Nate," Jenny said.

"What are you doing in the middle of Virginia?"

Dana's eyes widened at the sight of Jenny's frowning face in the glow of the instrument panel, and panic welled up in her chest, constricting her throat.

"How did you...?" Some thought wiped the surprise off Jenny's face. "Oh, your AmEx card. Sorry. It was an emergency. I'll pay you back."

His laughter filled the car. "You've carried a limitless charge card all this time and never used it once until now. And you use it to rent an economy SUV? You could have used it to *buy* a car, Jen. I certainly wouldn't have minded." His light tone grew serious. "Are you okay? You in trouble?"

"Are you keeping tabs on me?"

Dana squeezed herself against the door, suddenly unsure if she wanted any part of this.

"Oh, come on. No. Well, maybe a little. Look, I read about what happened a couple of weeks ago, and when AmEx alerted me to the charge on the card, I thought maybe you could use some help."

"You have been checking up on me."

Dana thought Jenny's tone was a little too indignant, given the fact that her husband actually wanted to be helpful.

"No, I haven't. Okay, yeah, once or twice I thought about where in the world you might be, and checked to see that you were all right."

"So you've been tracking my cell phone?"

"You got me." Nate's voice sounded weary, worried. "Never could fool you. Honest, though, it's not like I know where you are all the time. I've only done it a few times, like I said."

Jenny's face and tone softened. "That's sweet, Nate. Thanks. How are you, anyway?"

"I'm good. Things are good. How about you?" He sounded relieved.

"I've been better."

Dana stared at Jenny as if she were insane.

"I hate to ask, Nate," she said, "but you're right, we're in a little trouble."

"We?"

Jenny glanced at Dana and a corner of her mouth turned up wryly. "Nate, meet Dana, the Thelma to my Louise."

"Oh, boy. What the hell have you gotten yourself into? And nice to meet you, by the way, Dana."

"You, too," Dana said in a small voice. Her thoughts still reeled as she tried to understand the dynamics between the two.

Jenny gave him a quick rundown of the day's events.

"I need your eyes and ears, Nate. Dana and I are still in danger unless we can figure out who we're up against. We were witnesses to a crime on the train from D.C to Charlottesville. It should be making the news by now. Two bodies. Can you find out who the victim on the train was? The non-employee victim?"

"Should be easy enough. Hang on, let me check."

The car fell silent for a few miles, and Dana wondered if the call had been dropped. But Nate's voice suddenly broke the silence. Something about his tone seemed subdued.

"Got your answer, Jen. Not sure you're going to like it. Do you remember a guy in school, Mick Costanza?"

Jenny frowned, her brow furrowing. "Yeah, sort of."

"He was a few years younger."

"Wait. Mickey? In Billy's class?"

"That's the one. He and Billy hung out back then, if I remember right."

"You're not... He's the victim?"

"Yeah, sorry. Wish it was better news."

"I guess I am, too. It's just so weird. I mean, he always seemed a little lost as a kid. But how did he get himself into that situation on the train?"

"Hard to say what directions your life will take you. Look at us."

Jenny fell silent, and again Dana wondered what had transpired between her and Nate. She couldn't detect any acrimony between them, and from the sound of his voice she couldn't imagine why Jenny had left him. That much, at least, seemed obvious to her.

"Anyway," Nate went on, "I'm running a background search on him, figure out what he might have been up to that got him killed."

"Thanks, Nate."

They both paused, and the longer the silence lasted, the more Dana could sense the thoughts they left unsaid.

"You're going home, aren't you?" Nate said suddenly.

Jenny looked startled. "How did you know?"

"Just a feeling," Nate said. "After what happened in D.C. a few weeks ago, then the AmEx charge alert, you calling me... Just seemed like the place you'd head."

Jenny sighed. "Yeah, I figured it was time."

Nate didn't reply right away. "So, I'll call you when I have something for you."

"I appreciate it, really."

"No problem. It's good to talk to you, Jenny."

"You, too."

This time, Dana could tell from the silence that the call had disconnected. She stared at Jenny, mouth agape.

"That's it?" she said. "That's all you can say?"

"What do you mean?"

Dana curled against the door and stared out the windshield. "If I had a guy that sounded that nice, I wouldn't let him go. What happened to you two, anyway?"

"Long story. Let's just say I got married too young. I realized I wanted more from life."

"You couldn't do both? Have a career and a husband?"

"I don't know. Maybe. Things just worked out this way. What about you?"

"In case you hadn't noticed, I've got man troubles of my own," Dana mumbled. She folded her arms and scrunched down in the seat. "Never even been in love."

She wondered what it was about her that attracted the losers, the weirdoes and psychos. She wasn't unattractive. Many people, in fact, would have said she was pretty. Stealing a glance at the woman behind the wheel, though, Dana knew she wasn't a real looker, never had been. She'd been awkward and homely as an adolescent, and though she'd outgrown some of that by the time she graduated from high school she wasn't going to win any beauty contests.

Sitting next to Jenny, Dana could see the difference. Their resemblance was striking, even close up, and Dana could see why the killer aboard the train had mistaken Jenny for her. But Dana was an inch or so shorter, a dozen pounds heavier, her features coarser than Jenny's. Still, she wasn't plain, and certainly not ugly.

On a good night, with a little luck, she might be the prettiest girl in the room, but it seemed the few times she'd gone out drinking with people at work, the bars were always frequented by prettier girls than she, attractive women who were snapped up and swept away by handsome men long before midnight. Leaving her and others like her to be picked over by the remaining males, who were too drunk, too ugly, or too stupid to consider taking home.

Maybe, she thought, she exuded some scent that attracted a certain type of male. The smell of disappointment and, shattered dreams. The stench of her upbringing—the sweat from a hundred fights, stale beer spilled on the carpet on hundreds of nights, dried vomit, violent sex, greasy food heavily laced with garlic, all tinged with the coppery note of blood. It permeated her soul and leeched from her pores, a spoor for slavering beasts to track—

Stop! You are not your mother.

Dana batted the web of memories away with the same revulsion she reserved for spiders.

"You seem like a nice person," Jenny said, her voice yanking Dana back into the present. "Maybe it's time to do something about it."

Dana furrowed her brow, thinking back. "Which? Man trouble? Or falling in love?"

Jenny shrugged. "Both."

Dana tilted her head and considered the idea. She definitely deserved better. Maybe Jenny was right. But maybe tackling one task at a time would yield better results. Get an asshole out of her life first, and make room for love.

She brought her phone to life.

55

Sykes stewed, trying to force his brain to do what had come so naturally until the past twelve hours. *Think.* Unaccustomed as he was to anyone telling him to fuck off, let alone hanging up on him, he wasn't quite sure what to do about it. And that indecision bothered him. It was so foreign to him that it would have been humorous if he didn't feel that undercurrent of fear. That pissed him off. He'd never been afraid of anyone or anything in his life.

The concept sat him up, and he stared pensively, glittering, glistening strands of pearl headlights and ruby taillights strung out on the black ribbons of the interstate in front of him, kaleidoscoping in the raindrops on the windows. The only thing he feared, he realized, was failure. He'd never considered it, never calculated it into his plans as a possibility. Today had changed that. He'd let emotions rule, allowed his pride and anger to dictate his actions. Mick's theft had been impulsive, not planned. Mick couldn't possibly have known what was on the phone, how truly valuable it was beyond its actual cost. In response, Sykes had acted equally impetuously instead of planning his reprisal.

He shook his head, corners of his mouth turning down in disgust. He never should have gone after Mick. Like everything else he did, he should have distanced himself, sent men and stayed at arm's length while they reeled the boy in. He'd only fucked things up more with his impatience, and now he'd given Nastase another piece of leverage as well as a reason to worry. His mind raced. He needed a way to get back on top of the situation.

The sway of the car as George changed lanes jarred his thoughts loose.

Stop worrying like an old woman.

Nastase wasn't the issue. Sykes needed his damned phone, and he was on the way to getting it. That would resolve the problem. That was the goal now, his only focus.

The burner phone he'd been using vibrated in his pocket. The incoming number was blocked. He put the phone to his ear.

"Benton," said a familiar voice. "You've had quite the day, yes?"

Concrete coursed through Sykes's veins and started to set.

237

"What do you want, Volya?"

"What do I want?" Nastase's voice rose. "How about you show a little respect? One of my employees is dead. A good man."

"I can't help it if you send amateurs to do a simple job."

"Alexei says job was maybe not so simple. And now you want him to drive all the way to fucking Wisconsin? I'm beginning to wonder who the amateur is here."

Sykes held the phone way from his ear as Nastase's voice rose.

"What do you want?" he repeated.

"I want to know what the hell is in Wisconsin!" Nastase shouted. "I want to know why Mikhail is dead! I want to know why you have my resources chasing their shadows all over countryside."

"One of my employees inadvertently took my cell phone from my office," Sykes explained calmly. "He was severely punished, but unfortunately died before telling me what he did with it."

"All this for a fucking cell phone?"

Sykes sighed. "Volya, calm down. It's not just a phone. It's what's on the phone that matters."

Nastase was silent for a moment. "Sensitive information."

"Leverage. Isn't that what keeps us both in business?"

"Password-protected, of course."

"Of course."

"So, I don't understand problem. You've backed up this information to the cloud, yes?"

"I don't trust the cloud." Again, Sykes heard silence and wondered if the connection was broken.

When Nastase finally spoke, his voice was low, edged. "Your mistake. Not my problem."

Thoughts tumble-dried in his head like shirts, empty sleeves flailing for a grip on something. "Unfortunately, my errant employee made it your problem. The information on the phone could cost us both."

Nastase snorted. "What? Money? You don't pay me back, I simply take your business, sooner than later."

Sykes gritted his teeth and let the silence stretch this time, waiting for Nastase to fill it.

"You think the phone was sent to Wisconsin," Nastase said finally. Sykes nodded as though Nastase could see through the phone.

"I admit my mistake. So I am personally going to rectify it. I'm already on my way."

"And you want Alexei as backup. Why not risk your own

238

people?"

"I don't trust them. None of them know the extent of the business. Except Phillip, of course, and even he doesn't know everything. Better that way."

Nastase grunted. "I'll think about it. But I won't forgive. Or forget. I liked Mikhail. He made me laugh. And he had wife, kids. Going to cost you."

"Yeah, yeah." Sykes took a breath, let it go. "Add it to my tab."

"If you're fucking with me, Sykes, *ty troop*—you are dead."

56

Driving like an old fart in Florida, Alexei stared at the rain sheeting down through the dark. The hypnotizing thump-thump of the windshield wipers fueled his fantasy of turning the car southward and driving until the road petered out at the edge of the Caribbean. He'd find some boat captain or pilot willing to ferry him to an island, maybe the Bahamas. He could see himself retiring someplace where flip-flops, shorts and a T-shirt were the most he'd have to wear, and choosing his next drink the hardest decision he'd have to make on any given day. He could taste the salt air, feel the hot sun on his face, a cooling breeze taking the sting out of it. He could feel the sand between his toes, smell the brininess of the clear water and the fragrant sweetness of bougainvillea and hibiscus blooms.

He was barely middle-aged, but he felt far older than his years. Maybe that meant it was time to get out and retire. He had a little money set aside, not like Mikhail who had to plow every penny he earned into keeping his wife happy and his kids fed. Suddenly, Alexei wondered if Mikhail had been smart enough to buy life insurance.

He, himself, had a small policy he'd taken out when he'd first gotten married, so sodden with love for his Ekaterina that he'd recognized the enormous responsibility of taking care of another person when they'd gotten married. His beloved had seen things differently, had seen greener pastures in the form of a health club fitness coach named Boris.

Thinking back on it now, Alexei had no regrets. For nearly a year, he'd been blindly, blissfully happy. He didn't blame Ekaterina. Being married to someone who robbed and killed for a living and who couldn't, obviously, talk about his job, must have been deadly dull. Alexei had other interests—passable skills at chess, an interest in philately, and a fondness for nature walks—but Ekaterina had been more interested in nightlife, and the accoutrements that Alexei's fairly generous salary afforded them. He smiled at the thought of her receiving a $50,000 life insurance check. She might even remember him with affection.

The ring of the cell phone on the seat next to him gave him a start. He snatched it up and answered.

"Alexei? Volya."

"*Da.*"

"Sykes is a fucking liar. But I want you to follow him anyway."

"Boss?"

"I know, I know. I'm saddened by loss of Mikhail, too. And if I were in your shoes, I'd want to put a bullet in Sykes's brain. But I must know what the deal is. Why is his phone so important?"

"You want me to help him? After what he brought down on us?"

"No, I want you to make him think you are helping him. Find out where he's going, and let me know. In the meantime, I will make some phone calls, recruit some local help. Maybe Milwaukee or Chicago. Tomorrow morning I will fly to Chicago. You can pick me up there. I'll tell you where and when to meet me."

"You're coming? To Wisconsin?"

"I want to keep track of what this dickhead is up to."

"Okay. Fine. For Mikhail, I'll drive to fucking Wisconsin. I'll wait to hear from you in the morning."

"Good. Drink lots of coffee, Alexei. I don't want you sleeping at the wheel."

"No worries. My anger will keep me awake."

"My condolences, Alexei. He will be missed. Drive safely. I will see you tomorrow."

57

This compulsion was madness. Every mental attempt he threw out to slow his free-fall descent off the cliff failed as quickly as a branch breaking, an umbrella flipping inside out, a balloon popping, a rock ledge crumbling, a parachute collapsing. He never should have gone after Dana in the first place. He should have sicced the cops on her. Let the chips fall where they may. Maybe she didn't know anything about the missing money; he could have convinced them she did. With a little time and effort, he could make it look like she took it. Instead, he'd made himself look bad by trying to pull her out of a cab on a busy street, then killed some kind of Russian mobster.

He could still turn around. Go home to his condo in Georgetown and calm down with a couple fingers of excellent 20-year-old single malt Scotch, neat. Listen to some relaxing music. Think it through. And if he was still concerned, still harbored even an inkling that he faced insurmountable trouble, then pack a few things, grab his passport, and leave town. Head for Madagascar, or maybe the Marshall Islands. Someplace that didn't have an extradition treaty with the U.S.

Yet here he was, driving in the relentless rain, in the dark, following another mob associate—a *shestyorka*, if he remembered correctly—across the state. He'd gone insane, he decided. There was no other explanation for not turning around immediately and driving home, going back to his life. The parties—events, more like. The photos with the movers and shakers in D.C.—the world, even. Glad-handing with billionaires and world leaders. Meetings with CEOs of NGOs around the world—dinner in Paris, lunch on a yacht anchored in the Mediterranean off the Côte d'Azur, breakfast in Marrakesh.

People smiled when they gave Toby their money, relieving some personal guilt by helping the less fortunate, convinced they could influence their karma, save their souls. They heaped praise on him for his good works, for improving humanity's lot, for actually doing something to raise people out of poverty and help make them self-sufficient. He loved their adulation, loved the fact that the more self-effacing he behaved, the more they lionized him.

A huge sob suddenly wracked his chest, and tears threatened to pour down his cheeks in a torrent. He girded himself, sucked in his gut and held his breath, squeezing his emotions back down into the dark pit at his center. He couldn't go back to that life anymore. Never again would he taste that kind of acclaim. He'd known it the moment he'd stepped into the office that morning, confirmed it as soon as he'd confronted Dana. Life as he knew it was over. The best he could hope for now was to find out what she knew before he killed her, and then try to get away clean.

He turned up the volume on the Bang + Olufsen sound system and put a classical music CD in the player. He wasn't a huge fan of classical music, and would rather be tied on an anthill and smothered in honey than listen to a bombastic, depressing composer like Wagner. Even Beethoven could be ponderous, but he'd discovered a recording of Beethoven's Fifth performed by a German symphony at the fast tempo Beethoven intended. On the 16-speaker sound system, it was like Freddie Mercury and Queen on acid. It got his juices flowing even better than a shot of espresso.

He'd been following the now-familiar taillights of the Russian's big sedan for more than an hour on the interstate and was glad to have a distraction. The music helped keep him awake and alert. Still, the sight of the glowing red orbs ahead of him veering off to the right took him by surprise.

He slowed, taking the exit well behind the other vehicle so the Russian wouldn't spot him as a tail. By the time he reached the stop sign at the end of the exit ramp, he saw no sign of the Russian's car in either direction. A flash of brake lights across the road caught his eye, and he turned his gaze to see the taillights on the Russian's car wink out next to a gas pump at a service station on the opposite corner.

Quickly taking stock, Toby turned left and headed for another service station adjacent to it, the entrances only fifty yards apart. He wheeled up to a pump and got out to fill up his tank, keeping an eye on the Russian while he inserted a credit card and selected a pump handle. The big man stood motionless next to his car waiting, Toby assumed, for the gas tank to fill, just as he was. As soon as the Russian moved, Toby stopped the pump and hung up the handle even though his tank wasn't quite full. When the Russian got back in his car, Toby was already behind the wheel of the BMW with the engine running.

As the sedan pulled away from the pump at the other station, Toby matched the car's movement. But the Russian surprised him, stopping with a flash of brake lights and backing into a parking spot by the corner of the gas-station building. Leaning forward, arms wrapped over the top of the steering wheel, Toby watched the Russian climb out and walk around the car toward the front of the station. Quickly calculating how badly he needed to take a piss, Toby decided to chance it. He spun the car in a tight circle, nosed it into a parking spot, and got out, nearly sprinting into the station to find a bathroom.

58

We haven't been on the road that long—a couple hours, if that—but it feels like an eternity. Thankfully, the rain stopped, easing the strain of peering through the bleary windshield to see the road. We're still in Virginia, somewhere in a national forest about fifteen miles short of the state line, and my bladder is about to burst. I see signs for an exit up ahead, and goose the accelerator a bit in my hurry to find a gas station with a reasonably clean restroom.

Dana has been doing something on her phone for a while now, occasionally making notes on a scratch pad by the light of her phone screen. I'm curious, of course, but it's her business not mine. As I drift over to the exit ramp, she lifts her head to see where we are. I feel her gaze on me a few seconds later.

"What are you doing?" she says, her voice soft.

"I have to pee," I say. "And we need gas."

We don't really need gas—the tank's almost half full—but it doesn't sound as lame as me needing a bathroom. I'm surprised she doesn't, but she probably did her business on the train a few hours ago. My answer seems to mollify her; she turns back to her phone screen, fiddles with it, then closes the app, and puts the phone and scratch pad in her purse.

I brake to a stop at the end of the ramp and peer through the windshield at the two gas stations across the road. One has a mini mart. The other doesn't appear to have room inside for much more than a couple of vending machines. I pick the station with the c-store inside as more likely to have decent bathrooms and pull up to a gas pump. Dana waits in the car while I activate the pump and start filling the tank. A moment later she climbs out, stretches and walks around the front bumper toward the store. She glances at me and stops.

"I'm going to get a snack or something. I'm starved. Want anything?"

I shake my head and she looks away, then I change my mind. "Wait. Yeah, if you don't mind, could you get me a large coffee with cream and sugar?"

I dig my wallet out of my jacket pocket, take out some cash and hand it to her. "While you're at it, see if you can find a roll of tape. Duct tape or masking tape, if they have it."

Her brows furrow. "Tape?"

"Or a bumper sticker. Whatever. Something to cover the hole in the back window, make it less conspicuous."

Her mouth forms an "O" but no sound comes out. As she turns and walks to the mini mart, I'm glad I didn't say anything about what made the hole.

As soon as the tank's full, I get in the driver's seat and pull ahead then swing around and park at the edge of the paved lot opposite the front door, facing the way we came in. After locking up, I hustle across the lot before I wet my pants.

59

After Alexei had gassed up the sedan, he'd gone inside the service station to relieve himself and stock up on food and coffee for the long drive ahead. But once inside the restroom stall, his stomach had turned over and his bowels had erupted, draining him, the meanness of his day and his entire life now reflected back at him in the stench that filled the restroom. He felt sapped of strength and energy and sat motionless, bare ass on the cold plastic seat a reminder of his vulnerability, his mortality. He was, after all, just flesh and blood. The gun under his suit coat did not have the power to ward off disease or old age. Nor did the suit itself protect him from the bullets or knives of others. Mikhail had proved that.

He suddenly felt overwhelmed with shame and humiliation, and he shuddered as his chest tightened and his eyes welled. Just as suddenly, his disgust for acting like a frightened child, nearly whimpering like a baby, washed away the other emotions that sullied his self-image. After all, he'd not only accepted the code of the *vory v zakone* when Nastase made him a "thief-in-law," a proud member of the *Bratva*, all those years ago; he'd also worked hard and demonstrated his loyalty time and again to become a *boyevik*. Eventually, he might even be promoted to *bratok* or *avtoritet*, a step below Nastase, the *pakhan* himself.

Part of his shame came from the belief that he didn't really deserve his position. He wasn't a true *vor*, not like those in the previous generation who had paid their dues in Soviet gulags, who had earned the prison ink that marked them. Those hardened men had abandoned families, foresworn marriage or personal relationships that didn't involve another vor, had spent their lives resisting all forms of authority. In the old days and in the old country, Mikhail would have been killed for getting married and having children. Alexei, too, would have faced punishment for how he'd comported his personal life. He probably never would have been "made" since he'd spent so little time in prison.

But this was a different place, a different time. America was nothing like the old Soviet Union, and even the *Bratva* had changed. The *Organizatsaya* now was ruled and run by oligarchs in Russia and the Ukraine. It was all about big business, the global economy, now.

Even Putin was connected, though no one would ever mention let alone prove it. There was still room around the edges for people like Nastase, which made it possible for the likes of Alexei and Mikhail to survive and even thrive. And in America, they'd been encouraged to blend in, to ignore some of the tenets of the old code of honor. As Nastase liked to say, "Even the great writer Solzhenitsyn knew that a *vor* will bend the rules if it benefits him personally." At times like these, however, Alexei wondered if he deserved any of it.

He shook himself free of the stupor, wiped his ass, stood and pulled up his trousers. At the sink, he washed his hands carefully and splashed cold water on his face. He turned to get a towel and dried off, purposefully avoiding his reflection in the mirror. He didn't want to see the face of the man who experienced these sudden doubts. He couldn't turn into a pussy now. He'd given up everything for this, forgone any hope of a normal life. His marriage hadn't failed because of Bruno the personal trainer. It had failed because Alexei couldn't lie to his wife, so he hadn't really communicated with her at all. He'd never understood how Mikhail had been able to compartmentalize his two lives. But Alexei felt he owed it to Mikhail—he owed it to himself—to see this through.

The cold water refreshed him, and he walked out with more of a spring in his step than he'd entered with. Thinking about the journey ahead, he looked around the store for supplies. From a refrigerated case, he took a couple of sandwiches. He picked up a six-pack of water from a shelf, and realized he'd need a basket for it all before he finished. As he strode to the front of the store, the top of a woman's head an aisle over caught his eye, and his gaze instinctively shifted to check her out as he went by. Her back was turned so he couldn't see her face, but he did a double take as the familiarity of her clothes registered in his consciousness. He couldn't believe his luck, and with the sudden uptick in his respiration and pulse his moroseness of earlier quickly dissipated.

His brain shifted into a higher gear as he considered his options. If it really was the woman, he couldn't afford to let her spot him. And trying to take her in the store would attract too much attention. He unloaded the items he'd selected, leaving them on any bare space of shelving he could find, and walked out of the store without looking back. Taking an immediate right toward his car, he moved a few paces to the side of the door, out of view.

Nervous excitement poured into him, bubbling in his gut then filling his chest and expanding outward through his veins into his arms and hands and down into his toes. He pulled his gun out of its holster and tucked it in his coat pocket, the grip warm in the palm of his hand. If this worked, he wouldn't have to drive all the way to fucking Wisconsin. The job would be finished, and he could go home. Nastase would be pleased, maybe even promote him. If the other woman was with her, so much the better. He'd take them both, make them sit in the front seat of his car so he could keep the gun on them, direct them out into the forest somewhere, and shoot them both. If not... He shrugged. One step at a time.

He scanned the lot. A silver SUV was parked on the far side of the gas pumps. Two other cars were nosed into the curbs in front of the mini mart. He'd only seen one other customer, so he figured the other car belonged to the cashier. No other cars had driven up to the pumps, and despite the fact that it was still relatively early, maybe eight o'clock or so, only light traffic passed by on the highway. Even the soft whoosh from the interstate rose and fell in volume like gentle waves on sand instead of producing the steady dull roar he could hear in his apartment outside D.C. from the Beltway. He nodded to himself. The circumstances could not have been more fortuitous.

He tensed at the sound of the door opening, and had to force himself to slouch a little, as if killing time looking at the highway traffic while waiting for someone. He made a quarter turn so his back was to the door, but a slight turn of the head would show him who came out. He heard the clack-clack of footsteps. From the corner of his eye he could see the woman from the store heading toward the pumps with a plastic bag in her hand, walking to the SUV beyond, most likely. He let her get halfway to the pumps before pushing off the sidewalk. Light on his feet for such a large man, he closed the gap with big, silent strides. By the time she was aware of his presence she didn't even have time to scream.

She dropped the bag in surprise and started to turn. He quickly wrapped an arm around her shoulders, clamping his big hand over her mouth, and stuck the gun in her ribs. Her eyes widened and her body stiffened.

"Do not make sound," he growled softly, "or I kill you right here."

60

Dana stood glued to the pavement, paralyzed with shock, unable to move. It had happened so fast. The accented voice in her ear didn't belong to Toby, surely saving her from a heart attack. But gradual awareness of the painful pressure of the gun barrel bruising her ribs also turned a spigot, releasing a trickle of fear. She tried to shut it off before it became a torrent, tried to focus on the swirling questions in her head.

How did he find me? What does he want? I'm going to die. I'm going to die.

The Russian tugged at her shoulder, trying to uproot her and steer her in a different direction. The hand over her mouth had a fetid odor of rotting vegetation and dried blood, turning her stomach. His hot breath on her cheek smelled rank, too. Her fear grew, rising up like a monster wave that threatened to break over her head, suck her under and drown her. A voice in her head screamed at her to do something, to run, fight, bite, anything. But her mind still couldn't comprehend that this was really happening to her.

A soft pop registered over the white noise in her brain, and the Russian let her go as suddenly as he'd grabbed her, collapsing onto the pavement on one knee, his other bent at an odd angle. He yowled as the pain hit him. A dark blur of arms and legs behind him spun around with ferocious speed, planting the flat heel of a black boot in the Russian's kidney. Small and dressed all in black, to Dana the figure looked like a ninja as it whirled again, this time bringing a heel down on the Russian's outstretched arm, knocking the gun from his hand. As the big man craned his head to see his attacker, the black shadow stepped in and chopped at his exposed neck. The Russian's hands went to his throat, and he rolled over onto his side.

The ninja tugged at Dana's sleeve. "Come on!"

Dana stood transfixed. The big man lay on the pavement. Only seconds ago, he'd had her in his grasp, a gun in her side.

"The gun!" Dana said. "We have to get his gun." She whirled around, eyes scanning the ground for some sign of it.

"Leave it!" the shadow figure said. "We have to get out of here."

The bag she'd dropped caught her eye. No gun, fine; she wasn't leaving without something. She grabbed it, feeling the ninja tug on her other arm. Reluctantly, Dana let the figure pull her toward the SUV. Her brain finally began processing what she'd witnessed, what she'd felt, and she ran for the passenger door. Staring out the windshield, she barely registered the presence beside her as the SUV pulled out of the gas station and onto the road.

A sign pointed the way to the interstate entrance ramp blocks from where they'd gotten off. When they reached the entrance, the car didn't even slow as they passed it. Dana twisted in her seat to watch the entry and interstate signs recede behind them. She turned her gaze on Jenny for the first time since they'd left the gas station. In her black clothes and the black hat pulled down low over her eyes, Jenny almost did look like a ninja.

Dana opened her mouth to tell her she'd missed the entrance when Jenny spun the wheel to the right and turned onto a side street. Dana threw a hand out and braced herself against the center console to keep from tumbling into Jenny's lap. She quickly grabbed the seat belt, pulled it across her chest and latched it as the SUV accelerated, pinning her back in her seat. When she looked at Jenny again, the agent was rapidly moving her gaze from the road ahead to the GPS screen to the rearview mirror.

"What are you doing?" Dana said.

Jenny glanced at the mirror again. "We've got company."

Dana whirled around and saw headlights two blocks behind them.

"I told you we should have gotten his gun!"

"It's not the Russian," Jenny barked. "Calm down."

"Oh, God, someone else?" Dana could think of two other men worse than the Russian, and neither one made her feel calm. "Who?"

"I don't know. But I saw him pull out of a different gas station, so it isn't the guy I put down."

Jenny glanced at the GPS again, and told Dana, "Hang on."

Dana's knuckles went white in the light from the streetlamps from gripping the armrests as Jenny punched the accelerator, braked suddenly and accelerated through a left turn on a cross street. A block up she did the same thing, turning right this time. Dana watched the speedometer needle creep up past fifty, and was suddenly thrown forward against the shoulder belt as Jenny braked before gunning into a left turn. Dana glanced over her shoulder halfway through the turn and looked down the street they'd turned off. No sign of headlights. But just as her angle of vision was about to be cut off, beams of light raked the intersection down the street.

61

Inside the gas station, Toby hurried past a laconic cashier lounging behind the counter. Stringy hair the color of dusty hay hung over the collar of a bright red vest with the station logo on it. A scraggly mustache matching the man's hair drooped down both sides of his mouth. More interested in the action on a small TV screen on the counter, he paid Toby scant attention.

Toby turned his gaze away, spotted the restroom sign in the back and hurried toward it. He reached for the door handle and found it locked. Shifting his weight from one foot to the other, he waited twenty seconds and then knocked. No response. After giving it another ten seconds, he knocked louder. Still nothing.

A voice called out behind him. "Hey!"

Toby turned. The cashier waggled a wooden stick with a key ring attached to its end. A silver key dangled on the ring. "You need a key."

Toby strode to the counter, snatched the stick from the man's hand, and hurried back to unlock the door. The stench that assailed him as he entered nearly made him puke. The trash receptacle overflowed with dirty paper towels and take-out packaging coated with food remains, some of which looked moldy. Filth covered the floor, and the toilet looked as if it hadn't been cleaned in years. He choked back the bile rising in his throat and cautiously breathed through his mouth as he unzipped and stood over the toilet. Nothing happened.

He did a little dance to reposition himself and tried again with the same result. Stress had tightly clamped his bladder sphincter shut. He took a deep breath and tried to relax. Finally, a thin stream spilled into the bowl and grew stronger and steadier. But he felt an eternity pass before his bladder emptied. As worried as he was about taking the time to relieve himself, he realized now how full his bladder had been. Finally finished, he zipped up his trousers and washed his hands, careful not to touch anything.

Rushing out, he practically threw the key at the attendant with a barely muttered "Thanks." Afraid he'd already missed the Russian, he got in the car and started the engine before he even dared look. When he raised his head, the Russian's car was still parked in front of the other gas station. Toby hunkered down and waited.

When the Russian didn't come out, Toby started to worry. He

chided himself for being stupid. After all, he thought, where was the guy going to go? Even so, it bothered him that he didn't have a better angle, that he couldn't see the door and who was coming and going. He debated moving, but couldn't see any better vantage points that wouldn't give him away. He squirmed in his seat with indecision.

Shadows dancing in the parking lot and across the gas pumps sat him up straight a few minutes later. Something was going on, even if he couldn't actually see it. The shadow movement stopped almost as quickly as it started, replaced by two figures on the far side of the pumps running away from him. Small, they appeared to be kids. Maybe shoplifters. They ran to an SUV parked on the far side of the lot. So, maybe not kids, but women. As they got in, the passenger turned toward him for just a moment before swinging the door shut, revealing her face in the light.

He blinked, sure he was mistaken. He sat too far away to be sure, but he could have sworn the passenger was Dana. Two women. Silver-gray SUV. It couldn't be.... He slowly edged the car toward the road, timing it so they passed by as he reached it. The light silhouetted two women in the front seats, a ponytail poking out the back of a ball cap on the driver, and longish hair on the passenger, the one who looked like Dana. As the car passed, light glinted off the rear glass, limning a black hole.

Pulse racing, he waited a moment and turned onto the road behind them, barely able to contain his glee and his impatience. Only minutes before, he'd been moping about his situation, and suddenly the resolution presented itself. Maybe luck was like the weather: if you don't like it, wait a bit and it will change.

He wanted to cut them off and watch their faces as he strode back to their car with his gun in hand and a huge grin on his face. But he remembered that the hot one, the one who was not Dana, had a gun, too. He bit down on his lower lip and tucked his impatience in his pants, alongside the erection growing there at the thought of shooting that bitch Dana, then fucking the better looking woman before he offed her, too.

He stayed well behind them so as not to spook them, and figured they'd get back on the interstate. When they passed the entrance ramp, surprise and worry weighted his right foot, pressing it down harder on the accelerator. They turned right at the next corner, and by the time he followed, the SUV had gained a lot of distance. The driver had made him. She was smart as well as hot, he decided. Two could play that game. He tromped on the accelerator, and the big V8 engine almost effortlessly powered the car up through two gears.

Ahead, the SUV cornered again, its rear end nearly breaking loose. Toby's grin widened. The woman at the wheel might be a good driver, but her little SUV was no match for his BMW. He put on a burst of speed, tapped the brakes hard just before the corner, then used the paddle shifters on the wheel to downshift and accelerate around the corner. He made it just in time to see the SUV take another left turn a block up. He laughed from the sheer exhilaration of the chase, and let off the accelerator a little. No sense in ending the fun too soon. But when he turned to follow, the SUV had disappeared. He stomped on the gas until he reached the end of the block, and then rode the brakes to a squealing stop. He looked both ways at the intersection but saw no taillights in either direction.

Swearing at himself for his stupidity, he hesitated, turned right and pressed the accelerator to the floor. When he saw no sign of the SUV at the next intersection, he threw the gearshift into reverse, twisted in his seat and backed up on squealing, smoking tires straight through the intersection where he'd made the last turn to the next corner past that. With a shriek of rubber skidding on pavement, he braked to a stop in the middle of the intersection, and again looked both ways. Nothing. He beat on the steering wheel with both hands, stomach sinking, until his arms were tired and his palms bruised. Slumping forward, he rested his forehead on the wheel and closed his eyes.

What next? Think.... Shit, the Russian!

Sitting bolt upright, he put the car into gear and hurriedly retraced his route back to the gas station.

The parking spot where the Russian's car had been now sat empty.

62

From glimpses in the rearview mirror, I can tell the car behind us is a white BMW. Expensive, fast, and so ridiculously overmatched to my rental in every way possible that I don't have much hope of outrunning it. With every turn onto a new block, the BMW gains on us. So I have to think of a way to outsmart its driver.

Not surprising in a small town, streetlights are fewer and farther between than in a city, sometimes not even on every corner. The lighting leaves houses in the middle of the block a little more shrouded in shadow. I also notice a dearth of garages. Some of these older homes have an add-on shed roof that hangs over the driveway, creating a covered carport.

Dana starts shrieking every time the white car reappears around a corner a little closer behind us, and I can hardly think over the noise. But as I turn the next corner a plan formulates in my head, and I rapidly scan both sides of the street, almost immediately finding what I need about four houses down—a dark house with an empty carport. I spin the wheel to the right and jam on the brakes, shove the gearshift into reverse and kill the headlights as I back up the driveway. Under the carport, not even the front grill is visible from the corner. As soon as I brake to a stop, put the SUV in Park and shut off the engine, I place a hand on the back of Dana's neck and push her head toward the floor.

"Get down and stay there." Adrenaline and anger put enough menace in my voice that she doesn't let out a peep to object. I lean over the console, keep my head down and hold my breath.

The sound of a car engine grows louder as it accelerates up the street from the right, and slowly recedes as it moves to the left. I raise my head far enough to peek over the dashboard, and watch the BMW's taillights disappear around the corner up the street. I sit up, jerk the gearshift into Drive, and pull onto the street the way we came. At the corner, though, I turn left, not right, and check the navigation screen to be sure the street leads out of the neighborhood. I zig-zag a few more times just to be sure I've thrown off the tail. Probably due to my erratic driving, Dana still hasn't come up for air.

"You can sit up," I say. "We lost him."

She tentatively raises her head and gets her bearings. She's calmed down considerably, but her mouth is set in a grim line.

"How did they find us?" she says.

"I'm more concerned with who 'they' are," I say, although the how worries me, too. "If the Russians were double-teaming us, there may be others."

Dana shakes her head. "I know that white BMW." Her voice sounds as if she has swallowed soured milk. "That was Toby. Somebody must have put some kind of tracking device on your car."

Now my chin is swaying from side to side. "No way. It's a rental, and no one's gotten near it."

"What about back at the hotel? You left it in the parking lot."

She has a point, but I don't concede. "They could just as easily be tracking your phone. You've had it on most of the drive so far."

"Oh, shit." Dana rummages through her purse, retrieves her phone and shuts it off. She looks stricken.

My thoughts, simmering on a back burner since we picked up the tail, now smell done, and I relent.

"This is my fault. Look, as soon as we're out of town a ways, I'll check for bugs, but I think they got lucky. We were both on the train. It makes sense that we'd continue to head in the same direction. The interstate is the logical route. We just got off for gas at the same place."

Dana stares at me. "That's an awful lot of coincidence. The Russians and Toby and us, all stopping for gas at the same place at the same time?"

"Russian, singular," I say, pot now at a full boil. "I think his partner's dead, and I think your boss—"

"Former boss," she interrupts.

"—followed the Russian. Neither of them expected us to drop into their laps like that. Still, it's my fault for not thinking it through and choosing a less obvious route."

Which is why we're now heading north on a back road that will intersect with a state road miles out of town. From there I plan to continue north through the Monongahela National Forest until we can turn west again and catch I-79 up toward Pittsburgh. It will add hours to the drive but throw the dogs off the scent, I hope.

"Yeah, maybe," she says grudgingly.

Leaning over, she gingerly reaches into the bag on the floor, and pulls out a sandwich wrapped in plastic. Some sort of liquid dribbles off the end of it, and she holds it out over the bag so it won't drip on her clothes.

"Darn it." Her voice couldn't hold more disappointment than if she'd lost a favorite earring.

Finding a tissue in her purse, she uses it to delicately dab at the soggy package and peel away the plastic wrap.

"No, wait, it's okay." Her face lightens. She takes a bite and sighs with contentment.

"I can't believe you wouldn't leave without that bag. How can you eat at a time like this?"

She stops chewing and stares at me, eyebrows rising toward her hairline. "I'm hungry."

Her open-eyed innocence and chipmunk cheeks make me laugh. I can't help it. After a moment, she laughs, too, and soon we're teary and struggling for breath. For that brief span of time, all is forgotten. Even when laughter subsides to giggles and silence, the mood is lighter.

"I got you one, too," she says, leaning down again. "What a mess. There's coffee spilled all over everything."

The mention of coffee suddenly makes me aware that the smell of it has awakened a growling beast in the yawning cavern that is my stomach.

"No, wait a minute. This one didn't spill."

Dana holds a paper cup aloft in triumph. She pats down the exterior with tissues and hands it to me. I sip from it gratefully. It's terrible coffee, but it's still warm, sweet and caffeinated.

"I will have a sandwich," I tell her, "if you have an extra."

"Plenty. I told you, I got one for you. Turkey's okay I hope."

I nod. "Great. Thanks."

She dries and unwraps the sandwich in silence, and waits until I've holstered the coffee in a cup holder before handing it to me. There's little sound except the two of us chewing for a while, so her small voice takes me by surprise.

"Um, I'm not very good at this, but thanks."

"For what?"

"Well, I guess that's three times now you've saved my life."

I shrug and feel warmth creep up my neck. Seems I'm more uncomfortable accepting a compliment than she is dishing one out. I'm about to suggest that she would have done the same thing in my place when I realize that I don't know what she would have done. I don't know this person at all. Both of us obviously have secrets, but I'm taking her on faith. Given the number of rookie mistakes I've made since this morning that might be a bad idea. For the time being, we're stuck with each other.

"Seemed like the right thing to do," I finally murmur.

*****

It's two in the morning when Nate calls back. We're just outside Columbus, Ohio, and Dana has been asleep for hours. His voice is a warm and familiar beacon in the dark, though a little deeper than I remember, and I'm glad of the company.

"How are you?" he asks after I catch him up on our progress. I hear genuine concern in his voice.

"Tired. And a little frustrated." I tell him about our earlier adventure getting away from the Russian and Dana's now ex-boss a second time. I know I have to pin her down in the morning about the boss. I don't know many bosses who'd wage that kind of vendetta against a subordinate. There's obviously a lot she hasn't told me.

"You're okay to drive, though, right?" he says.

"Yeah, fine. If I start dozing off, I'll wake up Dana and let her drive a while."

"You're okay with that?"

"Why not? Where's she going to go? She's headed in this general direction anyway, even if she won't tell me where, exactly."

"I suppose. I might do a little background research on your friend. She is asleep, right?"

I listen to Dana's gentle snores. "Like a baby. So what have you found out?"

"Nothing good, I'm afraid. So, what I did was work backward. We know Costanza got on the train in D.C. Amtrak security cameras confirm it. We ran facial-recognition software to see where he'd been before that. We have him on foot in a couple of places on a track leading northwest from the station, so he walked from a neighborhood up there somewhere. You know D.C., so 'Adams Morgan' and 'Woodley Park' will mean more to you than me."

"Wait. What do you mean you ran facial recognition? On what? You have Mick on camera?"

"You're with the FBI, Jenny. I assume you know how many cameras there are in D.C."

"Well, yeah, but most of them are on city or federal security networks, like D.C. traffic, DHS and the U.S. Park Police. You need a warrant. Don't tell me you hacked into someone's network, Nate. Wait! I don't want to know."

He chuckled. "Boy, it has been a long time since we talked. More than half my business these days is government contracts. I have clearance. Way higher than yours."

"Clearance doesn't give you permission to surveil someone. I'm already in trouble. I don't want you getting screwed, too."

"Still pretty easy to get a judge to sign off on a FISA warrant." He pauses, but I don't bite. "Okay, so I fudge a little if someone asks and say it's part of another project we're working on. The point is that we don't have to rely on traffic cameras. Practically every new LED streetlight in D.C. has either a video camera, audio recording for

ShotSpotter, infrared sensors or all three. Doesn't matter. What I'm trying to tell you is that our software spotted Mick as a passenger in a town car coming out of Rock Creek Park about two-thirty yesterday morning."

I try to make sense of what he's telling me, but my head feels full of sludge. I need more coffee. "Sorry, I don't follow."

"Cummings? You know, congressman from the land of Lincoln? That's about the time he was killed."

"Oh, shit. Wait, you don't think Mick...."

"I ran a background check on him, Jen. Solid service record after high school. Multiple tours in Iraq and Afghanistan. Didn't re-up after his last tour. Probably not officer material. Practically no record of him after he got back. A couple of odd jobs that didn't last long and he fell off the radar."

It happens all the time. Some people—guys, mostly—don't adjust well to civilian life after spending time in a combat zone. They see too much that goes against everything they've been taught, everything they've experienced during their upbringing in the freest and richest country in the world. Those visions haunt them. I had no illusions about what I was getting myself into when I joined the army, or law enforcement, for that matter.

When I turned sixteen and got my driver's license, I'd come home from school and turn on the police scanner in the house. If a call came in that Dad or Bruce responded to, I borrowed the family car and drove to the scene to watch them work. Surreptitiously, or I would have caught hell from Dad. I never told him. As well prepared as I was for what I saw in Baghdad, the atrocities there still rattled me, etched themselves into my memory and scarred my soul. But it was what I signed up for. The ones who came home with PTSD never imagined, never prepared for, what they saw.

"Why would little Mickey Costanza be mixed up in something like that?" I can't get the picture of my kid brother's friend—wide grin, broad, freckled nose, jug ears—out of my head.

"Hired help, I'm thinking." He lets me chew on the idea. "Facial recognition ID'd the driver, too. George Kovacs. Served in Iraq with Costanza."

"Could be they were out reminiscing about old times."

"Yeah, except for the town car. Plates trace back to a shell corporation in the Cayman Islands."

"So you don't know who the car belongs to or who these boys might be working for."

"True. But we do know the town car is presently leased to a private club in D.C. that, interestingly enough, is owned by a different shell corporation in the Caymans."

"And the club...?"

"Very chi-chi. No way to get a list of members, but rumors say that the clientele is international, and only the top echelon powerbrokers and social elite get in."

"Who are we talking about?"

"Don't know for sure, like I said, but a few senior senators, a couple of Saudi princes, the Russian ambassador...."

"How do you even know this? I've never heard of it."

"I run in different circles than I used to."

Clearly, Nate's voice isn't the only thing about him that's deepened. This is a self-assured tech guru I'm talking to, someone who's grown comfortable contracting with powerful entities, not some nerdy whiz kid. I always knew he'd make something of himself, but he's far surpassed where I imagined he'd end up. I don't know why I'm surprised. I feel a twinge of guilt inside that I haven't followed his career nearly as closely as he seems to have followed mine. I force my thoughts back to the matter at hand.

"Who runs this place?"

"Not sure of that, either. The general manager is a fellow by the name of Philip Stevens, but he reports to someone else who stays largely behind the scenes. Benton Sykes, according to my sources. Keeps a very low profile."

"Nothing on his background?"

"Guy's a cipher."

My mind leapfrogs from one lily-pad thought to another, trying to make sense of all this.

"Can you get your hands on a photo of either of these two?"

"I can try. I'll text them if I do."

"Nate, any suggestion this club is tied to the *Organizatsiya*?

"The Russian mob? Not that I've heard. It's possible, I suppose. But then your people would be all over it."

He has a point.

Another question bubbles up in my head. "Did Kovacs come with the car?"

"I suppose."

"Okay, let's assume he's the chauffeur," I say. "Drives club members wherever they want to go. Picks up VIPs at the airport. He probably sees and hears a lot in that car. So he and army buddy Mick—who we know from our own school days—cook up some scheme. Blackmail, maybe. They squeeze Cummings and something goes wrong. Cummings ends up dead."

"Sounds plausible. But it doesn't tell us who killed Mick."

"No, it doesn't." I feel a sudden chill, as if a ghost has passed through me, and I shudder. "From what Dana's told me, whoever killed him was either one really sick individual, or he wanted something Mick had. He tortured Mick before he killed him."

"On an Amtrak train? Pretty bold."

We both fall silent, lost in our own thoughts. He finally breaks it.

"What else can I do, Jen?"

"You've already done way more than I asked. I can't thank you enough."

"No thanks necessary. What are friends for?"

I squirm at his use of the word "friends." A friend would've at least called once or twice in a decade, and I didn't even do that since I ran out on our marriage. I never even gave it a chance, never considered it any more than a convenience to get me out of Small Town, Wisconsin, like a Russian mail-order bride. At least he didn't say "husbands."

"Really, though. You've done enough. My God, what time is it there? You've already stayed up too late on this. Just call me in the morning if you know anything more about why Cummings was murdered."

"No problem. I'm usually up at this hour anyway. And I'll text photos as soon as I find some."

"Thanks. It's good to hear your voice."

"Yours, too. I've missed you, Jenny."

I feel heat rise into my face, and my tongue stumbles over an answer. I mumble a quick goodbye and start to disconnect when I hear his voice call out.

"Jenny? They're still after you, right?"

"Someone is."

"I'm coming to help. I'll meet you at your Dad's in the morning."

"Wait. Nate—"

He's gone before I can object.

And it's already morning; dawn is only a few hours away.

63

The car rolled to a gentle stop, the crunch of gravel under the tires bringing him up out of an uneasy sleep. Sykes opened his eyes to near total darkness, disorientation bringing on a momentary sense of panic. He blinked until his eyes adjusted, first picking out shapes—the curve of the steering wheel framed in the windshield, treetops off to his right. Slowly, he discerned more details—the ghostly white stripes marking the center of the road out the left-hand window, a row of fence posts marching up the hill along the other side of the road, stars in the sky behind them. Lastly, he saw movement, shadows shifting at the base of the trees that slowly took on the shape of men approaching the car. He counted six as they spread in a semi-circle around the car from front to back.

His unease grew as he realized the men carried guns, some with rifles, some with handguns. He instinctively reached inside the lapel of his coat for his own pistol, but his fingers encountered only soft cloth, not hard steel. He patted down his other pockets—all empty. Wondering where his gun went, he looked around his seat in a panic.

Where the fuck is George?

The men outside advanced until they stood thirty feet from the car. He slid to the far side, away from the guns that rose to point at him, and yanked on the door handle. Locked. He threw his shoulder into the door as he pulled on the handle again. The door didn't budge.

Nastase. So, it's come to this. What you sow, so will you reap.

He faced the dark figures outside and squared his shoulders. Muzzle flash from their guns lit up the night, and the explosive sounds reached his ears at the same time the windows shattered.

With a gasp, Sykes woke from the dream bathed in sweat. For the first time since his days doing wet work he could actually smell his own body odor, his own fear. He looked around to get his bearings. He sat in the back seat of the parked town car, where he'd spent the better part of a day. George was nowhere in sight. Sykes glanced at the simple, elegant Patek Phillipe on his wrist. Nearly three in the morning. Directly in front of the windshield stood a dozen gas pumps. So, a refueling stop. He opened the door and climbed out, back and joints stiff from sitting for so long.

Stretching first, he walked in a small circle next to the car to get his blood moving. The night air had grown cold enough that Sykes could see his breath. He jammed his hands in his pockets and pulled the coat tighter around him. Turning at the sound of a bell jangling, he saw George emerge from the convenience store, a plastic sack in each of his big hands. George strode rapidly to the car and set the bags on the roof to open the driver's door.

"Got coffee and water for both of us," he said. "A couple of sandwiches, too, if you're hungry. Want the coffee or water first?"

Sykes nodded his thanks. "Coffee, in a minute. Men's room first."

"Sure." George turned and leaned into the car with the bags as Sykes headed for the door. Inside, Sykes locked the restroom door behind him and stripped to the waist, carefully hanging his clothes on a hook on the back of the stall door. He washed himself as well as he could with hand soap, lukewarm water and paper towels. After relieving himself, he washed his hands once more and got dressed.

George had the car running and a cup of coffee waiting for him when Sykes got back in the town car. As soon as he settled back, George smoothly pulled out of the gas station.

Sykes took a sip of the hot liquid and felt it warm him inside on the way down his throat.

"Where are we?"

"Maybe thirty minutes outside of Indy."

"You've made good time. I didn't realize I slept so long. You must be tired."

"I'm okay. Thanks."

Back on the freeway, Sykes watched the sky brighten as they approached the city. Traffic was light at that time of morning, but he noticed that George kept the town car's speed about five miles per hour over the limit. Other cars occasionally passed in the left-hand lane. Sykes nodded to himself. George may not be the brightest bulb, but he was a good driver and knew when he could push it and when to hold back.

He leaned forward. "I'll take one of those sandwiches."

George glanced at him in the mirror. "Egg salad on whole wheat, or turkey and avocado on ciabatta?"

"The turkey, if you don't mind."

George fished in one of the sacks on the seat next to him and passed back a wrapped package and a stack of napkins. Sykes took it and settled back contentedly. George unwrapped a sandwich for himself and took a large bite.

After chewing for a moment, he swallowed and said, "When I was a kid, I always wanted to be a 'peterinarian' when I grew up. You

266

know, a veterinarian, but for pets—cats, dogs, maybe hamsters. Not like a vet in the country that works with livestock."

Sykes listened to the prattle with half an ear, wondering where George was going with it.

"Strange where life takes you," George said. "When you were a kid, ever think this is where you'd end up? I mean, no disrespect, but is this what you wanted?"

Sykes peered at him keenly now. "What, exactly, do you think 'this' is? I'm a successful businessman, no different than a thousand other CEOs. It's the American Dream: pull yourself up by your bootstraps and make your fortune. You have an issue with that?"

George rubbed the back of his neck with a big paw. "No, I only meant... I mean, we're out here in the middle of the night chasing down some skirt who probably didn't see nothing and don't know nothing."

Sykes felt his blood run hot, but when he spoke, icicles dripped from his words. "No, you're driving me to Wisconsin to help retrieve property that was stolen from me."

"See? There, that's what I mean. It's a phone. You killed a man over a phone. Like some street punk."

The veins in Sykes's neck pulsed and he clenched his jaw to contain the fury that boiled up inside him. He gripped the edge of the seat to keep his fingers from reaching for his gun, the feel of its weight assuring him that it rested securely in its holster, and turned to stare at the passing cars in the opposite lanes.

"I...I mean, not that you're a punk, Mr. Sykes," George stammered, realizing his mistake. "Just that it...well, it seems beneath you. Like you could've handled it some other way."

Sykes sensed his fear, could smell it. "Are you questioning my judgment, George, or my principles? You don't think Mick deserved the punishment I meted out? What, I should have only cut off his hands like they do in Arab countries?"

"I...I don't know," George mumbled.

Sykes studied him and let his anger cool. "Are you growing a conscience, George? You have some regrets about working for me?"

"Nah, that's not it. I like working for you just fine. I just..."

Sykes let the silence grow heavy. "Any time you want out, George, you just say the word."

"What? Walk away?"

"Well, after all, what would you say that wouldn't put you in jail for life? You held the camera that recorded Mick killing Congressman Cummings, right?"

"Sure. Yeah, I would never say nothing about you, or the club or any of it."

267

Sykes folded the wrapping over his sandwich and put it aside. He'd lost his appetite for the time being.

"I know, George. I know you'd never talk out of school." Sykes imagined the pistol in his hand, his finger on the trigger, an itch waiting to be scratched. Of course George wouldn't talk.

Dead men never do.

64

Dana heard voices, faint and distant. She thought they were calling her name. Just when she was about to approach an Adonis she'd been discreetly pursuing through the sun-drenched Greek countryside for most of a morning. Annoyed, she stopped, cocked her head and cupped a hand to her ear, glancing at the dusty track behind her. Nothing. She faced forward again, but the beautiful man-child had disappeared. She hurried forward, but the voices started again, stopping her in her tracks. She listened intently, and inexorably the voices grew more distinct, pulling her up into the blue Greek sky and out of her dream.

"...you ran facial recognition? On what? You have Mick on video camera?"

"You're with the agency, Jenny. I assume you know how many cameras there are in D.C." She recognized the voices now and saw no need to open her eyes. It was just Jenny talking to her husband on the phone. Nothing to worry about. But the incongruity of spending their ten-plus-year marriage apart brought her that much closer to full consciousness so that their topic of conversation finally registered. Video cameras. Everywhere. Keeping her eyes closed, she listened more attentively.

The voices faded as another part of Dana's brain worked on the tidbits of information Jenny's conversation had given her. *Security...video...facial recognition...cameras....*

Of course.... Jared had sent her copies of the cancelled checks deposited into the accounts she believed were suspect, the accounts where the embezzled money had been funneled. The checks were stamped with date, time and location of the deposit, along with coded bank information such as routing number, and so forth. Security cameras at each of those locations would have captured images of the person who deposited the checks at the moment they were time-stamped. A video record of the person responsible existed. Toby thought the person on those security camera images was her. All she had to do was access those images.

The voices intruded once more. Seemed there wasn't a lot Jenny's husband couldn't do when it came to computers and cyber security. Maybe, just maybe he could find a way into the bank systems that recorded videos of the thief depositing checks stolen from the foundation. She'd find a way to broach the subject with Jenny in the morning. Again, she wondered why and how Jenny could have let a guy like that go.

The vision of her Adonis popped into her head, and she let herself succumb to drowsiness and fall down through the clear Greek sky to go look for him.

65

Dawn had come cold and clear to the Midwest, high pressure pushing all the rain east, and now the sun was high enough that it warmed the interior of the car. Alexei cracked his window, letting some of the chill back in to keep him from falling asleep. He took a sip of water from the bottle in the cup holder, swallowed and winced. Putting the bottle down, he gently touched the bruised skin on his neck, and adjusted the mirror to catch a glimpse of it, wondering how badly it showed.

That fucking *bliyadischa*—that whore—had come up on his blind side last night and nearly killed him. It must have been her. Who else would have tried to stop him from taking the woman Sykes wanted dead? If he hadn't seen her strike at the last second and turned, her hand would have struck him in the larynx and crushed it. He would have been asphyxiated. As it was, he would have trouble eating for days.

She was good, too good. Alexei was a street brawler who'd learned a few dirty tricks. His size worked to his advantage, making most would-be assailants think twice before taking him on. The woman had been trained, and she carried a weapon. To Alexei, that suggested she was a cop of some kind, but she hadn't acted like a cop. She hadn't tried to arrest him or call in back-up either time they'd met. So, private security? Unallied, or unemployed?

It didn't matter now, since his objective had changed. He was unlikely to see either of the two women again. Only sheer luck had given him the opportunity to make good on the original job, and he'd been so dumbfounded and so excited at seeing the target that he hadn't even thought about the lookalike woman from the hotel. Fortunately, no one other than the two women knew he'd failed, and he certainly wasn't going to tell Sykes or Nastase what happened. If anyone noticed his bruised neck, he'd think up some plausible explanation.

Despite the sunshine, the flat, featureless countryside depressed him. He found it hard to believe anyone would live in such an environment given a choice. Perhaps with the green of summer instead of bare fields and brown, leafless branches of the few trees that stood in random copses, the Midwest would be more bearable. Maybe he just needed the hustle and bustle of a city with its glass- and steel-walled canyons, its hordes of people always moving with purpose to or from somewhere like ants in a colony.

His phone rang before his thoughts turned truly maudlin, and he gladly snatched it off the seat.

"*Da.*"

"Good morning, Alexei. I trust you're well." Nastase.

"Yes. All is well, thank you. And you?"

"Quite well, thank you. Ready to see what this *balvan*, this idiot Sykes is up to. The flight is boarding now. It's scheduled to land at eight-fifteen. Will you be able to make it in time?"

Alexei held the phone away from his ear and checked the time. "*Da*, I think so."

"*Spasibo*, friend." Nastase rattled off the airline and flight number. "See you in a couple of hours."

66

Movement darted across his peripheral vision. Instinctively, Toby tapped the brakes, sure that a dog or a deer was about to bound into the lane directly in front of him. But when he turned his head toward the impending disaster, he saw nothing coming across the median and nothing in the opposite lanes except normal traffic. He took a breath and unclenched the fingers that had turned white gripping the steering wheel.

He shook his head. Exhaustion had brought on the hallucinations half an hour earlier. He'd drained the last of his coffee a few hours before that, but he couldn't afford to stop for more. At least not until the gray sedan half a mile ahead of him decided to stop. He wasn't even sure he was following the right car, but in the bright sunshine of a new day, he didn't dare get any closer.

When he'd found the Russian's car gone from the service station parking lot the night before, Toby had nearly panicked. Not knowing what else to do, he'd gotten back on the interstate and put his foot down, pushing the BMW up to ninety, quickly overtaking traffic on the road, desperately trying to peer into every car that looked remotely like the Russian's as he passed.

After a harrowing twenty minutes, he'd finally come up behind a sedan with a single occupant in the driver's seat outlined by the lights of oncoming vehicles. Toby had passed to try to get a look inside, but could see little other than that the driver was large. Since the Russian had seen him earlier, he couldn't risk a closer look.

Maintaining his speed, he'd gotten far out in front of the car, and had taken the next exit. Immediately finding the entrance ramp, he'd waited on the shoulder until he'd seen the sedan drive by. He'd been following it ever since. The one time it had pulled off the interstate to gas up, Toby hadn't wanted to risk getting too close, but had gotten close enough to the station to see the driver get out to pump gas. The man's size and suit had matched what Toby recalled from the encounter at the hotel.

He was well past the point where coffee would do any good, he decided. If he didn't want to fall asleep at the wheel, or lose his focus and miss the sedan pulling off the highway, he needed to move to stronger stuff. With a free hand, he rummaged around in the center console until he felt what he was looking for—a plastic baggie with his drug stash.

He always kept a supply of various pharmaceuticals—ecstasy, Ritalin, Valium, oxycodone, Phenobarbital, roofies, a little hash, some blow—on hand for fundraisers and client events. You never knew when a potential donor in the mood to party just needed a little push to sign a big check. Toby rarely did any drugs himself except a line of coke now and then during an event just to keep him at the top of his game. Though he had used the roofies on occasion, slipping them into the cocktails of a few of the more attractive young women who'd come to fundraisers unchaperoned, taking care over the course of the evening to watch over them, cater to their needs, and eventually cull them from the herd.

He fished an Adderall out of the plastic bag and swallowed it dry. A surge of rage coursed through his system, and he suddenly realized why he was tailing the Russian, the real reason he felt compelled to find Dana and kill the bitch. He didn't care what she did or didn't know about the missing money. He cared that she'd turned him down. More than once. She'd rejected him. And for what? For no good reason. He was intelligent, well off, connected, a pretty decent looking guy, and damn good in bed. Who the fuck was she to reject him? She deserved to die. That's why he was on this fool's errand, driving halfway across the country on some Russian's bumper. He needed this.

The effects of the amphetamine started to kick in, making it easier to focus on the thickening traffic of morning rush hour. The big city skyline rose above the horizon miles ahead, many of its buildings—the former Sears—now Willis—Tower, the John Hancock, the Aon Center originally built as Standard Oil headquarters, the Prudential Building, the new Trump Tower—all so iconic that even though he'd never been here it seemed unmistakably Chicago.

Soon, cars and trucks ran bumper-to-bumper then slowed to a stop and expanded again like Slinky Dog in the Toy Story movies. Stuck so far behind the Russian's car that he couldn't see it, Toby got edgy, and cut from one lane to another when he saw openings to move ahead, drawing the ire and honking horns of two or three other drivers. When he finally drew close enough to see the sedan about six cars up in the next lane, he breathed a sigh of relief and stayed where he was.

By the time he reached downtown, traffic had picked up speed again as commuters exited, and he let the gap between his car and the gray sedan grow. He wasn't even sure it was the right car anymore, but he didn't have much choice at this point. The sedan continued heading northwest at the junction of the Kennedy and Edens expressways, and Toby sat back and relaxed somewhat, readjusting to cruise mode. The Russian surprised him, though, exiting toward O'Hare Airport.

Toby wondered why the man would drive all the way to Chicago only to take a plane somewhere else. But the Russian headed straight for the terminal, passing up chances to park. Smacking his forehead with the palm of his hand, Toby realized he must be meeting someone. But who? Surprising him again, the car stayed in the right hand lane leading to Departures. His chest constricted, and his pulse shot up as dread filled him again that he'd followed the wrong car. His heart sank as the realization hit him that he might have driven all this way for nothing. He had no choice now but to play it out, so he followed the line of heavy traffic heading in to disgorge passengers bound for early morning flights.

When he saw the sedan pull up in front of Terminal 1, Toby immediately swung to the curb well behind it and waited. Feeling conspicuous without a departing passenger, he looked around nervously. Sure enough, in the rearview mirror, he saw a cop at the end of the terminal slowly walking toward him along the edge of his lane, motioning drivers in the cars standing at the curb to move along if they weren't letting a passenger out. He turned his gaze ahead. The sedan hadn't moved. Toby stood his ground, keeping his eye on the sedan. The cop had covered half the distance the next time Toby checked. He tapped the steering wheel with his finger, and felt sweat roll down his sides under his shirt.

The rap on his window only a few moments later nearly made Toby jump out of his skin. He hadn't been keeping close enough tabs on the cop, and now a tall, beefy man in the uniform of Chicago's finest was motioning him to roll down his window. Toby gathered his wits and pushed a button to lower the window.

"You have to move, sir," the cop said. "No parking or standing."

Toby thought fast. "My wife is saying goodbye to a friend inside. She's coming right out."

The cop shook his head like he'd heard it all before. "You have to go around, then. Let's go."

He stood, waiting, until Toby put the car in gear, turned his signal on, and pulled away from the curb. Toby drove slowly, avoiding cars that darted to the curb in front of him. When he checked his mirror, the cop was already busy moving other cars along. Toby picked up a little speed and passed the sedan. The driver faced the terminal, not giving Toby a good look, but he was the right size. Toby's panic lessened slightly.

He saw curb space at the far end of the terminal, and swung his car into it. Leaving the motor running he waited again, knee bouncing up and down uncontrollably with nervous energy. Nearly five minutes went by before he glanced in the side mirror and saw the sedan pull away from the curb. He slid down in the seat until he could barely see over the lip of the window, watching the sedan approach in the mirror until it drew abreast. He turned to look and as the car went by, his eyes met the gaze of the passenger, a middle-aged man almost as large as the Russian with Slavic features—sharp cheekbones, strong jaw, thin, cruel upper lip, heavy lidded eyes. The man's gaze passed over Toby as if he were invisible. Toby sucked in a breath as he sat up, and checked traffic behind him before pulling out and following.

WISCONSIN

67

I experience momentary confusion when I open my eyes. My mind grasps at wisps of a fast-fading dream that features Machowski, my team leader Terry Hunt and a Citation CJ4 corporate jet. But the reality of the SUV solidifies under my sore—but cute, I'm told—butt, and the jet engines turn to road noise in my ears. I wet my lips and croak a question.

"Where are we?" My voice sounds as if I swallowed a wood rasp. I twist open a water bottle and take a sip.

Dana glances at me from the driver's seat, and quickly shifts her attention back to the road. Her hands grip the wheel at the classic ten-and-two positions, her shoulders tense. I can tell she hasn't had much time behind the wheel of a car, but when she offered to drive an hour after dawn, I gratefully accepted.

"We passed Madison a little while back," she says.

I blink the sleep from my eyes and look out the windows. The rolling pastures and crop fields, shorn, fallow and brown, interrupted by copses of oak and pine are capped by a brilliant blue sky cinched with a band of fluffy cumulus clouds on the horizon. It could be any of a dozen or more Midwestern states, but it feels like home to me, as quintessentially Wisconsin as cheese curds.

"You want me to drive?"

"It's okay." She lifts her shoulders. "I'm not tired."

"Let me know if you want to stop."

She nods without taking her eyes off the road. "How much farther?"

Billboards advertising the Tommy Bartlett Show, Dells Boat Tours and Dells Bells Wedding Chapel flash by, indicating we're getting close to—what else?—Wisconsin Dells.

I guess. "About an hour and a half."

Tourist season now long over, the Dells are quiet, empty. On an impulse, driven partly by curiosity and partly by a nagging feeling of being too exposed, I direct Dana off the interstate. We cross the Wisconsin River and cruise through the center of town, past the kitschy attractions and tourist traps—mini golf, paintball arcades, souvenir shops, fun houses, themed restaurants, and cheese shops on every block.

Once out of town, the terrain shifts again. I remember my grade-school state geography lessons. We're driving on the bed of a glacial lake that covered the middle third of the state. The soil is sandy, and the road is lined with more white and jack pine, as well as a few aspen, white- barked birch and tamaracks in brilliant fall colors mixed in with the scrub oaks. The tracts of trees are interspersed with miles of empty fields, some crisscrossed with snaking irrigation pipes centered in the hub of large wheels, idle now until summer. If it weren't for the trees, I think this part of the state would be as featureless as the Great Salt Desert.

But the flat horizon is misshapen occasionally by a sandstone mound that's been eroded by water and wind over the eons. Rarer, but soon to be more prevalent, are mesas and buttes that rise above the ancient lakebed like sentinels. They are still as familiar to me as the skin I live in. They are the Sunday summer picnic areas and afterschool playgrounds of my youth—Roche-A-Cri, Rabbit Rock, Ship Rock, Friendship Mound, Minnie Rock, Petenwell Mounds, Cottonville Rock, some on private property that we accessed with a wink and a nod from the owner, my father being the county sheriff and all.

Glaciers scoured the higher ground to the west; rocky, forested ranges of hills with valleys of pasture and cornfields between them run all the way to La Crosse and beyond the Mississippi River into Minnesota. The huge rivers of ice did the same to the east of the state, creating ridges and lowlands, essentially a huge moraine, a large swath of which is filled with "kettles," holes created when ice deposits left behind by the retreating glacier melted. Most of these are now good-sized lakes like Geneva and Elkhart. But the Central Sand Plains, as the state DNR—Department of Natural Resources—calls them, are as recumbent as flat-earthers believe the whole world is.

After a half-hour of this scenery, Dana finally breaks the silence. "You grew up here? Didn't it drive you nuts?"

"What?" I ask even though I think I know what she means.

"There's nothing here. It's like nobody lives here."

I don't dispute her point. I'm wrestling with mixed emotions the closer we get to our destination. My inner child takes delight in the well known, comforting scenery of "home." But now I'm more terrified of ghosts from the past than the elegantly-dressed assassin who nearly killed me less than twenty-four hours ago. At least I've been taught how to deal with the latter.

"I suppose that's why you left," she says a few minutes later.

My train of thought is so far down the tracks that it takes me a moment to remember what she's referring to.

"There were a lot of reasons," I murmur.

While the drive must seem hellishly long to her, it passes in a blink for me. We come upon landmarks so quickly I almost don't have time to warn Dana to slow for a turn onto an upcoming county road. From the turn, it's less than a mile to the gravel drive, bordered by trees on one side and grass on the other, that leads to a sturdy, old, two-story farmhouse—the house I called home for Act I of my life. Seeing it virtually unchanged fills me with a swell of feelings—joy, sadness, excitement, anticipation, trepidation—that brings me to the verge of tears. I blink them back ferociously. I'm not a child anymore.

"This is it?" Dana says, tires crunching to a stop as she brakes in front of the door. "This is where you lived?"

I nod. "It belonged to my grandparents, and it passed on to my mom when they died. They'd sold off most of the farmland before then since no one wanted to take it on. But they still had the house and about forty acres it sits on. We moved in when I was a baby."

We both get out, and I stand there a moment taking it in, listening to the SUV's engine tick in the silence as it cools. An eagle cries somewhere in the distance. Dana turns a full circle and looks at the house again.

"What did you do all the way out here?" she says.

I lift a shoulder and let it drop. "We made our own fun. Wasn't hard with four brothers and a lot of places to play. Plus, we could ride our bikes into town."

"How far is that?"

"Six or seven miles."

She regards me uncomprehendingly, as if I've suddenly switched from English to French.

"Where's the barn?" she says. "I thought farms had barns, and tractor and stuff."

I turn and point. "Across the road. My grandfather liked to keep home and work separate, and wanted the house closer in to the trees. Besides, keeps the bugs away. Barns attract flies. That all belongs to someone else now."

I walk over to the wrap-around porch, lean over and feel for the spare house key hanging on a nail under the stairs, no doubt another concept that Dana finds foreign. A lot of folks up here still don't lock their doors at all. My fingers find the key, and I step up to the front door and unlock it.

I crook my arm and wave my fingers. "Well, come on in."

She looks up at the house again, then climbs the stairs and walks through the door. I put the key away and follow her in. After the bright sunlight outside, the interior seems dim, and I stop to let my eyes adjust. The rooms come into focus as if transitioning from the unsubstantial nature of a dream to the defined edges of wakefulness. Everything is exactly the same as I remember it. Living room on the left, fireplace with oak mantelpiece centered on the far wall. Two beautifully carved wooden duck decoys sit atop the mantel, all that remain of my grandfather's decades-long hobby. Dining room on the right, oak table long enough to comfortably seat eight, ten in a pinch, surrounded by high-backed chairs, framed, faded antique botanical prints hanging on the walls.

Dark stained pine floors in the entry lead to stairs in the same material and down a hallway past them. A tall, narrow hall table stands opposite the stairs with an untidy collection of mail on its surface. At the end of the hall sit a large kitchen and a den, with laundry room and mudroom off the kitchen, and screened porch off the den. A half bath separates the two rooms.

I can picture the four bedrooms upstairs, two with twin beds for the boys, my parents' room, large enough to hold a king-size bed that replaced the twin beds my strait-laced grandparents slept in, a smaller room that had been mine, and two bathrooms. Nothing fancy, but big enough to hold us all, and comfortable enough to protect us from cold Midwestern winters and hot summers. I find it hard not to slip into a dissociative state. I've stepped into a time warp where the past decade or so doesn't exist. I know that only the house and its contents are fixed in time, not the events outside it.

Still, I have to shake off the sudden feeling of age regression and remember who I am now, and what has led me here.

I step into the hallway past Dana and gesture toward the stairs. "You're welcome to go up and shower. The small bedroom in the back corner is—was mine. You might even find some clothes that fit if you want to change into something else. Make yourself at home. I'm going to make some coffee, and then I have some things I have to do in town."

"You're going to leave me here?"

"Not for long. Don't worry. You'll be safe."

I never saw signs of a tail after we left Virginia, and I don't see how else we could be tracked. Then again, I haven't had much sleep. She doesn't look convinced.

"Most people around here know this house is where the sheriff lives," I assure her. "They tend not to mess with it."

"Gee, that's comforting. What if your dad comes home before you get back?"

"Introduce yourself." My remark doesn't elicit a smile. "I plan on seeing him when I'm in town. I'll explain what's going on."

Finally, she nods and heads up the stairs.

Twenty minutes later, the shower is still running as I head out the door. I call my little brother Billy on the way to town. He's the only family member I've really spoken to since I left.

"Hey, there," I say when he answers. "I'm home. Did Dad tell you?"

"Yeah, he mentioned it."

"Where are you? I'm headed into town."

"In my office—the diner, where else?"

"I'll meet you there in a half-hour. Will you still be there?"

"Unless I get a bond jumper in the next thirty minutes, yeah, I'll be here."

I drive to the grocery store in town first, and buy two small bouquets of flowers. Mums or marigolds, I'm not sure which. I'm not good at this. A few minutes on the other side of town, I turn into a cemetery and stop. It's changed, but I know where to go, and the headstones are easy to see in the bright sunlight, now filtered by high gauzy clouds. After a minute or two of walking across the closely-cut grass, still browned from the heat of summer, I find what I'm looking for. Two small headstones, maybe five by twelve inches, sit almost flush with the ground a yard apart. Only names and dates are carved on each, no memorials or tributes. Those who knew them knew what sort of people they were, and memories of them evoke far more emotions than a word or two cut in stone.

No one, least of all a fourth-grade girl, should have to attend the funerals of two family members within a month of each other. No one ever said life was fair, but nothing could have been crueler to these two people and the family they left behind than their deaths. I talked myself out in the years after, laying my grief and curses and tears on their grave markers. Now all I have to offer is an apology to each for the long gap between visits.

I place the flowers next to each stone, smiling at the irony that neither named person resides beneath the soil at my feet. We scattered my mother's ashes at the top of the rock formation at the back of our property, a place that she loved where she has a view of the creek and countryside below. And my brother's remains added an infinitesimal amount of height to the pitcher's mound on the field where he—and I—loved to play.

I don't know if they exist in any sense of the word anywhere in the cosmos. Certainly not in a form that can see my physical form or sense my thoughts and conflicted emotions. But the simple gesture of gifting their spirits with something beautiful makes me feel better. And with my stomach now tied in knots about what's to come, I can use all the happy juice I can find. I take a deep breath and turn to go meet the baby of the family.

The diner in town is old-school—vinyl-upholstered chrome stools at the counter, hard, molded plastic booths, padded seats wrapped in the same brown vinyl, with Formica-topped tables between them, floor checkered with linoleum tiles, photos of local celebrities and athletic teams, trophies and other memorabilia mounted on the walls, an American flag prominently displayed above the back counter over the soda dispenser, chalkboard menu over the pass-through window from the kitchen, jukebox in the corner, long, bare fluorescent light bulbs on the ceiling tinting everything a little blue-green.

Billy sits in a booth midway down the left wall, facing the door. He lifts his chin in greeting when he sees me, a smile spreading across his face. He looks the same, yet grown up, stopping me in my tracks for a moment until I can take it in. We've exchanged photos over the years via text, but seeing him in person is a shock, reminding me of how much time has passed. He's not a kid anymore. His face is leaner, harder, though still youthful, and while his grin comes as readily as it used to, I see a greater alertness, wariness, in his eyes. I realize I'm a fool for not visiting over the years and taking in the changes more gradually, more naturally. But I'm pleased to see him, and I hurry to the table.

He stands to give me a hug, and I see that despite becoming an adult, he's not much taller than I am, unlike Robbie and Bruce, who I remember always towering over me, even when I graduated from high school. He's lean and wiry, ropy muscles standing out in forearms bared by rolled up sleeves of his plaid shirt. A fleece vest, jeans and Green Bay Packers ball cap complete his outfit, a de facto uniform in this part of the country. Mom would have made him take the hat off inside I think as I sit across from him. But I'm not her.

He looks at the table, his face flushing, suddenly shy, and brings his gaze up to meet mine.

"I wasn't sure I'd recognize you," he says. "But you not only look like your pictures—better, in fact—there's no mistaking the family resemblance."

He's right, of course. I most closely resemble—resembled—Doug, the brother nearest to me in age, but none of us knows how Doug's features might have changed in adulthood. Billy's face is enough like the one I see in the mirror to know he's related, but he has more of Mom in him than I do.

"It's good to see you. How are you?"

He shrugs. "Can't complain. Enough assholes around jumping bail that I'm keeping my head above water. I know most of 'em, or their relatives, from high school, so it's not too tough. You know. Like, Bobby Morris's cousin was arrested on a DUI a few weeks ago. The other day he was supposed to appear in court but didn't show. The judge issued an FTA—a failure to appear—and since he was out on bail, Frank Chernanski, the bondsman, calls me. I call Bobby, who tells me his cousin is probably holed up with a girlfriend over in Baraboo. I drive over there and pick him up."

His shoulders rise and fall again. "No big deal. So how 'bout you? Why'd you come back?"

"Dad didn't tell you?"

His eyebrows knit and he shakes his head. "Communication is pretty much on a need-to-know basis with me and him. Guess he figured you'd rather tell me yourself."

I sigh. "I'm on leave. Officer-involved-shooting. It was clean, but my team leader won't own up to his own mistakes, so he let me out to dry. Sitting around my apartment for two weeks waiting to find out my fate would have driven me crazy, and I didn't know where else to go. Besides, it was time. It's been more than ten years."

"Closer to fifteen, Jen."

There's still a smile on his face, but I hear something in his tone that sounds like resentment. I let it go, and focus instead on his words. To my surprise, I realize he's right. And horrified that I've let so much time go by.

"I take it you haven't seen him?" he says.

"Not yet. I wanted to see you first. How is he?"

"The same." He pauses. "Hell, I don't know. Older. But he hasn't changed much. Of course, I don't know what the bad blood is between you two. And I don't know what he was like before Mom passed, either. Got nothing to compare him to. What do you want me to say?"

I keep my mouth shut, tamping down a reply.

"Besides, like I said, he doesn't talk to me. He looks like he's still in good health, and he seems to like his job. He's held onto it long enough."

Suddenly, I see him in a different light. "I'm sorry if I've put you in the middle all these years. I didn't mean to. I never thought...."

He waves a hand. "I get it. Look, I'm happy you kept in touch. Bruce and Robbie...well, they're so much older we never had much in common. Dad's okay, but if you remember, he kind of checked out after Mom died. I grew up mostly on my own. You always made me feel like I was part of the family, at least."

"Thanks," I murmur, feeling self-conscious. I change the subject. "Do you remember a guy in high school, Mick Costanza?"

He startles, then answers with a wary tone in his voice. "Yeah, why?"

"I take it you don't watch much news."

"No, not my concern. What about Mick?"

"He's dead. Murdered yesterday on an Amtrak train out of D.C. The one I was on. Killer thought I saw something and came after me."

"Holy shit!" His eyes widen. "Does this guy know who you are? Where you were going?"

I start to shake my head and stop. "I don't think so, but I'm not sure of anything. The woman who actually did see something drove here with me. We were on the road all night."

He pushes the cap up his forehead and scratches his head. "Man, this is weird. I haven't thought about Mick in years. After he joined the service, he blew out of town, and I never heard from him. He left a message on my voicemail yesterday. Said he couldn't talk, but he'd call again in a few days."

My pulse races. Mick reached out before he died. "Nothing else?"

He stares into the middle distance, concentrating. The little bell over the door behind me jangles, and I crane my neck to see a man dressed in a delivery-service uniform coming in with a package in his hand. He heads to the counter and hands the package to a woman behind the register. She signs his handheld scanner. As he turns around, he spots us, and his head bobs in recognition.

"*Yo*, Roberts," he calls as he walks.

Billy's eyes focus and he turns his head. "Hey, Bart, what's up?"

"I dropped off a package at your place a little bit ago. Best get it before someone else does."

"Oh, shit, I better," he says, sliding out of the booth.

"You can't stay a while?" I say.

He looks at me. "Lot of desperate people out there now stealing shit off people's front porches. Nothing's safe, or sacred, anymore. Besides, Dad'll be here soon for late-morning coffee if he's not out on a call. Since he knew you were coming, I'll bet he's staying close."

"You're avoiding him?" My own stomach started flopping like a perch on a hook at the thought of seeing him.

"Not exactly. We just give each other space. It's easier."

"Guess I'll see you later then."

"Sure. Give me a call."

He flashes me a grin and follows Bart out the door.

286

68

Sykes had managed a couple of hours of uncomfortable, restless sleep in the back seat. But he felt decidedly out of sorts as he surveyed the sleepy Wisconsin town. It represented everything he'd hated about his own life growing up and so much more—struggle, hardship, worry, hunger, pain.... All of that was compounded here by the glaring lack of refinement and culture. Even as a poor kid in New York he'd had access to one of the world's great storehouses of knowledge, the New York Public Library. And he'd been surrounded by art, sculpture, music, architecture. The most anyone would find here in the arts might be a country or polka band in a roadside bar, and hog-calling at the county fair in the summer.

His disdain for this part of the country and the people in it made him even more prickly. He itched for the old days, the release the kill brought from the tension, the build-up of cold rage. He almost wished one of these yahoos in a pickup truck would do something stupid like cut them off or ride their bumper like a New York cabbie just so he could get into an escalating altercation. Maybe even subtly antagonize the poor yokel into throwing the first punch, or better yet, brandishing a weapon so Sykes could kill the motherfucker in self-defense.

"Well, we're finally here," George said wearily.

"Yes, I can see that." Sykes couldn't keep the sarcasm from dripping off each word, and for the briefest moment, he even felt bad for taking out his pique on George. He knew George must be even more exhausted than he was.

If the mockery stung, George gave no sign of it. "Where to now?"

"The high school. You can drop me off there."

George nodded and didn't ask for further instructions. He fiddled with the navigation screen, and turned right at the next traffic light, half a mile up the street on the outskirts of town. Another half-mile down the road, the high school appeared on the right. George turned in and made his way slowly up to the main entrance.

Sykes climbed out, but leaned back in before closing the door.

"You look beat, George. Go get some coffee for both of us, freshen up somewhere, scout a decent place for lunch if there is such a thing in this burg, and be back here in an hour."

"Yes, sir. Thank you."

George pulled away as Sykes walked up to the door and stepped inside, the first time he'd seen the inside of any school since his own high-school days. The nature of his job back then had given him a lot of free time, and he'd spent much of it reading, devouring books of all kinds— philosophy, psychology, history, novels. He read the classics in literature from Shakespeare to Rand, Hemingway, Steinbeck and Faulkner. Science he learned from Newton, Darwin and more recently Stephen Hawking, among others. By the time he saved up enough to make the down payment on the club, he'd probably read enough to earn a half-dozen college degrees. He'd had no need for school after twelfth grade.

His footsteps echoed in the empty hallway as he looked for the administration office. He caught sight of his reflection in a pane of glass and changed direction mid-stride when he saw a restroom. He stepped up to the sink and took a closer look at himself, then splashed cold water on his face, wiping the sleep from his eyes and dried saliva off his chin. He washed his hands and combed his hair with his fingers before drying his hands and face. Satisfied, he straightened his tie and walked out in search of the office again.

Just steps away, he saw a sign on a door indicating he was in the right place. Sykes put himself into character and opened it. A matronly woman with lustrous chestnut hair grown out to reveal gray at the roots commandeered a desk big enough to block access to offices behind her. Plump fingers hovered over a computer keyboard, her gaze focused on a monitor standing a little off center. She glanced up at him over the frames of cheaters perched on her nose.

"Help you?" she said curtly.

"I hope so," he said softly, making her lean forward to hear him. "Please excuse my appearance. I've been traveling all night and just got into town. I wondered if you keep copies of old yearbooks, and if I could look at them."

"Oh, are you an alumnus?"

"No." Sykes let his face fall. "I don't know how to put this. I've been putting off this trip for too long. You see, a few years ago, my son came home from the service. He'd been killed overseas."

"I'm so sorry."

He waved away the apology. "Thank you, but you needn't apologize. It wasn't your fault. My son became good friends with someone he met in the service, but he never told me the friend's name. Or if he did, I must have forgotten. I never expected to have to remember. All I know is that he is from this area and graduated from this high school. He'd be about the same age as my son, so I have an idea of the year he might have graduated. If I could look through the yearbooks, I might find his name. I'd like to try to find him, ask him about my son and what happened to him."

"Of course, of course," the woman murmured. "We keep old yearbooks in the school library. I can give you a visitor's pass and send you down there. The librarian will be able to help you."

She opened a drawer and pulled out a name badge sticker and slid it across the desk along with a three-ring binder opened to a log-in sheet. She gave him direction to the library as Sykes chose a pen from a bunch in an empty mug on the desk and signed a fictitious name on the log-in. In large block letters, he printed "Ben" on the label, peeled off the backing and stuck it on his lapel.

He was about to step through the door when she stopped him with a question.

"Wait. How will you know if you've found him? How do you know what he looks like?"

Sykes patted the breast of his coat. "My son sent me a picture of the two of them. His friend can't have changed that much since high school, do you think?"

Without waiting for her answer, he closed the door behind him and followed her directions to the library.

When he explained what he wanted, the librarian helpfully steered him to the stacks holding the school's yearbooks, Stevens had provided Sykes with the year of Mick's graduation. Sykes picked that year's tribute as well as those for the three previous years. He carried the pile to a quiet table in the back of the library and sat down to slowly page through each one, starting with what would have been Mick's freshman year. The work was painstaking. Most of the photos had been shot by students on inexpensive cameras. Snapshots, really, that didn't reproduce well on the printed page. He scanned photos, stopping to check captions when a face seemed familiar.

He hit the jackpot in the third yearbook he opened. Toward the back in "Spring Sports," he found a shot of Mick in a four-by-two-hundred-yard relay passing the baton to a teammate. Mick's face turned up in the second row of the team photo on the next page, a goofy grin on his face, his arm slung around the shoulder of the kid next to him. Sykes studied the grainy picture carefully, cautiously tamping down a flicker of excitement. The other boy had a hand on Mick's shoulder, too. Letting his gaze rove to the caption, Sykes found the kid's name—W. Roberts.

Sykes closed the book and opened the last one, turning first to the back to find the sports section. He quickly riffled through the pages until he found "Track & Field," and perused each page slowly. His stomach knotted with disappointment when he didn't see Mick's picture on his first pass. When he went back through the pages again, he saw "Billy Roberts" in a group of runners straining for the finish line of a hundred-yard dash. Another speedster, apparently. In another photo, a wide-angle shot of the track's final curve and straightaway, Sykes suddenly saw Mick standing in a group of runners in the infield at the edge of the track, looking down toward the curve, their faces in profile, cheering on their teammate. And though not as chummy as in the previous year's photo, Mick and the Roberts kid were again standing next to each other in the team picture, big smiles on both their faces. Buddies. Exactly what Sykes had hoped for.

He closed that last book, put it on the pile and got up to take the yearbooks back to the stacks. On an impulse, he went up to the desk and asked the librarian if they shelved phone books anywhere, figuring the odds against it were enormous. No one he knew used or even had a phone book anymore. He doubted any of the younger employees in the club even knew what one was.

"Oh, goodness," she said, "we should. They're in the reference section. Sometimes they get 'borrowed' even though they're not supposed to be checked out. They'd be right over there, bottom shelf."

She pointed to a shelf against the wall with a desk in front of it. He thanked her and walked over to look. He didn't see any current directories, but found one that was a couple of years old. He thumbed through the pages until he found "Roberts," then scanned down the many listings until he saw "Roberts, William." After fishing his phone out of his pocket, he entered the name, number and address listed as a new contact. He put the directory back on the shelf, pocketed his phone and thanked the librarian on his way out, a smile on his face for the first time since he'd awakened in the car.

Less than thirty minutes later, he sat in the car and drained the last of the coffee George had brought him while he stared at the farmhouse down the road. George stood outside, bent over the open engine compartment, pretending to fiddle with a non-existent problem as Sykes weighed whether or not to go straight at the house without knowing anything about its occupants or the lay of the land here. He was tired and impatient. So far, he'd seen no sign of life at the house, no cars in the drive, no movement in the yard.

He rapped on the window, then opened it as George straightened and turned toward him.

"Let's go, George. Doesn't look like anyone's home, and it doesn't feel right. Why would a guy Mick's age live way out here in a house this big?"

"Maybe he's got a wife and six kids," George said as he eased his bulk behind the wheel.

Sykes barely paid attention as he typed the name William Roberts and the town into the browser on his phone. He ignored all the listings

290

for "public records" and zeroed in on one at a professional networking site. When the search results popped up, he gave a little grunt of satisfaction. Billy Roberts was listed as a bond-enforcement agent, but styled himself as a bounty hunter. Same thing, he knew, but the bounty hunter tag had a lot more machismo attached. It also meant Sykes needed to exercise caution; Roberts probably had a concealed-carry permit.

With a little more searching, Sykes found a bail bondsman listed a block away from the county courthouse.

"Where to, Mr. Sykes?" George asked.

Sykes read off the address.

69

Dana had actually begun to relax. The combination of a long, hot shower, clean clothes, a cup of coffee from the pot Jenny had brewed in the kitchen, and the quiet peacefulness of the bucolic setting had settled her nerves, had made her feel so removed from city life and the events of the past 24 hours that she'd finally felt safe.

That sense of security quickly was shattered by the sound of tires crepitating on gravel. Silently moving on bare feet to the living room, she looked out the window, careful to remain out of view. A county sheriff's SUV came up the drive and stopped in front. She should have felt relief, but the thought of being around cops still made her nervous.

Her unease grew when the uniformed deputy who got out of the driver's side appeared too young to be Jenny's father, and increased even more when the passenger door opened to discharge another man about the same age dressed in civilian clothes. He slung a backpack over one shoulder and met the deputy at the front of the SUV where they spoke a few words and shook hands.

Dana watched the deputy get back in his vehicle, turn around, and drive out to the road. By the time she turned her attention back to the other man, he was out of view, and she suddenly heard the sound of a key in the lock at the front door. Panicking, she looked around wildly, searching for a weapon in case she needed to defend herself. A voice in her head told her to stop, that someone in the company of a sheriff's deputy was not a bad guy, but her emotions had been so rattled and her nerves so frayed in the past day that she was beyond listening to reason. Spotting a set of fireplace tools, she quickly grabbed a poker and warily advanced toward the front hall as the door opened.

"Hello?" the man's voice called.

Dana raised the poker over her head, as the man stepped inside and shut the door. He turned and froze when he saw her, eyes blinking rapidly. His expression of surprise dissolved into a smile, which turned Dana's fear to anger. *Does he think I'm not serious?* She raised the poker even higher and waved it menacingly.

"Hey there," he said. "You must be Dana. I'm Nate."

She shook her head in confusion, thinking maybe the coffee

293

hadn't kicked in yet. She knew she'd heard that name... Suddenly, she felt herself flush.

"Oh, my God. Nate? Jenny's Nate?"

His smile broadened as she let the poker fall to her side. "I wouldn't say I'm Jenny's, exactly, but yes I'm that Nate."

"How did you get here?"

"One of my company's jets is small enough to squeak into the airstrip outside of town. I flew up this morning from Kansas City."

"You called the sheriff for taxi service?"

He laughed as he set the backpack down by the hall table. Dana liked the sound of it. It was unselfconscious and came from down deep. As he straightened and stepped into the light coming from the living room windows, Dana saw that he stood about six feet tall and had a well- proportioned body—broad shoulders under a gray sweatshirt, slim waist, muscular legs packed into snug, worn black jeans. He had a shock of unruly brown hair that somehow managed to look carefully mussed. His face wasn't leading-man handsome, but attractive enough. Real, Dana decided, a little boyish, but creased enough already to suggest he wasn't a kid anymore. She wondered again what the heck Jenny had been thinking when she'd dumped this guy. Dana instinctively knew she'd take a guy like this in a heartbeat.

"I smell coffee," he said, still grinning. "Any left?"

She nodded and followed him down the hall to the kitchen.

"The cop," he said as he poured himself a mug, "is Jenny's older brother Bruce."

"I thought you and Jenny hadn't even spoken to each other in however long."

He chuckled and faced her. "Doesn't mean I can't stay in touch with her family. Wouldn't be smart to invite myself to her dad's house if I was on the outs with her family. She told you they're all cops, right?"

Dana nodded, trying to wrap her head around the family relationships. She'd always thought her own family was pretty screwed up, but this one seemed to be messed up in a good way. She didn't know if Jenny would agree, but then she thought Jenny was nuts to have walked out on this guy. She gave up trying to figure it out and suddenly remembered the direction her thoughts had taken in the middle of the night.

"So, you're good with computers, right?" she said.

"I know my way around a keyboard, sure."

Her head bobbed. She took a deep breath. *Now or never.*

"I've got this situation. Jenny told you about my boss following me, right?"

"Sure, I remember."

"He thinks I know something about a lot of money that's gone missing from the foundation I work for. He's not a nice man. He tried to kill me. The only way I'm going to get him off my back and out of my life for good is to prove who embezzled the funds."

"Okay, I'm with you so far."

"I have access to the foundation's accounts, so yesterday I called a guy I know at the bank and asked him to send me cancelled checks written on the account to vendors I think may be fake. I wanted to see if I could figure out who was endorsing and depositing the checks. The names are different, but the signatures look similar, as if maybe the same person signed them."

"Clever, but I'm not sure where you're going with this or how I can help."

"The deposits are all time-stamped and coded with the name and location of the bank. Is there any way to maybe check video cameras at those locations, you know, like at ATM machines?"

She cringed, waiting for him to express ridicule at her suggestion, but he seemed to be puzzling the logistics of how it might be done.

A corner of his mouth turned up. "You probably know that accessing a bank's security cameras requires permission."

Her heart fell into the pit of her stomach. His smile only grew when he saw her disappointment.

"However," he went on, "there may be a couple of ways around the problem. One, I could illegally hack into one of the bank's systems and see what this theory of yours turns up. That approach could get us both in trouble—if I get caught. I haven't been caught yet. Two, I might be able to access different cameras close to the banks you've singled out and see if you can identify anyone going inside or coming out. Three, I can try to convince one of these banks that its security is threatened and get permission to review its camera feeds."

Dana's eyebrows rose. "You'd be willing to try?"

"Why not? You seem like a nice person."

He reached into his backpack, pulled out a laptop, set it on the counter and sat on a stool watching the screen while it booted up.

Dana sidled up behind him and looked over his shoulder. "I'm not sure, but Jenny thinks maybe I took the money, and that's why my ex-boss is so pissed."

"Maybe I'll hold judgment until I find out more. Want to give me some of that bank information you have?"

"Oh, right." She flushed and hurried upstairs to get her phone. When she returned to the kitchen, she pulled up copies of the cancelled checks that Jared had sent her and showed them to Nate. He studied them carefully then started working, fingers flying over the keyboard. The images on his laptop screen changed almost as fast as his keystrokes.

"Ah, we're getting somewhere," he murmured.

His typing continued for a bit before he spoke again.

"I know you're wondering what I'm doing. I probed the security of some of the banks, and found one that I think I can get into. The problem isn't hacking into a system; it's doing it in such a way that you don't leave tracks that lead back to you. I'm almost there, if I can just... Got it!"

A new screen came up, and he typed in some commands. After a moment, he turned the laptop so she could see the screen better.

"This is a shot from an ATM camera at the time of one of the deposits," he said.

Dana leaned in closer and squinted at the image on the screen. The face of the man on the screen wasn't the one she expected, but it was familiar. It took her brain a second to switch gears.

"Oh, my God, that's Greg," she said.

70

"Turn in here," Nastase said.

Alexei did as instructed, and drove into a parking lot. Ahead stood a rustic log building with two entrances. A sign over one said "Office," and the other said "Restaurant." Letters carved into a low wooden sign next to the walkway from the parking lot to the building said "River Inn." A row of small cabins lined up to the left, beyond the building, and Alexei caught a glimpse of sparkling blue-green between a few of them as the morning sun glinted off flowing water.

Alexei pulled up next to the walk and stopped.

"Supposed to be good food, comfortable rooms, and decent fishing," Nastase said. "At least that's what Gorovny tells me. But some people say Gorovny is nothing but a big liar."

"You think we'll be here a while?" Alexei said.

"I want to go home already, my friend, but even if we finish business with Sykes today, look at you. You should have good night's sleep before you drive all the way back to D.C. And me, maybe I go fishing if we conclude business successfully."

"You want me to get rooms?"

Nastase opened the car door. "No, no. All taken care of. I go tell desk we're here, and get some coffee in restaurant while I wait for Gorovny's people to show up. You, I want finding that *durak* Sykes, and learning why he's here and what he knows so far."

"*Da.* I will call you."

"*Spasibo*, Alexei."

Nastase leveraged his bulk out of the seat, closed the door, and walked toward the office. Alexei wheeled out of the lot and back onto the main road into town, pulled out his cell phone, and dialed.

Sykes answered. "What?"

"Where are you?" Alexei said.

"In the middle of this Podunk town in Wisconsin looking for a bail bondsman."

Alexei immediately worried, wondering what kind of trouble Sykes had gotten himself into now.

"What is wrong? What happened?"

"Not for me, you dumb Cossack."

"Watch your mouth," Alexei growled. "You are not boss, and I would be happy to repay you for what happened to Mikhail."

"I told you, not my fault. Find the courthouse in the center of town. There's a bail bond agency just up the block. Meet me there and I'll fill you in."

"Fifteen minutes."

Alexei stomped the accelerator, eager to find Sykes and put a bullet in his head. Less than ten minutes later he saw the county courthouse looming above the other downtown mom-and-pop businesses, and slowed to look for the bail bonds agency and a place to park. He spotted the agency storefront.

As he passed by, he noticed a town car parked at the curb close by, engine running, driver in the front seat. Half a block farther, Alexei saw a space at the curb and turned in. After locking up, he walked back the way he came, noting the businesses on the street—a law firm, insurance agency, tavern, pizza joint, chiropractic clinic, sundries shop—and how busy they were.

The bail bond agency wasn't busy. Alexei stepped into a reception area made dim by closed blinds pulled over the front window. A tall counter was set back a third of the way into the large room. An attempt to elevate the business to respectability had been made where Alexei stood with once plush though downscale vinyl-covered stuffed chairs around a maple veneer coffee table that evoked a 1950s living room. The furniture now stood tattered and coffee-stained, more accurately reflecting the business's true nature.

Beyond the empty counter sat three desks, each fronted by a straight-backed chair except the last, which had two and as a bald, fat man sitting behind it. He wore a powder blue dress shirt open at the collar, making room for the double chins below his jaw. Sykes stood in front of the desk despite the two chairs, and Alexei detoured to peruse the magazines on the table while he listened in on the conversation between the two. From the corner of his eye, he saw that the bald man noted his entrance and had tracked his progress.

"...Frank, is it?" Sykes was saying. "Frank, I have no beef with you. I don't even know you. But I do know that you don't want to have a problem with me. And if you don't answer my simple question, we will have a problem."

"Okay, fine, yes, I occasionally employ the services of the person you mentioned as a bail bond enforcement agent. But he works as an independent contractor, and even if I did know where he lives, I'm not supposed to give you his address."

"Surely you have his address on file here somewhere so you can send him a tax form at the end of the year."

Frank's gaze flicked to Alexei again over the counter, and Alexei shifted nervously. He wasn't sure what Sykes was up to, but until Sykes gave him some sort of signal, he didn't want to get involved.

"Suppose I pay this person in cash," Frank said, "so I don't have to get the IRS mixed up in my business or his?"

"You mean hypothetically, of course," Sykes said.

Frank's head bobbed.

"Then I would be very disappointed in you."

Frank hesitated. "Why do you want to see Billy again?"

"A mutual acquaintance sent him something that belongs to me. I want it back."

"Why not ask your mutual friend? Or call Billy?"

Sykes shook his head. "Billy doesn't know the item belongs to me. And our mutual friend unfortunately isn't in a position to give me the information." He paused. "Look, there's nothing illegal or nefarious about my intention here. I simply want to ask Mr. Roberts for something of mine that was sent to him by mistake."

Again, Frank glanced toward the front at Alexei.

"He can't help you," Sykes told Frank. "He's with me."

Alexei saw Frank's face harden, the words making up his mind for him. He sat up and opened a drawer in his desk with one hand. With the other, he grasped a cell phone lying on top.

"Here's what I think," Frank said. "I've been in this business long enough to know two hard cases when I see them. You clean up nice, but you've got 'criminal intent' written all over you. And you're friend up front is packing, and I don't think he has a concealed-carry license in this state. So unless the two of you walk out of here quietly, I'm going to call the cops."

"No," Alexei said. "No cops."

Frank turned toward him and stood up, hand coming out of the drawer. Before Alexei said another word, two loud pops punctuated the silence, and Alexei saw red spots bloom on Frank's shirt and forehead. Frank's eyes rolled up toward the hole in his forehead and he fell face first on the desk. Alexei saw Sykes slip a long-barreled pistol inside his coat. Not a barrel but a silencer, he realized.

"*Ahueyet...?*" Alexei shouted. "What the fuck? Why shoot him?"

"Lock the door. He had a gun, asshole. Now, lock it!"

Alexei took two strides to the door, locked it, and peered out at the street to see if anyone was coming. Traffic rolled by normally. A sign dangled in the middle of the door's glass pane that said, "Closed." Alexei flipped it so it faced outward. The door had no shade or blinds that he could close, so he stepped away from the glass, where he was less visible.

When he looked to the rear again, Sykes was pawing through a file cabinet behind the desk where the bail bondsman had sat. The body had disappeared, and when Alexei walked around the counter, he saw it had slipped to the floor. He turned up his nose as the smell of shit hit him full in the face from the man's bowels letting go.

"*U tebya cho ruki iz jopi rastut?*" Alexei muttered.

"Speak English," Sykes said, without turning from his task.

"I ask if your hands are growing from your ass. Are you crazy? What are you doing?"

"I'm getting the address that Frank, here, wouldn't part with. Oh, and you're welcome for not letting him shoot your ass."

"We need to leave. Now. What is address you want?"

Sykes sighed. "Some kid, a friend of Mick's. Mick sent him a package. That's why we're here. Kid's name is Roberts, Billy Roberts. Ah, here it is." Sykes pulled a folder from the drawer and opened it. He scanned it quickly, focused in on something on the page, then closed the file and replaced it.

"Now we can go," he said. "You go out the front. I'll call George and have him circle around and pick me up out back."

"First give me address. And tell me when you are going to visit this person."

"I'm going there now, idiot. What did you think? You can follow me."

"Okay, fine. I follow you."

Alexei checked the street again before unlocking the door and slipping out. As he hurried to his car, he pulled out his phone and called Nastase.

71

Trash littered the car's interior, fast food containers, soiled napkins, empty cups, candy wrappers bobbing with the car's motion like so much flotsam on an ocean swell. The small space reeked of garlic, stale gym locker, pepperoni pizza, coffee, urine and sour milk, and no amount of fresh air seemed to remove it. Tomato sauce stained the leather seats, Coffee and a chocolate milkshake had left residue on the carpet. Greasy fingerprints covered the steering wheel, armrests and dash. Not even a thorough detailing would remove all the evidence of this trip. Toby figured the car for a total loss. Might as well drive it into a tree and let the insurance company replace it.

He felt in worse condition than the car. He'd been reduced to something subhuman, a Kafka character searching for some semblance of closure. It had taken all his willpower not to turn into the so-called "inn" where the Russian had dropped off his passenger. The substandard housing afforded by the "rustic" cabins had tempted him more than anything else he'd lusted after in his life. To put his head down for twenty minutes and close his eyes. He felt so tired. But the Russian had driven out of the parking lot, and if he could do it, then Toby was determined to prove he could continue on, too. To keep himself going, he pictured the goal the Russian led him to—that bitch Dana.

After nearly soiling himself during the night, Toby had bought beverages only in wide- mouth glass bottles. As soon as he pulled over to the curb and parked to see what the Russian was up to, he drained the last of the apple juice in one of them, unzipped his trousers, and worked the mouth of the bottle over his penis so he could piss. He felt instant relief. He shook himself to deposit the last few drops in the bottle, accidentally bumped the bottle and spilled some of the contents on his suit trousers. He shouted, cursing the gods who had reduced him to this state. By the time he finished this journey, he'd need a haz-mat decontamination chamber. Now that the suit had followed in the wake of the shoes, they could incinerate the car and everything in it.

He zipped up and wiped off his trousers as well as he could with a fistful of paper napkins. He couldn't remember ever being this miserable. His crotch was moist, he couldn't stand the smell of himself, and his mood was just as foul. He was hungry and exhausted. His wretchedness was so profound that for the first time in his career he felt a small semblance of sympathy for the people his foundation supported. But they were used to their misery. It was the state of their existence. Discomfort was anathema to Toby, and his suffering only steeled his resolve to repay it in spades. Maybe Dana wouldn't be his only victim. Maybe he'd kill them all.

A few moments later, the Russian emerged from the storefront bail bond agency he'd been in for the past few minutes. He looked around nervously as he pulled out his phone and walked back to his car, and Toby wondered what had occurred inside to put him on his guard. A town car pulled away from the curb on the other side of the street and drove past him. Toby watched it in his mirror as it turned the corner behind him. The Russian had gotten into his car, but strangely, hadn't left yet. Toby's senses went fully alert, and his leg muscles twitched in nervous anticipation as he waited.

Minutes passed before the Russian's car pulled away from the curb. Toby let a couple of cars pass by before he swung out into the street and followed. He hadn't gone very far before he saw the Russian turn on a side street. He slowed and did the same. He nearly wet himself again when he saw a town car about a block ahead of the Russian. He suddenly realized that his BMW stuck out like the belly on a pregnant elephant in this hick town. He quickly turned into the first empty driveway he saw, and waited until the two cars turned a corner blocks up the street.

He backed out of the drive, and drove to the corner where the cars had turned. Slowing, he continued straight through the intersection, head swiveling to look down the cross street. Both cars were parked at the curb down the block. Toby pulled over as soon as he could, jumped out and jogged back to the corner, leaving the car running. Chest heaving from the exertion, he slowed and moved cautiously until he had a partial view of the two cars down the cross street.

The Russian and another, shorter man with silver hair and nicer clothes stood on the front stoop of a small house. A cottage, really. Maybe even smaller than his apartment in D.C. He couldn't imagine shoehorning much more into that house than a kitchen, bedroom, bathroom and tiny living room. Toby watched the Russian step to the door and bang on it with the heel of his fist. No one answered, and after another minute, the two men turned and came down the walk toward the street. Toby was about to turn and bolt for his car when the men stopped and faced off, seeming to argue about something. Their raised voices carried down the street, but Toby couldn't make out what they were saying. They apparently resolved it quickly, each turning and walking to his own car.

Toby hustled back to the BMW and had barely buckled himself in when his mirror showed the town car rounding the corner and heading the opposite direction. The Russian's car soon followed. Toby waited and watched until they were out of sight. Wearily, he put the car in gear, made a U-turn, and took up the rear.

He wanted to kill someone. He really did.

72

I take Billy's seat when he leaves and order a cup of coffee. My nerves are already frayed, but I need something to keep me awake. I order some fruit and a muffin, too. I know I should eat, but when it comes, all I can do is pick at it.

Before I'm ready, he's walking through the door. The rational, grown-up cop part of me assesses his appearance, his demeanor. He's not as tall as I remember, probably because I was shorter then. He has more gray hair salted in the short sandy brown cut he prefers, and the crow's feet at the corner's of his blue eyes have spread and grown deeper. He's softer, too, not just at the waistline where he's put on only a pound or two, but in his walk and in the way he carries himself. As if he doesn't have anything to prove anymore. As if he has more self-confidence in who he is, in his experience and his authority. But there's also a certain world-weariness in the wan smile, a weight that presses down on his shoulders. Maybe he's seen too much. I know how that feels.

The smile grows broader when he sees me, and the surprise of it, the genuineness of it, takes me aback. Now my grown-up self isn't so sure about how this encounter will go. And suddenly he's here, standing a foot from the end of the table, handsome in his uniform, clean and creased, as always. I don't know why I expected less. Maybe because Mom spent so much time fussing over his work clothes, making sure that he looked the part.

For all his self-assurance, he regards me warily now, as if I'm some exotic animal he's not sure might bite.

"You think after all this time I could maybe get a hug?"

Now I'm the chary one, but I see only good intentions in his eyes, and I slide out of the booth. With the feel of his strong arms around me and the familiar scent of him, I instantly revert to my five-year-old self, no longer Jenny, soldier, cop, agent, but Jenny, person, woman, daughter before all those experiences that made me who I am.

He gives me a last squeeze then grasps me by the shoulders and holds me at arm's length, his eyes searching my face. He lets go and motions to the booth.

"I didn't know if you wanted me to come," I murmur.

"Why wouldn't I?" he says as he slides in opposite me. "Jesus, Jenny, I've been waiting damn near fifteen years for you to come home."

"You're mad at me." I force the words out.

"No, I'm not mad. I'm... I worry about you. A father's supposed to be concerned about his daughter."

But he objected too quickly in a voice a few decibels more than necessary. He is angry, but as a cop and sheriff he's learned to smother his emotions, deprive them of oxygen so they don't burst into flames at inopportune moments. He does that now, smoothing the knit brows and clenched jaw into an amiable mask.

"So," he says, quietly now, "what did you do?"

I feel my brow furrow. "What do you mean?"

"They don't keep you on admin leave for no reason. You must have done something."

"I didn't do anything," I hear my voice rise, and I try to emulate him, suppress the knee-jerk reaction his off-hand comment elicits. "My god, Dad, give me a break. Cops are always put on leave during a shooting investigation. You know that."

"What I know is that based on the facts of the case, your leave should have lasted a couple of days, a week at the outside."

"Welcome to the federal government. An investigation can take weeks, and even if they managed to finish this huge one that quickly, I'd still have to get square with a bureau shrink before they put me back on duty. And that might be only desk duty until they decide to put me back in the field."

I recite chapter and verse of DOJ recommendations in an attempt to convince myself that everything about my leave is normal.

"It's been weeks," he says. "If it was a righteous shoot, you should be back at work. Since you're not, it makes sense you did something wrong."

"Sure, Dad. Whatever you say. I must have fucked up. Or maybe I just fucked somebody who decided I shouldn't get too uppity. Is that what you think?"

His face goes pale, but his neck reddens. I know I've shocked him, but I'm past caring. The five-year-old me is gone. I'm grown up now.

"I didn't say that, or even suggest it," he says.

"No, you said I must have done something wrong. Why? I'm a good agent, Dad. You don't know me, don't know what kind of a cop I am, but get this straight right now: I would never do anything like that. Isn't it just possible I'm still on leave not because I did something wrong, but because my dickhead of a team leader totally fucked up, and even though I tried to save his ass— hell, I did save his ass—he's hanging me out like yesterday's laundry? Isn't that possible, Dad?"

"Well, I suppose—"

I cut him off. "What the hell? Why can't you back up your own daughter instead of assuming I'm at fault? You're mad at me for running away. Is that it? You're angry that I didn't stick around and take care of you and the boys? I'm not Mom. Never was. And couldn't fill her shoes in this lifetime or the next. So don't put that on me."

He blinks at the verbal assault.

"Mad at you?" he says when he recovers. "I'm not angry. Hurt? Sure. You took off without a word. That stung, but I understood it."

He picks at a napkin on the table while a waitress comes over and sets a mug of coffee down in front of him.

"Here you go, Sheriff," she says.

He glances up. "Thanks, Cheryl."

She looks at me, more curious now that the sheriff is sitting across from me than she was when I sat alone. But our silence makes it clear we don't want company. She turns and leaves without comment.

"I'm sorry, Jen," he says when she's gone. "Maybe I should have been a better father."

I shake my head. My exhausted state has loosened my inhibitions. The words pour out of me without thought.

"We did this for too long when I lived here, Dad. Neither one of us was ever very good at reading minds. From the time I was little I could tell you and Mom had something special. I'll grant you, I had enough adolescent and teen angst going on after she died that I didn't stop to think about what her loss did to you. I only thought about my own loss. But I never blamed you, never thought you were less than the honorable, loving man I always knew."

He doesn't speak. Concern paints his face. Finally, he says, "How are you, Jenny?"

The abrupt change of topic surprises me, but I'm too frazzled to do anything but take the question at face value. "Tired—long trip. A little shell-shocked. But I'm fine."

His expression turns serious. "Really, are you okay?"

He asks as if he knows something.

"Why? What's going on?"

"I heard you might have got mixed up in something on your way out here."

Since Billy said they don't talk much, I can't figure out who told him.

"Yeah, I had a little trouble. You were bound to find out sooner or later—I brought a houseguest."

I quickly run through the events of the past twenty-four hours, sticking to the highlights. He interjects pertinent questions, quickly shifting gears from father to sheriff. When I have him pretty much up to speed, he leans back in the booth and stares at the counter for a bit, thinking.

"I don't understand," he says, shaking his head. "Why didn't you call 9-1-1 when this fellow chased you off the train."

I stare at him in disbelief. "He was trying to kill me."

He raises a hand, palm out. "I get that. But you outran him. Why not call once you saw you weren't being pursued? Why not call it in when you were hitching a ride to Charlottesville?"

"Excuse me for being a little skittish around cops after what's happened to me the past few weeks. I went to the agency field office as soon as I got to Charlottesville and reported in. And see where that got me."

"Jen, you know better. Call it in and the cops can quickly set up a search perimeter. You gave this asshole time to slip away."

"You think I haven't beaten myself up enough about that? Sure, I should have done it differently. Maybe you would have. But you weren't there, and you're not me."

By the time I'm finished, I'm halfway over the table, glaring at him. His jaw is set, and he looks like he's deciding which piece of his mind to give me when I catch sight of Billy coming through the door in a hurry. Dad twists in the booth to see what I'm looking at, but by then Billy's already at the table. He tosses a scuffed and slightly dirty padded envelope on the table and slides in next to me.

"It's from Mick," he says with a chin jut toward the package.

Dad looks at me with a raised eyebrow.

"Don't keep us in suspense," I say, dander not yet cool. "What's in it?"

"A phone." He grasps the envelope and starts to thrust a hand inside.

"Don't!"

Billy yanks his hand back at the sound of my sharp tone.

"That's what the man on the train wants?" Dad asks.

Billy looks at me.

I nod. "Didn't mean to startle you, Billy. Did you touch it when you opened the envelope?"

He shakes his head. "No, just looked inside."

"We know Mick's fingerprints are probably all over it, but we might be able to lift some that will tell us who the killer is."

"Oh, right. Sorry."

A look passes between Billy and Dad, and the air now is not only charged the way it feels right before a thunderstorm, but the pressure has dropped precipitously. Billy always was more impetuous, less disciplined than the rest of us, acting without thinking. I sense the rebelliousness in him now, and I don't have time for old family dynamics.

Surprising me, Dad lets it go and moves on. "Man wanted that phone pretty bad?"

"Bad enough to kill Mick for it," I say.

"Enough to figure out where Mick might have sent it, I warrant."

Now I feel like the dumb one. "You think he'll come here?" Of course he will, to finish what he started.

"I don't know," Billy says. "Been a long time since Mick lived here. Why would this guy think Mick would send a package here?"

I remember what I told Dana, why the Russian and her boss had found us.

"The train. It's a well-known D.C.-Chicago run. Why else would Mick be on it unless he was coming home?"

Dad chimes in. "Better to be on the safe side. I'll put word out to the deputies on patrol to keep their eyes peeled for anything unusual."

"We need to find out what's on that phone, quick," I say. "But I'm guessing it's password-protected."

"We know someone who can probably help with that," Billy says. He looks at Dad, and this time it isn't resentment on his face.

I face my father. "What?"

"Nate's at the house," he says in a quiet voice.

"Wait... How do you know?"

"He called me. I asked Bruce to pick him up at the airfield."

"Nate called you?" I'm bewildered, and a little angry, too.

My father shifts in his seat, and doesn't look at me for a moment. "What can I tell you, Jen? Nate calls me once in a while. He stayed in touch, gave me news—third-hand, I might add—about where you were, whether you were safe. And your brothers filled me in occasionally when you called. What, you didn't think I cared? Didn't think I was interested in what you were doing? Whether you were happy?"

It's too much to process. All these years, I avoided coming home, avoided my family, and the very people I'd run from had conspired to keep tabs on me.

"All these years, you've been in cahoots with my husband even though I ran out on him?"

He stares at me and blinks a few times. Finally, he says, "Nate's not your husband."

The words stun me so completely I'm not sure I heard him correctly.

"You were seventeen, Jenny," he says softly. "You weren't old enough, legally, to get married. Nate told me the whole story. He got a fake marriage license. He wasn't trying to coerce you. He wanted to see if you'd go through with it. It wasn't hard to understand why you did it."

My brain can't process the news. I glance at Billy. His face is tipped down toward the table, but his red face and guilty expression confirm the truth of what my father just told me. I always wondered why Nate never pressured me to have sex with him, to consummate our "marriage." He seemed content with me just sharing his bed and spooning in those few months we were together. It starts to make sense. But more important matters push the revelation out of my head.

"We'll talk about this later," I say through gritted teeth. "If you have the time, Sheriff, I think we should get this phone over to the house, dust it for prints, and let Nate get to work on it."

310

73

"Who's Greg?" Nate asked, swiveling on the stool.

As if she hadn't heard him, Dana muttered, "This doesn't make any sense at all. Greg?" She glanced at Nate. "Greg is my boss's assistant. I don't understand. Why would Toby try to kill me if Greg's the one who was embezzling the money?"

"Because Toby thinks it's you?" Nate said.

"No, no, that's not right. It's Toby. I'm sure of it. Toby's the one who has access to the accounts. Greg couldn't pull this off. Toby just wants everyone to think it's me!"

Nate held up a hand palm out in surrender. "No argument here."

They both started and turned toward the sudden sound of knocking on the front door. Nate looked at her.

"You expecting anyone?" he said softly.

She shook her head violently, her heart now racing.

"Who the hell would knock? Everyone knows where the key is," he muttered.

He stood as another knock came at the door, louder this time.

"Wait here."

Dana knew she should do as he said, but a sense of dread told her something was wrong, and it compelled her to follow Nate down the hall. She ducked into the dining room, out of sight as Nate opened the door. While they spoke, she cautiously peeked around the doorframe at the man outside the screen door. Her eyes widened in horror, and she shivered, feeling as if someone had jammed an icicle down her spine. She clamped a hand over her mouth to keep from screaming.

She wanted to warn Nate not to let the man in, but didn't dare for fear it would betray her presence. She stood motionless, paralyzed, and listened to the beat of her heart grow louder and louder.

74

George steered the town car onto the shoulder and let it coast to a stop. Trees lined the county blacktop on both sides, hemming them in. The sedan followed and stopped yards behind them. Dobrev got out and walked up to the town car. Sykes lowered his window.

"What we do here?" Dobrev said. "Why do you stop?"

Sykes pointed up the road to a break in the trees on both sides of the road. "There's a driveway up there on the left. Leads to a big old house. We came by earlier because it was listed as this guy's address in an old phone book. Now I'm thinking maybe it belongs to his family. Maybe he grew up there."

"So, why would he be there now?"

"If his family lives there, they can tell us where he might be, where he hangs out."

"I don't know. It's risky. One more place where people see your face."

"We find this guy and get my phone back, we're gone. Who cares if people in this shithole see me? They don't know who I am."

Dobrev nodded. "Okay. I wait here. You need help, you call."

"Let's go see if anyone's home," Sykes told George.

George started up the big car, and it purred the short distance to the driveway and turned in. Sykes watched for signs of life as they approached the house, but saw nothing to indicate anyone was home. When George pulled up in front of the front steps, Sykes got out and paused to stretch. Then he went up to the door and knocked loudly on the frame. No one answered. He looked for a doorbell, but didn't see one, so knocked again, louder this time. He was just about to go back to the car to get a lock pick set from his briefcase when he heard footsteps inside. He let his facial muscles relax, and shifted his weight to take some of the tension out of his legs.

The door swung inward, and a pleasant looking man who appeared to be in his thirties stepped up to the screen door into the light. He wore casual clothes—jeans and a crewneck pullover. Sykes thought he caught something on the man's face—a flicker of recognition or flash of surprise—but it was gone so fast he couldn't be sure the screen hadn't distorted the man's features.

"Can I help you?" The man's voice was calm, his manner friendly.

Sykes knew he looked out of place, so he decided to counter the formality of his attire with an informal, personal approach. "I'm looking for Bill—Billy Roberts. Do I have the right house?"

"No, I'm sorry. He doesn't live here."

"Are you sure? This is listed as his address."

The man smiled, and nodded. "Sure, used to be. This is his father's house. He hasn't lived here in a while that I know of."

"And you are...?"

"Family friend. Just visiting. You?"

Sykes matched the wattage in the man's smile. "An attorney," he replied vaguely. "You wouldn't happen to know where he does live, would you?"

"Somewhere in town, I think. I don't know the address offhand."

"You don't know where he spends his time when he's not at work, do you?"

The man shook his head. "Someone in town will probably know if you ask around. It's a small place."

"I'll do that," Sykes said genially. "Thanks for your time."

"Sorry I couldn't be of more help. Can I tell him who stopped by if I see him?"

Sykes waved a hand. "It's quite all right. I'm sure I'll find him."

"Have a good day." The man stepped back and closed the door.

Sykes turned and walked down the steps trying to put a finger on what didn't feel right about the brief conversation. It nagged at him all the way to the car.

75

Alexei leaned against the side of his car with his phone to his ear, watching the driveway down the road.

"How soon?" he said.

"Maybe fifteen, twenty minutes," Nastase replied. "They only arrived a little while ago and they wanted to take a piss and get something to eat."

"Make it quick. I don't trust him. He's too unpredictable."

"You're sure no one saw you leave the bail bond place?"

Alexei turned and glanced down the road. The white car was still on the shoulder maybe a quarter-mile back. Too far to see who was in it, but not too far to see the curved lines of the vehicle. Alexei had a pretty good idea who was driving. He'd seen the car before. Several times. He'd noticed it in town earlier, too slick and too sleek and too damned expensive for most people here. And that had gotten him to thinking about all the other times he'd seen a white BMW, all the way back to the asshole who had crossed a double yellow line to pass him and Mikhail on the way to Charlottesville.

"No one who can cause problems," he told Nastase finally. If the white car and its occupant ever got close enough, Alexei would happily shoot the bastard who had killed his friend.

"Then you should be able to handle Sykes for a few more minutes, yes?"

"And if he leaves?"

"Follow him, of course."

"What if he finds this person with the phone?"

"Stall him," Nastase growled. "Do what you have to. I want that phone."

"Okay. I get it."

Alexei disconnected and slipped the phone into his pocket as he watched the town car turn out of the driveway up ahead onto the road and cruise slowly toward him. When it drew abreast, the car stopped in the road and the rear window lowered with a barely audible whine.

"So, anybody home?" Alexei said as Sykes leaned toward the open window.

"Not the person I want," Sykes said. "Something hinky going on, though. I'm going to stick around and watch the place."

"You watch them, they see you."

Sykes pointed up the road toward town. "I noticed a track into the woods just a little way up the road. George can park the car out of sight and I'll walk back through the woods. You coming?"

Alexei grunted. "I come join you in a minute or two. First, I see if curiosity, how you say, kill the cat."

Sykes shrugged and sat back, the darkly tinted window slowly obscuring him as it closed. The town car pulled ahead and turned into the woods a few hundred yards away. Alexei checked on the white car again—still there—and got back into the sedan. *Time to pay a visit.*

76

I'm furious. Once again, the men in my life have decided what's best for me, but if I don't contain my anger and channel it, they'll be right. I won't be of any use if I act like a "hysterical woman." I wait, jaw clenched, for my father's reply. I'm not an agent of standing at the moment. I have to cede jurisdiction to the sheriff in this case. I want his support—and it would be nice to know my father's got my back—but I'll break the rules and go alone if I have to. Before he decides, my phone rings.

"Roberts," I answer, still staring at my father.

"The guy on the train..." It's Nate's voice. "Medium height? Silver-gray hair? Nice clothes?"

"Yeah, why?" I draw the question out, not sure I want to know the answer.

"He was here. At your dad's house. Stopped by looking for Billy."

"What did you tell him?"

"That Billy doesn't live here. I said I didn't know where Billy lives, which is true, and suggested he ask around in town."

"He left?"

"As far as I know. Showed up in a town car with a driver. Car's gone."

"Dana's there? You two are okay?"

"Dana's a little shook up. Kind of a shock for her."

"Stay there. Lock up tight. Stay away from windows. We'll be there in fifteen minutes." My voice sounds a lot calmer than I feel.

My stomach is in knots, and my heart is pounding. I turn to go, not waiting for permission. But my father raises a hand as he thumbs the mic on his radio.

"Bruce, you there?" he says.

"Yeah, Sheriff," my older brother responds. "I was about to give you a shout. What's up?"

"Could use your help at the house. We may have a situation."

"A lot of those cropping up all of a sudden. Just got word from Chief Lauby in town that Frank Chernanski got shot in his office. Wants help with the scene."

"How bad?"

"Frank's dead. Looks like a pro. One to the heart, one to the head. That's not all. Joe Santucci at the River Inn called in to say a guy with a Russian accent showed up to get a room and breakfast. Twenty minutes ago four hard cases in two cars join this guy for coffee."

My father swears softly. "Damn. We're going to need reinforcements." He thumbs the mic again. "Who's available?"

"No one," Bruce says. "Roy's on a domestic call. Fred's at an accident scene down south. Dispatch just sent two investigators to help Chief Lauby. Tom and Jake are working the burglaries over by Castle Rock Lake. Kyle and Kayleen took one of the dogs down to Grand Marsh to look into a tip about a meth lab down that way. Beth and Jim are in Appleton at that CSI refresher course at Fox Valley Technical."

"That's right. I forgot. And we haven't got anybody off-duty we can call in; Bert's taking his kids to the zoo in Milwaukee. What about state patrol? Where's Robbie?"

Robbie, my oldest brother.

"He got called out," Bruce tells him. "Morning fog caused a big ten-, twelve-car pile-up on the interstate. State's got its hands full."

My father thinks a moment. "All right, see if Lauby's okay, get everyone else to check in, and if no one needs you, get over as quick as you can. Have dispatch send everyone who becomes available as soon as they get free. And if you have time, give your brother a heads-up. Even if we can't pull him away from that pile-up, he'll want to know what's going on." He glances at me. "And be careful, Bruce. Those boys over at the inn could well be ringers the other team brought in. Don't want you to run into them without warning."

"Got it."

My father's still looking at me.

I match his stare. "Now can we go?"

"Nothing else you can tell us about what we're walking into?" he says.

I give my head a slow shake. "I think our answers are on that phone. Whatever it is, this guy chased us across the country for it. He's determined, resourceful and wants to tie up loose ends. Which means we're all in danger."

He nods as if agreeing with my assessment. "Okay, let's roll."

77

He'd held back on the deserted country road, and when they'd stopped, he'd pulled over, too, a good half-mile behind them. Too far to see what they were doing until he remembered the opera glasses stashed in the center console.

He'd bought them for that old hag Ida Rousseau, a filthy rich widow and high-society icon who wouldn't part with a dime for Toby's foundation until he took her to the opera. Toby hated opera with a fucking passion, but had invited her to one of the Wagner Ring Cycle operas, and had purchased two pairs of opera glasses for the occasion, an antique gold pair covered in mother-of-pearl, and a utilitarian black pair for himself, which he kept in the car.

Dressed up in his tux, he'd collected the Widow Rousseau at her Georgetown mansion in a town car, and presented her with the antique pair on the way to the theater. The glasses had set him back a pretty penny, but they'd been a write-off and an excellent investment. The widow had written a six-figure check to the foundation that night, and had donated a lot since, totaling more than a million so far.

He raised the tiny binoculars to his eyes and focused in on the two cars ahead. The Russian was standing in the road next to the town car, talking to someone inside—the same guy he'd seen earlier. After a moment, the town car continued down the road and turned onto a side road or driveway, he couldn't tell which from this distance. With only 3X magnification, the glasses didn't show him much at all, but they were better than nothing.

The Russian didn't move, just stood by his car. He glanced in Toby's direction a couple of times, but Toby didn't think much of it. After all, he could barely discern the Russian, recognizing him more from his size and the gray sedan than from his face. Minutes passed before the town car reappeared on the road and slowly approached the spot where the Russian was parked. Again, the pattern repeated with the big man appearing to exchange words with someone inside the town car, and the car moving on and turning once more onto some track into the woods.

When Toby trained the glasses on the Russian again, he was looking in Toby's direction. This time, Toby squirmed uncomfortably, feeling as if the big man were staring right at him. When the Russian

319

got in his car, swung it around in a wide U-turn and gunned it up the road, Toby yelped in panic and dropped the glasses onto the passenger seat. He'd been made. He had no idea what the Russian might do, but he wasn't going to sit around and find out. With fumbling fingers and thrumming nerves he jabbed at the start button three times before connecting. The engine finally roared to life, and Toby spun the car around on smoking, squealing tires and floored the accelerator.

He'd wasted precious seconds, and the car behind him was coming up fast. Toby knew his car could do a quarter mile in about twelve seconds but wondered if it would be enough to keep the other car at bay. It seemed dicey for a few seconds until he could tell he was out-accelerating the other car.

His shoulders relaxed as he quickly gained distance on the sedan until he could barely see it in his rearview mirror. It finally disappeared altogether. He slowed to the speed limit, and when the Russian's car didn't show up behind him he figured it had given up the chase. Realizing he was only a mile or so from town, he decided to find a side road and pull off to wait a while before heading back just to be safe. Before he could, a small convoy of vehicles approached at a high rate of speed. He checked the speedometer to make sure he was obeying the limit, and watched as two SUVs and a pickup truck blasted by in the oncoming lane.

He did a double take, craned his neck as they sped by and watched them recede in the rearview mirror to make sure. The lead vehicle had county sheriff's markings but ran without lights or siren. The pickup was unmarked. But the last vehicle, a silver-gray SUV, had a rectangle of black tape stuck to the rear window. Toby checked for traffic ahead and behind, then pulled onto the shoulder, swung the wheel hard, and made a fast U-turn.

His day had just gotten more interesting.

78

My father takes the envelope containing the phone—he's the only active sworn law enforcement officer among the three of us—to establish chain of custody. Since he's the sheriff, and we're headed to his house, he takes the lead out on the road, too. Billy follows in his pick-up, and I bring up the rear, the little SUV's engine straining to keep pace with the big vehicles accelerating ahead of me.

There's no traffic on the road save a single white car that passes us going the opposite direction. I'm so wrapped up worrying about what I'll say to Nate when I see him that the car doesn't register until I catch sight of it in my rearview mirror making a U-turn a long way back and following us. I try to recall what I saw when it passed by, whether I could remember the make or model. I know it was newer, more expensive than most cars in this part of the world.

I keep an eye on it as we barrel down the county road. It hangs pretty far back, so I can't tell what it is other than white. As the convoy slows approaching the house of my childhood, I check again, and the white car is gone, apparently turning off at the last crossroad more than a mile back.

Suddenly, we're there, turning in and rolling up the familiar drive, gravel crunching under our tires. We fan out and park, and then there's no time to be nervous.

"Jen, Billy," the sheriff calls as I climb out. We join him at the back of the county SUV. He takes out a crime-scene kit. "Unload the armory and bring it in the house."

"All of it?" I ask. "You expecting a war?"

He whirls on me, and his face is pinched. "I don't know what the hell to expect, but I sure as hell want to be prepared. I'm even more sure I don't want anyone outside getting their hands on this stuff while we're inside. Vests, too."

"Got it. Sir."

Billy opens up the lockbox in back. It contains an extra 12-guage shotgun besides the one racked up front within easy grasp of the driver's seat, an M24 sniper rifle, two AR-15 tactical rifles, a half-dozen flash bang grenades, smoke grenades, and hundreds of rounds of ammunition. Billy slings rifles and Kevlar vests over both shoulders, and I stuff boxes of ammunition into an empty duffle until it's almost too heavy to carry, and we follow the sheriff to his house.

Nate has already let my father in, and he mans the door as we follow with the armaments, closing and locking it behind us. My father is already on his way down the hall to the kitchen, but Billy and I pause to unload the gear in the hallway. I turn to greet Nate. He's smart enough not to move in for a hug, but his smile and greeting are warm, immediately putting some of my fears at ease.

I'm also taken in by the changes in the way he looks. His face is leaner, its features more angular, chiseled. His shoulders are broader, and there's more meat on his lean frame. The boy is gone except in the smile that crinkles the corners of his eyes, and the man that stands in his place is more self-assured than the cocky teen and, I grudgingly admit, far more attractive. Some of the fluttering in my stomach, though, is anger as I remember how he conspired with my father and brothers.

"We need to talk," he says amiably.

"Yes, we do," I murmur. "Later. Right now you have a job to do."

His smile fades and his brows rise. I gesture down the hall, and he precedes me to the kitchen. The sheriff has already gloved up, laid the phone on an old newspaper on the big center island, and is gently swirling a brush with fingerprint dust over its surface.

Pointing at it, I say, "Bad guy's phone. We think. You need to hack it. Can you do it?"

Nate walks to the counter and leans over to inspect the phone more closely. "If it's important enough to kill for, it probably has biometric and password protection. Not simple, but possible." He watches my father for a moment. "Any good prints?"

"Two or three so far."

"You photograph them, and then lift them?"

The sheriff nods. "Context. Photos document where the prints were found. I'll upload them right away to our digital crime-scene-management program and get someone to start looking for an AFIS match right away."

"Do me a favor," Nate says. "Don't lift them. I have an idea."

Dad glances at him, but doesn't ay anything as he turns back to his work, photographing the back of the phone with his own cell phone, then carefully turning the evidence over and dusting the front. Nate circles the island and sits on a stool in front of a laptop I assume is his and is soon absorbed in whatever he's pulling up on screen. Billy has helped himself to coffee and leans against the counter next to Dana. I walk over to the pot and pour myself a mug.

Raising the mug to my lips, I look at the pair and lift an eyebrow.

"You two introduced yourselves?"

They nod.

To Dana I say, "You're sure about the guy who came to the door?"

She shuddered. "After what I saw on the train I won't forget that man as long as I live."

"You told me you didn't get a good look at him."

She leans back, away from my tone, her eyes widening. "Not when he was in the compartment, no. I saw him chasing you off the train."

I sigh wearily. Fatigue is setting in, and I can't afford to lose focus. "Sorry. I'm sure you told me."

Billy assesses the two of us over the rim of his coffee mug, and I wonder if he thinks his big sister is a complete idiot, getting kicked out of the FBI and running home to Wisconsin chased by a well-dressed killer.

My father straightens up and put his phone in his pocket.

"All finished," he says.

Nate raises his head. "Great. Got any wood glue? Or school glue?"

My father looks at him askance and, after a beat, says, "Yeah, that might work. Should be some around here."

"Laundry room," I say. "Art cupboard."

He stares at me in disbelief, but goes to look anyway. He's back less than a minute later with the bottle of wood glue in his hand. He gives it to Nate, and the two of them hunch over the phone on the counter. The three of us crowd in for a look at what they're doing.

"...see here," the sheriff is saying, pointing at a spot on the phone "And here. Both good index fingers, I think."

Nate carefully applies a thin layer of glue to the phone, and waits a moment until it's tacky but not dry. Slowly peeling it off the phone, he looks at it closely and molds the back of it onto his own finger. The fingerprint dust sticks to the glue and will replicate the ridges and valleys of the real finger that left the print on the phone. A clever way to fool the biometric scanner on the phone—if it's the right print.

Dad's radio crackles to life.

"Sheriff, you there?" It's my brother Bruce.

"Yeah," my father answers.

"Just got a call from Joe. His out-of-town guests just bugged out. In a hurry, he says."

"Okay, sounds like we'll have company soon. Could sure use your help."

"I'll get loose as soon as I can. Do you want me to have dispatch pull Roy? Or Tom and Jake?"

I can see he's torn.

"No," he says after a pause. "We're no more important than

anyone else in the county."

"Not so sure about that," Bruce replies, "but I'll let dispatch know to send them here when they're finished with the calls they're on."

"Roger that. Be careful, son." He faces us. "Jenny, go pull the blinds and curtains. Every room, upstairs and down, then get extra vests for our guests. Billy, go unlock the gun cabinet in the den and get a pistol and extra magazines for Nate, here. Dana, is it? Dana, I want you here with Nate. Get him whatever he needs while he works on that phone. If things get ugly, we'll let you know. There's a safe room down in the basement that bolts shut from the inside."

There's no criticism or judgment in his voice, only calm assurance of a man ticking off checks on a planning list. And I barely hear his last instructions as I head for the den after pulling the blinds down over the kitchen windows. But I'm even more angry now, the list of people at whom I direct my wrath growing to include me most of all.

I should have seen this coming. All the pieces were there; I just hadn't put them together. I could blame it on fatigue, or preoccupation with my present non-status as an FBI employee, or the stress of the previous day's events. But that's all bullshit. I have no excuses. I'm an FBI agent—on leave, but still.... This is what I'm trained for.

When I'm finished yanking curtains and blinds closed, I go to the now-open gun cabinet in the den and take out a box of 9mm parabellums, I reload the magazine in my Sig, holster the pistol, and put the box back. Before returning to the kitchen, I find my backpack in the hall and retrieve the two extra magazines I packed, and grab two Kevlar vests. Dad glances up when I enter, sees me nod, and faces the laptop screen again.

"Any luck?" I ask Nate.

He doesn't look up, but the grin that spreads across his face makes him look like the boy I remember. "The fingerprint worked. Got the phone on, then spun up a new virtual phone on the laptop, imaged and booted it. Been working on hacking the password to get into the phone files, and it just cracked. I'm in."

"Good," my father says, climbing off his stool. "Let us know what you find."

"Where do you want us?" I say.

"They're from out of town. They don't know the land." He's thinking out loud. "I'm guessing they'll come at us from the front. If they're smart, maybe come through the woods on the west. Too open on the east side. I don't think they'll try to circle all the way around to the back. Too hard. They'll try to hammer our defenses head-on."

"Could be they don't know what they're messing with," Billy says.

"They'll sure as hell figure that out once they see the Sheriff's vehicle in the drive, now, won't they?" my father says.

Billy gives a pained nod.

"Guns up front," my father says. "Eyes in back. Dana, can you do that?"

"Do what?" She blinks.

"Keep a lookout back here," he says. "Move from here to the mudroom to the den. Watch for movement in the trees, back by the garage, that sort of thing. You okay with that?"

She nods.

"Then let's all put vests on and get ready."

Michael W. Sherer

79

Sykes heard the vehicles long before he saw them, the rush and hum of tires on macadam drawing near and passing by first, then the bite of rubber on gravel up ahead somewhere. By the time he pushed through the undergrowth to a point where he could see through the remaining trees, three vehicles had parked in front of the farmhouse. The one in the middle had a light bar on the roof. An emergency vehicle of some kind, but he couldn't see the markings from where he stood. From the color, not a fire or EMT truck.

Two people pushed through the front door, a man and a woman. The woman in the rear carried duffle bags, but she blocked his view of the man ahead of her. He recognized the woman, and neither she nor the young man who'd disappeared inside wore uniforms. So, the driver of the middle vehicle likely was already inside. Three people, one of whom likely was some kind of cop. And he couldn't underestimate the woman. At least one more person inside.

Snapping twigs and swishing branches signaled George's unconcealed approach. Sykes thought a large bear crashing through the underbrush would be stealthier than George. The big man's expression revealed obvious displeasure with his surroundings. It turned to surprise when he pulled up short next to Sykes.

George stared through the trees, breathing heavily. "Where'd they come from?"

"Where, indeed," Sykes murmured.

The stakes had just gone up. Cop or no cop, he had to get that phone. Without it he was as good as ruined, and if the people inside the house had it and figured out how to hack it, he was as good as dead. Everything he'd worked for was tied up in that simple, elegant piece of technology. And one hick cop and a country bumpkin bounty hunter weren't going to get in his way. He had nothing to lose.

He held out his hand. "Give me the keys."

"You're not going to leave, are you?"

Sykes rolled his eyes. "I need to get into the trunk. And I want to talk to that idiot Russian before we make a move here."

George dug the key fob out of his trousers.

"Keep an eye on the place," Sykes said. "And for fuck's sake call me if anything happens."

Sykes backtracked through the woods almost soundlessly, and came out in the clearing where they'd left the town car. Dobrev's sedan sat parked twenty yards away, on the track that led in from the road. The Russian climbed out from behind the wheel as Sykes walked to the town car and popped the trunk.

"They're here," Sykes said as Dobrev approached. "Where's your backup?"

"I called them. They're on their way. Where is phone?"

"In the house. Go meet your friends and tell them to barricade the driveway in the front with their cars."

"And what you do?"

Sykes reached into a locker in the deep trunk and took out an HK MP7 personal defense weapon, a handy little machine pistol that could empty its 40-round magazine in about two-and- a-half seconds.

"I'm going to go back through those woods and take up a position," he said. "I'll call and ask the people inside to give me back my phone. Nicely. If they don't, we go in and take it."

80

She finished two circuits—kitchen, mudroom, den, kitchen—peering in every direction through every window, the sound of the others loading weapons, familiar from television, drifting back from the front of the house. She turned away from the window and watched Nate's hands fly over the laptop keyboard. She couldn't decipher the scrolling lines of numbers and figures on the screen.

"What are you doing?"

Nate replied without taking his eyes off the screen. "I created a virtual duplicate of the phone so I could crack the password without getting locked out of the phone itself."

"So you're looking at what's on the phone on your laptop?"

Nate frowned. "No. There's a little of the standard stuff on the phone. A few apps, a contacts list. It seems that other than making phone calls, the phone's primary use is linking to a private server. I streamed all this information to my server network back at the office. They have a lot more processing power and should be able to get into this guy's server faster."

Dana shook her head. None of it made any sense to her. She turned back to the window and felt the back of her neck get damp as her heart beat faster. She stiffened as she saw movement, then realized that it was only a branch that had been ruffled by the breeze.

"Damn it!" Nate's sharp tone made Dana jump.

"What's wrong?"

"Whoever set this up booby-trapped it in a half-dozen ways. Maybe more. Kind of like playing a videogame and never getting past the first level."

"How many chances do you get?"

"If I was trying to get into the server itself, I would have been locked out by now. Game over. Fortunately, I have unlimited lives. Once I crack the virtual version, then I can have a go at the real McCoy. Yep, there it is. Gotcha."

Remembering herself, Dana turned back to the window and anxiously scanned in all directions for movement, afraid she'd missed something. Behind her, laptop keys clacked softly. She saw nothing in the woods, the only movement a crow hopping in the grass, scavenging for something to eat, and a hawk lazily riding the air currents high overhead.

Nate swore softly, then called out, "Jen, you better come see this."

Dana stayed at her post until she heard footsteps entering the kitchen. Unable to help herself, she sidled away from the window until she could see the laptop over Nate's shoulder as Jenny joined him. He queued up a video. The scene was so dark that Dana could barely make out a figure lit up in the center of the screen, holding an umbrella.

Jenny bent suddenly and leaned in closer. "Wait, I recognize him. That's Congressman Cummings."

"Wait for it," Nate said. Dana saw movement on the edge of the beams of light centered on the man in the video.

Nothing happened for a moment. Then another man stepped into the light toward the man facing the camera. She saw a flash of silver and the man Jenny said was Cummings went down on one knee with a howl. He looked up, pleading in anguish and pain. There was another flash of silver as the man with his back to the camera raised a bat and brought it down with crushing force on the fallen man's skull. Dana spun away, and quickly covered her mouth with her hand. She thought she might be sick.

"Jesus," she heard Nate say. "Brutal. That square with what you remember about Mick?"

"I hate what the service does to some guys," Jenny replied, "but, yeah, Mick always seemed to skate on the edge. You'd have to ask Billy, though; he knew Mick better."

"Well, now we know who killed the congressman."

"I don't get it," Jenny said. "You told me Mick was with the chauffeur. This is Sykes's phone."

"Actually," Nate said, "the phone just uploads all its content to a server. Had a hell of a time getting in. I picked this file because it's the most recent one uploaded."

"You think Sykes was there when Cummings was killed?"

"From what we know about him, he's too smart for that. Probably had the accomplice stream the video to his phone."

"If Sykes did order Mick to kill Cummings, he must have had a reason," Jenny said. "See what else you can find on that server."

81

Alexei trudged down the dirt track back to the road. It wasn't far, and leaving his car parked behind the limo effectively blocked any attempt Sykes might make to leave. But weariness settled in his bones, weighing him down and turning his legs to lead. This whole affair had gone sour from the beginning, and fatigue now pushed him to the brink of forsaking his vow of loyalty. Volya had been good to him, but was all this worth it? What did he owe Nastase, anyway? Nastase was wealthy and powerful because of men like Alexei. Alexei had given him years of loyal service, and what did he have to show for it? Indigestion, hemorrhoids, and his boyhood friend dead.

He savagely kicked a small branch lying on the track and slipped. His arms flailed, windmilling as he fought to keep his balance. As he regained his footing, he felt a small muscle in his lower back pop. The pain nearly buckled his knees. Slowly straightening, he pressed a hand to the spot and gingerly took a few steps. It didn't seem too bad, but he cursed his luck and his advancing age. He was still sore from being ambushed by the woman. He didn't need to add to his aches and pains. His mood now as foul as his breath, he picked up his pace. As much as he might want to quit, to retire right now and find that island shack, he wasn't about to test Nastase's patience.

Another twig on the track tempted him, but Alexei carefully nudged this one aside with a toe. He blamed Sykes for all of this. He wasn't privy to the details of Volya's business dealings with Sykes, but he knew Sykes owed his boss money, enough to put Sykes in Nastase's pocket. Why Volya continued to grant Sykes favors, though—like loaning him Alexei's and Mikhail's services to track down the kid—mystified Alexei. Protecting his investment, Alexei surmised. But Sykes was dangerous. Alexei sensed he always had been; Sykes had toughness, hardness, under the refined veneer that hinted at a past not unlike Alexei's own. Lately, though, he'd been moody and unpredictable. And this business with Mick had sent him over the edge. Sykes had taken crazy risks and, smelling blood, Nastase had insisted on moving in for the kill. Recklessly, Alexei thought.

His mind churned as he approached the road. He saw no way out at the moment, but vowed he would navigate his way through this situation as carefully as possible. He wanted to live to be an old man.

But whatever happened, Sykes would pay for Mikhail's death, as would the man who killed him, the driver of the white BMW.

Alexei stayed back near the cover of the trees until he heard the distant rush of wheels on pavement. He leaned out to peer down the road, and saw not one car but two in close succession barreling down. When they were still a few hundred yards away, he stepped out into the open by the side of the road. He made no signal. If it were Nastase and the hired help from Milwaukee they would stop. If not, he would attract no attention other than passing curiosity.

The two cars slowed, and the lead car stopped as it pulled abreast, its rear window already rolling down as Alexei walked into the road to greet it. Nastase poked his head out of the open window, but Alexei eyed the two men in the front seat before turning his attention to Nastase. Large men, at least through the chest and arms, both had close-cropped hair and were in their mid-30s. Both wore sunglasses and stared straight ahead, though Alexei knew they'd checked him out before stopping. The driver's hands gripped the top of the wheel, revealing tattoos on all four fingers between the knuckles and first finger joints. Both wore casual dress—windbreakers over a button-down shirt for the driver; a turtleneck for the man in the passenger seat to hide prison ink on his neck, Alexei guessed. Hard cases.

"So?" Nastase said as Alexei neared the car.

Alexei described the situation, pointing out the track he'd taken out of the woods and the driveway a hundred yards down the road.

Nastase nodded. "Okay, I'll let you know when we're in position. You tell Sykes to make the call. We see what happens."

"Yes, we'll see," Alexei agreed.

"Oh, and Alexei, if Sykes gets the phone—"

"I kill him," Alexei said, finishing the thought.

82

Practically every step he took made Toby shudder in revulsion and horror. Trees hemmed him in on every side, and the thick underbrush, despite being half-denuded by the changing season, pawed and pulled at his clothing. His attempts at stealth failed miserably as the uneven terrain and obstacles in his path kept him constantly off balance.

Already he'd walked face-first into a spider's web, found ticks crawling up his overcoat, and nearly swallowed a moth that had surprised him, fluttering furiously off a branch disturbed in passing. Now, he swatted at every twitch of his clothing, twisting away from imagined attacks by ferocious predators, both insect and mammalian. He couldn't imagine how unbearable this place must be in the summer, when the woods were full of horseflies and deerflies and mosquitoes, which he'd heard referred to as the state "bird." His slogging was a little easier now that he skirted the edge of a long narrow strip of pasture adjacent to the road.

When he'd seen that the caravan was leading back to the spot where the Russian and others had stopped, he'd turned off on a side road, knowing he couldn't chance approaching directly. He'd assumed the Russian and the new guy, whoever he was, were still there, lying in wait. And maybe they'd already ambushed the convoy. Toby's only chance was to find another access point. He'd consulted his navigation system after turning, and found that the county had laid out roads in a relatively neat grid where the landscape permitted it. All he'd had to do was traverse three sides of a square and come in from the east.

Wondering why the Russian had picked that particular spot, he'd pulled up an aerial view of the area on his phone and zoomed in. He'd discovered that the limo had turned off on a driveway leading to a house. He'd also found the track where the limo and the Russian had turned off the road into the woods. Noting the farm buildings across the road from the house, and the general topography, he'd formulated a plan to get close and find out what was happening.

As soon as he'd seen the barn and other outbuildings that sat across the road from the house, he'd found a place to get off the road and park. And had started his trek through these impossible woods.

As he struggled through the foliage, he actually heard himself whimpering. Only the adrenaline triggered by each difficulty kept fatigue from forcing him to quit, to turn around, crawl back to the car and flee. Stumbling over a log hidden under leaves and pine needles, he nearly fell onto a trail of some sort. The well-trodden path provided surer footing and fewer obstacles, and Toby felt his spirits lift. He couldn't imagine that people walked out here in the middle of nowhere often enough to create this track. That left animals. Toby shuddered to think of what kind he might encounter.

As if to frighten him more, the brush ahead rustled, and a branch arching over the bushes on the side of the trail swayed. Toby froze and held his breath. The muffled crackling grew louder, closer. Suddenly, the tall, thick grass at the edge of the path parted as a short, fat black creature waddled onto the path, heading straight for Toby.

Toby slapped a hand across his mouth to muzzle his shriek of terror. The startled creature raised its snout and emitted a squeal of its own when it spied Toby. Then it turned tail and started to scamper down the path in the opposite direction. That's when Toby saw the wide white stripe down the black fur of the creature's back. *Skunk!*

He recoiled in horror as a cloud of mist rose from under the creature's raised tail and drifted down the path toward him. The smell reached him before the cloud rolled over him, giving him just enough time to backpedal and crash through some bushes alongside the trail deeper into the woods.

He ran, branches whipping his face, leaving welts, barking his shins as he tried to jump over fallen tree trunks, churning legs carrying him only ten or fifteen yards before his toe tripped on something unseen. He went flying, and landed with enough force to knock the breath from his lungs. He lay there gasping, knowing that even though the skunk hadn't scored a direct hit, he wouldn't get the smell out of his nostrils for days.

When he finally sat up and took an inventory of his bumps, bruises, and scrapes, he realized his humiliation was complete. He couldn't sink any lower. There was only one thing left for him.

Now more than ever, he was determined to kill Dana or die trying.

83

"Who's Cummings?"

Billy's voice startles me. I wasn't aware that both he and my father followed me into the kitchen and have been silently watching the video over my shoulder. My father turns and strides out of the room without a word, his mouth a grim line. I focus on Billy.

"Congressman from Illinois," I say.

"Not good," he mutters.

"Billy," my father calls. "Get in here."

Billy's face pinkens. He gives an apologetic shrug and heads down the hall. The sound of something heavy scraping the floor drifts into the kitchen. Curious, I follow Billy. He's rushing to grab the other end of a sideboard from the dining room that my father is dragging toward the front door. As they place it up against the door, my father's gaze meets mine.

"Don't just stand there," he says. "Move whatever you can in front of the windows in the living room. Billy, let's get the couch over here, too."

I haven't moved. Exhaustion is fogging my brain, and his precautions seem over the top.

"We're cops," I say. "You expecting a military assault?"

He stops, straightens and puts his hands on his hips. "He shot at you, didn't he?"

"I never identified myself."

"I saw the video," he says. "You said this man killed someone to get that phone back. He's chased you all the way from Washington. Yes, I expect an assault. I don't think this guy gives a rat's ass if we're cops or how many of us he puts in a box. Now, move."

I'm still incredulous, but I automatically respond to the familiar ring in his voice and hurry into the living room. I drag a heavy easy chair to the front window and go back for another. I stack the coffee table and end tables on top of the chairs. They've already stolen the couch. As I turn to survey what other furniture I can move, the sound of crunching gravel reaches my ears. Hardly daring to breathe, I step to the side of the window and pull the curtain back an inch. Two sedans have driven halfway in from the road and are jockeying so they are angled nose to nose across the driveway. Bright, filtered sunlight reflects off the darkened glass of the windows, making it hard to see who's inside, but from the movement I discern, there are large men in each.

"We have company," I call out.

"I see them," the sheriff responds from the dining room across the hall. "Might be a good time to check your loads and body armor. Billy, see to it that the civilians in the kitchen are strapped into some Kevlar and get them down on the floor. Might get busy soon."

I hurry to the pile of supplies we dumped on the hall floor, checking my gun as I go, and pick out a vest that, though too big, fits well enough. Then I return to the stake I've claimed in the living room. For what seems like hours, I hear nothing but my heartbeat.

There are footsteps in the hallway and Billy calls out, "I'm going upstairs, see if I can get a good vantage point."

Silence falls again, and with it a heavy mantle of dread. Somehow, I've managed to put everyone truly close to me in deadly danger. I don't know anything about the cars outside or the men in them, but the events of the past twenty-four hours have snowballed, and we are about to get hit by the avalanche.

Suddenly, a phone rings. I frown. It isn't mine. The sound is coming from the kitchen. "Jen?" Nate calls. "I think maybe you ought to get this."

I hustle to the kitchen. Sykes's phone rings on the counter, the vibrations shifting it slightly. Footsteps clatter down the stairs and in the hallway as Billy and my father join us. I look around at the anxious faces and swipe the screen to answer, but say nothing.

There's a moment's hesitation, then a man's voice intones, "Whoever you are, you have my property. I'd like it returned. You have sixty seconds to send someone outside with it and surrender it to one of the gentlemen in the cars in your driveway. Sixty seconds. Otherwise, we will come in and take it."

The call disconnects.

I turn to my father. "Your decision. I'll give it to him right now if you want."

He snorts. "The man tried to kill you already. You think he won't kill you now just because you give him his phone? He has one play—kill us all."

Dana emits a whimper, and clamps a hand over her mouth to keep it from turning to a scream. He ignores her and goes on. "We have two choices: let him, or don't. Frankly, the latter appeals more to me."

He actually smiles, and for a moment I think everything is okay. That he's angry at the asshole on the other end of the phone, at the situation, not at me. But his expression quickly turns somber.

"We just used up about forty of our sixty seconds, so we better get in position. It could be a long fight before Bruce finds reinforcements."

Billy turns on his heel and races out, his boots clomping up the stairs before we leave the kitchen. I glance at Nate, and he flashes me a weak grin and a thumbs-up signal. It's the best I can hope for right now. I pray there's time for apologies later.

On the way down the hall I grab an AR-15 and a stack of magazines. I hunker down behind one of the chairs I pushed in front of the window, lay the magazines on the floor within easy reach, and use the rifle barrel to pull the curtain aside an inch or two.

"They're out of the cars," Billy calls. "And here it comes."

No sooner than he says it, while I'm raising my head to peek out, there's an ear-splitting chatter of automatic weapons fire, glass breaking, wood splintering, and at least one person screaming. The noise seems to go on forever, and by the time there's a moment's respite, I discover that I'm scrunched into a ball on the floor. My heart is pounding against my ribs, my ears are ringing, and my jaw is clenched so tight it aches.

I know the tactic—shock and awe. The army used it all the time. Hit your enemies so hard, with so many munitions that they piss in their pants with fear. In Iraq, though, the enemy's tactics of hit-and-run and roadside IEDs were equally demoralizing, if not more so.

I hear the loud *pop-pop-pop* of guns inside the house, and realize that it's time to shove aside the pre-game jitters and get off the sidelines. I slither up to the window, ignoring the glass shards sticking me through the thick denim fabric of my jeans. The curtain is shredded. I rest the rifle barrel on the sill and raise my head enough to look out and see men bobbing and weaving behind the cars blocking the drive. I lean into the sights, take a bead on one of them and squeeze off a shot, then another. Both miss, but the *whang* of bullets on metal is enough to drop him to the ground. Sporadic and strategic shots from upstairs and across the hall are keeping other heads down, too.

Suddenly, more automatic weapons fire erupts, from a new direction this time, and it takes my brain a half-second to recognize that the windows to my right on both sides of the fireplace are exploding inward under a hail of lead. I drop the rifle and cover my head to keep the glass from embedding itself in my face. The new onslaught distracts Billy and my father just long enough to let the men out front finish seating new magazines and starting round two of the frontal siege. The attack apparently isn't coordinated well enough to include the upstairs because I hear bursts of fire from the floor above and a triumphant war whoop.

"I got one!" Billy yells.

As the firing continues for another few seconds, however, his yell turns to a yelp, and there's sudden silence as the men out front again run through the ammunition in their magazines and have to reload. Billy's on his own. We can't spare anyone to check on him without putting them in jeopardy, too.

I'm now more frightened than I've ever been in a firefight, but also angrier than I've been in a long time, and I focus on that. I scramble up onto my knees, grab the rifle and level the barrel on the windowsill again, firing bursts of three shots into the doors and windows of the cars the men hide behind, giving them the same bombast in return, going for maximum effect of shattered glass and punctured metal.

The fire from my flank concerns me, though, and I quickly change magazines and roll across the floor to the nearest side window. A quick scan of the woods reveals nothing, so I start firing bursts, moving the barrel slowly left to right. In the sights, I see chunks of bark blown off some trees and get the desired response an instant later—muzzle flashes and the explosive rip of sound from an automatic weapon. I dive for the floor as bullets whiz over me like so many angry wasps. These boys have badass and highly illegal weaponry, which makes me even angrier.

When the fusillade from the side stops, the assault in front recommences. I slide to the window on the right of the fireplace, farther away from and under the line of fire from out front. Using the stone fireplace as a shield, I lean toward the window and concentrate my fire on the spot where the muzzle flash came from. But a moment or so later, a burst erupts from the trees several yards away from where I've been planting lead.

I duck back and lean against the cool stone, as the shooter fires a long burst, raking the entire side of the house. The gunfire elicits more shrieking from Dana, and the din is so deafening I see rather than hear Nate make a U-turn in the hall and disappear as he charges up the stairs.

"Nate, don't!" I yell, but it's too late. I don't want him close to any part of the house where bullets are flying through walls and shot-out windows. He must have heard Billy and run to help if he can.

I don't have time to think about it. From my vantage point on the floor, light shines through the constellation of bullet holes in the front door. It's a wonder the door is still on its hinges. The wall opposite the fireplace is nothing but shredded plaster and lath. The automatic weapons fire ceases again as our assailants stop to reload, and I swing around onto my knees and face the window again, ready to fire. I want to wait this time, however, for a target instead of indiscriminately shooting trees.

From across the hall comes a steady *boom-boom-boom* as my father fires one of the 12-gauge riot guns. And suddenly, I hear a distant *craack* of a single shot from a rifle or carbine. Sounds like someone's .30-06 deer rifle, something I heard a lot during hunting season as a kid. It's followed almost immediately by a whoop from my father.

"It's Bruce!" he shouts. "He got one! Set himself up in the barn across the road."

There's another crack, and another shout of triumph from the dining room before the assault weapons outside start up again. I keep my eyes on the tree line, searching for movement. Five men showed up in two cars out front. It sounds as if three have been dispatched, or at least are down. But perhaps not out. They could still pose a danger. And I don't know how many are in the woods. I've seen muzzle flashes from only one weapon, but I'm sure there must be more than one shooter.

As if to prove me right, shots suddenly ring out across the large expanse of yard between the house and the trees. They are quickly spaced, but not the rapid fire of a rifle, and the sound suggests a semi-automatic pistol. Those are joined by the assault rifle in bursts of three rounds. I hold a moment, face hidden, then lean out and into the rifle sights and squeeze off single shots in quick succession at the new targets. I'm frustrated that I haven't hit any of the bastards yet, but am consoled somewhat by the fact that we've held them off and evened the odds a bit. The sniper rifle is silent, so Bruce either doesn't have a target, is pinned down by return fire or is dead. I gloss over the last possibility as too improbable.

Shots become more infrequent and stop once again. I wonder if these assholes will ever run out of ammunition.

During the lull, Nate calls down from upstairs, "Billy's okay. Just a flesh wound. A lot of blood, but not too much damage."

A grunt emanates from across the hall, my father's manner of expressing his relief. I feel as if someone invisible just stopped sitting on my chest, and for an instant, I feel a presence still nearby. I wonder if my brother Doug is watching over the proceedings, seeing his childhood home literally shot to pieces. The quiet continues for too long, and I start tightening up again as if bracing for a body blow.

"Sheriff?" I call.

"I feel it, too," he says. "Nothing out here."

Something's not right, but I can't put my finger on it. I crane my neck, scanning almost a full 180 degrees outside the window, searching for movement. Finally, a sound penetrates the silence and registers through the ringing in my ears. A powerful motor running at a high rpm in the near distance and closing fast.

"Holy...!" my father shouts.

I sidle quickly to the front windows just in time to see a dark blue sedan with a white stripe from wheel well to wheel well careen down the drive toward the house—a Wisconsin State Patrol car running without siren or lights. The rear end slews as the wheels spin in the gravel with a roar of the engine, kicking up rocks and dust. Heading directly at the double-car roadblock, it smashes into the front quarter panel of both vehicles with a loud whump and screech of metal, the push bumper helping it force its way between the two cars.

The crash flushes two men out of hiding behind open doors of the two cars. One stands, turns and starts firing at the patrol car, now slewing toward the woods, bullets thudding into the trunk and blowing holes in the rear window. The other man turns and runs down the drive toward the road. Another assault weapon fires from the woods at the patrol car. As bullets punch lines of holes in the sheet metal, I'm afraid the driver won't last long under the onslaught. I'm even more afraid that this isn't some random officer coming to help, but my oldest brother Robbie. The driver throws the wheel the other way, and the car slides and skids to a stop at a forty-five-degree angle, its nose pointed at the house.

Without thinking, I spring into a crouch and sprint down the hall. I realize there's an off chance they managed to get someone around back to cover the rear, so I change course for the basement stairs and take them down two at a time. At the far end, under the den, another set of stairs climbs to a storm cellar door leading outside. On my way up, I shoot the lock out, raise my arms over my head with the rifle in both hands, shove the two doors apart and burst out into the bright daylight, hoping the element of surprise throws off anyone guarding the rear. No one shoots at me, which I take as a good sign.

As I round the corner of the house, a man strides out of the trees toward the car. His long greatcoat flaps around his legs as he runs, his silver hair waving in the breeze. *Sykes.* But this time he's holding an ugly, black personal defense weapon that appears a hundred times larger in his hand than the pistol he used on the train. I recognize it as the type our Special Forces guys use because it accommodates hardened-steel, armor-piercing ammunition.

Once again, my father was right—this has been a military-style assault. I'm willing to bet most of these men have served in some military before becoming career criminals. I've been wrong about almost everything since stepping outside my door a day ago, my confidence shaken by what my peers and superiors have done to me. But I know I'm good at what I do. Time to start acting like it.

The door of the patrol car pops open and a burly officer tumbles out onto the dry, brown grass. Feathered shirt fabric splays out from the holes in his uniform where bullets have punched through the car door and deep into his vest. Blood smears cover one hand and the side of his face. I still can't tell if it's my brother, but it makes no difference. He needs help. Sykes is intent on his prey as he moves in, and it's clear that he means to finish the job. The thin veneer of elegance that provided my first impression no longer hides what this man is—walking evil. He doesn't see me yet but even the element of surprise may not be enough this time. I'm too late and too far away.

Sykes extends his arm as he takes the last few steps until the barrel of the PDW nearly touches the cop's head. The cop's face is recognizable as he looks up. It's Robbie. My heart stops. I can't get a clear shot off on the run, and there's no time for anything else but a scream of frustration and rage.

84

The sudden onset of gunfire stopped Toby in his tracks, and its closeness and ferocity buckled his knees with fear. A sob broke from deep inside, and his eyes brimmed with tears as he fought to keep from pissing his pants. It sounded like World War III. No way could he walk into that. He wasn't a stone killer like the Russians. Sure, he'd acted tough, shot a man, but that wasn't who he was. He was just a guy who'd gotten in too deep. Selfish, narcissistic, greedy, sure, but he wasn't like them. He must be losing his mind. Why else would he be out here in the middle of fucking nowhere with a pea-shooter in his pocket when all around him it sounded like cannons going off.

Get a grip.

He swiped at his eyes with his coat sleeve. They weren't shooting at him, so he was safe for the moment. But surely someone was going to get hurt, probably killed. The fighting was too fierce for everyone to dodge all those bullets. And that might work in his favor. Dana might be one of the people caught in the crossfire. They might do his job for him. The smart thing, if he kept his wits about him, would be to watch and wait until they all kill each other. And if she somehow escaped, he'd be there to finish her off.

He got to his feet. Forging ahead, he spotted the house through the trees a moment later. He continued to creep through the woods until he was nearly even with it. Not more than twenty or thirty yards of sparsely wooded ground lay between the denser forest where he stood and the back of the house. One of the two cars blocking the drive was still visible, two men using it for cover while they fired assault rifles at the house. Most of the gunfire seemed to be coming from the front of the house, though he heard some echoing from the far side. He couldn't believe they'd left the rear unguarded. Suspicious, he waited, gaze flicking back and forth, checking the covered windows for signs of movement inside. Nothing registered.

He heard the distant, echoing report of a rifle, twice. The automatic weapons fire increased in volume and intensity and decreased in waves, and in the middle somewhere came the roar of a car engine and crash of metal and glass. The gunfire from other side died out. Suddenly, the muffled *pop-pop-pop* of a gun reached his ears, much closer than any of the others. With a thump, the storm cellar doors at the back of the house flew up and banged open. A woman with an assault rifle bounded out of the blackness from beneath the house and sprinted around the corner.

Toby's feet moved before recognition dawned on him that she was the other one, the bitch who was not Dana. Which meant Dana was still in the house, with one fewer person to protect her. And he'd just been shown a way in.

The fact that he even contemplated going in there confirmed that he was losing his sanity. Or maybe he was just plain crazy. The open door beckoned, the answer to his problems. Get rid of Dana, and no one would know he stole from the foundation.

He took the gun out of his coat pocket and hefted it in his hand, its weight as comforting as a glass of warm milk at bedtime.

85

Alexei shook his head in bewilderment. They were insane, all of them. Shooting at *cops*. Sure, part of the oath he'd sworn, the thieves' code, said not to help the authorities in any way. But attacking them, trying to kill them...? For what? A phone? Might as well put the gun to his temple and pull the trigger.

He'd heard the triumphant yells from inside, had seen one of the Russian muscle-heads from Milwaukee go down. Bullets had ripped into the trees nearby as someone in the house tried to flush him and Sykes out from cover. He'd nearly been deafened by Sykes's vicious fusillade in response from twenty yards away. He'd heard two sharp reports of a more distant rifle—across the road, perhaps—and had seen two more fall in front of the house.

He half-heartedly pulled the trigger of his pistol a few times, throwing shots in the general direction of the house. He'd lost his enthusiasm for this fight, and the way things were going, his boss might not be in it much longer, either. As they said here in America, Alexei had no skin in the game. Only loyalty to his boss and a desire to avenge Mikhail had brought him this far. But he was no use to Nastase, nor could he exact vengeance, if he died. A strategic retreat felt like the right thing to do.

His mind made up, he glanced off to his left and saw that Sykes was so fixated on the battle scene outside the house that he paid no attention to Alexei or his own driver. Slowly and quietly, Alexei backed away, and as the gunfire abated, he heard the rising growl of a powerful engine. As it drew closer, Alexei continued to retreat farther into the woods. He suddenly caught a glimpse of a state cop car ramming the two vehicles blocking the drive, sending Nastase and the last man from Milwaukee scattering. When he saw Sykes step toward the car that had suddenly crashed in on the scene, he turned and ran back through the trees to his parked vehicle.

As he climbed in, he had an epiphany. He suddenly realized why the woman seemed so familiar—the good-looking one, not the horsey lookalike. He'd seen her on TV. Her face had been everywhere for a couple of days after that aborted terrorist attack in D.C. She was a fucking fed, for shit's sake. FBI. The joke was on Sykes. Or maybe it was on all of them, he thought. Maybe the whole fucking mess had been a sting from the beginning, a way to bring down both Sykes and Nastase. Alexei now had even more reason to flee.

The car fairly flew over the rutted track as Alexei mashed the gas pedal to the floor, and the tires squealed and smoked as they fought for purchase when he reached the asphalt county road. For a brief moment he debated which way to turn, but once again loyalty won out. He spun the wheel and accelerated toward the house, fearing he was already too late.

Nastase burst onto the road a hundred yards ahead, legs churning, arms pumping. His head turned at the sound of Alexei's car and, raising an arm as though hailing a taxi, he suddenly changed direction, then staggered as a bullet struck him. Alexei took his foot off the pedal, already knowing Nastase's fate was sealed. Another bullet ripped through the front of Nastase's jacket, and Alexei's boss crumpled to the ground.

Alexei jammed on the brakes. Before the car skidded to a stop, he slammed the gearshift into reverse. Tires smoking once more, shrieking in protest, the car sped backwards with Alexei gripping the wheel hard, craning his neck to look out the rear window, fighting to maintain control. He heard rather than saw a bullet *thunk* into metal, and then another. He kept going until the front end started weaving back and forth despite his efforts to keep the car straight. He spun the wheel and slammed a foot on the brake pedal at the same time. The car slewed and did a one-eighty. He threw it into Drive and took off.

With a growing sense of resignation, Alexei slumped in his seat, sadness settling on his shoulders for a moment. The life he'd known was over. And just as suddenly, the weight lifted like a bird taking flight as the realization sank in.

His old life was over.

Finally, he was a free man.

86

The noise filled Dana's head, crowding out everything except the fear that clutched at her heart like a crone's bony talons. She clapped her hands over her ears and shrieked, trying to drown out the bombast of assault weapons, splintering wood, shattering glass, rending metal.... This time she was going to die. She knew it. She threw herself on the floor to protect herself, but that only made matters worse. She didn't want to die on her hands and knees, cowering in a corner. Besides, they'd given her a job to do.

She took deep breaths and got to her feet. The assaults, she reasoned, came from the front and one side of the house. She stood a better chance here in the kitchen than anywhere else. As long as no one attacked the rear. Her one job.... She hurried to the side window, hooked a finger along the edge of the blind and pulled it out far enough to peek outside. She scanned the expanse of grassy field to the east, and slowly panned her gaze along the edge of the woods back toward the house. Nothing moved except a few leaves fluttering and some tufts of tall grass swaying in the light breeze. She slowly let the blind fall flush with the window and let her breath out with a sigh.

Moving fast but quietly to the den, she positioned herself next to the window and did the same with the curtain there, drawing it aside just enough to peer out. As soon as she did, she gasped and yanked her head back, quickly covering her mouth with her free hand and biting down on it to keep from screaming.

Toby had stepped out of the dense woods and was making his way furtively to the back of the house, using trunks of the few trees in the yard as cover. Dana quickly stole out onto the screened porch and glanced down. A black maw leading into the earth below yawned widely. A storm cellar door. He was coming in.

Dana ran back to the kitchen. The time for stealth was over. The time had come to defend the Robertses' home. Grim determination gripped her now, squeezing aside the fear. She wasn't going to relinquish ground to anyone, least of all the misogynistic bastard who'd controlled her life for too long. No way in hell was he getting past her.

Nate had left the pistol on the kitchen counter next to his laptop when he'd run off to help Billy. She grabbed it. Its weight surprised her, and she nearly dropped it. Gripping it more tightly, she grabbed on with her other hand as well. An image flashed through her brain, and she nodded to herself. Now she knew why all those hot actresses playing cops or FBI agents on TV used a two-handed grip. She moved into the hallway and stopped ten feet away from the door to the basement. Her knees quaked, and she wasn't sure she could stand.

She thought of what Toby had done, how he'd harassed her at work, how he'd treated not just her but so many of the foundation's employees like chattel, looking down on them all. She thought of how he'd shot the Russian without any qualms whatsoever, and her anger started to mount. She stared at the basement doorknob and thought of how many starving children and their parents had been deprived of simple necessities like clean water because Toby, not Dana, had been ripping off the foundation for years. She knew the truth now. All she needed was to hear Toby say it, admit what he'd done.

Almost imperceptibly, the knob turned ever so slightly, then slowly some more. She stared even harder, gripping the pistol tightly and raising her arms straight out until the barrel pointed at the center of the door. Gunfire sounded outside, masking any noise the knob or even the door itself might make as it was opened. The knob stopped turning, and the door inched open a crack, then opened wider still until someone stepped into the hall and swung it partially closed. Toby. He turned and froze as he saw her. She noted his right arm hanging at his side, the hand hidden behind the folds of his overcoat. He smiled, and a chill ran through her.

"Put the gun down, Dana," he said. "You're not going to use that. Put it down and tell me what you did."

She blinked. "What I did?"

"Yes, you little bitch. You've made my life a living hell. Now put the gun down!"

He took a step toward her.

She shook her head and held her ground, aiming the gun at his chest. "You're going to jail, Toby. We've got it all—bank records, video of the deposits Greg made in your accounts.... The police are going to arrest him, too. You don't think he'll squeal like a pig when they start asking him questions?"

Toby's face reddened. She'd hit a nerve. She knew it, knew she'd been right all along. Ever since she'd first suspected someone was embezzling, she'd been certain it had to be Toby. And to think that he'd accused her of being the thief.

"I'm not going to jail, Dana." His voice was so soft she almost didn't hear him, but she saw the menace in his expression. "Who's going to make me? You? I know you. You're a scared little girl whose slut for a mother got the shit beat out of her every night. You won't

348

stop me."

Dana paled, her stomach sinking through the floor. Her hands shook, the barrel of the gun noticeably wobbling in front of her. How did he know? How had he found out about her past? It didn't matter. She wasn't that little girl anymore. She'd wised up. He couldn't take away her accomplishments, and he couldn't deny the truth.

Toby took another step, and she saw him tense. Her anger returned in a wave, washing away her uncertainty. She swallowed hard, gripped the pistol tighter and raised it until it pointed dead center at his forehead.

"Not another move, Toby, or I will shoot you. You're right, I don't want to shoot you. I'd rather see you rot in jail for the rest of your life, but take one more step and I'll pull the trigger."

"You're bluffing," he said, and lifted one foot to take another step.

Dana swung the gun down toward the floor and pulled the trigger. Both the sound of the shot and the pistol's recoil made her jump back in surprise. She hadn't expected the gun to be so loud or so powerful. But judging from his open mouth and wide eyes. Toby was far more surprised, and she recovered more quickly.

"Facedown on the floor!" she said.

"You crazy bitch!" he screamed.

His arm rose, the gun in his hand now visible, and he straightened, preparing to advance. Dana raised her gun and pointed it at his chest again. She saw sudden movement over Toby's shoulder.

"Don't move!" the sheriff said, moving up the hall behind Toby. "Drop the weapon and get your hands in the air."

There was a clatter of shoes down the stairs, and Nate appeared behind the sheriff.

"Whoa!" Toby said in a calm voice, slowly raising his hands. "Everybody just chill out here."

Dana noted the gun was still in Toby's hand as he raised his arms. She focused on it, tightening the grip on her own gun.

"What's going on here?" the sheriff said, pointing a pistol at Toby. "Who the hell are you?"

"I'm her boss," Toby said casually. "I've been following her because she stole millions from the foundation I run."

"That's bullshit, Doug." Nate said quietly. "Dana's actually pretty brave. She found evidence that this asshole has been embezzling funds for years. He tried to kill her yesterday."

"Hey, hey!" Toby protested. "You're lying. I don't know who you are, but you're full of shit."

"Well, Nate," the sheriff said, "which is it? I need to know what's going on before they start shooting again outside."

Dana saw the sheriff let down his guard for half a second to glance over his shoulder at Nate, and knew Toby saw it, too. Toby brought his gun arm down and swung it toward the sheriff.

She didn't hesitate.

"Look out!" she yelled, and pulled the trigger again.

87

Sykes stands over Robbie, gun to his head as I scream. He lifts his head and sees me, distracted for just an instant. It's enough. Robbie manages to get his hands up and grab Sykes's gun. Robbie twists it, not hard enough to break Sykes's grip, but enough to throw Sykes a little off balance. Now his attention is divided between Robbie and me. He tries to wrench the gun out of Robbie's grasp and, as they struggle, I squeeze off a shot to further confuse him. Only the hammer falls on an empty chamber. Horrified, I run faster.

Sykes's finger tightens on the PDW's trigger, loosing an abrupt burst that sprays the ground next to Robbie with bullets and flying chunks of dirt and grass. Robbie's arms shake with the gun's recoil, and he suddenly lets go as the hot barrel blisters his palm. Sykes jerks the gun away and smashes the butt into the side of Robbie's face, knocking him aside, unconscious.

Sykes turns toward me, but he's too late. I'm already on him. He wheels the PDW in my direction, but I'm already swinging my rifle by the barrel as I charge. I plant a foot, rotate my hips and put all that momentum from running into it, focusing on his moving trigger hand as if it was a baseball, just like the old days. I connect with the trigger guard and front folding stock, a hair off a homerun but a solid double that knocks the gun up out of his hands and sends it spinning through the air.

I continue rotating and whirl into him with a roundhouse kick that catches him just above the hip, hitting mostly muscle, not high enough to do any real damage. But it moves him aside enough to give me room to step closer, swinging the rifle again. He winces as it smacks his upper arm, but quick as a snake he shoots his hand up and curls his arm around it, latches on and yanks it out of my hands. I let it go and move in with short, hard strikes a Krav Maga instructor showed me after I came home from Baghdad and left the army.

Sykes is way faster and in far better shape than his appearance suggests, and he parries almost every strike I throw at him. He deflects the blows I land enough to render them largely ineffective. My surprise and frustration throw my rhythm off, and he's quick to take advantage, following defensive blocks with strikes of his own. I thump a flat palm strike against his chest that lands half on his sternum and half on his solar plexus. He grunts but it doesn't incapacitate him. I stomp on his toes, and knee him in the groin, but he shifts enough to catch the brunt of it on his thigh. His counter-punches sail at me just as fast, and it's all I can do to avoid strikes to the ribs, thigh and the fist heading for my face that almost ends it all. I see it in time to jerk away; instead, it rakes my cheekbone and ear as it whistles past.

Stars explode in my vision, and pain rattles my brain. I may be a fraction of a second faster, but he has weight and power that I can't match, and fear starts to circle the ring. I refuse to look at it, but knowing it's there prompts me to change strategy. My Krav Maga instructor was five times tougher on me than any drill sergeant. He knew why I wanted to learn the techniques, and his lessons imprinted deeply within me. I heed them now and dance back a step to reach inside my jacket for my pistol.

But Sykes doesn't pause when I retreat. Instead, he advances quickly, going on the offensive with the same flurry of hand strikes I threw at him. My hand hasn't cleared my jacket as I try to fend him off, and by the time I get the pistol out of the holster, I am stumbling backward to avoid his blows. I get both hands up, the pistol useless, and he easily swats the gun out of my hand with his assault.

Now I have no choice but to go back to the original strategy—strike until my opponent is incapacitated. If I can't overpower him, I have to fight dirtier. I thrust a two-finger strike into his jugular notch, digging my nails into the skin. I block his counter and fake a spear-hand strike to his eyes and claw my other hand up into his groin until I cup his testicles and squeeze.

He roars and head-butts me. Blood pours down from split skin at my hairline, and I stagger back as the world grays around me. When it comes back into focus, Sykes is facing me ten feet away, pointing the pistol with the suppressor on it at the center of my forehead.

He smiles. "What's your name?"

"Fuck you."

A huge man in a black suit has appeared from nowhere behind Sykes and approaches slowly, a sad expression on his face. I recognize him—the man on the train platform in Charlottesville— and realize I've seen his picture, too. Of course...the chauffeur. Mick's buddy. Sykes seems to be aware of his presence but pays him no attention.

Sykes shrugs. "Odd name for parents to saddle a child with. I'm still going to enjoy killing you even if I don't know who you are."

The chauffeur—Kovacs—stops behind Sykes. His gaze still rests on my face, and I can't read his expression.

"George," Sykes says, "meet Fuck You, the woman from the train. And say your goodbyes."

Sykes trigger finger whitens, and I involuntarily tense, waiting for the bullet that will render all my worries, all my regrets, moot. Before he can fire, Kovacs wraps his arms around Sykes from behind, pinning Sykes's arms to his sides. I hear the gun fire, but I'm still standing, still breathing.

Sykes roars and swears a blue streak as George lifts him off the ground. George gives me a last look then concentrates on the man squirming in his grasp. I turn and run. I need to end this, but I no longer have a weapon, and I refuse to put the rest of family in danger any longer. I need to lead Sykes away from the house, and I know just the place.

I hear the suppressed gun fire again, and another roar, but from a different voice this time. And then Sykes saying loudly, angrily, "George, you stupid, stupid, son of a bitch."

The gun fires one last time and goes silent. I can't hear Sykes's footsteps, but I know he's following me. I reach the edge of the woods, crash through the first ten yards like a wounded deer, so Sykes knows where to go, then dart to the right onto a well-known but hard-to-see trail that leads north, deeper into the trees.

88

Toby lay sprawled on the floor, blood pooling on the dark wood next to him. Dana stood over him, gun in both hands still pointed at his chest. Sheriff Roberts kneeled next to Toby, picked up the pistol in Toby's hand, and handcuffed him.

"Is he...?"

The sheriff glanced up at her. "He'll live, but he's not going anywhere. You can put that gun away now."

"Good," Dana said, surprised by the vehemence in her own voice. She lowered the pistol to her side. "Let him rot in prison."

Nate walked up to her and gently took the pistol out of her hand.

"Damn nice shot," someone else said.

Dana looked up and saw Billy at the foot of the stairs, one hand pressing a towel against his shoulder. She thought maybe he was making fun of her—after all, how tough is it to shoot someone from a few feet away? But his expression approached awe, as if he suddenly saw her in a different light. She thought she saw something else on his face...but, no, that couldn't be possible. They'd just met. She pushed the notions out of her head and cocked her head as the sheriff thumbed the mic on his radio and spoke.

"Bruce? You okay?"

"Yeah, Sheriff. Just fine."

"Sounds like it's all over. We've got two wounded in here. Call in an ambulance and then come over and secure the scene here."

"Got it. Be there in a few."

"Be careful. We don't know who else is out there, and I don't know if everyone we put down will stay down."

"Will do. Out."

The sheriff scanned the faces around him one by one, his gaze finally stopping on Billy.

"You all right?"

Billy shrugged and winced as his shoulder moved, a shade of pink moving from his neck up into his face.

"Yeah, I'm fine. Just a scratch."

Roberts nodded and looked around again as he stood. The corners of his mouth turned down.

"Where's Jenny?"

Dana saw blank expressions on the other faces, and her mind started to churn. She wasn't surprised when Roberts turned his gaze on her.

"Did you see her go past you? Out the back maybe?"

Dana shook her head.

"Well, she didn't go out the front, and she's not here. Where the hell is she?"

Swallowing hard, moistening her mouth to speak, Dana said, "I think she left the same way Toby got in."

Roberts looked down, his expression turning to surprise. Toby stirred and groaned. Dana realized they hadn't yet considered how Toby had gotten into the house.

"The storm cellar doors are open outside," Dana said. "I saw Toby come out of the woods and head for the house. When I looked down, I saw the open doors. Jenny must have left that way."

The sheriff's head bobbed now, and his confusion vanished as he took charge again.

"I know where she went. She's probably trying to lead Sykes away from the house. I'll go find her."

"I'm going with you," Nate said.

The tone of his voice made Dana turn and look at him carefully. She could see it written all over his face—he still cared about Jenny, deeply. She wondered again what had happened between them.

"No," the sheriff said. "I need you here, Nate. See if you can keep this asshole from bleeding to death on my floor before the EMTs get here. Billy, keep watch and keep everyone safe until Bruce clears the scene and joins you."

"Wait," Billy said as the sheriff walked toward the kitchen. "Where are you going? I mean in case you get in trouble, we need to know where to look."

"The mound," Roberts replied over his shoulder as he went out the back door.

89

The sky darkens and the temperature suddenly drops ten degrees or more. It isn't just an effect of the shade the trees provide. The branches above me rustle and sway as the breeze picks up and works its way down to the forest floor. A front is moving in, and it's moving fast. Goosebumps rise on my arms, and a shiver runs through me despite the fact that I'm perspiring from exertion.

I run as fast as I can over the rough and broken terrain. Already, the ground rises ahead, and my lungs and heart work harder to keep my muscles oxygenated as I attack the grade. Gradual at first, it soon ascends more quickly. The steep climb parallels the length of the mound. About three-quarters of the way up, a switchback leads to the top, the path now little more than a goat track squeezing between trees and over large boulders.

The trail comes out on the lower shoulder of the mound, a relatively flat expanse of solid rock covered with dirt in spots the length of a football field that varies from ten to twenty feet wide. While trees rise up from the side of the mound, half of the mesa is bare except for a few scrubby bushes and some grass growing from the dirt in the fissures. I run along the spine of the mound toward the highest spot where trees grow more densely, covering the other half of the narrowing rock spine. My lungs are burning from the climb, but I don't slow or stop. I don't want to be caught out in the open.

The sky now is leaden, and the wind whips so intensely it throws me off course for a moment. I dance-step back to the middle and keep going. The flat rock at the highest point narrows to perhaps ten feet with a precipitous drop into the trees on one side and an almost sheer rock face on the other. Nearly seventy feet below is a river. There are only two ways off this precipice—the way I came, or a jump into the river. But I know a secret. Two of them. The mound has another descent continuing along the spine, though it's not actually a trail and it's a long and difficult climb down.

But past the high point that juts out toward the river, down an incline, is a large red cedar growing in a cleft up from below. Some of its low branches hide a chimney in the rock. Chest heaving from the run, I pull aside one of the branches and scoot under it on my butt, feet first into the chimney. The curved passage slides steeply down and to the left, stopping at a ledge about fifteen feet below and to the right of the precipice above. When I reach the ledge, I look out over the river.

A sharp line of demarcation across the western sky where lead turns to charcoal marks the border of the front. The dark clouds are rapidly eating what's left of the blue sky far to the east. The wind howls up at this height, and the first scattered drops of rain slap my cheeks and arms. Rain...

*****

Driven by the wind, the storm marches toward me. A thunderclap peals across the sky, resonating so loudly that I feel it as much as hear it. A wall of water descends from the edge of the front, moving ever closer. Below, the glassy flowing surface of the water downriver froths under the onslaught of rain.

Suddenly, I sense him on the crag above me.

"Jump!" The wind rips the word from his mouth and carries it past me so quickly that I hear a whisper not a shout.

I look down, and fear grips me. The height, the swirling water and the wind combine forces to dizzying effect.

"Come on, Jen," Doug calls. "I double-dare you. You can do it."

I raise my head and squint against the drops and see my brother hopping, dancing at the edge of the rock face with nervous energy. The jump is a right of passage. Robbie, Bruce and all their friends have done it many times on hot summer days. Doug and his friends have, too. Billy's way too young. Which leaves me.

While the day was perfect earlier—bright sun in a cloudless sky, heat and humidity typical of mid-August—the oncoming storm front has turned it ominous, full of foreboding. I shake my head as the downpour sweeps over us, drenching us in seconds. The temperature drops further, and the wind on my wet skin makes me shiver. I can't stop.

"No!" I shout. "I'm too cold."

"Do it, Jenny! Just jump and we'll go back to the house and get warm. I promise."

"No. I want to go home."

"You're such a baby," he yells, leaning over the edge to get a better look at me as I scrunch into a ball to fend off the rain. "Okay, I'll go first and wait for you in the river. All right?"

"I'm not going. Not today."

"Come on!" His voice fills with frustration and anger.

He flings his arms out and across his chest a few times and hops up and down. I can tell he's getting cold, too, but won't admit it.

"Okay, I'm going. This is your last chance. If you don't jump, I will."

"Fine!" I shout. "Go ahead."

"Don't think I won't," he says, shifting his feet in time to some internal

rhythm.

His foot slips on the rain-soaked rock, and I watch in horror as he goes over the edge, arms flailing. He cartwheels through the air, crashes into the rock face and bounces off to sail end over end down into the river. I hear someone scream his name, and wonder if it's me, or a voice inside my head. A geyser of froth erupts from the river's surface where he hits, but the sound of the splash is drowned out by the rain. When it subsides, he isn't visible in the water.

Huddled on the ledge, frozen in shock, I turn my head at the sound of someone scrabbling down the chute. Mom crawls over to me, pulls me close, and holds me tight, stroking my hair.

"Jenny, thank God you're okay," she murmurs in my ear.

90

He stopped to listen. Over the sound of the wind rustling in the trees, he heard the sound of running feet. As he crashed through the underbrush in their general direction, he almost missed the faint indentation in the forest floor that indicated a well-traveled trail. He imagined all manner of forest creatures used it, including the woman he sought. He followed it, picking up his pace now that it was somewhat easier to maintain an even footing. Even then it wasn't easy.

He ducked under a large tree limb arching across the trail and leaped over the trunk of a fallen tree a few yards farther. He knew he couldn't catch her, not after seeing the relative ease with which she'd left him behind when he'd followed her off the train. But if he managed to keep pace, he could use her panic against her and follow the sound of her flight.

Sykes was so sure of his plan that he let his mind wander to other issues, like how he would get into the house to retrieve his phone once the woman was dispatched. The frontal assault had failed, but perhaps that meant that they wouldn't expect a single man to infiltrate their defenses and take them out. And he did need to take them all out. He'd known all along that this would be inevitable, but now he had no choice. He'd come too far, and already had lost too much.

He didn't think his old life was salvageable. The club was as good as gone. He couldn't go back. Surely, they'd figured out by now who he was. If Nastase was still alive, he could have the club. Let the feds harass him, Sykes figured. As long as he had his phone, he could still produce income. He knew too much about too many people, and he could use the leverage to squeeze them from anywhere in the world.

His anger mounted again as he thought of not only Mick, whose betrayal created this whole mess, but now George, one of the people he'd trusted most next to Stevens. Big, dumb George. Sykes had been convinced George was content enough, and smart enough, not to cross him. But the stupid mope really had grown a conscience. Sykes almost regretted killing him, but he'd had no choice, and he couldn't abide disloyalty. Nor could he let anything get in the way of catching the woman. With her as a hostage they'd have to give him the phone.

Absorbed in his own stew of emotions, Sykes almost missed the change in direction of the woman's attempted escape. The trail continued ahead, but Sykes suddenly heard scrabbling footsteps above and behind him. He quickly turned his attention back to the trail ahead, now difficult to discern in the fading light. The sky had darkened ominously and the wind had picked up. But he managed to spot the fork in the path ahead, a less-worn trail veering off to the left. He took it, and it immediately grew steeper. Suddenly, it switched back and headed the opposite direction, climbing steadily now, the ground underfoot getting rockier, the earthen path broken by stretches of bare stone, boulders jutting from the side of the steep hill.

He had to hand it to the woman. She made an admirable adversary. And there was no doubt she could fight. Only the fact that he had trained so hard himself to stave off his advancing years had saved him. His reflexes were a shade slower than they'd been as a younger man, but his instincts had helped him anticipate her moves, and he'd had the advantages of size and strength. As his lungs burned from the climb, he realized that he'd need those assets to defeat her once he caught her.

His confidence grew the higher they climbed. He doubted there were many points of access or egress from wherever she was headed. Which meant she'd made a fatal error. She would be trapped up on top of this hill or whatever it was. He smiled to himself despite the ache in his legs and his ragged breathing. His bloodlust barely whetted, Sykes could taste the sweet satisfaction he would experience when he squeezed the life out of her and saw the light in her eyes fade. But first, the phone.

The path suddenly ended at a rocky table that ran the length of the ridge. The woman was nowhere in sight. As Sykes started up the stone spine he felt rain on his face, and turned to face the gusting winds. A quarter mile away, a curtain of rain so heavy he almost couldn't see through it waved and rippled toward him. It drowned the forest so rapidly he knew it would be on him in a matter of seconds, not minutes. He increased his pace until he reached the highest point, and slowed to a walk. He still saw no sign of the woman.

At the peak, the rocky spine descended a gradual incline until it broke off into jutting boulders among into trees so thick he doubted it was possible to traverse the hill in that direction. Instead, he made his way to the edge of the table and looked over. Far down a sheer cliff lay a black ribbon of water that now churned and frothed in the wind and rain. The edge of the storm flew over him now, drenching him with cold rain and icy pellets. The wind tore at his coat and found its way into every opening and through the thick fabric, chilling him. A bolt of lightning crackled nearby, its flash nearly blinding him, followed almost instantaneously by a crack of thunder that shook the ground under his feet and rumbled on for another twenty seconds.

The storm stoked the burning pit of anger in his belly and sent a surge of energy through him, as if the electricity from the lightning had coursed through the ground and snaked up through his feet into his body. He breathed deeply, pulling the ionized air into his lungs, recharging his muscles with oxygen as he surveyed the view from his perch. And as he completed a scan of the surroundings, another bolt of lightning illuminated a flash of white on a rock ledge in the cliff side below him, almost as if a deer had turned tail and run. He quickly locked in on the spot and saw her, huddled against the downpour, clothes and hair blending in with the dark grays around her.

She was his now.

91

My mother's face dissolves as the memory fades. I realize there are tears mixed with the rainwater streaming down my cheeks. I thought I left these ghosts behind years ago. For a time after Doug's death, I dreamt about it on a nightly basis, the terror waking me in a cold sweat. When the nightmares lessened and finally stopped, I refused to relive the memories ever again. I buried them deep.

Now they've exposed a wound that never healed, and the pain is raw and excruciating. I can't blame myself for what happened to Doug, but even after all these years, even after time spent in therapy, I still feel twinges of guilt. It was my idea to "initiate" myself, to make the famous jump for the first time. Doug was only too happy to come along. What happened was an accident. No one's fault, really. If I wanted to assign blame, I should blame Doug for hopping around on slippery rock.

My mother, on the other hand, would not have been there getting soaked in the cold rain were it not for me.

Rain... I hate fucking rain.

The sudden presence I sense jerks me back to my present situation, again postponing my reckoning with the ghosts surrounding my mom's death. I glance up and see a dark figure standing on the edge of the precipice, silhouetted against the sky. He's here. The chill I feel is due to more than the cold rain and hail loosed by the thunderstorm. I wrap my arms closer around me, huddling on the rock, sensing the dragon in the dark recesses of my mind hovering just out of sight. I can't succumb to it, can't let fear's black wings envelop me. I will my mind to focus, and summon my fury at this invader, at the havoc he has wreaked on so many lives in so short a time. That anger glows hot and bright, banishing the dragon from sight and sense.

I had no plan as I climbed up here to one of my favorite childhood spots before the accident, only a desire to lure Sykes away from my family. But a glimmer of hope percolates in the back of my brain. He doesn't know about the chute. I might be able to circle around behind him. And if he finds the chimney and tries to attack, I have the advantage, even without a weapon. I turn to see that the hidey-hole looks smaller than I remember; still, there's enough room to move around.

As I scrabble back from the ledge, chips of rock fly up from the spot where I'd been. At the same moment, I hear a pop that's quickly ripped away by the wind. The bastard's shooting at me. I duck into the chimney where he can't see me from above, sheltered by both the cliff and the big cedar that guards the door to my fortress. In the rubble of loose rock lining the chute, I find a fallen branch as thick as my wrist on one end, the spread of smaller branches with feathery brown cedar needles on the other. I lean it against the side of the chimney and stomp on it, breaking it in two. I'm left with a three-foot club. Better than nothing.

Slowly, I crawl toward the edge to see if he's moved. The rain stings my upturned face like hailstones or a million small bees. I have to wipe the rain out of my eyes with my sleeve before I allow myself to believe what I see. Sykes has stripped off his overcoat, suit coat and shoes, and has lowered himself over the edge of the precipice, stockinged feet perched precariously in a crevice in the rock face. In shocked amazement, I watch him blindly find purchase with his toes even lower until he clings to the cliff side, his head now below the edge. Apparently, he's convinced there's a third way down off this mound.

I put the branch down and change strategy, pulling back from the edge and turning around to collect some baseball-size rocks from the ground near the chimney. The pitiless wind drives the rain sideways into the sheltered alcove, and the treetops bow to its will. I creep as far out on the ledge as I dare, the wind threatening to grab hold of my clothes and drag me off, and throw a rock at Sykes. He's already moved down and over a few feet, and he scrunches his shoulders as the rock hits the wall next to him and bounces off.

I wind up and throw another, aiming more carefully this time, sacrificing some speed for accuracy. It thunks into his ribs under his shoulder blade, and I hear a grunt of pain over the constant rush of wind and rain. A third hits him in the temple, forcing him to let go with one arm. It flails and falls to his side. He sags, and for a moment I think he'll black out and fall, but he straightens his legs and repositions his fingers in another cleft a little lower, finds a toehold and comes down another foot.

His progress makes me more nervous, as if the muscle beating against my ribs to get out and the trembling in my arms and legs from an oversaturation of adrenaline aren't enough. My arm is limber now, and I throw one as hard as I dare on the narrow ledge. It hits him in the back with a satisfying thud. He roars in pain, arching his back. His fingers dig into the rock face until they're bone-white, and he turns his head to snarl at me, rain and blood streaming down his face.

"Fucking cunt! I'll kill you."

The wind rips the words from his mouth and flings them at me. They cannot hurt me after all I've been through. They only serve to fuel my anger. I want to beat some basic manners into his skull.

He shifts slightly, reaffirming his hold, and uses his left hand to pull his pistol from his waistband. I duck back under cover as he fires. The bullet ricochets off three surfaces before zipping out over the river. I turn my face to the chimney wall and cover my head with my hands as he fires two rounds in quick succession even farther inside the shelter; they bounce and whiz around the space like angry horseflies. I feel a twitch on my arm, as if someone has pinched my sleeve and pulled. I ignore it, and wait for the deafening echoes to die down. When he doesn't fire again, I worry, and slide along the nearest wall toward the edge to peek around the corner.

He's repositioning himself again, but he hasn't loosened his grip on the gun. He glances down, and when he sees me, raises his arm to shoot. I sidestep and wildly hurl another rock that hits his wrist with enough force that he lets go, and the gun spins down toward the river and out of sight. The pain seems to motivate him even more. He winces as he finds another handhold. I'm sure I've fractured a bone in his wrist.

But he clamps his lips together, grits his teeth and moves even faster down the cliff face toward me, now only a body length above and to the side of me. I have no clear throw. And if I climb up the chute now to get above him, he'll have time to make it on to the ledge. Stalemate. I have to end it now. My only chance is the short length of cedar branch and whatever strength I have left when he attempts his final assault.

Staying out of sight, I step closer to the edge, hoping when he drops I might be able to take him by surprise and knock him off balance. But when he comes, he finds a way to swing his body into the opening instead of dropping straight down onto the ledge. I'm unprepared, and his momentum carries him into me. He pushes me back with a flurry of short, sharp blows to my ribs. I try to take them on my arms and elbows, but he's relentless, backing me up into the chute where my feet slip on the loose rock and I go down.

He raises his knee to drive a foot into my chest, and I barely have time to block it holding the branch in both hands. The blow lands with such force that it snaps the club in two, and drives the breath from my lungs. The wood absorbs enough force that I'm not completely winded, and I suck in a deep breath as I roll to avoid another pile driver. I hear a crunch as his foot lands awkwardly on the rocks. He howls in pain and I know he's broken his foot or ankle.

I scramble to my feet and don't hesitate to attack with the same types of blows that he aimed at me, but I slash and jab at his eyes, his throat, his armpits, his groin, and drive him back against the rock wall, its curve bending him nearly in half. He lashes out wildly, his fist connecting with the side of my head, but not before I stomp on his broken foot. The pain stops him long enough for me to step back and shake my head, trying to clear black spots dancing in front of my eyes.

He comes at me, undeterred, and I hear the beat of the dragon's wings in my head, fear gnawing at the edges of my consciousness. Again, I work the bellows stoking the rage that has kept me upright and fighting. My vision narrows until all I see is the evil in front of me. As he charges, I dance toward the chimney at the last second, out of reach. He has trouble stopping and pivoting on the injured foot, and now he stands between me and a black sky full of wind and water.

"Sykes!" a voice roars from above, followed by a gunshot.

It startles him, distracting him for the instant I need to take a running step, plant a foot and put all my remaining strength into a snap-kick that lands squarely in the middle of his chest. He staggers back, and as I collapse on the cold, wet stone, exhausted, he disappears over the edge.

92

Stones and small rocks clack and clatter, cascading down the chute as a form quickly slides down the chimney. Rain smears my vision, and my head aches terribly.

I hear my own voice over the wind, small and irresolute. "Mom? Is that you?"

But the kind, grizzled face that approaches and the strong arms that envelope me are those of my father.

"Jesus, Jenny. Are you all right? Thank God you're alive."

He pulls my head to his chest and strokes my wet hair.

"I thought I lost you again," he murmurs.

Thunder rumbles across the sky, and the wind whips the rain in circles, blowing it into the little bit of shelter we have. But it's the tears streaming down my face that soak me now.

"I'm sorry, I'm sorry," I sob. "Don't be mad. Please, don't be angry with me."

"Why would I be mad at you?"

I can't bear to look at him, can't face the accusation and disappointment on his face. I can't find the right words, but I force some out anyway.

"You know... For... for what happened to Mom."

I feel him pull away to look at me. He cups my chin in his hand and gently turns my face up toward his.

"I'm not angry with you. What's this about, Jenny?"

Tears of anger, frustration and grief, too, brim and spill out over my eyelids.

"I killed her, Dad. It was my fault. If I hadn't been out here that day, she wouldn't have gotten soaked. She wouldn't have gotten sick."

The days after Doug's accident come back to me in a rush, my mother's sneezing and runny nose worsening until she was bedridden, then days of visiting her at the hospital, her face drawn and pale against the sheets, tubes running out of her arms. In time, she seemed to get better. She came home, and life started to resume. But suddenly, a week or two later she was gone.

His brows lift. He seems genuinely puzzled. Then his features dissolve into an expression of profound sadness. He puts his hand on my cheek and gently swipes away a tear with his thumb.

"I'm sorry, Jen, so sorry," he says.

I have to strain to hear his voice over the patter of rain.

"I had no idea you thought that all these years. You had nothing to do with your mother's death. She did get sick--pneumonia, in fact. But that wasn't what killed her."

He stops and looks away. His Adam's apple bobs as he swallows hard, and when he faces me again, his eyes are red. I can't tell if the water rolling down his cheek is rain dripping from his soaked hair or tears.

"Your mom had a weak heart," he says, voice choked with emotion. "Never let on. I didn't even know until Doc Bruin told me at the hospital just before she died. Said it was a wonder she'd managed to raise five kids and do all the stuff she did with you."

I blink away the tears, trying to process what he's telling me. I've been carrying my weight in guilt ever since the day I learned to hate rain, and now find no one else thought it was my fault but me.

"All this time," he goes on, "I thought *you* were mad at *me*."

I shake my head, trying to empty the confusion out through my ears. "For what?"

He drops his gaze to the ground, and his face flushes. He makes two false starts before he raises his eyes and actually speaks.

"I let you down."

His voice is so quiet I lean in to hear him.

"Not just you," he goes on. "I let all you kids down. When Katie—when your mom died, I couldn't handle it. I'm ashamed to admit it. I was supposed to be there for you. I was supposed to be strong for all of us. Your mom was the strong one, Jenny. She was the glue that kept us all together. And I loved her..."

He presses his lips together and looks out over the river. Wind blows wet strands of hair off his forehead. He faces me again.

"I loved her so much that the pain I felt was almost more than I could bear. I hardly knew how to be a sheriff in the months after her funeral, let alone how to be a parent. Especially for you. Lord, help me, the boys could fend for themselves. But I didn't know how to replace her in your eyes, how to give you all the things she did. I know now how foolish that notion is, but back then...."

He pulls me close and hugs me. I wince as pain shoot through my chest. He senses it and holds me at arm's length again, eyes searching my face.

"Ribs," I gasp. "Bruised, for sure. Maybe cracked one or two."

"You think you can make it down on your own?"

I nod. He lets go of my arms and stands, then looks at the blood on his hand. It's only then that I feel my arm burn with pain. I look at the tear in the sleeve of my soaked leather jacket, and shake my head.

"It's nothing. Just a scratch. Asshole ruined an expensive jacket, though."

He smiles and helps me to my feet.

"So, maybe we'll see more of you around here from now on?" he says, earnestness wiping away his smile.

I laugh and cry at the same time as the pain hits me.

"Let's see how this visit goes first."

93

The rain tapers off to a drizzle once the edge of the front passes. Red and blue strobe lights bounce through the trees, reflecting off wet bark. As we break out of the woods into the yard behind the house, the scene looks like one of Dad's sheriffs conventions, or maybe a public safety conference, with cop cars, EMT wagons, fire trucks and medical examiner's car parked from the drive all the way out to the road. Dad has an arm around my shoulder to help support me. As we round the corner of the house to the front, I see a half-circle of responders ringing the perimeter of what has become a crime scene that swirls with activity.

A couple of M.E. staff members crouch over a body by the wrecked cars. Strobe flashes from different sides of the yard pinpoint locations of two sheriff's deputies taking photos of the scene. One goes inside; the other trades his still camera for a video camera and works his way from the driveway in toward the house. Two officers in state patrol uniforms set out plastic, numbered tents next to groups of shell casings that litter the ground. There are too many to mark individually. EMTs load Robbie onto a stretcher next to his patrol car. He glances my way and stays one of them with his hand. Dad walks me over.

Robbie manages to smile through the pain contorting his features. "Hey, little sister. 'Bout time you came for a visit."

I lean over and kiss him on the cheek, getting it wet with tears—of happiness this time. He gives me a one-handed hug that makes me wince.

"Just had to bring your own excitement," he says when I pull away. "I see you're still kicking butt like when you were a kid."

Impatient to get him to the hospital, the EMTs slowly roll the stretcher away from us.

"We'll talk soon," I tell him with a short wave.

As we turn for the house, I see Bruce conversing with a man in a suit. He hurries toward us when he sees us.

"I was starting to worry," he says as he closes the gap. He nods at me in greeting as if he saw me just yesterday. "You got him?"

"He went over the edge into the river," Dad says, and shrugs.

"Couldn't see him after that."

"I'll send some of the fire and rescue guys to search."

"It's your crime scene," Dad says.

Bruce smiles for the first time. "Well, technically it's not, since I'm involved. I handed it off to Travis, but he'll listen to suggestions."

"Good idea," Dad nods. "Travis will handle it properly."

I give a nod over Bruce's shoulder toward the man in the suit. "Is that who I think it is?"

He glances back. "Active duty or not, you're a cop, Jenny. The bureau needed to know one of its own was in trouble."

I sigh, wondering what sort of shitstorm this will stir up. No use worrying about it now.

Bruce looks at Dad again. "They're going to start taking statements. You might want to join the others inside while you still have a chance."

He's right. I want to know what's happened to everyone else since I ran out of the house, and we'll be separated as soon as they send investigators in to take out statements.

Dad puts a hand on Bruce's shoulder. "You did good work, Bruce. Thanks for saving our butts."

Bruce colors, gives a nod of thanks and turns away, quickly walking back to the FBI agent. He's never been much for mushy sentiment.

Dad wraps his arm around me again and steers me toward the house. "Come on."

The façade shocks me. Every window is shattered, curtains behind them hanging in tatters. The wood siding is splintered and dotted with holes everywhere. There's almost nothing left of the paneled front door but the outer frame. We climb the steps, push it open and step over the wreckage. Two EMTs block the hallway as they work on someone on the floor. I stop dead and gasp, my hand flying to my mouth and my heart dropping through the floor.

Dad quickly pulls me into a gentle embrace. "It's okay, it's okay. It's one of the bad guys."

I recognize the clothing then, my eyes widening in surprise. It's Dana's now-ex-boss Toby, the gunslinger on the hotel balcony. It seems like eons ago.

We squeeze past and hurry into the kitchen. A ring of faces turns to look as we enter, and relief and smiles flood all their expressions. A babble of voices erupts as everyone offers greetings and words of comfort and gratitude all at once. Tears spill unbidden down my face again even as a smile threatens to split it in half.

"We haven't got much time," Dad says over the din. The voices fade and die. "We can share notes later, but anyone have anything important to say? If so, now's the time."

I look at Dana. "You okay?"

Her head bobs. "Toby's going to jail for a long time. We found the evidence to prove he stole the money."

I glance at Nate, who squirms and reddens as I mouth a silent thank-you. He shrugs and his expression turns serious.

"You need to hear this," he says, "before they come for statements. I got into Sykes's phone and the server it leads to. The server has enough information on it to keep the FBI busy for months, years."

I frown. "Like what?"

"Sykes blackmailed dozens of men who frequented his club. Important men, from all over the world. He used the club to feed their vices. He gained their trust by granting their every wish and treating them like royalty. Hell, some were royalty anyway. But he recorded everything, and used it to squeeze them for money or favors. The server also has the club's real set of books, not the ones he gave to his accountants and auditors. I can't even imagine what'll turn up there."

I'm glad he's found information that will help justify what we did to defend ourselves, but my brain is so fogged with exhaustion and pain I don't see what he's getting at.

He glances at Dad. "If I don't say anything, no one else will figure out how to break into Sykes's phone."

"Why not tell them?" I still don't understand. "It's motive for what Sykes did, all of it."

Again, Nate's eyes flick to Dad and back to my face.

"It's not my investigation, son," Dad says. "What you say or don't say is up to you."

Nate's shoulders relax. "You can use this, Jenny. It's a bargaining chip. A huge one. When the bureau finds out what you've got, they'll reinstate you. Hell, they should give you a medal."

I hesitate. "They'll take the phone as evidence."

He shakes his head. "Like I said, they'll never get into the phone, and if they do, the server is booby-trapped."

He isn't boasting, and I suddenly remember that his quiet self-confidence was always one of the things about him that attracted me most. Now, I realize despite the pain and fatigue, he has a lot of other attributes attracting my attention.

"They'll take your laptop, too."

"Doesn't matter. I transferred of all the data on the server to my company servers in K.C. and wiped the laptop."

"They'll compel you with a subpoena to give them what you have."

"I'm sure you can work something out before that happens."

I feel everyone's eyes on me, as if their fate, not mine, hangs in the balance. My mind churns sluggishly, but weighs the pros and cons nonetheless. A commotion sounds from the front of the house, and men's voices float back to the kitchen. The investigators have arrived.

I give my father's arm a squeeze, quickly stride around the island to stand next to Nate. The men in my life need serious educating. But I think I didn't give this one half the chance he deserved. Gingerly draping my arms around his neck, I lean in and kiss him softly on the lips.

He doesn't hesitate to kiss me back.

Acknowledgements

Thanks to Ed Stackler, who has a terrific eye for story and whose keen editing shaped the final book; Tim Hallinan, who encouraged me to try "pantsing" and let the characters tell me who they are and where they want to go; Robin Burcell, who suggested I make one more pass at the book with a focus on structure; and to all the fans who continue to support me and read my stories.

I've tried to be as accurate as possible in describing actual places and things, but this is a work of fiction, and any resemblance of settings, situations, or characters to real people in real life is purely coincidental. Any mistakes are mine.

About the Author

Michael W. Sherer is the author of *Stolen Identity*, four books in the Seattle-based Blake Sanders series, including *Night Strike* and *Night Blind*, which was nominated for an ITW Thriller Award in 2013. His other books include the award-winning Emerson Ward mystery series, the stand-alone suspense novel, *Island Life*, and the Tess Barrett new/young adult thriller series. He and his family reside in the Seattle area.

Please visit him at michaelwsherer.com, or follow him on Facebook at www.facebook.com/thrillerauthor or on Twitter @MysteryNovelist.

Photo: Valarie Kaye-Sherer